FRAGMENTS OF AMERICA

BLACK AUTUMN: BOOK 5, SHORT STORIES OF THE APOCALYPSE

JEFF KIRKHAM   JASON ROSS   L.L. AKERS

JOSH BROOKS   BOYD CRAVEN   ARTHUR DORST

ADAM FULLMAN   GEORGE GRIMM   PAUL KNOCH

CHRIS SERFUSTINI   R. CHRIS YATES

ReadyMan
PUBLISHING

THE BLACK AUTUMN SERIES

FOREWORD

At ReadyMan, we can't leave well enough alone. We poke and prod at every fixed belief in the survivalist world and we forever ask "why the heck does everyone think that?"

We hate people who do that too, and we wanted you to know that we know this about ourselves—that we're a pain in the ass.

Oh, by the way. We've recruited a bunch of friends to help us overturn more apple carts.

You're welcome.

As you probably know, a small nuclear bomb will detonate in Los Angeles harbor and over seventeen days America will become a living hell. That's the kick-off for the *Black Autumn Series*, which we recommend you read, before or after *Fragments of America*, it doesn't much matter. All the books in the Black Autumn Series happen during the same seventeen days.

As we sit in our La-Z-Boy chairs, sipping Black Rifle Coffee, reading post-apocalyptic fiction, we survivalists are pretty sure we're familiar with this coming hell. We've pondered it. Watched a hundred movies about it. Read half a thousand books about it. When the apocalypse comes rolling around the corner, we plan to have our shit wired tight, strapped down and squared away.

But what if the apocalypse doesn't cooperate? What if *our own damn minds* don't cooperate?

In 2019, ReadyMan invited both experienced writers and new writers to pick at these strings—to find their own frayed ends and to follow the threads, wherever they may lead. Fragments of America was half written by published post-apocalyptic fiction writers and half written by first-time authors. Many of the stories themselves are heavily co-written between new writers and old. By mixing "new wine in old skins," I think you'll see that we've crafted a strange, new brew. Most of the themes in this book are entirely new to the post-apocalyptic genre.

By bringing in a bumper crop of fresh blood, we ventured outside of the old tropes (*forgiveably-flawed guy uses his ample preps and commando-worthy gun skills to make the apocalyptic world his bitch.*)

We wanted to poke holes in the steely-eyed hero of prepperdom. We wanted to have more fun with the apocalypse than just kicking its ass. Jeff Kirkham and I hope you enjoy the end result as much as we have.

A word about writing fiction: if you've never tried it before: it's a cast iron, up-at-dawn, butt whipping. The psychological anguish inflicted upon these new writers to get their work up-to-snuff with our readers' fussy literary standards has resulted in a noticeable bump in the consumption of both alcohol and therapy in the ReadyMan Writer's Group. These guys took a holy beating to write their stories, and they took the blows in their tender parts. It's a unique brand of courage to write fiction, and every author herein proves their mettle ten times over.

Thank you to our longsuffering editors: L.L. Akers, Paul Knoch and Linda Orvis. For every story that made it through the meat grinder to become one of these small miracles, there was another author and another story that's still churning about in "English

Composition 101" where the editor and the writer try to make delicious sausage together but don't always succeed.

Please tell us which story you enjoyed the most and why. Join the private group on Facebook at Readymen Group and let's talk post-apocalyptic fiction. And, if you feel you have a short story rattling around inside you that absolutely must be told, let's make some sausage together.

What's the worst that could happen, I mean, compared to a nuclear bomb in Los Angeles harbor?

--Jason Ross

1

A WALK IN THE PARK

BY ADAM FULLMAN

ONE OF MY DEAREST, lifelong friends, Adam Fullman brings a lawyer's eye and a wicked-sharp pen to the brink of the Black Autumn collapse. As he rolled slowly to work each morning in stop-and-go, Los Angeles traffic, he reflected on the bleak reality of escaping L.A. during a wildfire apocalypse and he crafted this wire-tight cautionary tale of sin and black heartedness.

If there was ever any doubt, the apocalypse won't likely erase dark deeds. If anything, they will come due with interest.

-Jason Ross

IF YOU'RE smart about it, there are few things as fun and fulfilling as cheating on your spouse. At the low, low price of just a few extra lies to his wife, Case Richards had doubled the amount of sex he was having as a married man. Hell, he'd tripled it at least. The kind of chick who'll fuck a married man is the kind of chick who is DTF at pretty much any given moment.

And all the stuff that comes from having a family? Case had all that too. His wife, Jane was a solid life partner, though perhaps not particularly gifted in the brains department. She was a good mom to his son, Jimmy, and although she might not have the tight body that had attracted Case to his girlfriend, Evie, Jane was still put together pretty well. He loved Jane. She was the kind of woman a man could happily grow old with.

To the innocents who thought life was like one of the weak romantic comedies out of Hollywood, loving Jane while also fucking around would look like a contradiction. How could he claim to love his wife when he wouldn't keep his dick in his pants? To Case, whose ability to parse words and draw the finest logical distinctions made him a rock star legal advocate for corporate America, there was no contradiction. The two were simply not related.

This was not a new concept. Case had heard a proverb from the days when the British navy was still using sailing ships to control England's now collapsed empire. It went something like "Saltwater washes vows away." Case never went so far as to think that a short commuter flight washed his wedding vows away. He simply enjoyed a little side tail when on the road. True, things were simpler when his forays into extra-marital sex had been limited to trips for out-of-town depositions and meetings, but Case had no intention of fucking things up with Jane. He had no intention of fucking things up with Jane when he first asked Evie, his waitress at the time, about the tattoo on her cleavage. He had no intention of fucking things up with Jane when he asked Evie what time she got off work, while unconsciously touching the condom in his pocket. And he had no intention of messing things up with Jane when he bought a pair of burner phones and started "the Evie thing" as a longer-term project.

Yep. For the right guy, for the smart guy, fucking around could be a ticket to a perfect life.

But Case was no fool. Even perfect lives are subject to the whims of larger forces. Case had known for a long time that it only took a few additional bad decisions, on any given day, by the all-powerful and all too stupid folks in Washington, or The Kremlin, or Beijing, or even a cave in Afghanistan to bring it all down. Case knew that the whole interdependent socio-economic system that his perfect life was built on was only a hop, skip and a jump from spiraling into a digital wasteland of useless bank accounts and a physical apocalypse of rubble, chaos, and death. But if you are smart enough, you can plan for anything, even the end of the world. Case was smart. Case had planned. Now, it was time to get the hell out of Dodge.

Case pulled down on the steering wheel of his Toyota Rav4 hybrid, boosting himself up to peer farther down the bumper to bumper line of vehicles in front of him. Turnpike traffic was becoming problematic. The economy tanking over the last few weeks had been problematic. If Case were to be honest with himself, which was an idea his subconscious had been toying with since that nuke went off in Saudi Arabia, the last 12 months had been problematic.

Case had been listening to Fox news on this way into the City that morning. He'd arrived at 9 a.m., and immediately tuned in to Fox News on the television in his office. By 10 a.m. He'd decided that things were bad enough out there to trigger their bug-out. He'd walked into the office of one of his team's associate attorneys and informed her that he was taking the rest of the day off and starting a long weekend visiting family. He dropped a thick file on the associate's desk.

"The client's discovery responses are due Monday. You should get right on that."

The associate had been paying attention to the news as well, and as he left, her expression showed her skepticism of Case's reason behind his sudden departure. Case didn't care. Though he was only a junior partner, he was still above her. Besides, he never really cared for the younger attorney; her tits were too small.

Unfortunately, it seemed that half the City had the same idea. Late morning traffic out of the City was horrendous and Case still had that little glitch in his plans to work out before they could truly hit the road. If Case did not get home a lot sooner than the ETA on his Google Maps display, any chance he might have to resolve the glitch while limiting damage to his bugout plans would be gone like a Saudi oil field, leaving nothing but melted glowing sand.

The problem was not with the plan *per se*. The plan, also known ironically as "A Walk in the Park" by Case and Jane, was pristine in and of itself: the route home from work--including an alternate foot route if needed, the bug out preparations, bug out route, again with alternate routes, the firearm training that even Jane had been competent at, and the crown jewel--convincing his brother, Ray to turn the apple farm that Ray had bought from their parents into a well-stocked, deep well-fed, solar-powered Richards Family haven in case of financial and/or political collapse. That's where Ray and his family lived and cared for the senior Richards, that's where their brother Chris and his family would be headed, and that's where Case and his family would also be headed as soon as he could get his ass home.

At home Jane would be gathering together the last odds and ends for herself and Case, and for their five-year-old son, James. As soon as Case got home from today's (his last?) 50-mile round trip commute, he and Jane would load James's and Jane's bug out bags into the Rav, along with the larger "bug out boxes" and head to the farm. Case's older brother, Ray, was an attorney, like Case himself. But unlike Case, who earned over a quarter million dollars per year working long hours as a junior partner in a medium sized firm in The City, his brother had built a small but solid internet-based business helping consumers and small businesses fight debt collectors. Although Ray earned half as much money as Case, Ray's lack of drive (as Case saw it) was perfect for allowing time to fiddle with, and eventually fully embrace, prepping. Case had been the one to first insert the topic into holiday dinners, but it was not long before Ray and their brother Chris were 100% onboard.

The apple farm, their dad's idea of semi-retirement after taking an early pension from his teaching position, had never been profitable. After buying the farm, Ray had been content to shut down any remaining efforts at commercial apple growing and live the quiet life of self-employment, sticking it to the occasional debt collector, and stockpiling supplies and skills for post apocalypse life with his wife, their twin ten year-old boys and the rest of the Richards clan. Ray's wife Cindy loved Jane, and the twins were always happy to let little James tag along as they explored the orchards and the adults drank wine and planned for the end of the world. Jane, Cindy, and Chris's wife Maria seemed to mostly take prepping as an excuse to get together and gossip while canning fruit. That was fine. Case and his brothers had the rest covered.

Yes. Operation Walk in the Park would work, as long as he was smart about it. But he still had to take care of the little problem that had been growing in his mind since the economy started to tank. The thing he had come to think of as "the glitch."

A car horn snapped Case's attention back to the road. Ah, there was a two car-length gap in the stopped traffic that Case had failed to instantly pull forward into, drawing the ire of another frustrated commuter. He considered flipping off the horn-happy asshole behind him, but thought better of it. Tensions were running high and he and Mr. Honker would be stuck in traffic together for a while to come. There was no need to escalate the tension.

Case began to consider the first Walk in the Park alternate route, the trails. In planning his bugout, Case had been forced to acknowledge the potentially problematic issue of his daily, God awful, 26-mile commute from the City to his suburban home. Under normal traffic conditions, it took 45 minutes to drive home in the late afternoon. Although his long working hours meant that he would often stay in the office until well after normal traffic had died down, Case had needed his bugout for all times of the day. On a Friday before a holiday weekend it could take over 90 minutes to get home, and in case of societal upheaval, who knew? He'd once had the perfect excuse to spend the night in the City when a truck carrying 20,000 cans of sardines overturned on the turnpike. The Fire Authority had decided to shut everything down to clean up the "potentially flammable" sardine oil. Sounded like an excuse to gouge the taxpayers for hazard pay. But the shut-down had only been outbound, not into the City, and Evie had been willing to drive in from her apartment for a little booty call around midnight, so that had worked out just fine.

Getting stuck in the city (or halfway between the City and home) was not an option for TEOTWAWKI. So Case, as he had done so often and so successfully for his firm's clients, began to work the problem, to find a way over it, around it, and if necessary, right the hell through it.

Just outside The City was the Senator Matthew Robinson Wildlife Preserve. A state wildlife refuge where hunting, fishing, smoking, campfires, and naughty language were banned. Half of Case's 26-mile commute consisted of a large, lazy loop around the Wildlife Preserve. Case's and Jane's neighborhood backed right up to the state preserve area, which was crisscrossed with hiking trails and a few rural homes that had been grandfathered in when the preserve was created in the 1970s. Case had identified two points of ingress off of his commute route which gave him a couple trail choices for a six to seven-mile hike across the preserve to his home--mostly downhill. The area was underused by the City folk who preferred staring at video screens to hiking in the Great Outdoors during their free time.

Case mentioned the ingress points to Jane over their usual late dinner one evening. She had responded by reminding him to take out the trash cans for collection the next morning. That evening, as he trundled the garbage can, recycling can, and the other recycling can to the curb, Case Richards had decided to take up trail running.

Case's attention was caught by activity in the convertible Volkswagen Beetle in front of him. The driver had the top down and now he threw his hands up in the air, grabbed his own head in a sort of hug, and then reached for his dashboard. The VW driver fiddled around for a few moments while casting frightened looks at the sky. Then the convertible's motorized top reached into the sky and closed itself up like a lambskin pith helmet.

Case had switched to a satellite radio music station. He changed back to a news station and sat in shock while listening to the news of a nuclear explosion in Southern California. Details were sketchy, but it was clear that a nuclear bomb had been detonated in or near Los Angeles. He looked around at the drivers sitting in motionless cars around him. Some were stunned and frozen, some talking and making wild gestures to passengers in their cars or through open windows to neighboring drivers. Their voices were quickly rising to panic, despite the fact that they were not in California and were far enough away to be (probably) safe from any wind-carried radioactive fallout.

Case heard a screeching noise and looked back to see a Ford F150 accelerating from the stopped slow lane over to the right shoulder in what was obviously a panicked maneuver. The driver, a man in his 20s, immediately lost control, and the F150 caromed off the railing, rebounded, and crashed nearly nose-first into a minivan in the slow lane, completely blocking the right shoulder. The driver of the minivan, a red headed soccer mom type, promptly exited her vehicle, walked around to the F150, and emptied a pink "key-ring size" can of pepper spray into the F150 driver's open window. This prompted the Ford's female passenger to lean over and spray the red head's face with what Case assumed was her own pepper spray. Next a dozen other people left their cars and chose sides in what was quickly becoming a general melee.

Enough of this shit, thought Case. He slowly maneuvered over to the left shoulder. Then, as there was no rail here, he slowly drove completely off the road onto the grass that topped the slope descending from the turnpike. He turned off the Rav's engine, checked to make sure the key fob was in his pocket, and hit the button to unlock the cargo door. He exited and walked around to the rear of the Rav, ignoring a few inaudible shouts from the people still on the road. Whether they were teasing him for what they assumed was a pee break, or asking what he was doing, Case did not care. He had no desire to discuss his plans with these sheep.

In the cargo area of the Rav, he lifted up the floor cover to expose the storage beneath. His battle belt, light pack, and partially disassembled AR were all wrapped in a light tarp. Case had no intention of kitting up and assembling his rifle on the side of the road. He took up the bundle, locked the Rav, and walked down the slope without looking back.

The tree line began 10 yards from the bottom of the slope. Once inside the tree line, he stepped around a large enough tree trunk to completely conceal him from the road. He put his back to the tree and rolled out the tarp.

Case finished assembly of the AR first. He'd practiced this perhaps two dozen times. That was not enough practice to be able to rely on muscle memory, but the job was quickly done, nonetheless. He finished kitting up with his belt and pack. He checked the water supply and noticed that one of the two bottles was missing. He remembered that he'd used it when Jimmy had gotten thirsty on a trip to the farm last month. He'd be fine. He'd just finished a Diet Snapple Peach Tea he grabbed from the law firm's break room on his way out.

He pulled out a weather resistant topographical map of the wildlife preserve and studied it. He was still a couple miles from a trailhead, but he could jog along the edge of the tree line to get there. That shouldn't be a problem.

But there still was a problem. The glitch. And he was running out of time to fix it. He was still not sure how to do that, which was why he'd been putting it off this last week. The glitch wasn't a problem he could bluff, bluster, or maneuver around, nor could be ignore it any longer. It'd grown in his mind daily, until now the little glitch filled him with thoughts of responsibility, fear, and yes, even love. He had to admit to the love, because the glitch in Case Richard's plan was his daughter, Lucy. He dug out his cell phone and typed a message.

An hour later Case stood just below the top of a ridge. The trail forked, splitting around one of the private homesteads that had been grandfathered into the public reserve. This was not his usual trail for practice runs and he needed to check his map. He took the opportunity to unsling the AR. He hadn't practiced running with the rifle, and it was more awkward than he'd expected.

The sound of the gunshot startled the shit out of Case. It took him a moment to gather enough of his wits to hit the ground. He slid forward down the slope. He knew there was no time to scramble back over the exposed ground on this side of the ridge. He threw himself down, which became a 50-foot tumble that landed him in a tangle of heavy brush and tree trunks. The ridge behind him cut off about one hundred and eighty degrees of exposure to bullets. He peered through the brush downhill. There, at the foot of the slope, about a hundred and fifty yards below him, was a house. Case couldn't see the shooter, but he assumed that the shot was related to the house. Shit! Some fucking old coot who had refused to sell his shitty shack when the Preserve was made had just taken a shot at him.

What the fuck! Why are they shooting!

It didn't occur to Case to call out to the shooter. If he had thought about it, he might have considered how scary he looked, standing on the hill above the isolated house with an AR during a time of economic uncertainty and social stress, if not outright disorder. If he had thought of that, he might have been tempted to try to open a dialogue with the shooter. Then again, if he had thought further, he would have realized how dangerous giving away his position would be in the first place. But he didn't think of any of these things. Lawyers in general love to talk, but he wasn't some hack cranking out wills and trusts in a small-town practice. He was a litigator in the city, whose favorite part of the job was beating the other guy. It was that ingrained response to life in general that took over.

In this situation, beating the shooter did not mean killing him. Case had seen that immediately--like analyzing a new case and knowing it was a loser--because the facts were stacked against him.

Yeah, this situation was a like a case with bad facts.

Case still didn't see the shooter. He knew he couldn't let himself get pinned down. He considered the amount of brush and tree cover between himself and the house and between the house and the direction he needed to go. It was a long run, but at the bottom of the hill he could see a trail which made a sharp turn and disappeared behind an outcropping in the hill, forming a little valley, or ravine, or whatever the fuck it was called. If he ran full tilt, downhill and angled away from the house, he could keep heavy brush between himself and the shooter's likely location. Case could burst out of the brush and onto the path, but only for a few yards. He'd make that turn and put some solid earth and rock between himself and the shooter. Then he could haul ass toward home.

He found himself hesitating. There was no getting around the fact that he was going to be exposed as shit at several points during this run. He overcame the fear with a childhood trick.

"I go on three," he said aloud. "1...2...3!"

JANE RICHARDS SAT at her kitchen table and re-read the hand-written letter she had worked on over the course of three days.

"I've known about your wandering penis for two years, Case. You were so careful and so smart, certainly smarter than I am. But wives have certain advantages of their own. It was your laundry, of course, you dumb motherfucker."

Jane had read that the division of domestic responsibilities in American households was approximately eighty-twenty. That meant that, as a result of relational dynamics, an average married woman, even a married woman with a full-time job, like Jane, was responsible for eighty percent of the housework and child-rearing. This was for the straight sub-group discussed in the magazine article she had picked up at the pediatrician's office. Gays have their own problems. For the Richards household, this was closer to ninety-ten.

She continued re-reading her letter to Case. "I gave up hope of anything more than token help with Jimmy long ago, but if you took the time to handle ANY of your own shit, you might have gotten away with it longer, maybe forever. I'm sure you thought you were checking your pockets carefully, and you probably did, most of the time. But it amazes me that you never learned from those testosterone-driven war books you love that you can't ever let your guard down. Because it only takes one. One bullet. One landmine. One mistake. One momentary lapse of attention."

"Total evidence clean-up ninety-five percent of the time equals getting caught. Ninety-five percent. That's nineteen out of twenty, Case. Sound like good odds? Maybe you knew you weren't perfect, but you took it as a calculated risk. I mean, after all, you are so smart and I am so dumb, so blonde. But, oh randy husband of mine, you failed to calculate something: it's not just the fucking. It's not just covering up the physical act of sleeping with another woman, it's every text message, every email, every internet interaction which shows a history, every gift given, every dick pic, every dinner - every weekend away, like the one when she finally let you fuck her ass (yeah, rack your brain trying to figure out how I learned about that. You disgust me)."

Jane had stopped writing for the day after that. She'd continued the letter the next day.

"I didn't like how that last part felt to write. I didn't like the taste of the words. But I'm not re-writing or editing any of this.

"Let me give you an idea of how dumb you really are. Once I suspected, really suspected, that you were fucking around, what could possibly stop me from learning everything? A secret credit card with bills sent to your office instead of home? Brilliant! Do you know what gets reported on your credit reports? Credit cards! Even secret "side-fuck" credit cards. And do you know what you need to access a credit report? DOB, SSN, mother's maiden name, and the name of three other credit accounts appearing on your record. Your online card billing statements are just as easy--and do you know who knows ALL THAT SHIT? Your wife. Oh, and if I wanted to hijack your accounts, I could reset all your passwords because I know that your favorite childhood television character is RacerX, and even though you tell everyone that your favorite food is Thai, the answer you use for security questions is pizza.

But, let's get back to you being a shitty helper around the house. When your default action is to dump your clothing on the floor at the end of the day, and to kick it into a pile after I complain, guess what? You'll forget to check your pockets from time to time. Because, Baby, you are a secret slob. You're the kind of guy who puts on a sharp dressed show for the outside world while strewing his dirty underwear around the bedroom and leaving the bathroom vanity looking like sticky fingered toddlers shaved a cat in there each morning. Even when you figured out that you should put your clothes in the laundry when coming directly back from rubbing against some perfumed whore, you still kept dropping your clothes on the floor *each and every other time*. I know you've never been impressed with my intellect, but the odds were in my favor to win at least a few of those games of 'one of these nights is not like the others.'

"So why not tell you I knew? Why not divorce you and take you for everything I could? That was certainly my first thought when I learned that you were screwing around with one-night stands. Jesus, Case, *Tinder*?! I almost hired a lawyer when I figured out that you'd taken up with an actual, fucking, long-term mistress!

"And then you got her pregnant.

"I talked about my options long and hard with Cindy. She never told your brother because I asked her not to. You never understood the sisterhood I have with Maria and Cindy. None of us have biological sisters, and I haven't spoken with my family since I testified against my father. And that, more than anything, was why I stayed with you, Case. It was the family. It was me, and you (you asshole!) and James, and Ray and Cindy and the boys, and Chris and Maria and little Richie, and your parents.

"And it was the Farm. That's something else you never understood. You are so proud of yourself and your preparations. So proud of your training, your guns and your fucking plans. You never understood that it was OUR training, OUR plans, and yes, OUR guns. The Plan, the Walk in the Park is OUR plan, OUR Walk in the Park. As the world has gotten scarier this last year I have been thinking about the Farm and about OUR family gathering there. I bet I think of it much more than you do.

"And now we are going. We are going for our Walk in the Park and we are going to save our family and I will not let you throw that away."

Jane had nearly finished the letter that morning. Now she wiped tears from her eyes, and snot from her nose, and she continued.

"I got your texts. I've had time to think about them, and they still don't seem real. My family is broken in a way I never saw coming, and you won't even let me grieve, because you had to ask. Of course, you had to fucking ask, but not now. Not like this. Not in those Goddamn texts."

She continued to write furiously for another ten minutes. Then she wiped her eyes and started grabbing gear.

EVIE HAD NOT BEEN able to move since she had opened her door and found herself confronted by The Ferocious Woman with the Guns. The Ferocious Woman, wearing a pistol at her side and a terrible looking rifle over her shoulder, held Evie transfixed while she read her ranting letter. She'd been going for five minutes, flipping the handwritten pages from front to back. Some of the words tumbled out so fast that Evie's startled mind could not follow them. The letter was almost over before Evie realized she was facing Case's armed wife. But the avatar, Ferocious Woman, continued to stick in Evie's mind even after she had recalled that the woman was named Jane.

Ferocious Woman finished the letter. "So now I have your stuff, and I have your guns and I'm on my way to get that whore's ass. I'm going to get your brat too."

Ferocious Woman looked up from the letter. For a moment their eyes locked. Evie saw so many emotions in Ferocious Woman's eyes: anger, grief, desperation... Such a person could do, would do, anything.

Evie burst into action. She flung the door to close it, but Ferocious Woman stopped it with her sturdy hiking boot.

Evie was across the room in a flash, snatching up her daughter and spinning around to flee. But Ferocious Woman was already coming around the door, her pistol up in front of her, aimed directly at Evie and baby Lucy.

Evie screamed, and it was a sad sign of the times when no

neighbor came barging to the rescue after such a scream. But times were sad, and no one came.

"Knock that off!"

Evie knelt down and bent over her baby, her voice was hardly audible over her now crying infant. She focused on her daughter's face. "Don't kill us. My daughter. Don't kill Lucy."

"You're surprised. I guess that's a point for the wife."

Evie did not move, she was frozen into a shell, a protective cocoon around her child.

"You need to read this." Ferocious Woman's voice was softer now, cracked with emotion. Evie looked up to see that Ferocious Woman was not holding a pistol at all. Her pistol was still on her belt. It was a cell phone in her hands. She was holding the phone out with both hands, so the screen faced Evie.

As FEROCIOUS WOMAN slowly walked closer, the screen came into focus.

12:14 pm.

Jane, I'm leaving the Rav and I am going to try do the trail run. Don't worry, I'll be fine. Honey there is something we need to talk about when I GET HOME

1:32 pm

pick up.

1:33 pm

Honey answer the phone.

. . .

1:35 pm

> *Honey I'm shot. I don't think it's too bad.*
> *He shot me in the back!*

1:36 pm

> *I need you to pick up.*

EVIE REACHED up with trembling hands and took the cell phone from the equally trembling hands of Ferocious Woman. Ferocious Woman's grip tightened for a moment when their fingers touched, but then she released the phone. Evie scrolled down on the screen.

1:38 pm

> *Okay It's been while and I don't think*
> *he's coming down after me. I've stopped*
> *the bleeding I think.*
> *It's my chest. Breathing is hard. It's*
> *downhill here so am going to crawl for*
> *a bit and then walk.*

1:40 pm

> *You'll need to meet me on one*
> *of the truck trails on the route maps.*
> *Your car has a full set. PLEASE Call me*
> *when you get this!*

1:52 PM

> *I can't move it hurts too much. I'm in*

the same place. I'm calling to the
man in the house he might help me.
But he's not answering. I'm bleeding a lot honey

1:54 pm

He's not answering. I'm bleeding too much.

1:54

I'm bleeding too much.
Honey I have to tell you

1:57 pm

328 W. New Row Road
Her name is Eve Martinez
I wanted to tell you.
I think maybe you knew

1:58 pm

we have a daughter.
I have a daughter Lucy and
I'm sorry. I love you.

1:59 pm

Listen. Jane. Take Lucy
to the farm. Don't let Evie
stop you. You're stronger than
she is. Take Lucy to the farm,
Jane. Please.

. . .

EVIE FELT an ice ball forming in her belly, but she continued to scroll as the replies came to the bottom of the screen. All caps.

"BABY WHERE ARE YOU! I CAN MEET YOU! WHERE..."

JANE GRABBED the phone from Evie. "That's it." She snapped. Her face grew hard again, angry.

Evie had begun to think of this woman as Jane, Case's wife. But now Evie again saw the Ferocious Woman. And now Ferocious Woman looked like she regretted letting Evie see the personal message! She was furious at Evie for starting to read the replies! She looked into the eyes again. There it was: anger, grief, desperation... Such a person would do anything: kidnapping, certainly. But Evie did not fear a kidnapping now. At this moment, more than anything else, Evie feared was a rival female, like the meerkats and monkeys she's seen in a documentary. Jealous females sought to eliminate their offspring's competition for resources--by infanticide. Evie didn't recall the details of the documentary. She sensed the danger on an instinctual level.

Evie looked quickly down, practically prostrating herself before the Ferocious Woman. She had to direct the anger away from Lucy. There was silence for a moment. Then Evie's voice was very low. Practically a whisper.

"She looks like Case", she said.

Ferocious Woman did not seem to notice the words. She stood staring forward, speaking more to herself than the woman whose home she'd just invaded, "My phone was on silent. I saw all the messages at once. He didn't answer. I called and texted. It's been hours. 911 goes to voice mail."

"You don't have to kill her. Jane, she looks like Case. She looks like James. Please don't kill my daughter."

"...I can't even use the iPhone finder. He keeps his location off, so I won't catch him cheating."

"She looks like Case. She looks like James. She could be your daughter. I don't have to live. If Lucy lives, it's okay. I don't have to live. "

Jane finally seemed to notice Evie. She looked down at her. "I don't want your daughter."

Jane lurched forward and reached for them. Evie cried in terror and cowered lower over Lucy while blindly swinging a fist above her head in a weak defense. Jane easily pushed the arm away and grabbed Evie. Evie tried to roll away, but Jane was much stronger.

"Hey! Hey! Stop it. Stop!" Jane gripped Evie by her shoulders.

It took several moments for Evie to realize she and her Lucy were not being murdered. When she looked at Jane's face, she saw shock and remorse layered over a bedrock of grief. Jane pulled Evie into a hug. When she released her, Evie saw something else in Jane's eyes: empathy. Maybe even the shadow of a shadow of something else that might someday be sisterhood.

"But the messages. Case said to take..."

"LISTEN, EVE," interrupted Jane, "I loved Case. And I know he loved James and me, to the best his wiring allowed. But Case never took the time to try to understand women. He didn't understand me, and I'd bet he didn't understand you either."

The words tumbled out now. "I'm sorry about the letter," Jane said. "I wrote it to my cheating husband, and I really needed someone to hear it. Those are things I wanted to say to Case. The crazy things. The things I should have been able to say. To yell. But I can't now. You're scared, and I'm scared, and your daughter is my son's sister, and they're only halves. Case can't make any more now, so halves will have to do, and the world is ending, and I'm still really mad at Case and I'm really mad at you."

Without another word Jane turned on her heels and walked out the door she had just forced herself through. Evie sat on the floor holding her daughter, still trying to make sense of what had just happened. Jane was back in less than a minute. She was holding her son. Evie looked up at Jane as porchlight backlit her striking figure. The Warrior Mother. Not ferocious, but fierce. Evie could not take her eyes away. She was drawn to this woman. She wanted to trust her.

Jane looked down at Evie. "But you have to come with me and James now. It's getting late."

Jane shifted James to her other hip and held out a hand to Evie. "I secretly made a bug-out bag for you and Lucy about a month ago. I don't know why I did it. I didn't have any plans. I just thought someone should do it, and I just knew Case wouldn't. I had to guess on some of the personal details for your bag. None of the receipts I found in his pants showed which diapers Lucy wears."

Then Evie saw something that surprised her. A wry smile lifting up one side of Jane's mouth.

"He never bought you diapers, did he? I mean, I know he helped support you. I figured out how he funneled the money to you. But he never brought over anything other than wine and condoms, did he?"

They both looked down at Lucy as they realized what Jane had just said. But it had been an attempt at humor, a sort of humor, and Evie's mind had caught up enough to appreciate that. So, after a moment Evie tried too. "If he'd brought condoms, I wouldn't have had to give up the wine."

Each of them recognized that this was actually pretty funny. Neither of them laughed, but each managed an ironic smile. Jane's hand still reached out. Evie hesitated, then took it.

"Case's family will be hurt to lose him," Jane said. "But they'll welcome us. All of us. And James and I will mourn Case, and I guess you will too. And I'm going to have to allow that. We'll allow for each other."

The two paused for a moment, and Jane's lip came up in another wry smile. "I might still shoot you; you know."

Evie knew that Jane was not entirely kidding. And that made Evie trust her all the more.

2

BLACK FLAGS RISING

by Josh Brooks

I CHOSE *this short story as the cover story for a few reasons. First, after I read the first draft, I wanted to seduce Josh Brooks into writing a full novel together. I may have succeeded. Second, the action scenes bristle with raw power and Josh's firsthand experience in combat becomes immediately obvious. A combat seasoned enlisted man can bring something to a story nobody else can. Third, as you can probably tell from the writing, Josh is likeable and funny and I'd enjoy writing with him. He and I have already planned the full novel sequel to this hard-hitting tale and it's going to kick ass. Expect to see* White Wasteland: Black Flags Rising *published sometime before early 2021.*

What I didn't know about **real world** *Detroit raised hairs on the back of my neck. I'm not any more worried about Muslims than anyone else when it comes to my family's safety. My own preparedness group includes several Muslim families. I am, however, worried about* **every** *organized community, post-collapse.*

Modern America has so few tight-knit communities that even a small, united church group or well-lead Elk's club could leverage an oversized influence on any given town in a post-apocalyptic world.

What if a leader arises among the 300,000 Muslim Arabs currently living in and around Detroit and he decides that the Black Autumn collapse was his god-anointed opportunity to make Sharia the law of the land? Who would stand in his way?

With the National Guard in shambles and the Michigan Militia forced into the northern half of the state, a ragtag group of security guards stands watch over the one weapon with enough destructive power to turn Detroit and the Great Lakes into a thousand year wasteland: **the Enrico Fermi II Nuclear Power Plant.**

   -Jason Ross

"LIFE ON EARTH is at the ever-increasing risk of being wiped out by a disaster, such as sudden global nuclear war, a genetically engineered virus or other dangers we have not yet thought of." – Stephen William Hawking

SUNDAY, September 24th

Somewhere in Detroit, Michigan

A fireball rolled toward the heavens, like an upper-cut to God himself. From his position in the convoy, Sergeant Malone watched chunks of his up-armored vehicle rain down on the concrete.

"Contact left!" His turret gunner began rattling off rounds at a target Malone couldn't see.

Supersonic chunks of metal hammered into the Humvee and yanked his attention from the explosion in front of him. Those pieces of lead meant silent death, and he was on the wrong side of this one-sided engagement.

The radio barked to life with the familiar sound of his Platoon Sergeant's calm voice at the rear of the column. "All vehicles, this is

One Bravo. Contact left, contact left. Push forward and establish a perimeter at LT's truck. We need to establish fire support... Shit!"

Another flash backlit the convoy and an explosion rocked Malones Humvee on its leaf springs. He looked to the side mirror and realized he was now the senior sergeant. He picked up the radio handset, his hands shaking.

"All vehicles, this is Malone." He swallowed hard. "I need the back half of the convoy to push and establish a perimeter around One Bravo's truck. Check for casualties. First half, you're on me, same fire mission. Out." He hoped he'd sounded half as composed as his likely-dead platoon sergeant. It was the least he could do to honor the man.

Malone dropped the handset and glanced to his left. His driver looked like a turtle tucking his head into the shell of his flak jacket. "You ready, Jensen?"

"No, Sergeant."

"GOOD. PUNCH IT." Malone studied the side mirror of the vehicle to make sure the four others were following. His soldiers were doing exactly as trained.

That's the best we can do at this point. When it's FUBAR, is when training pays off the most.

A burst of machine-gun fire raked across the hood, vaporizing one of the zip ties that held the concertina wire in place. The wire slid to the side just as the hummer came to a screeching halt next to the burning vehicle that used to belong to his platoon commander.

Malone could feel the immense heat coming off the wreckage. The smell of burning human flesh intermixed with the pasty smoke of rubber and plastic. The remains of an unidentifiable passenger vehicle twined with the charred Humvee engine block.

Mother fucking car bomb. In Detroit. America. Was this like Red Dawn? How had hajjis suddenly appeared in fucking Detroit?

He had to see if the dead vehicle's radio was still operational, and he'd have to pick through his dead friends to do it. That radio was the only link they had left with their command unit in Camp Grayling.

"Heft, I'm getting out with Bower and Jackson. Pick up that fire when we jump out." Malone reached over and tapped the turret gunner on the legs to ensure he'd heard him. The kid was a nine-teen-year-old private, but his disciplined rate of fire told Malone the kid had the bones of a warrior. Today was the day he'd learn that truth.

"I got you, Sergeant." Heft yelled down the turret hatch, "Bower. I need another can of ammo."

Malone looked back to Bower and Jackson. Bower shook like a terrified Chihuahua as he dug out a can of 7.62. Jackson's hand was on the door. Malone gave them a nod.

"On me!" Malone grabbed his door handle and glared through the bulletproof glass into the new, dystopian world of Dearborn, Michigan. This wasn't supposed to be happening, but this was no time to bitch. At the end of this road of death, stood the Enrico Fermi II Nuclear Power Plant, and if these shit eaters took that target down, Southern Michigan would be erased from the map. Everyone he loved, liked, and knew would be dead or dying from some ghastly form of radiation poisoning or eventually cancer. If ever there was a good reason to give his life, this was it.

He shoved the door open and the sounds and smells of battle jerked the marrow of his bones back to the streets of Baghdad. Like a twisted, recurring nightmare, Kalashnikov fire bespoke the chaos of an all-out street fight.

"Bower, Jackson, take up positions at the front and back of the vehicle and give me some cover!" Malone shouted as the three men sprinted toward the wreckage.

The other two soldiers braced against the dead vehicle as soon as they arrived and took well-aimed shots at the rooftops that surrounded them. Malone seized the black door handle and yanked hard. Nothing happened. He swiped his gloved hand over the cracked glass to clean off some of the muck, but he still couldn't see a damned thing. He tried the rear passenger door, and it dumped the burning body of a soldier to the pavement.

Flames roared out of the cab, licking after the soldier as though following the fresh meat.

"Sergeant?" Jackson yelled at Malone as a deafening volley of enemy fire battered the burning vehicle they were using for cover. Malone pointed toward their Humvee. "Get back to the truck! They're gone. The radio is toast too."

Malone started shooting before he could see targets. He sighted down his ACOG and picked out the familiar wooden fore end of an AK firing down on their position from the rooftop of a Halal restaurant.

"You first, Bower. I'm set." Malone poured direct fire into the AK-47 when it poked back over the wall. The barrel of the gun took a round, causing the shooter to drop it to the sidewalk below.

"Moving," Bower yelled as he sprinted back to their Humvee. Sliding like a member of the Detroit Tigers, Bower hit the front of the vehicle and jumped back up to a kneeling position. "Set!"

"Jackson, go." Malone didn't pull back from the ACOG, hunting for threats.

"Moving," Jackson sprinted across the gap to the safety of the armored hummer as rounds tore into the concrete around him. "Set!"

"Moving." Malone hesitated as he jumped back and prepared to run.

At the rear of the convoy, men from his unit were fighting hand-to-hand combat with men in all black robes. Sergeant Jones had an enemy pinned to the ground and was smashing him repeatedly in the face with his helmet. When the man stopped moving, Jones looked up. The man beneath Sergeant Jones exploded.

Malone was thrown across the burning asphalt. As soon as his wits returned, he gathered himself off the ground and sprinted for the hummer. Several more explosions ripped across the rear of the column, each one knocking Malone to the ground yet again. Eventually, an explosion slapped him into his Humvee, where he scrambled for something to hold him upright. He ripped open the door to his car and dove inside, grabbing his handset.

"Jensen, we're moving!" he screamed.

Heft continued firing from the turret. "Bower! Ammo," he shouted down into the hull of the Humvee.

"All vehicles, this is Malone. Assault through contact. I say again, PUSH THROUGH! Stay right on my ass."

"Sergeant, what about... "

"Break, break, break. I say again. We are LEAVING!" Malone slapped Jensen on the helmet hard, pointing straight ahead.

The five remaining Humvees pushed forward as fire rained down on them. The turret gunners returned fire in controlled bursts, leveling anything they could see.

They rounded their first corner, and the road ahead appeared to be clear.

"Malone. What the hell?" Corporal Adams came over the radio, throwing radio etiquette out the window. "Our guys were being overrun back there!"

"They WERE overrun. We have to Charlie Mike and get our asses to that power plant before whatever the hell this is reaches nuclear fucking fusion. Maintain comms discipline. Malone, out." Malone threw the handset of his radio at the windshield and punched the dash repeatedly until he could feel knuckles bleeding under his Mechanix. Leaving men behind wasn't something Malone could have ever imagined himself doing.

Even during the worst times in Iraq, he'd never left a brother behind. He had no idea if the men at the rear were dead. All he knew was that they were in danger of being completely overrun and staying behind to save his brothers could have gotten them all killed. At least now they were a dozen blocks outside the ambush, and he could still field a fighting force.

"Uhh, Sergeant?" Jensen's voice pulled Malone back to the present. "I think we have a problem."

A massive crowd of civilians thronged ahead, blocking the road. Men in the crowd waved black flags and shouted in Arabic. Malone recognized it in an instant. They were the black flags of the Islamic State.

"Stop the damn truck, Jensen." Malone growled. He popped open his door and stepped out, grabbing the bullhorn from under his seat. "Disperse or we will be forced to fire." Malone could barely hear the megaphone over the shouts of the crowd.

A rock impacted the armored door. Malone lifted his rifle into the air and let out three rounds. More rocks answered in protest.

A single gunshot splatted on the armored window.

"Fuck this." Malone tossed the bullhorn on the ground and climbed back in as another round smacked the glass in front of Jensen. "Drive, Jensen. They'll move or we'll fucking smash them."

Jensen rolled forward at a slow pace. The crowd moved out of the way for the vehicle but surged around it as it passed, rocking it back and forth.

"Private Heft. Button up." Malone reached back and grabbed the private by his legs and pulled him down. "All vehicles engage your combat locks and button your gunners up inside. We're pushing through."

More gunshots rattled outside, cracking the glass next to Malone's face.

"We're done here. Step on it, Jensen." Malone looked over at his driver. Jensen's face turned pale as he accelerated. The vehicle's engine revved as it gained speed. Members of the crowd ran to get out of the way. Rocks skittered across the hood. A burst of automatic fire sounded at the rear of their convoy.

"All vehicles sitrep," Malone barked, watching a man in a black ski-mask try to open his door.

"Two, we're good."

"Three, all set here. I think these guys are waving the ISIS flag, Malone."

"Four, doing fine."

No response came from the fifth vehicle.

"Five, this is One. I need a situation report, over," Malone said into his handset.

The throaty thump of a hand grenade detonated in the rear of the convoy. Malone couldn't see what was happening at the back because of how tight the crowd packed against his Humvee.

"Fuck me," Malone said. "All vehicles, this is Malone. Ram through this crowd. Kill anyone in the way."

A woman jumped onto the hood of their Humvee as Jensen accelerated. The jolt from the vehicle rocking forward made her lose her footing in the concertina wire. She slipped and her head impacted the side of the truck. Some of her hair was torn away in the razor wire. Her body tumbled forward and disappeared under the front bumper. The Humvee lurched and Jensen hit the brakes.

"Just drive, Jensen!" Heft yelled.

Jensen hit the gas and the Humvee slammed into the crowd, like a bear tearing through rats. Bodies slammed into the grill, the hood and the windshield. Jensen craned his neck left then right, trying to find a clear view of the road. The Humvee bumped and bounced like it was driving across a tilled field. After what seemed like forever, they broke free of the mob and raced onto clear asphalt.

Malone focused on his passenger side mirror, counting the vehicles behind them.

"ONE...TWO...THREE..." Then nothing. They'd lost another one of their trucks. All of the surviving vehicles were covered in gore. "And we're four."

"Jesus, God forgive us." Malone threw himself back into his seat and held his face in his hands.

FIVE DAYS BEFORE...

WEDNESDAY, September 20th
   Stony Point, Michigan
   Near the Enrico Fermi II Nuclear Power Plant

THIRD SHIFT WAS ALWAYS boring at the Enrico Fermi II Nuclear Power Plant. Getting put on third shift at the change of each rotation meant you and eleven co-workers would be spending the next month living like vampires from old black and white horror movies.

Vasean Miller hated third shift, but would never complain because the salary was high, and it wasn't like Iraqi insurgents were driving car bombs into the gate here.

It was twenty minutes until shift change, and that meant Vasean had another five minutes to finish his cigarette in the car and listen to the last of the evening news. Even after two years out of the Marine Corps, he still showed up fifteen minutes early to everything.

As he took a deep drag of his Newport, he listened to the hosts bickering on the news about the stock market closing. The commotion had something to do with a dirty bomb detonating somewhere in Saudi Arabia. He took one last drag and rolled the window down to flick the butt.

Man, why's it always gotta be the Middle East messing it up for decent parts of the world? Don't they know what century we're in?

He rolled up his window and shut off his car. Roll call would take place at the security office.

"Hey Vee!" a voice shouted from behind him as he swayed toward the office while strapping on his duty belt. "You hear about the dirty bomb in Saudi Arabia, man? Sounds like some pretty wild shit, dude. I bet they raise our Force Pro levels. Might even bust out the rifles and Kevlar!"

"Man, you always on some dumb shit, Phil. The last thing we want is to stand around all night kitted up because some idiots in Saudi Arabia got blown up." Vasean said over his shoulder. "Besides, why the heck we gonna need Kevlar? You think a pack of rabid squirrels with machine guns are gonna attack this place? No one cares, man. This place is a non-factor."

Phil chuckled at the statement "I dunno Vee, you think they'd be paying us 80k a year to stand guard if this joint was a non-factor?"

"Nah man, they pay us 80k a year because we came pre-packaged with the training they need. There's a reason the company only takes combat veterans and veteran police officers. It saves them money teaching us how to stand post and stare at nothing. Besides, we're contractors. We pay a good chunk of that 80k to Uncle Sam at the end of the year anyway," Vee said as he swiped his ID card and entered the first of three security checkpoints into the building. "Let's go, man, roll call is in 15 minutes, and I want to grab a coffee from the break room before we start. I'm not in vampire mode yet. Oh, and I'm gonna punch you in the gut if they have the Kevlar out. You gotta stop jinxing us, bro."

Sure enough, as soon as they entered the security checkpoint for roll call, the QRF from the previous shift was pulling Eagle Industries SAPI plate carriers and Advanced Combat Helmets from the armory and setting a neat stack by the door. Vee glared at Phil as other members of the shift walked in and assumed their customary seats on the left side of the room. Most of them wore the same look of frustration, but a few were already checking their phones to make sure they'd have enough juice to get some selfies in the high speed kit.

"Gentleman, as I'm sure most of you have already figured out, we have been upgraded to Force Protection Condition Alpha." Jerry began the brief as soon as he entered the room. He braced himself on the podium. "The dirty bomb attack last night shut down our stock market today. We have received zero guidance from the company on the situation, but this is a decision the other shift leaders and I have already discussed and agreed upon. We will be in FPCON Alpha until things stabilize in the stock market. Before the shift change, does anyone have any comments or concerns?"

Situations like this happened all the time, and most force protection elevations were usually de-escalated back to their previous levels within two shifts.

"Hearing no complaints then, we'll go ahead and conduct the shift change. We have no post changes or absences tonight. The only difference between tonight and last night is that you'll be standing your posts in full gear with a rifle. After you grab your kit on the way out, report to the armory to pull your pistol and rifle." Jerry spoke as if he had given this exact speech every night for the past ten years ... because he had. "Then report to your post with your counter-parts and conduct the change of duty. I'll see you out there through the night. Don't be dicking around with the rifles, and if I catch any of you posting pictures of our elevated FPCON status to Instagram, you'll be fired. You know company policy."

Vee stood from the table, walked over to the pile of gear and grabbed a set, hot seat style. You got what you grabbed at the beginning of your shift and turned it in for the next guy to pick up at the next roll call. On his way to the pile of gear, he shot Phil a look that said *I'm gonna kick your ass.* Phil shrugged and gave his best shit-eating grin. He obviously hadn't had his fill of wearing SAPI plates, but that would change. Spending a duty shift feeling like you're stuffed into a coffee cup drained the piss and vinegar out of any man.

OUT ON POST, everything seemed normal, except for the damned plates. Vee sat in his usual box at the Fisher Street entrance to the power plant and contemplated stepping outside to have another smoke. Newports were the second worst thing to ever happen to him in Iraq. One of his buddies sent him a care package with two fresh cartons of Newports on his first deployment. His intentions had been to use them as a bartering chip to get snacks, but curiosity got the better of him, and before he even knew it, he developed an addiction to nicotine that followed him back to Detroit.

Shifting the weight of his plate carrier, Vee made the decision to step outside of his box and grab a smoke. He picked up his rifle, feeling the familiar weight, and strapped it to himself with the company's two-point sling. As he stood in the middle of the road, leaning on the cross bar, he heard the heavy footfalls of his shift leader.

"Hey Jerry," Vee said without looking over his shoulder.

"Damn, son. How'd you know it was me?"

"You ask me that every single time, Jerry. How long you been trying to sneak up on me now? Two years? It's never gonna happen. I can hear you stomping in those clod hoppers from a mile away. Plus you always show up at the same time." Vee lit the cigarette.

"Yeah, I suppose." Jerry sighed. "Can I bum one of those off you? I left mine back in the office."

"Yeah, sure," Vee said as he rattled the box of cigarettes. "So, hey man, for real. You guys think this Saudi thing is something serious? I only caught a little bit on the news."

Jerry took the cigarette from Vee, pulled an old Zippo out of his pocket and lit the cigarette with a deep inhale. "I don't know, Vee.

Tell you the truth, the company puts us on FPCON Alpha whenever the stock market goes wonky. In all those times, the stock market has never stayed closed for an entire day of trading. All I know is that it's some bad juju. So the supers all got together and called the security level increase."

"You mean the company hasn't called yet?" Vee asked.

"Nope. And that's not normal. Generally, the site manager would have been here by now to upgrade us," Jerry said as he flicked the ash on his bummed smoke.

"That's heavy shit. You don't think they forgot about us, do you? I mean, we're one of three nuclear power plants in the state of Michigan. Something goes tits up here, we're talking about not only a lot of people losing power, but potentially a large portion of that big lake out there," Vee said tossing a thumb over his shoulder in the direction of Lake Erie.

"Yeah, I dunno, Vee. The company doesn't only cover down on nuke sites. They've got banks, casinos, and super rich guys to worry about. Maybe they're just too busy dealing with screaming rich dudes who lost five percent of their portfolios to take a second for us ground-pounders," Jerry said, tossing his cigarette into the butt can next to Vee's post. "Just stay awake. I doubt anything's gonna happen here, but there wouldn't be a job for washed up jarheads and cops like you and me if someone, somewhere didn't think this place might get shot at someday."

"Hey, you might be washed up and old, Jerry, but I can still bang hammers. I was banging in Iraq and Afghanistan not even two years back!" Vee argued, tossing his smoke in the bucket.

"Yeah, yeah." Jerry waved a hand over his shoulder as he turned back up the road toward his security office in the main facility. "Whatever you say, kid. Iraq this, Afghanistan that. You want me to thank you for your service now or just go straight to sucking your root?"

Vee laughed and watched Jerry hobble back toward HQ. Vee

went back to his post and pulled his phone out of his pocket. It was almost six in the morning. The sun would be coming up in about an hour, and his shift was halfway done. At noon, he'd be cut loose. Then he could head into the hospital and visit his Mom for an hour before sleep. This job and its schedule was taxing, but it afforded him the opportunity to keep his mother in an up-scale hospital in Detroit where she could receive the end-of-life care she deserved. After she was gone, Vee knew he'd be on his own. The thought of losing her still made his head swim a bit, even after all these months of seeing it coming like a slow-moving storm across the valley. He'd lost her a bit at a time, and that was a mercy in a way. But when she finally went, he worried that he wouldn't handle it well. He'd lost people before, and it hadn't been pretty. Not at all.

The hours ticked by slowly, and as usual, nothing happened until around nine in the morning, when the first plant employees started showing up for work. The people who came in the Fisher Street entrance were, for the most part, commuting from Detroit. Most of them lived in South Detroit and held minor jobs at the facility, like grounds keepers and janitors. A lot of these folks grew up in the same neighborhood as Vee but made significantly less than him. He made an effort to treat them as equals.

"Hey, Vasean. They got you on night shift again, boy?" Aliyah laughed as she handed her ID out the window of her Honda to Vee.

"You know it, girl. I'm here for the sunrise. Hey, when you gonna let me take you out?" Vee scanned her ID and handed it back.

"I dunno, when you gonna stop working from midnight to noon?" she answered with a sly grin, taking back her ID card.

"I see how it is. You get me this job, then you go dark on me because we work opposite shifts." Vee flashed his moneymaker at the girl. Even at the end of a night shift, he still "had it."

"You got my number. You just give me a call when your shift changes, then maybe we can talk about getting a bite to eat. Oh hey. Get gas on your way home. We're up to four dollars a gallon because of this bomb thing." She rolled up her window and drove into the plant.

Damn, that's a big spike in gas prices overnight, Vee thought to himself as he took the next ID and scanned the employee in. *I hope it doesn't go up much more before I get out of here. This Saudi thing must be big.*

Checking his phone again, Vasean could see the complaints from his friends on Facebook. Gas prices were indeed skyrocketing, and according to Funker530, one of the veteran news pages he followed, the Saudi's were already blaming Iran and the Houthi rebels for the dirty bomb attacks. Things were heating up around the world. The AK he had tactically acquired in Iraq would need to come out tonight. Better safe than dead.

At 11:42 in the morning, just 18 minutes before his shift change, Vasean's radio came alive with Jerry's voice.

"All posts, this is your shift leader Jerry McCuellcek. A nuclear weapon has detonated off the coast of Los Angeles. You are to stay on post, Condition One and ready to defend this location. The next shift will be relieving you soon. Roll call is cancelled. Once you are relieved from post, you are to report to me. This shift will be staying on site to reinforce the QRF. Second shift has been recalled as well. If you go home at the end of your shift, your contract with the company will be terminated."

Vasean could barely believe what he was hearing. He stared out the bullet proof glass, stunned. A feeling of dread took hold. A nuclear weapon had just detonated on the west coast of the United States, and there wasn't anything he could do for his mother. He could call on his break. That was all. Vee found himself looking at his hands, as though they'd somehow betrayed him. He wondered how many people had been killed? Were his friends in Camp Pendleton okay? Did the opening shots of World War III just get fired? What would happen now?

Round and round the questions flew as he scanned ID cards.

Many of these people would probably turn around to be with their families as soon as they found out. Almost forty-five minutes passed before Vee's relief arrived at the post. Nothing about this shift change was normal. The woman who relieved him was in full-kit, her face a roadmap of distress, scrunched and folded like a topographical map.

As she approached, she held up her hand to silence Vee before he could say a word. "This is bullshit, Vee. The company is holding our paychecks hostage, and there could be Russian Paratroopers landing in our backyards by dinner tonight. I have half a mind to say screw it and leave right now."

"Whoa, don't take it out on me. I don't make the rules." He slung his rifle around his back. "Do we know it was the Russians?"

"We don't know who did it. If I don't get solid intel by the end of my shift, I'm going home, and the company can keep the damn paycheck. I've got to protect my kids." She set the rifle to condition one in the clearing barrel.

"I'll let you know what I find out, Sarah. Don't worry." Vee unloaded his rifle in the same clearing barrel, showing her the rifle was clear before heading to the security office.

It was already getting cold. On the walk back to the conference room where he was hoping there would be some kind of brief, Vee stabbed his hands into his plate carrier and walked against the wind. Autumn was in full swing in Michigan, and the morning frost was hanging around longer and longer each day. It was past noon, and the grass on either side of the foot path was still wet with melting frost, turning the ground black underneath the dying grass.

Damn Russians couldn't have thought of a worse time to do this. I suppose winter isn't anything to those guys though. Vee picked up his pace and approached the first security checkpoint.

Outside of the conference room, Jerry was arguing quietly with the next shift's supervisor. Vee had a feeling that the men were arguing over whether Jerry's shift should be allowed to go home. As he approached, the two men stopped and waved Vee inside the conference room. His phone had yielded no information yet, just that things seemed to be getting worse by the hour. It appeared as if the grid was going out in most of California and in large parts of the west coast.

"Ladies and gentlemen, please take your seats," Jerry asked. "As you have all heard, there has been a nuclear attack on the West Coast. At this time, we have not heard from the company other than to inform us of the attack itself. First shift is currently all present and accounted for, and they're already on post as we speak. Third shift is all present and accounted for as well. We have placed emergency calls to each member of second shift, but so far have only heard back from their supervisor. He's telling us that things inside Detroit are deteriorating rapidly, and that we shouldn't hold our breaths for our co-workers to arrive. The 75 is blocked bumper to bumper both in and out, and the police are swamped because the banks have closed and people are looting."

He paused and looked toward Michael, the other shift supervisor. The man appeared shaken, like a bird that had just flown headfirst into a window at full speed. Jerry sighed as Michael answered his cell phone and stepped out into the hallway.

"The decision to keep you here was made by me." Jerry paused and looked at the faces of his shift members. "Michael wants to head home to be with his family, and I honestly don't blame him. I won't blame any of you if you follow him. I can't make the decision to hold your paychecks and fire you. Those of you who stay will be paid overtime, but let me make something perfectly clear..." Another pause...

"The company didn't hire a bunch of retired law enforcement officers and combat veterans to stand guard at this location for window dressing. As you all know, this location, and locations like it, provide electricity to a lot of people. On top of that, we're about a stone's throw away from Lake Eerie, which bleeds over into Lake

Ontario. We all know Chernobyl. An attack on our facility could put a lot of people, not only out of power, but it could kill and maim millions of Americans. Right now, you are the ones keeping this location secure until the Michigan National Guard arrives, which may or may not happen within the next few days." Jerry looked in the eyes of each member of both shifts as he spoke.

The atmosphere in the room darkened when the first hand went up. "Sir, with all due respect, I'm going home to my family unless you can confirm that this was a random one-off terror attack and not an act of war by a nuclear superpower. I get it about the red, white and blue, but I'm a father before all that." It was Thomas, a former street cop from third shift.

"I can't confirm a damn thing," Jerry said, trying to dig himself out of an impossible hole. "I'm also not going to keep any of you here that don't want to be here. Once I know who's staying and who's going, we're going to set up a post rotation to man all six posts around the clock. The plant itself is stripped to a skeleton crew, and all non-essential people are being sent home."

Vee raised his hand and waited for Jerry to acknowledge him. "Jerry, this place provides power to the hospital in downtown Detroit, right?"

"I think it does," Jerry replied.

"Then I'm staying. My mom is in that hospital." Vee crossed his arms and looked at the others. "A lot of people depend on this place. That's probably true of your families, too."

"Very well." Jerry said. "Who else is staying?"

Only four other hands went up. The other six members of third shift stood and walked toward the door where Michael was standing. Michael gave Jerry a nod and left.

"What about the shift on post right now?" Phil asked rubbing his temples.

"We'll give them the same opportunity when their shift is over. For now, I want the five of you to go to the staging area with the

Quick Reaction Force. See how many of them will stay. We have six stations to man, which means each of us is going to be standing in the box for a hell of a long time with no sleep unless a few of the others decide to stay. I'm going to go see what the manpower situation is with the crew at the plant. Maybe we can convince a few of the civilians to stay on board to help keep security up and running." Jerry drew a hasty outline of the compound on the white board and wrote down the names of each shift member remaining.

What did I just get myself into? Vee asked himself. "I'm going to hit the posts, see who I can talk into staying. I know Sarah will bail as soon as her shift is over," Vee said to Jerry.

"You do that, Vee. Let me know what you find out as soon as you can. This is going to get worse before it gets better." Jerry let out a sigh. "Protocol says Michigan National Guard is supposed to reinforce the plant within forty-eight hours of any type of CBRN attack inside the U.S. I hope we hear from the company and FEMA by the end of the day."

Vee cocked his head. "My grandpa used to say, hold hope in one hand and bullshit in the other. Just see which fills up first."

"WE MIGHT BE on the brink of an apocalypse if, instead of poor people with suicide bombs killing middle class guys, middle-class people with suicide bombs started killing rich guys." – Bruce Sterling

SUNDAY, September 24th
    Dearborn, Michigan
    Intersection of Shaeffer Hwy and West Warren Avenue

. . .

IMAM MOHAMED ABDUL-HAADY had gathered his most trusted followers into the back room where they sat cross-legged in a circle. In a hushed tone, the men spoke to one another while the Imam waited. These men were going to serve as the commanders in his army, and together they would sweep through Dearborn, Michigan, block-by-block until they had full control.

After that, they would attack deep into the heart of Detroit and purge the city of all that was not pure under Shariah Law. Haady had been in contact with members of the Islamic State in both Iraq and Syria. Baghdadi himself had told Haady to bide his time and gather his people. Haady had been ordered to stockpile weapons and ammunition. They bid him, "Train them in Jihad, and strike out when the time of Allah dawned on America"

This was the time. The brothers in Iraq and Syria sent the bomb against the Californians. The weapon used against the Saudis had been the trigger. The glorious attack against the United States had been the response. The global Jihad had begun. Every major news network had confirmed his expectations.

Indeed, now was the time to move forward with the war they'd been preparing for many years.

As the men whispered back and forth, an air of electricity filled the mosque. When it reached its apex, the imam spoke.

"Brothers. Today is the day that we gather and strike." He stood and raised his voice. "In two hours, I will call the people to prayer. They will fill the mosque, and I will tell them our plan. You, my commanders, will bring more brothers with you, as well as the supplies we have stockpiled. Muslims who refuse us will die. Those who join will become the Soldiers of Allah, and we will be the hammer that strikes the wickedness that is Detroit."

The men whispered agreement.

"We will attack like a lightning bolt. The army and the police are hiding from the wrath of Allah, at home with their women and chil-dren--soft targets." Haady's voice rose over the excited whispers.

"Once we secure Dearborn, we move into the streets of Detroit and seize control of key infrastructure. The streets will run red with the blood of infidels. We will slaughter them by the tens of thousands. The Detroit river will run as red as the sands of our ancestors. Our time is now!"

The men shouted and ululated. Their passion filled the mosque to the rafters, like heat rising.

"*Allah Akbar! Allah Akbar!*"

Haady continued and the ululation hushed. "Brother Kaatib. Your Chaldean Mafia has been operating openly for some time. Are the brothers prepared to strike the first blow?"

"Yes. We are ready Imam. The warriors are gathered and armed," Kaatib answered, pride filling his voice. "We will strike Dearborn as soon as I give the word. First, we destroy the remaining police. Our martyr is prepared with his car bomb. *Inshallah* he will find success. Our follow-on attack against the precinct will be swift."

"Good," Haady responded, nodding and smiling. "Strike now while I make the call to prayer. After you destroy the precinct, I want you to take control of the other mosques and have your *hajis* step in where the other imams will not. Ensure that all our people join the jihad. We will bring the infidels to their knees. We will enslave them where they are of use to us and kill them where they are not. This is the will of Allah. Our war begins today. Our law shall be eternal."

"*ALLAHU AKBAR! ALLAHU AKBAR!*" The shouts drowned out all else in the tiny smoke-filled chamber. The men rose as Haady lifted his hands to heaven. Their shouts pulsated, the men losing themselves in the blood-dipped vengeance of an outraged god.

Haady shouted at the top of his lungs, "In these days, we will hang the black flag of the caliphate from the city capital--for all to see. Go brothers. Gather our people and bring holy jihad!"

The imam stepped down from the lectern and left the room, the men carried in the passion of righteousness. Haady smiled as he walked silently through the halls toward the loudspeaker that would call his people to prayer. In these last years, more and more of his people appeared at the Mosque to pray. This would be the perfect time for Allah's holy ultimatum. In these desperate times of need, his flock arrived in numbers he had never seen in the United States.

Haady stepped into his office and knelt on his prayer rug. He closed his eyes and communed with Allah for a moment in silence. God filled the room with white hot light, cleansing the imam with pure purpose and holy anointing.

He pulled the microphone from his tiny wood desk down to the head of his prayer rug. He had prayed on this rug since boyhood— since his days as a dirty urchin on the streets of Riyadh. Tattered cords of cloth hung from the edges and the color had all but drained to gray. He used a newer prayer rug when he led prayer in the mosque. But here in his private office, when he prayed alone, he preferred to remember how Allah had lifted him from filth to the head of one of the most powerful *ummah* within the United States. Haady bowed low, clicked the loudspeaker and began the morning call to prayer.

Even from inside the walls of his office, he could hear his soldiers shout.

"ALLAHU AKBAR! ALLAHU AKBAR! ALLAHU AKBAR!"

"APOCALYPSE DOES NOT POINT to a fiery Armageddon but to the fact that our ignorance and our complacency are coming to an end," – Joseph Campbell

SUNDAY, September 24th – Late Evening.

Stony Point, Michigan
Enrico Fermi II Nuclear Power Plant

FIVE FULL DAYS had passed since Vee last left the nuclear power plant, and he had no idea if his mother was alive or dead. As far as the eye could see, massive clouds of smoke rose into the evening sky. Even their Canadian neighbors in Windsor appeared to be on fire.

Vee wanted to scream his rage at the sickly-orange sunset. He wanted to charge into that smoke with his AR and kill every criminal motherfucker he could find. He wanted to rush that hospital, scoop his mother out of her bed and carry her to safety.

And then she would die right then in his arms. Those electricity-sucking machines were the only thing keeping her alive. So, standing here with his dick in his hands, protecting the power plant was the best he could do. At his back, those turbines turned out the power that kept his mom alive. He wasn't going anywhere, as much as every cell in his body screamed for him to take direct action.

Out of the twelve security team members from his shift, only six remained. Jerry had convinced seven members of another shift to stay as well. He pulled that off by inviting their families to come onsite, which would've gotten him fired in a heartbeat if anyone at corporate knew or cared. The site kept extensive supplies that would allow the security team and the skeleton crew to stay operational for several months without any outside support. Essentially, he'd bribed them, which was fine with Vee. He'd much rather hold the line with men and women who were also protecting their families.

As a result, the twelve men and women faced a relentless shift cycle of twelve hours on post, twelve hours on what was called quick reaction force, or QRF. While the team members were on QRF, they could sleep, eat and shower, but they had to remain within arms-reach of their equipment. Jerry was the only shift supervisor, and it seemed like the man never slept. Vee wasn't sure how the old man managed it.

This wasn't entirely new to the members of the security team. Every person hired by the company had the experience of working in either ground combat or extensive law enforcement history. High operational tempo was the name of the game in those trades.

Vee's radio came to life. "Post four, this is Jerry, radio check over."

"Roger, I got you lickin' chicken." Loud and clear.

"You doing okay, Vee?" Jerry asked.

"I would probably kill someone for a Newport right now, but yeah, I'm good." He'd run out of cigarettes the first day and was only just climbing out from underneath the craving for nicotine. "Guess this is one way to quit smoking."

"Roger that. I just got word that three National Guard trucks are coming in. They'll hit your entrance any minute. Let me know when you have eyes on."

"Maybe those guys got some smokes. What took them so long?"

"Things got hairy for them." Jerry's voice trailed off. "I'll talk to you when they get here."

Vasean put the radio down on his table and rubbed his face. He hadn't trimmed his beard in days.

The contingency plan for nuclear power plants in Michigan was to have members of the National Guard on-site within 24-hours of any disaster or attack. It'd been four days.

Only four trucks? Vee thought to himself. *There's supposed to be an entire platoon. We've trained with these guys three times and they show up with twelve trucks and at least forty dudes.*

As if on cue, the first green M1114 Humvee rolled up to the gate. Behind it, two more trucks rumbled to a stop. The trucks and Humvee looked like they'd just done the Cannonball Run-through Ambush Alley in A Nasiriyah. The glass in the windshield of the first truck was pock-marked with bullet holes. To the left of the driver, two holes spiderwebbed out and joined a third hole where the driver's face had been. On the hood, a bail of concertina was festooned with cloth and hair. The front apron of the vehicle was covered in blood and scorch marks. Even the bumper had several huge dents. It looked like they'd hit several hundred deer on the way to the plant.

A tall, wiry man in ACU fatigues that Vee instantly recognized from their annual training programs stepped out of the Hummer. "We're what's left of the CAAT unit from Grayling. We're here to reinforce you."

"Yeah. Right. Malone, what the hell happened to you guys?" Vee asked. He sidestepped to check out the damage to the rest of the trucks. They were every bit as trashed as the lead Humvee.

"You're still at your post, Vee?" Malone asked and walked forward to shake hands.

"Yeah, what the hell?" Vee held his arms out, mouth still agape.

"Man, we got straight-up ambushed in Dearborn. Some psychos drove a car bomb into our lead vehicle, and they cut us off at the rear. Had us in a kill-box and started raking us with PKM fire. PKM fire, dude. Like we were back in Afghanistan." Sergeant Malone shook his head. "We fought through the contact; most of the trucks followed us. Couple of blocks past that, we got ambushed again by an angry mob waving the damn flag of the Islamic State. Let me say that again for you, *ISIS dude*. We lost some trucks. We rammed our way through a nuts-to-butts-thick crowd of people. How did America turn into Beirut in five days?"

"*ISIS?*" Vee tried to get his mind around what he'd just heard.

"That's just what we saw in Dearborn. Past that, we saw the mafia gangbangers shooting it out with those Chaldeans. It's an all-out warzone in there right now." Malone kept patting down his plate carrier vest, as though he still couldn't believe that it hadn't taken rounds. "Task Force Wolverine show up yet?"

"Who the hell is Task Force Wolverine?" Vee's voice jumped an octave. He had so many questions he didn't know where to start.

"We're supposed to link up with some militia dudes here. Apparently, they're pipe hitters--not the fat kids you see playing with guns on YouTube." Malone pulled out a cigarette and stuck it in his mouth. "You going to let us in man? We need to get to work shoring this place up and squaring our own shit away."

"Yeah, man. Hold on a sec." Vee dug around in his pocket for the VIP pass for the gate. "You just dropped some heavy shit on me, telling me ISIS is fighting with the black mafia and shit. Hey, let me bum one of them smokes off ya." Vasean licked his lips at the thought of a cigarette.

"Sure." Malone reached inside the hummer. "Take a pack. We got plenty."

"I'll hit you up in a bit, Malone. I get relieved in thirty minutes," Vee said. He caught the Marlboro cigarettes and packed it against his wrist. "Sounds like we got some catching up to do."

"Damn straight, brother," Malone said. He got back in the vehicle and closed the door.

Vee scanned the special access card four times over the keypad and waved the Guard vehicles onto the premises.

Marlboros weren't exactly Vee's favorite cigarette, but he'd have to make do. He lit the first cigarette as soon as the last vehicle rolled through, and by the time his relief showed up thirty minutes later, he'd burned through three more.

Vee walked toward the staging area and caught a chill on the way. He hungered for info on a gut-deep level and it'd been all he could do to keep from radioing Jerry to ask. The news that blew in with the Nasty Girls amped Vee's concern for his mom a thousand percent. Out on the horizon, fires were burning so bright that an eerie orange glow had replaced the night canopy. Black columns broke up the flickering orange, and it appeared as if both the cities of Windsor and Detroit were massive, burning candles. He recognized the familiar smell of burning plastic, rubber and maybe the slight scent of human flesh. It was a smell from a world he thought he left behind him in third world warzones where the apocalypse was already happening. Thoughts of his mother haunted him.

Outside the main security building, three Humvees were now staged bumper to bumper. Several of the National Guard troops were squaring away the trucks-- washing away the blood the best they could with a hose. Others went from truck to truck with green cans of 7.62 ammo for the two M240 Bravo medium machine guns. Vee noticed that one truck had an M2 Browning heavy machine gun, and the other was loaded for bear with a MK-19 automatic grenade launcher. These boys were indeed rolling heavy. Vee was sure they gave better than they got back at that ambush. A lot of people died to kill a couple dozen National Guardsmen. Maybe hundreds.

Who the fuck would do that in America?

Inside the security building, Jerry spoke quietly with Sergeant Malone. Judging by the way Jerry ground his teeth, Vee would bet that the Sergeant was telling Jerry the same story he'd heard at the gate. Other members of the security team were offloading their gear, and Vee spotted Phil floating around collecting bits of news.

"Hey Phil." Vee motioned for his friend to come talk while he shrugged out of his plate carrier.

"Yeah man, whatsup?" Phil asked.

"Smoky treat?" Vee teased holding up the pack of smokes.

"How'd you score those?" Phil smiled.

Vee tossed his friend a cigarette from the pack. "I have a way with people. Let's chat before Jerry and Malone over there put us on sandbag duty."

"Sandbag duty?" Phil looked confused. "What, are we in Afghanistan now?"

"Maybe. Come on."

Once outside, Vee lit his cigarette and tossed the lighter to Phil. He relayed everything he'd heard from Sergeant Malone.

"Are you serious?"

"As serious as cancer in your throat." Vee nodded, pointing at Phil's neck with his cigarette pinched between two fingers.

"So, let me get this straight, you're telling me that the *Islamic State* is out there right now fighting a war inside of Detroit, and that they're using car bombs to hit National Guard and gangsters?" Phil took a long drag from his bummed Marlboro. "Where the hell is the actual military?"

"That's all the boys in gray told me," Vee said, scratching the top of his head. "It sounds like the whole damn city has gone internal-- turned into Mosul--and no help is coming."

The door cracked open and Jerry joined them. He stood stock still for a moment, sighed heavily, and then pulled three cigars out of his pocket. "I just discovered this cigar company two months ago boys: Warfighter Tobacco Company. I was saving them in the office for winter when we had a cold night. Hand rolled in Nicaragua. Looks like that night is tonight."

"What's the plan, Jerry?" Phil asked, taking one of the cigars with a nod and reaching into his pants for a pocketknife to cut the tip.

"Well, we can count the National Guard out, except for these guys. As far as you're concerned, I'm not going to hold anyone here against their will. I think it's safe to say the company is gone, or they just don't give a rat's ass about us anymore."

Jerry lit his cigar and pulled on it a few times to get it burning. "That said, if what these boys are saying is true about that ISIS stuff and the car bombs, I think I'm going to stay. The last thing we need right now is for ISIS to start playing reindeer games with a nuclear power plant."

"Yeah, me too," Phil said after a long puff. "I've got nowhere else to be right now, and nothing better to do. Count me in."

Both men turned to Vee.

"The power goes out, and my mom dies. On the other hand, if the city burns to the ground, it'll take the hospital with it." Vee looked at his boots. "Tonight, just keeps getting heavier and heavier."

"We need you here, Vee," Jerry said with a sigh. "I know I can't force you to stay. All I can do is ask. If you go into that city right now, who's to say you even make it to the hospital? In the south, the black mafia is conscripting up every brother they got and going to war with what sounds like the Islamic State of Syria. Their Tec-9s and Hi-Points aren't going to beat PKMs. Even if you didn't get sucked in, you'd have to be one hell of a Rambo-ass mofo to fight your way to that hospital."

Phil just smoked his cigar in silence.

After a long pause, Vee gave voice to his thoughts. "She probably wouldn't survive long away from the machines, but at least I'd be there with her when she passed." Vee took an inhale of his cigar and stared at the blazing orange sky.

"It's a tough choice, Vee. What would she want you to do?" Jerry asked.

"She would want me to stay here and survive. She'd want me to keep the lights on for everyone else."

"Survive, huh?" Phil echoed. "So, you're with us?"

"I'm with you guys," Vee decided. "*Moms* would kick my ass if she got to heaven and I was there already because I got myself killed for nothing... Damn it. That woman was never anyone's charity case."

"Sounds like my kind of lady," Jerry said with a laugh.

"You keep my momma outta your spank-bank, Jerry." The three men laughed and smoked in silence for a few minutes. It was a bittersweet interlude of brotherhood, one that they all knew would end too soon and would likely end in pain.

ON THE WHITEBOARD inside the conference room, Sergeant Malone studied a rough sketch of the perimeter. The entire plant was surrounded by reinforced chain-link fence, topped with razor wire. East of the plant was Lake Erie. To the South sat the small city of Stony Point. To the west, a small open field surrounded by a line of tall elms. To the north was the city of Detroit.

There were only two ways into the plant by vehicle, and both entrances were blocked by powered sliding chain-link gates. One entry came in from Fisher Street, and one from Stony Point. Locking down those two entrances would be as easy as adding sandbags at the guard shacks and bringing the M240B medium machine guns to bear.

"Alright, Jerry," Sergeant Malone said, pointing at the sketch. "We can put one 240 at each entrance. What's changed since the last time me and my guys trained with you?"

"Not a lot." Jerry stared at the map. "To be honest, the only real thing that's changed is the war inside Detroit and America eating itself for dinner. We are the only cavalry we're going to get."

"Got it," Sergeant Malone agreed. "So our old plan should stand. Your guys are going to stay instead of turning security over to us, right?"

"Well, most of them are staying—most of the men and women still here," Jerry said.

"I brought twenty. You have eleven including yourself, correct?"

"Yes. That puts us at thirty-one shooters." Jerry wrote the number on the board and then wrote the names. "I'll set a guard rotation. Can I get eight bodies from you so the guys can stop standing twelve on, twelve off?"

"We'll all chip in and start a full rotation. Six people will always be on post, with another twelve on QRF at the gun trucks. The six coming off post will go into a rest period while the remainder is on work details." Malone picked up a marker and wrote the names of his own men on the board. "That plan should stay the same. We need to lay in defense in depth and prepare for the shit storm in Detroit to reach us here. I don't want to count on the combat fairy to protect us from ISIS. They know exactly where we live."

"Agreed. What's our plan for defense in depth outside of sand-bagging the two entry points?"

"We're going to have trip flares in the tree line, here." Malone pointed toward the trees. "That will alert us of anyone coming in from that direction. We'll also send a patrol through there periodically to make sure no one is eyeballing us, and to make sure the flares aren't disarmed. Following that, we'll build alternate and supplementary positions at each post so the guys there can fall back."

"Okay. Good," Jerry agreed, scratching his chin and analyzing the sergeant's plan. "We might also want to build improvised positions around the control facility where the civilians and families live."

"I don't think it will come to that, but it's not a bad idea. We can get that done after we lay in the other defenses." Malone added it to the bottom of the checklist. "We also need to establish a solid line of communication with Camp Grayling. We would usually use our command vehicle, but we lost the LT and his truck to the car bomb. Any idea where we could set it up?"

"Uhh... I got nothing on that Sarge." Jerry shook his head. "We generally rely on land lines and cell phones here. That's outside of my wheelhouse. What's up with this whole Task Force Wolverine thing? Sounds like something Hollywood dreamed up."

"They're Michigan State Militia, which isn't as lame-sauce as it sounds. But we have no radio comms with them. All I was told was that the full bird in Grayling linked up with that old dude, Bryce, from the Michigan Militia, and they sent one of their 'Special Operations' teams to reinforce us." Malone made finger quotation marks when he said Special Operations. "According to the commo guy in Grayling, those dudes are the real deal, but I don't know them from Adam."

Thunder rumbled from the north and Malone's radio came to life.

"Sergeant, just had another explosion out of South Detroit. We saw the fireball this time." The radio chirped twice after the transmission, indicating that his battery was starting to die.

"Roger. Not our problem. Have the boys prep for a brief," Malone responded.

"Roger 'at, Sarge," the radio came back, triggering another electronic double-chirp from Malone's hip.

"Guess that's our cue to get back to work," Jerry said. "I'll get my people briefed." He headed out the door and stopped. "When we're pinning all our hopes and dreams on the same guys Obama pegged as 'domestic terrorists,' that means we've officially entered the Twilight Zone. Am I correct, Sergeant?"

"That's an affirmative, my brother."

"Civilization is like a thin layer of ice upon a deep ocean of chaos and darkness." – Werner Herzog

Monday, September 25th – Just after Midnight.
Clinton Township, Michigan
I-94 South

Eight men of the militia's Task Force Wolverine barreled southbound down I-94 in three matching Crown Victoria sedans. Two years ago, when the task force had hardened into the commando core of the Michigan State Militia, they'd chipped in and picked up the police surplus Crown Vics. The muscular police cruisers had become their team symbol—three flat black harbingers of militia doom. Now they were rolling for real, and they looked like death.

There wasn't much traffic in the southbound lane that led into the city of Detroit. In the opposite lane however, leading out of Detroit, traffic was at an absolute standstill.

The entire city of Detroit burned. Even though it was just past midnight, the glow from large buildings afire lit the night sky. Ash rained down, making it appear as if the season had changed to winter in the three hours they had been on the road.

What should have been less than a thirty-minute drive down the 94 had, so far, turned into an absolute slog for the three vehicles and their occupants. At multiple points in the journey, they'd been blocked by accidents which required the men to get out and render aid or move blockages.

Now as Task Force Wolverine entered Clinton Township, north of Detroit, things seemed to be clearing up, at least on the road.

A multitude of gun fights echoed across the cityscape. Captain Randall Myers had no intentions of involving Task Force Wolverine in any of them, though they'd come prepared to dominate. He was under strict orders from the militia's Colonel to race directly to the Enrico Fermi Nuclear Power Plant and keep it out of the hands of Queen Mother Chaos.

En route to the power plant he was to recon the city. This was a secondary mission that he'd tasked to his two former MARSOC operators, Sanders and Wulf. They sat in the backseats of his minivan taking pictures with a Canon EOS 70D. Each picture was instantly uploaded to a high-end Toughbook laptop, then uploaded to the militia command center located in Camp Grayling.

Keeping one hand on the steering wheel, Myers squeezed the

handset and broadcast to the vehicles behind him. "Stay on 94 until we hit the interchange with 53. How copy?"

"Vic Two, solid copy"

"Vic Three, that's a copy. You sure we want to do that? It's a secondary objective. And the pictures are for shit at night," Xiong replied from the rear of their convoy. X, as they called him, had been a SEAL Team communications guy and had done a stint working alongside the Kurds in Northern Iraq. Like most Team guys, X liked sticking to the book. He got antsy when things grew hair.

"Our orders are to recon Detroit and we are more than capable of taking on looters and gangbangers." Myers let off his handset long enough to signal there was more information. "Stay right on me. We're going to drive through this shit show like Baghdad. Engage any threat."

Myers loved this moment: when fear and excitement fused in a chemical cocktail. He could almost feel his pecs contracting and his vision tightening. He could follow each flake of ash floating to the ground in front of the massive bumper he'd bolted onto his Crown Vic. Sounds amplified and the warm glow from the fires became as bright as the sun. The smell of burning rubber and flesh cranked his intensity to Defcon One.

The adrenaline hit him in waves, tuning the sounds of gunfire coming out of the city to the point where he was almost able to pinpoint the location of the shooters.

A huge explosion in the distance rattled the windows of the Vic, followed by a crescendo of automatic weapon's fire and several whumps from what he could've sworn were grenades. The unmistakable chatter of PKM machine gun fire gave Myers pause. As familiar as it was, he'd never heard such a thing in the U. S. of A. Underneath the heavy machine gun reports, he swore he could pick out Kalashnikovs. Periodically, the sound of a shotgun or an explosion would punctuate the symphony of destruction. This wasn't a gangbanger thing.

"Cap, we got a pickup on our tail. They're flying some kind of flag off the back. Can't tell if friend or ..." The radio cut off mid-sentence. Then, "CONTACT! SIX O'CLOCK!"

Myers picked out the familiar flicker of burning tires silhouetting two cars blocking the road a hundred meters ahead. "Roadblock! I'm ramming through. Increase your intervals!"

Stealing a glance into his rearview mirror, Myers could see the second vehicle slow down. Wulf and Sanders in the backseat, had their windows down and were searching for targets. They opened fire, filling the vehicle with thunder.

Off Myers' fenders, two pickup trucks flying black flags hemmed him in. The trucks each absorbed a half a mag from Wulf and Sanders before veering away down side streets.

The men at the roadblock raised their rifles and fired. The muzzle flashes from their Kalashnikovs overrode Myers's adrenaline and dumped a heavy dose of dread. He couldn't avoid the reality: they had driven into something much worse than civil disorder. "Get down!" Myers shouted over the roar of gunfire.

Taking one last look at the two vehicles blocking the road, Myers made sure the frame of his vehicle would connect with the wheels of the two trucks, then ducked low behind the steering wheel to position his body behind the engine block. As he ducked, Myers mashed his foot down on the skinny pedal. He counted down in his head toward impact.

7.62mm rounds ripped through the unarmored windshield like passing through paper. A large caliber round punched the roof of the Vic and ricocheted off into the rear.

Men shouted in a foreign language, likely fleeing the roadblock. The Crown Victoria slammed into heavy metal, and all three men were flung forward against their seat belts. The airbag exploded, and Myers sat up, stabbing at it with his hands as he accelerated through.

"Wulf, Samson? You good?"

Both men opened fire a split-second after impact, dumping magazines at the men on the side of the street. In the rearview mirror, which had miraculously survived the fusillade, Myers saw the other two vehicles rocket through the opening.

"Sitrep," Myers commanded into the radio.

"Vic two good," Johnson replied instantly, the sound of gunfire echoing over the radio.

"Vic Three good," X replied. "Still got our tail. Think we got the guy in the back of the truck, but the passenger is still shooting,"

"Roger. Close intervals, I want us tight-tight. Two move out to the right lane and see if you can help put some fire down on our tail."

"On it."

The small convoy closed their intervals before the second vehicle veered out into the right lane. Vic Three sped up to come alongside Vic Two. A roar of gunshots competed against a smattering of incoming AK fire. Within a heartbeat, the pickup truck veered to the left like a wounded animal, crashed into a guardrail and rolled hard. Myers caught a glimpse of a familiar logo on the flag as it snapped in two.

"Job jobbed. Zero casualties on our end," Xiong reported from the rear of their high-speed convoy.

"Keep it tight, stay right on me. The Vic seems to be holding up fine. Two, take point and keep en route to the nuke plant."

"Roger. Two taking point now. Same-same for us. No casualties," Johnson reported as the second vehicle in the convoy pulled out and passed Myers.

"You guys good back there?" Myers glanced over his shoulder at the two men in the back of his vehicle. "That got nasty."

"Wulf caught a round to his leg, Cap!" Samson laughed.

"You're full of shit."

"No really, look." Wulf held his prosthetic leg for Myers to see. "Fuckers shot me in the ankle!"

Myers rolled his eyes, the adrenaline bleeding off bit by bit. "You two keep snapping pictures. That was the flag of the Islamic State on those trucks, which makes no sense at all. That intel changes everything for HQ, yet you two idiots grab ass like it's just another day in the Corps."

"Every meal a feast," said Wulf as he ratcheted his leg bag into place.

"Every formation a family reunion," replied Samson.

Myers reminded himself that joking and the military platitudes were how men celebrated not being dead.

As the convoy sped down Gratiot Avenue, the chaos transformed into what looked like open warfare in the streets. Team Wolverine kept a high rate of speed, but that didn't stop them from having two close calls with sniper fire, nor did it keep them from driving past several firefights that were none of their business. Myers wasn't nearly as pumped up on himself and his team as he'd been at the beginning of this drive. They were hitters, for sure, but they weren't invincible. And these were no douchebag, side-shooting gangbangers. Somehow, this was ISIS in Detroit.

Myers had to run his windshield wipers to clear the falling ash near the heart of the city. The scraping of the wipers over bullet holes in the windshield grated on his nerves. In the backseat, Wulf and Samson snapped pictures. Hopefully, the information was being relayed to their command center in Grayling. Who knew if any of that high tech shit was even working now?

"You wanna pick up the pace?" Johnson asked over the radio. Given what they'd just seen, the nuclear power plant was anything but safe.

"Affirm. I think we've seen enough, break," Myers spoke into his radio as he drove. "We may need to pull off once we get past the south side of Detroit. My *check engine* light just came on. Vic One might shit the bed." They hadn't seen another vehicle since the ISIS-mobiles.

The enemy always gets a vote, fluttered through Myers's mind unbidden.

"Solid copy. Once we're through I'll find us a place to pull off and we can execute the bump plan," Johnson said. "We're coming up on the interchange by the stadium."

"Got it. I would set up an ambush here," Myers said. "They start shooting, we turn this convoy into a death blossom, and we keep pushing. We are not stopping."

As if on cue, Johnson began to increase speed in the lead vehicle. Myers accelerated with him. Below the interchange sat Ford Field and Commercial Park. Many times, Myers had come here with his son to watch the Tigers play baseball. What he saw now put a knot in his gut the size of a major league baseball.

"Lights out. Lights out. Go dark," Myers hissed into the radio. Both vehicles went dark and the convoy slowed.

"I see it, boss," Xiong radioed.

"We just going to let this happen?" Johnson asked from Vic Two.

Myers knew that stopping the convoy and engaging would put their mission at risk. But they were Wolverines—the best of the best America had once fielded in the Global War on Terror. And now the shiteaters had brought their hell to his home. He wouldn't allow it.

At the entrance to Ford Field, at least three dozen men wearing black hoods stood in a circle. Four pickup trucks shined their lights into the middle. A man shouted in the center of the pool of light, holding a machete above his head. A man knelt on the ground before him, a black hood over his head.

In a flash, the machete came down, thunking into the back of the man's neck. Blood shot up toward the sky as the executioner drew the machete out of the ragged wound. Twice more the machete fell before the man's head dropped and rolled to the executioner's feet. The body slumped sideways and went still.

"Execute the bump plan now," Myers snarled into the radio.

The next person was being blindfolded and pushed toward the headsman. The dead body was carted to a pile of other headless bodies. The head was collected and put in a separate pile.

"We're going to buy these people a chance."

"One pulling off," Johnson replied.

"Three pulling off," Xiong followed on the radio.

They veered off to the side of the overpass in unison instead of taking the exit that would lead them toward the power plant.

"Wulf, Samson, get Johnson, Rodriguez, and Berryman to move our gear to Vic Two. Then rally at the rear," Myers ordered as he popped the trunk and leapt out of the dying Crown Victoria.

"On it," Samson and Wulf replied.

Myers grabbed his go to hell bag and high-cut ballistic helmet from the trunk as he ran back toward Vic Three. He fished around in the bag and pulled out a PVS-14-night vision monocle and clipped it to his helmet. People wailed and screamed from Ford Field, and Myers threw the bag on the ground behind Vic Three as he strapped on his helmet and prepared to go to war.

Ford Field was one of the few structures inside of the city that wasn't on fire. Undoubtedly, it was being used by the city to house refugees. It was common practice for relief agencies.

Myers stepped to the guardrail beside the Vic and pulled his monocle down over his eye.

Xiong and McDaniels approached, also pulling their night vision. "What's the plan?" Xiong asked.

Myers held up a finger and surveyed the killing grounds. Another victim was already on his knees, and the butcher was giving a long speech in English now.

In front of the butcher, a camera operator recorded the executions. Who would ever see them now that broadcast was dead, remained a mystery? More than a dozen black-clad men stood behind the butcher with Kalashnikov rifles. A man on each end held the black flag of the Islamic State. Drifting around the perimeter of light, another two dozen men, more or less, mulled about, getting their rocks off from the murders. Most of them wore coyote tan chest rigs and carried AK style rifles with varying degrees of uniformity.

In a flicker of reflected light, the machete came down and again failed to fully sever the head. Several more whacks failed to remove it, and the butcher began the grisly work of sawing through the man's vertebrae with the dinged-up edge of his blade. Once the spine had been separated at the base of the skull, he gave the neck another strike and the head fell away. He tossed the dulled machete to the side and called for a new one.

Myers looked back at his men. They all stood beside him; all emotion concealed by the NVGs covering their faces. But Myers knew what they felt.

Rage.

Samson stepped up the overpass rail with his Remington 700, and unslung it from his shoulder.

"That's part of the plan," Myers said to Samson, finally gutting out the Redman chew he had been working for an hour. He slung it onto the side of the road with a vicious whip of his hand.

From the crowd below, Myers heard the struggle of the next victim being dragged to the executioner's block. Women screamed over the sound of a diesel generator.

"Johnson, Rodriguez, Berryman, X and I are all going to rappel down. Wulf, Samson, McDaniels, you're on overwatch. Two minutes after the last guy hits solid ground, I want you two to take out the guy with the machete. You are the trigger. Then everyone's weapons free to start killing men in black pajamas. I want those truck lights out fast, so we can go to work with our NODs."

"The light coming off the fire is going to screw us either way. We don't get to be the night stalkers this time," Berryman pointed out. "We'll have to make them dead very quickly, before their eyes adjust."

"Twins, you take Vic Two. McDaniels take Vic Three. We'll rendezvous at the intersection of Brush and Madison. If that's untenable, the five of us will snag a few of those ISIS trucks and meet you on the road. You'll know it's us because we'll be rolling blacked out." Myers had whipped the plan together. Even to him, it sounded a bit thin. But people were dying—getting their heads lopped off. He heard a thunk and whipped around so see another American die beneath a fanatic's blade.

The enemy always gets a vote.

He watched the black-clad fuck-stick saw at a woman's head, her long hair tangling his blade.

"That fucker dies first." Myers flipped up his NVGs.

The seven other men of Task Force Wolverine nodded in unison and got to work. Berryman and Rodriguez walked to the back of Xiong's vehicle, pulled out the rope and rigged a hasty rappel line down to street level.

Myers, Xiong, and Johnson all made themselves Swiss seats while the Twins set up their elevated shooting position across the concrete barricade. McDaniels trotted to the front of the convoy to provide the Twins with rear security.

"All members of Wolverine, this is Myers," Myers spoke over his personal radio. "Roger up on comms so I know all channels are open."

Each member of Wolverine rogered up as Berryman kicked the last rappel line over the ledge. Berryman buzzed down the rope first.

It had been a year or so since Myers had practiced a rappelling operation, but he dropped down smooth as silk.

When his feet hit terra firma, he found himself in a tight 360-degree perimeter made up of his four men. Each man in this circle had done this exact thing dozens, if not hundreds of times with their units in places like Bosnia, Iraq, Afghanistan, and Somalia. Myers checked the glow of his wristwatch and marked the position of the second hand. Two minutes.

Berryman and Rodriquez, the two former Army Rangers, fell into a quick groove. Johnson had been a para rescue jumper with the Air Force. He acted as medic for Wolverine and looked more like a doctor than a pipe hitter. With him, Xiong held the southern half of the perimeter. X, a former Navy SEAL was a dead ringer for a math nerd. But they were hardened killers, each one.

"Wolverine, moving." Myers keyed his radio. "Stay in cover, optics down."

Sixty seconds later, Samson's Remington 700 boomed, followed by the confused shouts of Islamic State fighters.

Myers and his team rushed forward behind the low swell of the once-manicured park strip. The Remington 700 cracked overhead, dropping targets. Kalashnikovs responded immediately. At first, in dribbles, then in a roar.

Rodriguez and Berryman were already perched across a concrete divider outside the parking lot. Berryman's belt-fed M249, another gift from the militia's Colonel, roared as soon as he got the bipod jammed up against the divider, his shoulder into the weapon.

Rodriguez was taking aimed shots with his smaller rifle at the truck lights, knocking them out one at a time. Johnson joined him on the lights as X and Myers laid waste to the men in black pajamas. The ISIS fighters didn't appear to realize they were taking rounds from ground level.

"Do not let them get to their trucks," Myers spoke in a mastered voice into his radio, leveling the red dot of his rifle on a fighter trying to take cover on the wrong side of the diesel generator. "Wulf, what you got?"

"We got a bunch of confused bad guys shooting at us. Machete man is facedown, chewing concrete."

"Roger. Berryman, Rodriguez, lay the hate on my mark. X, Johnson, that'll be your sign to bum rush their trucks." Myers slammed a fresh magazine home and slapped the bolt release of his AR. "Go."

For a few seconds, all hell broke loose in front of them.

Berryman's M249 unleashed hellfire. Any doubt about his position was erased. Return fire pinged around him and Rodriguez. Flecks of concrete flew off the divider, challenging their focus. Rodriguez leaned into the fight, and Berryman dropped down to swap his belt.

Johnson and Xiong bounced up and ran at a dead sprint toward the six parked pickup trucks, taking shots on the move.

One fighter climbed into the back of a pickup truck with a mounted PKM medium machine gun. He caught a Remington round through his chest. It exploded out his back and continued into the windshield of the truck behind him. The fighter flopped to the ground screaming. A split-second later, his body exploded in a flash of light and thunder.

"What the hell?" Xiong skidded to a brief stop. "Suicide Vests!"

Xiong and Johnson hit their target trucks in a few seconds. They had fixed and flanked a numerically superior force, and now laid down a withering level of suppressing fire that allowed Samson and Wulf to put down targets from overwatch.

Civilians rushed past Berryman and Rodriguez's position in a wave that overwhelmed their ability to target identify. Even so, the fight slid in their favor. Return fire from the pockets of ISIS fell off.

"X, Johnson, I'm coming to you," Myers radioed. "Increase your rate of fire. Berryman, Rodriguez. Lay it down."

Myers rushed toward his two men behind the trucks. He baseball-slid between the two men and popped up, slamming his shoulder into the side of the truck.

"What do you have?" He heaved, catching his breath from the sprint.

"Four of them left, Cap," Johnson replied, ducking down behind the truck and flinging a magazine out of his rifle to slam a new one home. "I think they're trying to get back inside the stadium."

"Not gonna happen," Xiong smiled, looking over his sights in the direction of the last enemy position and holding his fire.

A Kalashnikov raised over the concrete and started "spraying and praying."

X fired a single round that smashed the upper receiver of the AK and ripped it out of the man's hand.

"Cap, we got a serious problem up here," McDaniels barked over the radio, sounding panicked.

"Go ahead, Mac?" Meyers replied.

"A whole convoy of technicals is coming our way from the direction we're supposed to egress. What's the play?" He sounded like he was already repositioning.

"Hold them off. We're heading back to you," Myers ordered.

"Not a chance, Cap." Several PKM medium machine guns opened up on the overpass and were met with the sound of Wolverine's smaller rifles. "We gotta beat feet or these guys are going to overrun us. Suggest you go with Plan B," Mac huffed into his mic, running for his life.

"Roger that. Rodriguez, Berryman, move to our position now. McDaniels, meet us at the power plant." Myers turned to X and Johnson. "Johnson, get this truck running, X, you're on me. We finish this before those guys up top get into a position to fire down on us."

Myers signaled for Xiong to break around the back of the truck as he moved up to the engine block. In unison, both men stepped out from behind cover and rushed toward the remaining Islamic State fighters.

They bounded together, firing and maneuvering, taking up positions of cover and laying down a rate of fire that did not allow the enemy to poke their heads out. In an ideal scenario, they would toss a hand grenade and be done with it, but militia didn't allow for

explosives. They'd been lucky enough to get the Colonel to use his firearms license to get the single belt-fed for each team in Wolverine.

Myers ducked beside the generator with a dead guy next to it and reloaded. The magazine flew out, and another went in almost the same second. He slammed the bolt release and went back to work. Xiong took a knee, swapped mags and headed left. A small caliber pistol round pinged off the generator, ricocheting into the dead body.

The two men continued their ballet together. Moving. Shooting. Reloading. Keeping the four remaining Islamic State fighters pinned behind a never ending curtain of lead. Myers and X were within feet of the fighters when time seemed to slow. Seconds felt like hours. Meyers caught a 9mm round to his SAPI plate. He shrugged it off and pushed the assault.

Just as he cleared the top of the barrier, and the enemies' heads came into view in Myers' reticle, they shouted to Allah in unison. And the world went white.

MYERS CAME to in the bed of a pickup truck with Johnson hovering over him like a protective mother hen.

"Cap, wake up!" Johnson shouted over automatic gunfire as he smacked Myers on the side of helmet. "Not a good place to take a nap, boss."

"What—what happened?" Myers choked on his dry throat.

"S-Vests. Fuckers blew you up. You're good though--had your bell rung and you took a small caliber round to the chest. Didn't even break your plate. Can't say the same about your lid though." Johnson, swiveling his body like a tank turret to the rear of the bouncing truck, aimed down his sights at the technical that shadowed them on the freeway overpass.

Myers sat up and shook his head. A burst of machine gun fire rattled from above.

"Move it!" Myers shouted and flopped onto the roof of the pick-up truck his men had stolen from IS of Detroit. "Xiong good?"

Johnson rocked forward and slammed his knee into the tailgate of the truck as it accelerated. "Yeah, he's good. The explosion didn't catch him like you. We aren't out of this yet, you wanna help me out here?" The trucks above were racing to keep up. They'd apparently figured out that enemy forces were getting away with one of their vehicles. The overpass above Ford Field followed the frontage road for another quarter mile then veered away. They needed to hold the technical off for another sixty seconds and they'd be in the clear.

Myers shouldered his weapon and popped off precision shots at the driver of the lead technical. The shuddering and pitching of the truck and his double-vision made each shot feel like an impossible feat. But even his wild shots were enough to give the driver of the truck above them pause, and it slowed long enough for them to get out of range of the large caliber machine gun in the back. Between the two of them, they succeeded in keeping the machine gunner from getting accurate dope on their position. As the PKM fire dwindled, and their roads separated, the tension of battle drained away. Myers slumped against the back of the truck cab.

"How long was I out?"

"A few minutes at the most," Johnson replied, keeping his weapon aimed toward the vanishing overpass.

"Anything from Mac and the Twins?" Myers rubbed his temples and removed his helmet to examine the damage.

"Negative, we lost comms with them just before the explosion."

"Shit." Myers pulled a chunk of rock from his helmet and tossed it from the truck. He replaced the ruined helmet on his head and keyed his radio. "Xiong, keep trying to get the Twins or Mac on comms."

"Roger. Berryman says we should hit the nuke plant in about forty-five minutes, not counting what else we run into."

"Good, copy. We need to pump the brakes once we hit the northern outskirts of the plant. I want to infil on foot to make sure this place isn't already captured. If you reach Mac or the Twins, tell them to link up with us at that location." Myers put his head back on the truck and gazed at the night sky. Not a single star was visible through the smoke and firelight.

He'd lost three men. There was a good chance they were still alive, but they'd be running and gunning, unsafe and disconnected from their team. He'd essentially traded those three men for a whack at an ISIS death squad—and maybe that swap now left him without enough force strength to hold the nuclear power plant.

The math didn't lie: it wasn't a trade he could afford.

But the enemy always gets a vote.

How could he have known they faced much smarter, better organized enemies than Detroit gangbangers? The answer: a combat leader can never know who the enemy might be or what they have planned. That's why combat leaders train to play it smart, even under fire. Even in the throes of rage.

But we could not let those people die!

(They are dying anyway, even now.)

Fuck you! Myers remonstrated with himself. *They were Americans.*

(And so are the people downriver of the Enrico Fermi nuclear power plant and everyone else in this area if these guys cause a meltdown at the reactor.)

"APOCALYPSE HAS COME AND GONE. *We're just grubbing in the ashes.*" – Samuel R. Delany

. . .

MONDAY, September 25th – Just after Sunrise.

Stony Point, Michigan

Outside of the Enrico Fermi II Nuclear Power Plant

Myers stuck his face into the cab of the truck through the sliding window. "Berryman, pull over. We'll move on foot from here."

The sun had begun to rise as Task Force Wolverine cleared the smoldering remains of Southern Detroit. They'd lost three members of their team to a superior attacking force, and the five remaining members of Wolverine had come down hard from their combat high. Adrenaline fled their bodies in waves, and fatigue filled the hollow it left. It'd been years since any of them had been in a gunfight, and each man slumped sullenly in the bouncing truck, wrestling with memories and exhaustion.

After the battle at the stadium, Wolverine had been engaged by Islamic State fighters twice more. What should have been a forty-five-minute drive to Stony Point had taken close to six hours. They'd also dealt with near white-out conditions from falling ash and a flat tire. Being a "god of war" had never felt so humbling.

Berryman pulled off the main road and parked the truck behind a tumbledown shed.

"Have we managed to get comms with the guys at the power plant?" Myers asked for the third time.

"Negative man. Maybe they're not using the same HAM freqs," Xiong guessed, cracking the passenger door to the vehicle. "I think I heard Mac for a split second on our personal radios, but he was weak and unreadable. Or maybe I was imagining things."

"Let's jock up and move," Myers ordered, not sure if even he had the energy to continue with the mission. "If my GPS is correct, on the other side of that tree line, we should be able to see the Fisher Street entrance to the power plant. Hopefully, those ISIS shitbags haven't beaten us here. If they have, sure as hogs are made of bacon, plant security is going to shoot at us the instant they spot us. Stay frosty. Rodriguez you're on point."

"You got it, Cap." Rodriguez stifled a yawn and reached for his toes like a man getting ready to run the hundred-yard dash. His rifle butt banged the ground. "Moving," he said as he stood up and headed for the trees.

FROM HIS POST, Vasean could hear faint, staccato refrains of gunfire coming from Detroit eight miles away. Looking out from his guard shack, smoke rose into the morning sky from a hundred columns flattening out in a black haze that muted even the sunrise. Ash rained down upon the frosty earth, a malignant likeness of early winter.

Vee had made numerous attempts to reach the hospital to check on the condition of his mother, but none of the phone lines were working in the city.

He pulled out his last pack of Marlboros. With a tap on his wrist, he flipped the box open and made a mental calculation. He had twenty left, and he might just make them last two days. After his last cigarette, he wasn't sure he'd still care enough to stand guard. The idea of survival had lost some of its shine in the last twenty-four hours.

She had to be dead. The smoke wasn't coming from barbecue parties. One of those columns had to be his mother's care facility.

Plucking a cig from the pack, he pulled it out and fumbled for his lighter with his left hand while he held the stock of his rifle with his right.

Once he got the cigarette going, he surveyed his sector of fire. Since the National Guard had shown up, they'd built a fighting position with an M240 Bravo medium machine gun behind a ring of sandbags. Like it or not, he'd been conscripted into the defense of this location.

The fresh smoke filled his lungs, and he indulged in the rare moment of pleasure. He walked toward the machine gun position and smacked the buttstock of his AR, causing fresh ash to fall from his smoke.

Vee shivered against the wind and looked out toward the distant tree line. From his position, the M240 would cut down anyone moving through the open field. Even a numerically superior fighting force would have to contend with grazing fire for 500 yards of open terrain. In that time, the QRF could move one of the heavy machine guns into battery. If he couldn't save his mother, at least he could put hate on the animals that killed her.

Jerry appeared behind Vee and stepped over the sandbags. He slumped down, putting his back against the wind. "Let me get a hit off that, man. It's damn cold out here."

"Yeah. Here you go," Vasean said, handing the cigarette to Jerry. "So, how long we gotta stay like this? What's the word?"

"I wish I had something for you, but I don't." Jerry took a drag, the cherry lighting bright orange before he handed it back to Vee. "Ten SF types from the militia should've been here last night. We hold tight until this thing blows over."

"And if it doesn't blow over?" Vasean asked as he looked crosswise at Jerry.

Jerry scrutinized the tree line. "We haven't gotten that figured... What the hell is that?"

The first of several trip flares fired into the sky like roman candles. Vee dumped his AR against the sandbags and swiveled the machine gun in the direction of the flare. He searched for targets down the weapon's magnified optic.

"Whoa, brother. There's a chance that's our SF guys coming in." Jerry put his hand on Vee's shoulder.

"More likely it's ISIS. I'm pretty sure SF dudes don't fall over trip wires. Better get the QRF out here," Vee said as he set the cigarette down on the traversing bar of the tripod.

"Malone, this is Jerry, go ahead and spin up the QRF and get them to the Fisher Street post now. Trip flares just went off in the tree line."

"Solid copy, QRF is en route," Sergeant Malone replied.

Vee raised his voice an octave. "I got five guys in multi-cam. High cut helmets, packing AR-style rifles at the edge of the tree line. A big ass white dude with a biker beard is in the lead with his hands up."

"They got anything on them that says they might be our guys?" Jerry said.

"Other than them being white? I ain't never heard of no white, ISIS, multi-cam, high cut ballistic helmet wearing biker traveling with a Hispanic dude and an Asian." Still, Vee pulled the buttstock deeper into his shoulder. "Does that make me a racist?"

"Pretty sure it does," Jerry answered. He unslung his rifle and stood up on the sandbags. He waved both hands over his head. "What are they doing now?"

"Looks like the short Hispanic guy up front is glassing us. The rest of them got their weapons lowered and are taking a knee." Vasean said. "Asian guy is carrying a handset with a whip antenna. Definitely only five guys in the clear."

An M1114 Humvee skidded to a halt behind them. Sergeant Malone jumped down from the vehicle and brought his scoped rifle to bear in the direction Vee aimed.

"Talk to me Vee, what am I looking for?" Malone shouted over the rumble of the Humvee.

"Five dudes at the edge of the tree line, facing us," Vasean shouted back over his shoulder. "Looks like the little dude is waving back. Are those our guys?"

"Only one way to find out." Malone dropped his rifle down to the low ready. He turned and climbed back into the passenger seat of the Humvee. After a moment, they drove over the curb and headed out into no-man's-land toward the strangers.

Vee kept the 240 on them, covering the armored vehicle as it rolled out to meet them. "Either those are our guys, or they're the most ethnically diverse motorcycle club in all of Southern Michigan."

MYERS WALKED STRAIGHT to the white board inside the command center of the power plant and studied the drawing of the perimeter.

"Sergeant Malone, do you have a radio operator, or somebody that can pass for one?"

"Hold on, Captain America." Sergeant Malone stepped halfway between Myers and the white board. "Let's hear your story and *then* figure out our next steps. This facility is my responsibility—me and Jerry over there. He's acting head of plant security. I'm what's left of the National Guard unit with orders to defend this plant."

The rest of Task Force Wolverine filed into the briefing room along with a few of the National Guard troopers and Jerry.

"Are you the hot-shit militia team they told us was coming in here with ten certified members of the Pipe Hitters Union to save the day?" Jerry extended a hand and smiled.

"I'm Captain Myers, Task Force Wolverine." Myers reached out and shook the man's hand. "And you are?"

"I'm Jerry, like the man said. I'm the security shift supervisor who inherited this shit sandwich." Jerry stared into Myers's eyes.

"Right." Myers chewed on the inside of his cheek. "You guys haven't had any outside comms since all of this started?"

"None. All we know is what Sergeant Malone and his guys brought in with them. They say ISIS is coming for us, and they have the bullet holes to prove it. We do have a satellite phone if your man has someone on the other end who will actually answer a call."

Jerry dug a sat phone out of his vest and Xiong grabbed it and went right to work while the big dogs spoke.

"Islamic State," Myers's voice trailed off. "Who they are is beside the point. Long story sucks, so I'll give you the short one."

Jerry and Malone both seemed to concede the floor, at least for the time being. They both took a seat at the folding table facing Myers and the white board. The rest of the men in the room sat down in the plastic chairs.

"America is falling apart everywhere. I've seen this dozens of times in other countries." Myers established his bona fides right up front. "With the government and economy failing, there's a power vacuum. It's not so unusual to see tight-knit groups like the Islamic State of America stepping up. Who else around here has that level of command and control when the telephones and paychecks stop? We can only hope Camp Grayling and the militia are still functional. We don't have anything but our personal radios at this point."

Malone shook his head and Jerry stared at a blank wall. Xiong stepped outside with the sat phone.

"And the entire United States government is doing absolutely nothing about it? What about the police? What about the rest of the military?" Malone asked.

Myers raised both hands. "Cops went home to protect their families. A majority of the military probably did the same."

Malone nodded in concession. "Even four days ago when our unit got activated, only half our people showed up."

"We're surprised you guys are still here." Myers scratched his chin. "So, what's the plan? I need to understand the battlespace."

Xiong came back in and interrupted. "Comms are up, Cap. I passed our sitrep, the Colonel wants to speak to you."

"I need a list from you. What you have and what you need," Myers told Sergeant Malone. Then he strode to the back of the room and took the phone from X.

"Colonel, this is Captain Myers, our situation is as follows," He took a breath while looking at Xiong. "Wolverine Alpha is down to five pax. Wulf, Samson, and McDaniels are missing in action. We are with the standing unit leader for the National Guard CAAT unit, Sergeant Malone. The security team that was on duty when everything fell apart is currently standing at ten pax. The CAAT unit is standing at twenty with four vehicles."

"Shit, that's a lot of bad news bears, Myers. Wait one." The sat phone went silent. Colonel Bryce was probably briefing Camp Grayling's commander and preparing follow on orders.

During the pause, Jerry approached Myers with a sheet of paper torn from Sergeant Malone's notebook. Myers cringed at the shoddy handwriting and the items on the list. He'd been expecting it to contain full counts of their current ammunition and weapons. Instead Myers was reminded that Sergeant Malone was no staff non-com or Platoon Sergeant but was just probably the highest ranking enlisted fighting man left alive.

Myers waved over his man Johnson. "Take this list and un-fuck it with Sergeant Malone, quick-time."

"Myers. Standby to copy." The phone came back to life in his ear.

"Standing by."

"I've spoken to the bird here at Grayling, and I want you to know that you are officially in command of Operation Shawnee. Your mission is to hold that power plant and keep it running. If you are unable to hold the power plant, you must conduct a full shut down of the facility. It may be a few weeks before we're able to reinforce you.

"Solid copy on that Colonel. We're about a platoon-sized element here. What do we have for air assets?" Myers would've liked to challenge the Colonel on the notion that the National Guard couldn't spare troops to protect a damned nuclear power plant, but he didn't want to sound like *one of those guys*—an officer who bitched about allocation of resources.

"All we have is a resupply and that's coming straight out of my ass, son. Assume you will be alone and unafraid for the next few weeks, over." Colonel Bryce's confidence didn't mean much to Myers. The facts were the facts and the words were the words. He and these men had just been asked to defend the Alamo. They'd have to pin their hopes on the chance that ISIS in America didn't give a shit about eighteen million uranium pellets.

"We're working on that resupply list as we speak. Do you have a sitrep for us?"

"No good news, I'm afraid. The Marines are digging in a battalion-wide defensive position along the rifle line, holding every major bridge and freeway that they can. We're trying to spread the word about the Islamic State, but the truth is most people are too damn hungry and scared to see the forest for the trees. I wish I could tell you that you were the first militia commander to be taking command of a National Guard unit, but at this point our guys are practically running the show in this state. The bird here hasn't heard from his superiors in two days."

"We'll report back when we have our resupply needs. Give us a shout if you get any more information, sir. Out." Myers handed the sat phone back to Xiong with a grim look.

"What's the word, boss?" Xiong asked, stowing the handset.

"Operation Shawnee." Myers laughed. "We're holding this position until we're reinforced or overrun. If we're overrun, or in danger of it, we shut the plant down. Get that wish list tossed up to higher. I want us resupplied as soon as possible. I'm going to get with Johnson, Malone, and Jerry to see if we can't figure out how to keep 10,000 screaming jihadis from kicking down our front gate."

"Guess the only easy day really was yesterday," Xiong sighed.

***

THE SUN HAD REACHED its midday peak, but the temperature still hovered in the low sixties. The smoke-choked sky muddled the earth, stealing all color. Everything smelled of burning plastic, even this far from town.

The militia guys, Berryman and Rodriguez, marched toward Vee's guard shed in step with two privates from the National Guard and two members of the security team.

"Vee," Berryman called out. "I need you to pace out our LZ and make sure the Hueys fit. We're going to put both birds down simultaneously if we can right over there."

"All right, man," Vasean said, squaring up to the two privates. "Give us security while the big man and his little friend work their magic with the radios."

Berryman gave Vasean a nod and a fist bump and stepped out into the open field just past Vee's security station. The two men had only just met a few hours prior when Berryman pulled the vehicle in, but they had an immediate attachment with each other. Both understood the hardships that came with growing up in south Detroit, and both also shared the common bond of serving their country to escape that hardship.

"Rodriguez, where we at on comms?" Berryman asked. He took a knee and switched his personal radio over to the channel that would connect him with Captain Myers.

"When did they say the birds would be here?" Rodriguez asked.

"They left Grayling about an hour ago. Should be in range of your radio pretty soon. At least that's what Xiong told me." Berryman clicked his push-to-talk. "Wolverine Six, this is Berryman. Radio check, over."

"Berryman, this is Six, I got you loud and clear. Standby to copy." Myers voice was like a spike through the cold wind. "Hueys are inbound over Detroit right now. They should be in range of handhelds. They're packing quite a bit of gear. Once you get it off-loaded, I need security on the LZ. We'll be sending Malone and two gun trucks with a pickup. How copy?" Myers said.

"That's a solid copy. Out," Berryman said, the radio handset hanging over his shoulder. He racked the bolt of his M249 SAW back to the rear and engaged the safety near the trigger housing, looking towards Rodriguez. "Anything?"

Rodriguez held up a finger, nodding and spoke into his handset.

"What's the play?" Vee asked tossing a thumb back over his shoulder toward the landing pad.

"Birds land. We help the crew chiefs unload a couple of M249s, some crates of ammo and the chow, then we post far side security in the tree line until the gear's packed away. Good? Birds came in over Detroit, so I'm going to get with the pilots and see if they saw anything headed our way."

"If something is headed our way?" Phil asked, worrying out loud. He press-checked his rifle to ensure a round was in the chamber.

"We'll fuck that goat when we get to it, man," Berryman said, smiling. He'd seen the elephant in the last twenty-four hours, so the terror of combat had smoldered down to standard-issue dread.

The other two men smiled as well when the two Privates made a disgusted face.

The unmistakable sound of rotary-wing aircraft thumped out of the north. The two Vietnam era UH-1 Huey helicopters stood out against the gray sky with their dark green silhouettes. Visible on the side of the lead Huey was the insignia of the Michigan Militia, two golden deer holding a shield with two crossed, red lightning bolts.

"Birds think they see the LZ," Rodriguez reported, holding the handset against his shoulder. "Pop smoke."

Berryman pulled the smoke canister from the MOLLE loops on his vest. He pulled the pin and tossed the canister into the middle of the LZ. It landed with a thump and spewed a bright red smoke.

"Short Final," Rodriguez yelled over the increasing volume of the two aircraft. The ground shook as their noses flared back and the skids touched down.

"Go. Go," Phil yelled, giving one of the two privates a push. "It's just a helicopter, kid. This is still a working party. Move your ass!"

"Wolverine Six, this is Berryman. Birds are on the deck. Ready for the work party."

"Work party en route. Who's UH-1s are they?" Myers came back.

"Both are Militia. Looks like the Colonel wasn't messing with you when he said this resupply was coming out of his ass. Don't we only have four of these things?" Berryman walked toward the helos.

"Affirm. National Guard and the Reserve must be way over-tasked if the resupply is coming from us." The radio paused momentarily; Berryman could feel the frustration in his Captain's voice. "Watch your ass. Wolverine Six, out."

Vee and Berryman ran toward the lead helicopter, knowing that it'd flown by the senior of the two pilots. Berryman pounded on the window, and the pilot kicked open the side door and lifted her visor.

"Whatsup, Berryman? Just you and Rod out here, where are Wulf and Samson?" the pilot shouted over the still-beating rotor blades. Vee helped offload gear while he listened in on the conversation.

"MIA in Detroit. Hey listen, Murph, I need to know what you saw on the way in. We don't have much time. Myers and the Colonel want you guys back in the air ASAFP."

"Shit... They're MIA back there?" Murph tossed a thumb over her shoulder. "Brother, there ain't nothing good going on back there. We had guys taking pot shots at us with a DShK heavy machine gun."

"You see anything headed our way?" Berryman asked, glancing over his shoulder to check on the two security contractors furiously unloading supplies into a pile on the dying grass.

"Not sure what was going where. Why, what's up?" The pilot pulled a cigarette from the cargo pocket of her flight suit and put it to her lips.

"This is a pretty obvious target. We can't imagine the hajis Islamic State will leave us alone forever." Berryman eyed the cigarette. "How many of those you got left?"

"I knew you boys would ask. Make sure you look under the bench seat. Got a couple cartons in there for you." The pilot flashed a mischievous grin. "We'll risk another flyover on the way out of here."

"Roger. Appreciate you." Berryman reached up and snagged the already lit cigarette out of the woman's mouth. "Ima steal this one real quick too."

"Hah! You do t—" Murph's laughter was cut short by the sound of a rifle firing on automatic.

Vee caught movement as he unloaded a crate, looking through the open doors of the Huey. A mass of black-clad men was rushing the landing zone. He pushed through the open door of the helo with his rifle, braced his foregrip and laid rounds into the running bodies. The other security contractor dropped to the turf and fired through the skids.

"Best get outta here, Murph!" Berryman yelled at the pilot, then dropped to the ground and joined the other shooters in laying down hate onto the attackers.

The pilot frantically worked the controls of her aircraft while yelling at the co-pilot. It was all background noise to Vee, who was running his rifle like a penny slot machine.

An explosion shook the ground. Vee glanced back to see smoke rising from the second helo just as Murph pulled the pitch on her aircraft and leapt off the ground. Vee pitched back and out of the huey, landing on his ass. He saw incoming rifle fire rake the side of the helicopter as it fought to distance itself.

Berryman stood and shouldered his M249 and spewed half a

belt of 5.56mm in the direction of the tree line. Most of the black-robed runners had either died, dropped in the grass or retreated into the trees. But the whizzing and pinging of incoming rounds didn't slow down in the slightest.

Vee maneuvered toward the sandbag emplacement, stopping along the way to cycle rounds through his rifle.

Looking up again, he could now see the second helicopter burned brilliantly as the first heeled off into the sky. Both of Vee's National Guard privates still lay on the ground.

"Set!" Vee shouted over the chaos.

"Moving!" Phil yelled back. Vee hammered at a hillock in the grass as Phil ran.

Berryman picked up with Phil and the two men positioned to either side of Vee. All three took a prone position. "Wolverine Six, this is Berryman. We are in direct contact with an unknown number of enemy fighters. We have one UH-1 down, and at least two KIA, over!"

"Roger that Berryman, gun trucks are on the move. They should be to you in seconds." The radio clicked off.

The three shooters continued to lay a devastating amount of fire into the tree line. None knew where the enemy was, but killing the enemy wasn't the only way to beat him.

Rule number one in a gunfight is to get fire superiority over the enemy as soon as possible. A gun fight cannot be won from behind the curve.

From the direction of the power plant, the sound of an M240B machinegun joined the chorus, its throaty barks overpowering the sound of the two rifles and the light machinegun.

"Let's move to the Huey," Berryman shouted. "Once I pick it up, you two bound. Gun trucks are en route."

Vee and Phil nodded without looking up from their rifles.

Lifting the feed tray cover of his M249, Berryman swiped the remnants of the last belt of ammunition away. Rolling to his side, he pulled another 100 round cloth drum from a pouch on his vest and slipped it into the locking mechanism on the bottom of the receiver. He pulled the 14-round lead belt out of what was commonly referred to as the nut-sack and slapped it onto the feed tray and slammed the cover down.

"Move," Berryman shouted as he rose to a knee and started sweeping the tree line with his M249. He saw the back of a man retreating into the woods and dumped a short burst into his body.

Vee and Phil moved laterally behind the concealment of the burning Huey, stopping at each of the two National Guard soldiers. They were both dead. Vee moved to the front and Phil to the rear of the aircraft and scanned for targets. Return fire had nearly vanished.

"Set!" Vasean shouted as he stood scanning around the burning airframe.

"Moving to you," Berryman responded.

"Contact!" Phil yelled as he raised his rifle at a target in the grass. An AK round punched Phil's chest and threw him backward.

More rifle shots came from the dip in the grass, and Berryman sprayed it down with his M249. Vee caught sight of AK rounds tearing through Phil's legs and mid-section. He dialed in on faint muzzle flashes and carefully dumped a mag into the depression, shooting through the dry grass, hopefully grazing the heads that had to be shooting from prone. The reports from the AKs fell silent.

In the distance, the M240 was drowned out by the beefy thumps of a .50 caliber machine gun cutting into the tree line. Every few second the .50's fire would pause; the turret gunner forced to cycle the action to clear a malfunction of some unknown origin and get the gun back into the fight. The Humvee bumped over the rough terrain, and with the sound of that heavy machine gun, all incoming fire from the tree line ceased.

"Vee, check the pilots," Berryman put his finger to the throat of the two privates again, but Vee already knew that outcome. One had caught a round to his chin, his face laid split open like a banana with his tongue hanging limply over his throat. The other lay face down in the grass, his entire body a charred mess from the explosion that destroyed the helo.

Vee looked inside the Huey and saw the pilot and copilot, utterly blackened and dead. He ran over to check on his friend, but found Rodriquez supine in the grass halfway there. Vee felt for a pulse but got nothing. He pushed up from the dead militiaman and continued to Phil. Berryman was already there administering aid.

"Hold on, brother, I got you. I'm here." Berryman rolled Phil to his side and emptied the contents of the man's emergency first aid kit. Pulling out his knife, he cut away his pants to reveal the injuries.

"Oh no. Oh shit man. No. They got me. I'm going to die, man," Phil began to ramble. His face was already starting to turn pale from blood loss. "Shit. Shit, man. Shit."

"It's okay, Phil, I got you brother. Just stay with me." Once Berryman had removed the man's pants, he saw the true extent of the injuries. No less than eight 7.62x39mm rounds had penetrated his upper legs. Blood sprayed bright red from his left thigh as dark red blood pooled around another entry wound in his groin.

"Alright, buddy, I'm going put a tourniquet up by your junk. I need you to hang in here with me. Once we get that one, I can start packing this wound up by your hip. You're going to be okay." Vee had no idea how Phil could possibly survive, but he ripped Phil's tourniquet off his shoulder and handed it to Berryman. Berryman was grinding his knee on a spraying arterial bleed on Phil's upper thigh.

Vee took a knee next to Phil and grabbed his hand. He shared a look with Berryman and did not like what he saw.

"Rodriguez?" Berryman asked as he slid the tourniquet underneath Phil's leg.

Vee shook his head.

"Shit." Berryman struggled to feed the strap through the eyelet in the tourniquet, which would be required to cinch it tight. "Too much... too much freaking blood, man."

Several seconds passed before Berryman finally managed to feed the strap through and cinch it tight. Vee pulled another tourniquet off his own vest and started prepping it as Berryman twisted the windlass. More blood pooled in Phil's groin as he ratcheted on the windless, tightening it as tight as it would go.

"You monitor that TQ," Berryman said. "If he starts bleeding again, put this one on just above that one. Get started on it now because he's going to pass out once I start packing the wound."

Vee nodded. Another Kalashnikov fired on full auto from the trees. It was quickly silenced with return fire from machine guns on the trucks.

Phil was still talking, "Vee. I love you, man. I love you, man. Don't let me die. Not like this."

"You ain't gonna die, Phil. You're a tough son of a bitch." Vee gripped his friend's hand harder and watched as the Ranger crammed several inches of gauze into the gaping wound. Just as Berryman had predicted, Phil passed out immediately.

"These other wounds are superficial. He's not going to walk again anytime soon, but if I get this packed and we stop the bleeding here, there's a chance Johnson can do surgery back at the plant. Watch that arterial. If you see so much as a drop come out, you get that other tourniquet on fast, then re-tighten the original." Berryman strained as he packed inch after inch of gauze into the gaping wound. Blood pooled out of the injury, and each time it did, Berryman wiped it away with a gloved hand and packed in more gauze.

As he was coming to the end of the gauze, Berryman shouted. "Shit!"

A surge of blood shot from the gunshot wound in Phil's thigh like a geyser.

"Second tourniquet, get it on. Get it tight," Berryman said, unrolling another ball of gauze and packing it into the groin wound. "I'm almost done. Once you have that second TQ on, tighten the first and we can move him. He's going to make it, Vee."

Vee cranked on the second tourniquet's windlass. On his fourth rotation, it snapped with a loud *crack*. The blood surged again.

"Not good!" Berryman yelled. "Tighten the first tourniquet. Do not screw it up or this man dies. Right here, right now."

"Here we go," Vee said, unstrapping the windless and letting it loose. It rotored twice in the opposite direction before he could get a hand on it. As he tightened it again, Phil woke up.

"*Oh shit! Oh no! Mama!*" Phil screamed and struggled. His legs flailed, causing Vee to lose his grip. "*Help me!*"

Berryman mounted the man, pinning his shoulders to the ground and put his face inches away from Phil.

"Calm down. You're going to be okay. Listen," Berryman whispered. "I need you to listen to me. Calm down. I've got you, brother."

Blood shot from the wound in an arc, leaving a crimson trail across Vee's black vest. But there wasn't much to the second spurt of blood. By the time Vasean got back to his knees from being knocked over, the bleeding had almost completely stopped.

Phil passed out for the last time.

———

"*THE WORLD IS VERY different now. For man holds in his mortal hands the power to abolish all forms of human poverty and all forms of human life.*"
– *John F. Kennedy*

MONDAY, September 26th – Early Afternoon.
Stony Point, Michigan
Inside the Enrico Fermi II Nuclear Power Plant

Not hours after escaping Detroit, Rodriguez, two privates and a security contractor had died while conducting a routine resupply. Myers had no illusions: the terror organization knew right where they were, and they weren't taking a pass on the nuclear power plant. He and his mixed bag of patriot fighters were all that stood between ISIS and an inconceivable loss of American life.

Rodriguez's death hit all of Task Force Wolverine hard. They'd trained with the man for years, and he had become their brother. When they recovered his body there wasn't much left. The force of the explosion in the helo took off an arm and a portion of his head.

Myers reminded himself: people die in combat. It's the unit that overcomes the loss first that wins the next fight.

He made his way to the staff room that they'd turned into a hasty bunkhouse. Vee was up against the wall, tossing and turning in his sleep. Myers took a knee next to the younger man and gave him a nudge. "Hey kid. Time to wake up. You good?"

Vasean's eyes flew open and he pushed himself away from the man's touch as if he had poked him with a hot iron. "The heck man?"

"Meeting in fifteen. I need to know if you're still with us?" Myers whispered so none of the sleeping would hear.

"Shit man. I just watched my best friend bleed to death screaming for his mom. I don't even know if my own mom is alive or dead." Vasean rubbed his head and pulled his knees up.

"Where'd you serve?" Myers asked, changing the subject.

"Ramadi in oh-six. Nowzad in oh-nine. Was an oh-three-eleven with Second Battalion, Third Marines. Why?" Vasean looked up at the man.

"Rough years. Look kid, Berryman told me how you handled yourself out there." Myers sighed and crouched lower. "Half these National Guard kids haven't seen combat outside of that ambush in Detroit. We need you solid."

Vee got up and stood in front of Myers. "Those cats that attacked us ain't playin'. They're the real deal. I took this job to be done with jihadis driving car bombs into my shit. Guess *the best laid plans of mice and men*, eh?"

Myers chuckled. "So, you going to be good?"

Vee looked at Myers and nodded. "I guess this is how the story ends. Hey, I thought you were the bad asses come to save us all." Vee smiled.

"To be honest, I thought that too. Now, I think maybe we all might be speed bumps in the road of Master Mayhem." Myers clapped him on the shoulder. "But I'll be damned if I let them get their filthy, psycho hands on this place."

Vee chuckled. "Heard that."

Myers clapped the man on his shoulder and walked to where Xiong was monitoring the shortwave radio. He looked down at the man's notes, and then up to him. "That whack job with the stolen Humvee still broadcasting from Texas?"

"Yeah man, that dude's funny as hell. Pretty sure he's drunk every time he picks up the microphone." Xiong laughed.

"Yup. Put your specialist here on the radio." Myers turned and looked toward the front of the room. Berryman was making wide arcs with his hands. Malone and Jerry nodded, but still looked confused.

"Look Malone, I'm not bullshitting you. We take the rear leg out of the back of the tripod, put it up front to give us a high angle, and then use the Mk-19 grenade launcher to shoot the opposite side of the trees from inside the compound." Berryman sounded frustrated. "We don't have a gunner's quadrant, so my math is going to be Kentucky windage, but I'm sure the Captain will approve us to test fire and register the gun. It's going to be useless during a close in fight anyway."

"What am I approving, Berryman?" Myers crossed his arms, taking a classic infantry commander's pose.

"I was explaining to these fine gentlemen that we can take the

MK-19 and set it up inside the wire here and use it as an indirect fire weapon." Berryman shrugged. "Malone's not having it. He wants the Mk on a gun truck to maneuver wherever our points of friction are."

Myers nodded. "That's a killer idea, Berryman. As soon as this meeting is done, I want you to grab a couple guys and get that set up. Make sure they know how to operate the weapon system, and then register your preset targets." Myers turned to Malone. "We're not trying to step on your dick here. Berryman knows what he's talking about, and the Mk-19 isn't going to serve us as well as the extra 240s in the gun trucks. We're surrounded by some pretty flat land here, and we need the grazing fire."

Malone shrugged. "You're the boss."

"I'll teach you." Berryman grinned. "It's going to be badass. Trust me."

"Alright, gents. Listen up," Myers said. "Yesterday around five in the evening we were attacked by a unit of Islamic State fighters during our resupply. As you are all aware, we lost Chief Warrant Officer Rawlings and his co-pilot Mr. Basset. Also, among the dead are Sergeant First Class Rodriguez, Privates Walker and Ellis, and Mr. Phil Ballew, one of the security contractors from the facility. May God give them peace."

Myers glanced out at the men, gauging their resolve. They looked ready for payback. Anger was good. Better that than fear.

"We confirmed five enemy killed in action, several more escaped in a pick-up truck. I think we can consider the attack a probe, and since they managed to kill a helicopter, I doubt they're running scared." Myers hesitated, unsure if he should be giving his enemy this much credit. "But they will also know that the people defending this location aren't just going to roll over and let them take it."

Myers swallowed hard and picked up his coffee cup. "We don't know how or when they're going to attack, but we can guess that with the lake at our backs to the east, they will most likely not attack us during the morning. If they do, we should consider that a win, as they'll be firing into the sun. If they attack at night, we have the advantage of night vision." Myers took a sip from his coffee.

"We also know that this enemy is capable of conducting suicide attacks. They have explosive weapon systems, and access to machine guns, including DShK heavy machine guns. Our enemy's most likely to hit us just before sunset when they have the sun at their backs. If I were them, I'd use a car bomb to hit a gate, and then flood in."

He turned and pointed to the hand-drawn map on the white board. "We're going to be ready for them. Any vehicle that passes this line without prior clearance from us is considered hostile." Myers turned as he drew a solid red line in front of both entrances. "Three hundred meters. You open fire and shoot to kill."

The men nodded.

"If they detonate a suicide attack at our gates, we're going to fall into these supplementary and alternative firing positions to reinforce the gate with our QRF. If we're pushed back to the power plant, the engineers will begin the emergency shut down procedures. That requires roughly ten minutes and during that time we hold the perimeter at all costs.

"Jerry, you and your boys will set up fighting positions from this point back to the reactor control room. I want four of your men inside of that control room with the engineers at all times."

"If we lose control of this power plant with the control rods still hot, lots of people will die. Plain and simple. Senior Master Sergeant Johnson, brief everyone on the logistics of my defense plan, please. Xiong, you're with me."

"Alright, to piggy-back off of what the Sir said..." Johnson pointed to the map. Myers and Xiong walked out of the room.

Xiong closed the door to the briefing room behind him.

"I need you to follow orders without questioning me on this, X.,"

Myers started. "If we get pushed back to the plant and are forced to start the emergency shut down, you get on the satellite phone, call up our situation, and then grab the closest shooter to you and egress. Got it?"

"You expect me to run out on a fight, Myers?" Xiong crossed his arms. "You serious?"

"If this shit goes south, I need you to hit the lake and get the hell out of here. We're going to get hit hard, and if we lose the fight, someone needs to inform command of the abilities of ISIS and the status of the nuclear material. If we can fend them off until reinforcements arrive, it's all good." Myers took one step toward Xiong and grabbed him by the arm. "But if we are losing this fight, then Colonel Bryce has seriously underestimated these people. Will you follow my order?"

"Why me?" Xiong asked.

"You're the only guy I know who can swim the hell out of here."

———————

VEE LAID in the grass with a National Guard private next to him. He looked through his binos at the first target they were attempting to register on the Mk-19.

"Make sure you don't mess up and drop rounds on us. Over," Vasean said on his radio. He signaled for the private to watch the opposite direction for threats. The man seemed like a flake—he kept catching him sketching out. Vee didn't trust him. He shouldn't have to point out that the man should be providing security.

"Roger, break, break." The radio paused. "All stations: we're registering the Mk-19. You'll hear a series of detonations, and it's nothing to be concerned with. Sending it now. Wolverine Five, out."

Seconds later, the Mk-19 clunked from somewhere inside the power plant yard. The gun sounded like a gang of lumberjacks chopping wood. The first three rounds impacted just short of their intended target-- a small bridge just beyond the trees. "Come up about fifty meters, over."

"Good, copy. Up fifty. Standby," Berryman replied.

The clunking of the gun sounded again. Vee thought he could hear the whistle of the rounds traveling over his head, but it was hard to say, since his ears were still jacked from the gunfight the day before. When the grenade rounds impacted, they were dead on target.

"Confirm target. You are dead on. Over." The Private tapped Vee on the shoulder. He pointed across the road and held up two fingers.

Vee scrambled for his binos and picked out two men moving laterally to their position across the street.

"Break, break. We have two men directly across the street. Requesting permission to engage."

"Vee this is Wolverine Six," Captain Myers said. "If they are military-aged males and they are armed, cut them down."

The Private had gone pale. He stabbed his finger repeatedly toward the tree line

With his naked eye, Vee saw at least thirty men moving through the trees.

"Actual, we have thirty hostiles on the tree line, break," he said, his voice barely a whisper. A wave of adrenaline hit Vee and he became Corporal Vasean again. "Berryman, Vee. Shift fire from your current point of aim three hundred fifty meters west. Traverse west to east and give me fifteen rounds, over."

The roar of the heavy machine gun blotted out any response, but Vee thought he heard the lumberjacks going to work again behind him.

Vee's blood ran cold as one man, then another, popped into view, maneuvered and then disappeared again. There was no question; they were being attacked.

The tree line erupted with 40mm explosions. HEDP rounds

impacted trees and the ground, sending steel, earth and wood in deadly blooms—cutting men down and tossing them around like ragdolls. In the short breaks of the heavy machine guns, Vee heard the screams of the wounded, already rolling across the fresh battlefield.

Many screamed in English. This was his hometown, and these ISIS fighters had been his neighbors. They had probably purchased their AKs in the same gun stores where Vee went to buy ammo and ogle assault rifles. Americans were killing Americans, and it was only the beginning of the slaughter.

"Down twenty and give me one traverse with the same number of rounds. Over," Vee whispered into his radio. He knew that he was the killer. The guns fired blindly from behind the perimeter, but Vee pulled the trigger. Unbidden, the memory of Phil's artery dumping his lifeblood, and the sounds of his cries for his mother hit Vee. His blood went cold and he prayed a blessing on the HEDP rounds as they whistled overhead.

Tear their limbs from their bodies—these men we welcomed into Detroit from foreign countries and who repay our grace with murder...

The bellow from the heavy machine gun split the battlespace in half and another blanket of death tore through the tree line. The chorus of screams intensified.

Come mayhem. Come death. Burn, motherfuckers.

Vee keyed the handset. "Repeat fire-mission. Over."

"Sending," Berryman replied.

The tree line came alive with bursts of light, showers of frag and the greedy fingers of death. A huge elm tilted, then fell over.

"Face the Reaper..."

The private tugged on Vee's shoulder again. He shouted over the booming grenades, "They're trying to bail in that van."

Vee keyed his radio. "Berryman this is Vee, hit our first registered target, we have a van trying to squirt."

"Break, break. This is Myers. Let the van go. We're better off if they retreat." Myers stepped on Berryman's transmission.

"We should take them out now! We've got the shot," Vee interjected.

"Negative. Let them go. Wolverine Six out." The discussion was over.

Looking toward the bridge, Vee could see the van had already escaped. He slammed his fist into the dirt. "Fucking bullshit. We should've blown those guys up."

The battlefield had gone suddenly quiet, except for screams.

"Should we do something about the injured?" the Private asked. His face looked green.

"Nah, man. Let them suffer. Let's finish registering the Mk-19," Vasean replied. "Get used to the sound, man. We're in a new world, and this isn't over yet."

The private vomited in the grass.

"Berryman, this is Vee. Good impacts on those last three fire-missions. Have the QRF spin up. We're going to need a patrol."

"Solid copy. Standby for next rounds." Berryman's reply was business as usual.

THE SUN WAS SETTING, and a sickly-orange glow fell on the nuclear power plant. Inside the combat operations center, Myers examined the hand drawn map and double checked his registered targets. Xiong monitored the radio in silence. Jerry walked in with Berryman and Vee in tow.

"Malone is supervising the Mk-19 pit," Berryman announced to the room. "He's running them through some drills. I think he intends to ride out the night at that position."

"What's our BDA? Myers asked.

"We put down twenty of the bastards." Vee took a seat at one of the tables. "If you guys don't need me, I'll head to the trucks and standby with the QRF."

"Hold on a minute, Vee. We need you here. About to call up a sitrep to the Colonel," Myers said over his shoulder without taking his eyes off the map. "That is, if you're with Wolverine now."

"Yeah, I'm with ya'll." Vee looked to Jerry for support, and the supervisor nodded. The moment of war had overtaken them all.

"CAP, Colonel on the hook for you." Xiong shook the sat phone in the air with his right hand. He leaned his head on the left. "I'm going with Vee to work the QRF as soon as we're done here. The Specialist can camp on the radio."

Myers didn't like it that X had just told him how it was going to be, but he nodded as he grabbed the phone.

"Colonel this is Wolverine Actual, send traffic."

"Sounds like you boys have been chewing them up."

The Colonel made it sound like good times, which cut across Myer's looming dread. Since this position had already cost the militia one helicopter and two pilots that could never be replaced, Myers cut the Colonel some slack.

"I have good news and bad news, son. Which do you want first?"

"I could use some good news, Colonel."

"The good news is that we're going to get a platoon of Marines out to you tomorrow afternoon. We have an entire Marine Expeditionary Unit coming through the locks in about six hours. Bird tasked them to secure key infrastructure. You boys are our top priority."

"Well, that is the best damn news I've heard in a week. What's the bad news?" Myers wrote *Marines coming tomorrow!* on a sheet of paper and held it up for the other men to see.

"Bad news is, you boys are in for some chop tonight. Intel tells us

ISIS is planning to hit you with everything they got. Sounds like your little trick with the indirect fire made the wrong person look weak, and they're pissed. All you've got to do is hold out for the night. Captain, I would like your word of honor that you boys will survive until those Marines arrive." Colonel Bryce's voice went solid as granite.

"Roger that, sir. We're too angry to die at this point." He gave the men in the room the universal hand and arm signal to circle the wagons and get ready for the whirlwind.

"May God be with you." The phone went silent and Myers waved Jerry over.

Myers scratched the back of his head. "They have intel that we kicked the radical Islam hornets' nest with that last beating we gave them. Turns out, I probably shouldn't have let that van go. We pissed in some imam's cornflakes. They're coming for us any minute."

There was a flurry of movement as vests were strapped and rifles made ready. Each man jocked up. Every man in the room froze for a split second as a machine gun barked outside. Rifle fire followed.

Xiong grabbed Vee and ran for the door. Just as he opened it a massive explosion rocked the room. Vee and Xiong were tossed back inside. Jerry hit the floor. The rest scrambled for cover. A second explosion followed, and the machine gun fell silent.

"Move! Move!" Myers shouted. "Jensen on me. Call command and tell them we are in *direct contact* with the enemy."

Berryman

Berryman sprinted in the direction of the Mk-19. Three of the National Guard soldiers were prepping the weapon while Sergeant Malone barked commands.

The sun had just begun to set. Berryman could see the flickering light from fires burning at both entrances. The machine gun emplacements had been erased from the earth.

"Malone," Berryman said, stepping into the fighting position. "I'm re-tasking you. Get with the QRF, we're probably going to need to split the gun trucks and send them to the entrances,"

"Shit man, I have no idea what's going on. Both ECPs started popping off at the same time, and then the explosions hit us back to back." Malone fiddled with the chin strap on his helmet. "I'm guessing they were suicide bombs, but who knows?"

The three soldiers were cramming the Mk-19 full of fresh lubricant. The stuff was a heavy paste, and they applied it liberally to every surface inside the weapon. "Malone go link up with X and Vee. They're going to need you at the South Gate. Get me a situation report and call out targets. This will be the last position before we fall back to the Alamo."

"On it." Malone ran toward the QRF's staging area.

"Dial in on AB1001. That's the northern entrance on Fisher Street," Berryman barked. "What are your damn names again?"

"I'm Corporal Bower, that's Specialist Jackson and that's PFC Heft." Bower looked like a chubby, up-north hunter. He racked the weapon's action to the rear a second time to get it into fighting condition. "We're ready, Berryman... Is it cool if we call you Berryman?"

"I've been militia long enough to not give a shit about rank. Do what I say, and we might survive the night. I got good news; a whole platoon of active duty Infantry Marines is coming first thing in the morning." Berryman clapped Bower on the shoulder. "AB 1001, That's the Fisher Street bridge."

Vasean

Xiong had taken charge and Vee was more than happy to be following the SEAL.

Xiong rattled off orders like a man possessed. "Malone, take an M249 and M240 gun truck down to the south entrance with ten guys. Fill in those fighting positions and standby for contact. I want you to spread out four guys, two in each of the other positions with security contractors. Vee, you're with me. We're taking a fifty up to the Fisher street entrance with an M249. Let's go people! Barn doors are wide open here."

"Xiong, this is Johnson." Xiong's radio crackled to life.

"Go for X." He continued directing traffic as he jumped into the passenger seat of the Humvee with Vee at the wheel.

"You and Malone get me a sit-rep the moment you hit those gates. If we have injured, I'll come to you with the pick-up and move them back to the main casualty collection point. Self-aid then buddy-aid. You know the drill. Over."

"Roger on all, X out."

Xiong looked over to Vee and extended a fist. "You ready?"

"Time for payback." Vee hit the accelerator and the truck roared in the direction of the rubble that once was his post.

On the way to reinforce the position, Vee was struck by the eerie beauty of the scene. The sun setting behind the trees, cast an orange glow that was only marred by the smoke rising from the burning hulk of a charred vehicle.

It was one of the most beautiful sunsets X had seen in a long time. It was as if the earth did not care that the human race was tearing itself apart. Men, women, and even children were terrified and suffering, dying by the hour, yet the planet kept spinning on its axis, striding through the detritus like an untouched bride stepping over a grave.

Movement at the burning wreckage came into view. Shadows from the churning smoke and dying light combined to make it difficult for Vee to threat identify. He saw an arm reach up from the ground and he realized that the security contractor was probably still alive.

A bullet flecked off the armor of the Humvee and Vee accelerated forward.

"Contact front," Xiong said. He reached back with his elbow and hit the turret gunner. "Aim below the muzzle flashes, kid. Light them up."

The Browning heavy machine gun raged from the turret over their heads, interrupted only by the gunner's curses as he cycled the action to keep it in the fight, clearing the mysterious malfunctions given to him by the combat fairy.

Myers

Captain Myers had run out of the briefing room with everyone else, and he had a vague idea he should head toward high ground so he could see the battlefield as it took shape. The tallest, most central building would be Main Engineering. But every time he ran toward it, another radio call came in, and he'd have to stop to hear what the hell they were saying.

"Go for Myers."

"This is Jerry. We're spinning up the emergency shut down procedure as a precaution. They tell me they can cancel it at the push of a button. Over," Jerry's voice came through the radio smooth, like he was informing Myers about his golf score last weekend instead of telling him he was poised to cut power to most of inner-city Detroit.

"Good, copy on that, Jerry. Break. Break." Myers released the handset. "I'm hearing shooting, X, give me a situation report."

"Standby, approaching the site. Multiple contacts in the tree line engaging the fifty," Xiong yelled. Myers stood in an empty parking lot—his hands over his Peltors to cut the noise. This was no time to botch a transmission.

"Roger. Berryman adjust fire from AB1001 to AB1007, the tree line across the street and drop two hundred to get impacts in the tree line. Fire when ready. Spot those rounds X. Break." Myers released his handset and took off running.

"Break. Break. X this is Berryman, standby for rounds, over."

"Captain Myers, Malone here. All's quiet on the southern front. We have no activity. Post got hit hard by the VBIEDs, over."

"Shot over," Berryman said.

"Shot out," X replied.

The chunking of the closer Mk-19 barely registered over the thundering of the .50 caliber heavy machine gun. Kalashnikov fire traded off with the 5.56mm of friendly forces. Chaos began to overtake order, and Myers harnessed that chaos. If he was successful tonight, he would save lives by creating openings for his outnumbered force to strike back. If he failed, then they would all die. Myers mashed his Peltors with one hand, and held his binos with the other, trying to catch windows of the north tree line through gaps in the buildings. He couldn't see anything of value, so he started running toward Main Engineering again, struggling to catch every word over the radio.

Moving the right unit to the appropriate point of friction at the perfect moment would mean the difference between surviving the night or landing twisted up and naked in a pile of bodies by morning. Myers's job was to fight his own men first--control their prey drive—and hopefully, join them in seeing the sunrise.

As he ran for high ground, Myers thought about putting a sniper team on overwatch. Those were men he had wasted in his bloodlust, his failure to think, to lead. Three of his best wandered Detroit at this moment, set adrift from the life-and-death struggle of Team Wolverine. It was his fault that Mac and the Twins weren't here to serve their critical role.

Over the squat admin buildings, Myers saw the north-eastern tree line erupt in 40mm explosions. The ambient gunfire took a breather, but cranked up once the explosions stopped. From his position, Myers needed to know how effective the grenades had been. Placing himself on ground level sucked. He took off, sprinting across the acres of power plant grounds. He slowed only to hear his men's report.

"Berryman this is X, repeat fire-mission. I need double that to take the heat off my fifty gunner. Break." The background of the radio-chatter from Xiong competed with a heavy volume of fire, both incoming and out-going. "Johnson this is X. I have three wounded up here. My gunner got tagged in the cheek. He's alive but unconscious. I have two other urgent surgicals. We need tac med, bad."

"X, Johnson. En route. Be at your pos in three mikes."

"Damnit! Go higher," Myers said to no one. He broke into a run. He'd caught himself thinking the ISIS force was superior. He'd never felt that way before—like he had reacted instead of owning his enemy. With air assets, intel, and the endless ability to stack advantages one on top of the other, he had dominated every battlefield in his career before this. Now, in Detroit, America, he ran like a desperate, confused rookie, thinking a jihadi lurked at every turn.

The enemy always gets a vote. If you'd respected that truth from the beginning, maybe you wouldn't be so far behind.

Myers slammed into the door of Main Engineering hard enough to send a shockwave of pain up his arm. Once inside, he ran for the stairs.

Xiong

"Talk to me, Vee. How we doing up there?" X shouted to be heard over the roar of the heavy machine gun's clunking.

"Lotta bad guys out here, man. But none of them are maneuvering, yet." Vee had taken the place of the private on the Ma Deuce.

"Tell Berry to keep that Mk-19 going. They hug the dirt every time a volley goes out."

"Roger!" X picked up his handset. "Berryman, I need you to pick up the rate of fire on that tree line."

"Solid copy on that X." Xiong strapped the handset of his radio back onto his shoulder and kicked the door of the Humvee open. He moved up to the front tire.

The National Guard troops had formed a tight skirmish line. Three of them were on the ground and two more were administering aid to the fallen. They couldn't maintain this for long. Xiong moved up to the injured men in the half-destroyed sandbag bunker.

"I can't figure out this nasal, man. It won't go in. It keeps getting stuck. We're going to lose him." A National Guard corporal panicked, his face a mask of terror.

Stepping over the turret gunner with a round through and through his cheeks, X kneeled next to the corporal and pulled the nasal phalangeal airway out of the unconscious man's nose. He tossed it over his shoulder and ripped into a first aid kit to pull out a fresh airway.

"I don't have time to show you again," Xiong opened the airway packaging and then slathered it in blood from one of the other men's shrapnel wounds. "This is lube. Insert the nasal till you feel resistance, twist and push through until it's all the way in. Take off your glove and make sure he's breathing through the tube."

While he'd been helping save the private, the firefight had gone high-order. The Mk-19 must have run into issues because the *thump-thump-thumping* had stopped and the *clack-clack-clacking* of AK-47 fire had doubled, then tripled.

The whistling brakes of a Humvee broke into Xiong's attention on the wounded. Medevac had arrived, but he couldn't spare a second to catch them up. They'd figure it out.

He dropped down in the skirmish line, shouldered his rifle and squinted down his ACOG to get a picture of the fight in front of him. He wasn't aiming to take shots; the eight National Guardsmen and Vee were already hammering anything that moved.

X couldn't see a damn thing other than sporadic muzzle flashes, barely visible in the light of the setting sun. He had shooters in the field, shooters in the tree line and shooters converging from the sectors to the left and the right of their position. It looked like every American hater in Michigan was coming to kill them.

Myers

"XIONG, MALONE. SIT REP," Myers barked into his radio as he slammed open the door to the roof of Main Engineering and barreled out into the chill air of coming darkness. He kicked himself for not setting up a sniper's position here. The overwatch would've made all the difference.

"Captain, this is X. They're wearing us down here. We're burning ammo while they stack more and more dudes against us. We can't do this all night, bro."

"This is Malone. We've got nothing here on the north. No movement."

Myers took a knee behind the half-wall that surrounded the rooftop. Placing his pack on the ledge, he braced his binos and glassed Xiong's position.

They would need to switch to NVGs soon. He picked out a line of a dozen pickup trucks moving across the bridge with mounted machine guns in the beds. Myers closed his eyes and took a deep breath. He was the last guy who could allow himself to panic.

"Berryman, this is Myers." He picked up his handset while holding the binoculars with the other hand. "Shift fire back to AB 1001. We have multiple technicals crossing the bridge right now."

"On it. AB1001."

Four of the technical vehicles managed to cross the bridge unmolested before the first 40mm grenades dropped out of the sky onto their heads. Each explosion bloomed and flashed the area with yellow light. The concussions took a full second to reach Myers on the roof of the building.

The first truck went up in flames with three direct hits. Myers watched the gunner incinerate in a ball of fire. The driver jumped out and ran while the truck behind slammed into the back and rammed it over top of the fleeing man.

Myers dug in his vest for his satellite phone. He hit the speed dial to Grayling.

"Sir, this is Myers."

"Go for Bryce."

"We have a dozen plus technical vehicles crossing the bridge into our AO. Our Mk-19 is only going to stop about a third of them. We have an unknown number of ground fighters hitting us from the tree line to our west. Do you have any air support for us?" Myers chewed the inside of his lip.

"Negative, Myers." His commanding officer sounded frustrated, but that didn't help the situation.

"Copy. Myers out." He hung up the sat phone without being dismissed.

Myers could see that Xiong and his half of the QRF had the situation under control for the moment. The Islamic State fighters couldn't move forward because of the withering machine gun fire across the open field. If he still had ammunition, Xiong would probably hold.

"Berryman, shift the Mk-19 back to the tree line. Drop one hundred. Technical vehicles are parked in there somewhere behind the trees."

"Roger. Shifting fire," Berryman's voice came back.

Just as Myers was about switch to the other side of the building to check Malone's position, six thumps and six streaks of light sliced through the air from the tree line. Myers heard shouts of "*Arrr-pee-gee!*" on the icy, evening breeze.

One of the security contractor's posts by Xiong erupted into a fireball. Even in the failing light, Myers could see the body of a man being thrown from the post. A half-second later, the concussion slammed into Myers's gut.

Malone

"WHAT THE HELL WAS THAT?" Malone shouted. "Someone get eyes on it."

"Sounds like RPGs!" Malone's turret gunner yelled. "Should we get ready to haul ass over there, Sergeant?"

"Negative. We're holding here. We're not leaving our sector unless Myers orders us." Malone held his handset to his ear hoping for information.

"X, this is Myers. Sitrep, over." Over the radio, Myers didn't sound like he was panicking. Malone, on the other hand, was barely holding back a wicked case of diarrhea. This whole scene reminded him of getting blown up in the middle of Detroit. He cursed his bowels and their betrayal. If he was going to die, he sure as fuck didn't want to die with his pants full of shit. This had never happened in Iraq. Why the hell now?

"Cap, this is X. RPG gunners in the tree line. We need Berryman to put the pressure on or I'm going to run out of guys." Xiong's voice had jumped an octave since his last transmission. Malone rubbed his hand furiously across the line where his helmet met his forehead.

"This is Berryman. We're shifting fire now. Wait one."

Malone's turret gunner screamed, "Sergeant! I've got something big coming toward us. Two hundred meters. What the hell... "

Malone whipped around and saw what looked like the eighteen-wheeler from Hell roaring toward his position. A massive steel cow-pusher had been welded onto the grill. Its windshield had been replaced by slotted, armor plating.

"Kill it!" Malone shouted, his terror driving his voice into a high-pitched wail.

He shouldered his rifle and fired into the chinks in the armor, but he was standing, and the target was moving—a chill poured down his spine like an injection of ice water.

100 meters.

His turret gunner followed his lead and dumped rounds into the metal behemoth. Malone's hope broke loose, like a dinghy in the winds of the tempest. If this was another suicide attack, they were dead men standing. But at least they would die for their friends.

50 meters.

Malone flipped his mag out and loaded another, sliding into a sense of calm born of resolve—a quiet surrender to the last seconds of his life. He smacked the bolt release and his body stilled. His bowels quieted. His vision sharpened. Then he fired his weapon.

He watched, in crystal clarity, as one of his rounds carved directly through the slit in the armor, and he saw the driver's face cave in on itself. He continued to fire, but victory was his. The truck would not stop but neither would pass his post--his bit of dirt on the outer ring of a nuclear power plant.

10 meters.

The truck accelerated.

Clean, white light consumed his world.

Myers

Myers heard a burst of shooting from Malone's position and raced to that side of the building. Halfway there, the building lurched and Myers' feet were swept out from under him. Glass shattered; car alarms blared. The largest explosion he'd ever seen fireballed into the sky where Malone and his men once stood. Even five hundred meters from the blast, a blistering heat knocked Myers to the ground.

He already knew Malone and his men had been erased from the planet, but he grabbed for his handset anyway.

"Malone, this is Myers. Come in. Malone. Come in!"

"This is Berryman. There's nothing left there. Move on, Captain. I've got two trucks flying up the same road. Over."

"Holy Lord," Myers mumbled to himself. He watched trucks barrel toward the opening left in the wake of the massive IED. Two dozen enemy popped up from the fields and rushed the opening on foot. Myers narrowed his eyes and took a deep breath.

"Berryman. Shift fire, now. Plug that hole. Break...Johnson, I need you to drop what you're doing and reinforce Berryman's position. Please copy."

An RPG streaked toward the contractor post, which was spraying 5.56mm from an M249 into the fields. It connected with the bottom of the post and punched straight out the back without detonating, then hit the ground a few feet behind it. The M249 stopped firing.

"Get there now, Johnson! I'm on the way. Myers out." He didn't wait for Johnson's copy.

Myers sprinted for the stairs. As he rumbled down the stairwell, he could hear the muffled sounds of bedlam outside. He kept his radio to his ear, but the airwaves were dead. For six agonizing floors, he was alone with his remorse, set to the drums of the death song of his brothers. The Islamic State had played him. They'd played them all—biding their time for the moment when their fanatic devotion would make them the strongest tribe left in Michigan. Americans' soft lives resulted in gross overconfidence—militia and civilian alike. Now he would die at their hands. After surviving a hundred one-sided battles in the homeland of ISIS, they would step over his dead body on American soil.

He slammed open the door on the bottom floor and ran for open air. Johnson was only a few steps ahead of him, and another man he didn't know ran behind. They cleared the three hundred yards to Berryman's position in silence, punctuated only by their heavy breathing.

The sun had finally set beyond the western horizon. The three men jumped into the sandbagged emplacement where Berryman was sluicing rounds from his M249 across the southern entrance in disciplined bursts. The enemy trucks had pulled behind cover, probably coordinating how best to attack their next ring of defense. A round smashed into a sandbag beneath Berryman's bipod, throwing fragments into the air and causing the gun to hop up out of position. Berryman blew the sand out of his face, shifted the weapon and continued firing.

"I'm hit, but I'm still good," Berryman reported. Myers couldn't see any wounds in the dark, but he believed him.

Myers and Johnson shouldered their weapons and began firing in the direction of the smoking ruin that had once been Malone's position.

Berryman shouted over the stupefying din. "'Bout damn time. Thought I was going to have to kill all these assholes myself." Some men's balls went Triple X when facing death. Myers smiled as he worked his AR. *Damn, he loved these guys.*

Three men from the National Guard struggled to rotate the Mk-19 back into position. Myers moved over to Berryman and yanked him away from the SAW. Berryman looked up and Myers grinned at his friend with the eyes of a lunatic.

"Give me that fucking thing. Get that Mark back into the fight." Myers dropped down behind the M249 and went to work on the shadowy edge of their sector of fire.

"I see how it is, Cap'n," Berryman laughed and shouted as he worked on the grenade launcher. "You three come over to a party at *my house* and I get sent back to the kitchen to do the dishes. Fucking *officers*."

The three guardsmen who had been working on the Mk-19 dropped to the sandbags and shot rounds at the muzzle flashes from the edge of the dark.

The Mk-19 started putting rounds down range again. Myers looked over his shoulder and saw the big man had removed the traversing and elevation tool from the tripod and was firing it from the standing position. Each thunking round sent the immense blowback into the man's arms.

"Bower, feed that gun." Johnson shouted with a grin at one of the guardsmen. "The big man wants to play Rambo."

An ISIS pickup truck nudged toward their position out from behind a building, trying to get their belt-fed into the fight. The front of the truck erupted as a 40mm grenade cratered the hood and blew the engine block into frag. Berryman walked rounds back and forth across the truck before the Mark went silent again.

"Shit! Get the feed throat, dude. The gun's not feeding with just your hands." Berryman lifted the feed tray cover and swiped the bulky 40mm rounds off the weapon system. He jammed a cleaning rod into the receiver and dumped a jammed round out of the ejection slot. Enemy fire immediately heightened as several PKM machine guns joined from the black of night.

The guardsman working the Mk-19 screamed. "Fuck, I'm hit!" He dropped back to the cover of the sandbags.

Myers radio blared. "Captain, they're maneuvering on us!" Xiong called out. "We need help on this side."

Myers grabbed a PFC by the shoulder strap. "You know how to use this thing?"

"The SAW sir?" he asked.

"No. My dick. Are you trained on the SAW or not?" Myers pushed the butt stock toward the kid.

"Yes, sir."

"Go to work." Myers pulled the handset to his ear. "Xiong, pull back to the facility. We are being overrun at our position. Move to phase two of the defensive plan. We'll make them fight for it inside."

A series of explosions clapped to the north, and Myers could see the fireballs erupting as the barking of Kalashnikov and PKM fire continued to escalate. The return reports of 5.56mm rifles and automatic weapons seemed like nothing in comparison.

"Xiong, how copy my last?" Myers cursed, looking at his radio. No response.

"Jerry, this is Myers. We're moving inside to you. Over." Myers turned to Johnson, who held a dead soldier in his arms. "Johnson, Berryman, Heft, Bower, we're falling back to the facility to give the engineers time to shut this place down. We ain't winning this."

A fresh swarm of buzzing, whirring bullets smashed into their position. One of the young guardsmen dropped completely into the emplacement and looked to Berryman. Berryman looked to Bowers, then Johnson and Myers.

"Negative, sir. You and Johnson get inside with Jerry and Alamo up. The three of us will cover your movement."

The guardsman nodded and got back up, bracing the bipod against the sandbags and firing the weapon into the gap, sweeping it in arcs.

"Move, you goldbricken' pansies!" Berryman shouted. He gave Myers an evil grin. "An honor, sir. Make 'em bleed in there." Berryman turned back to the Mk-19.

Myers and Johnson ran for the nuclear control facility for all they were worth.

Xiong

"Myers, this is Xiong. We are overrun. I say again, we are overrun," Xiong whispered into his radio, unsure if anyone could hear him. He dropped the handset and lay underneath the Humvee, watching a dozen Islamic State fighters move past his position.

Vasean lay next to him with a gunshot wound through his right bicep. He grit his teeth against the pain.

"Vee, can you swim?" Xiong whispered. "Your arm. Can you swim?"

Vee nodded and put his face in the dirt.

All around the two men feet scurried by. Xiong lost track of the number.

Five National Guard soldiers had died holding the line. Once the massive suicide vehicle had detonated, and the MK-19 shifted fire to defend the southern flank, the Islamic State fighters rushed across the field in the face of the withering fire from the M2 Browning.

The big gun had jammed at the worst possible moment, and Vee had scrambled to get it back up. In the process, he'd taken a round. Seconds later, RPGs rained down on their position. That opening cascaded into a rout.

Xiong looked to Vasean again. "We're overrun, brother. They'll be shutting the plant down now. We wait until these fucks get past us, and then crawl out to Eerie, then swim up the Detroit River. Can you handle that?"

Vasean whispered, "I dunno, man."

"Just stick with me. If you start to struggle, I'll swim for the both of us." Xiong locked eyes with him. "Do exactly what I say or we both die."

Berryman

"Last can!" the guardsman yelled to Berryman.

"I'm on my last drum!" The other guardsman looked back over his shoulder, his eyes as big as eight balls.

"Boys, let's take as many of them as we can!" Berryman's booming laugh cut through the tension as he slammed the feed tray cover and racked the Mk-19's action back. "Bowers, get over by Heft and start putting rounds down range. Feed that M249 rifle mags if you have to."

Berryman swung the MK-19 toward the enemy and laid down a volley of fire only a hundred meters in front of him. A group of fighters had taken up position behind a cluster of dumpsters. With one burst from the MK-19, the fighters ceased to exist.

Another group of fighters rushed up to a small stand of trees and put rounds on Berryman. One ricocheted off the feed tray cover, taking the leaf sight clean off. Berryman gave them a burst from the grenade launcher and took both the men down together with huge fragments of the tree trunks.

Bower, one of the guardsmen, screamed.

Risking a glance over his shoulder, Berryman could see the man had been shot just below his vest. "Get pressure on that, Bower! Heft, keep shooting, little brother. Keep shooting!"

Berryman looked down to check how many rounds were left in his last belt and a round hammered the top of his helmet, knocking him square on his back.

"I'm out!" Heft yelled.

This close, Berryman could hear the Islamic State fighters yelling their crackpot bullshit, *but in English.*

Berryman struggled to his feet in time to see a fighter wearing black jeans and a black Puma t-shirt jump into his position and stab Heft in the chest with a bayonet.

Berryman whipped out his pistol and fired five rounds into Puma man.

Another fighter jumped in behind him. Berryman shot him seven times; the last round caught in the ejection port of the pistol. "Well, shit," he swore.

Berryman slapped the bottom of his pistol magazine and

worked the action just as another fighter hurdled the sandbags.

The two men shot each other to death.

Myers

"What about the injured in the COC?" Johnson asked as the two men sprinted through the hallways of the control building. The explosions of 40mm Mk-19 fire shook the building as they impacted way too close. "We can't just leave them."

Myers stopped. "Yes, we can, we have to."

"Captain. I swore a damn oath, 'so that others may live.'" Johnson looked him in the eyes. He'd been an Air Force Pararescue operator in a past life.

"I need you. We don't have time to move the injured. Berryman and those National Guard kids aren't going to last long and we're talking about a good chunk of America's fresh water supply. Ever heard of Chernobyl, man?"

"Please. This is how I die, Captain. They're going to have to run directly past our COC to get to you anyways." Johnson snatched two M67 fragmentation grenades off Myers pouch. "Let me and the wounded have this."

"Are you sure, man?" Myers unslung his rifle and stared at the man. The medic nodded. "Take my rifle and mags. We have shotguns staged in the control room."

Johnson took the rifle and two mags, turned and ran in the direction of the COC.

Myers called out on his radio as he ran the corridors. "Jerry this is Myers. I'm on my way to you. We have bad guys incoming."

The sound of a violent firefight broke out behind him as he ran. Six grenades exploded in succession followed by rifle fire. It was cut short by an explosion that was much louder than any hand grenade.

"Myers, this is Jerry. How much time do we have?"

"None. Get one of those shotguns ready for me."

Xiong

After Berryman's position was overrun, total silence fell over the power plant.

Dozens of men poured into the front entrance past Xiong and Vee. It had destroyed X to watch Berryman get overrun, but there was nothing he could do for them. His orders had been to get himself and Vee away from the power plant and into Lake Eerie.

"Vee. We're going to crawl out of here. Once we hit the lake we're swimming south for a bit. Are you good, dude?"

"Yeah, I think so. This is fucked," Vee said.

Xiong nodded and began to crawl.

For what felt like an eternity the two men scuttled through the tall grass along a fence that descended toward Lake Eerie. At one point, Xiong heard a succession of grenades go off inside of the facility. Then, more shooting, more explosions. Then, silence.

Every light in the power plant cut out. Seconds later Detroit went dark. A few more shots were fired, then everything went quiet.

Vee and Xiong slid into the cold, dark waters of the lake. They swam in silence around the power plant, then Stony Point, then around the small neighborhood to the south of the plant. As they made their escape, succumbing to hypothermia by degrees, they slid past the homes, streets and parks of what used to be the United States of America. They could hear people driven into the street by the power outage, talking in hushed tones.

To the two men, drifting past the civilians in the night, the darkness that had devoured the region represented something more than a frightening loss of electricity. It meant that the Enrico Fermi II Nuclear Power Plant could not become a weapon.

To them, the darkness had been won with the lives of their friends.

3

THE OBSERVER

BY PAUL KNOCH

WE TRIED *every angle to talk Paul Knoch into carpooling to Utah with another ReadyMan to experience the 2019 RMI series of combat and survival training events. Instead of joining us, he went to work on the question, "what if a ReadyMan got stranded away from home when the Big Enchilada hit?" That led to an even more insidious question: "to what lengths is a man willing to go in order to see his family again?"*

When he's not digging for razor clams, Paul manages human resources for a Christian conference center and teaches creative writing on the Oregon coast. Living along the Cascade Volcanic Arc and enjoying life in a tsunami zone has convinced Paul and his family that preparedness is the price of admission to live amidst the natural beauty of the Pacific Northwest.

We're pleased to report that not once during the 2019 RMI event series did the apocalypse strike.

-Jason Ross

. . .

NOAH STARED at the Smith and Wesson .40 caliber round held lightly between his fingers and returned it to his front pocket. He felt the slightest tinge of embarrassment. What a cliché. Like a scene from a bad action movie. But the last twenty-four hours showed him that real evil existed just beneath the crumbling veneer of society. There was worse that could be done to you than a bullet in the brain, and worse that you could do to yourself.

The afternoon sun crept down the hillside where Noah sat hidden behind scrub brush. He shifted slightly to remain at least partially shaded from the sun that beat down upon the ruined landscape. He scoped the length of the road to the bridge but nothing had changed. The unmoving cars remained mute and still. The bodies, some disturbingly small, lay as they had. A few cars still smoldered, strewn about at odd angles along the highway. It was unclear where the vehicles were going or where they'd been. Most seemed to have been traveling north on highway 45 toward Interstate 84. All appeared ransacked: doors left open, unwanted items discarded on the ground.

From the map he found in the glovebox, and the signs he'd passed, Noah determined he was at Walter's Ferry on highway 45. The bridge would lead him over the Snake River and eventually highway 45 would reconnect with Interstate 84 and take him home to Oregon. But first he had to cross this bridge alive. He'd been watching it for several hours, waiting for a vehicle to attempt the crossing. From his vantage point, he could see through binoculars that the bridge was blockaded on both sides and guarded by men with rifles. The specter of burning cars and dead bodies massed near the entrance to the bridge was not comforting.

There was no compelling reason for Noah to cross the bridge unless it was safe to do so. He had other options. Returning to Interstate 84 would have normally been the fastest and most direct route home, but Noah knew nothing was likely normal anymore.

His thoughts ranged back five days earlier. Just five days. It was hard to believe. It felt more like five years.

He had agreed to travel to Salt Lake City for a weekend of... Noah couldn't even categorize it. Prepper? Military? Survival training? A buddy of his sent him the invitation. A weekend of survival and firearms training. *Hone your skills. Get ready for the apocalypse.* "Prepared, Not Scared!" the flyer promised. This particular weekend was just one of several that were planned – each focused on a different survival skill: bush craft, foraging, force on force combat. To Noah, the concept was appealing and total bullshit at the same time.

He'd been surprised when he told his wife Lynn about the invitation and she had been enthusiastic. In some part of his brain, Noah could not help but interpret his wife's support as an indication of her skepticism of Noah's abilities as a provider and protector. Normally, getting approval for a weekend with his buddies required significant diplomacy. She seemed almost too eager to have him go.

The invitation had a catch, however. There was a guy named Dave who lived in Vancouver, Washington who also wanted to attend the weekend training. He owned a truck and was looking for someone to ride with him from the same general area and share the gas cost. Adding a thirteen hour drive each way to the weekend of training, made the whole idea increasingly unattractive to Noah. When it was first suggested, he envisioned a gathering of slightly overweight guys decked out in camo, bragging about their bugout bags and SHTF preparations.

Noah was familiar with the type. Living on the coast of Oregon was his introduction into the world of "preparedness." The possibility of a massive earthquake along the Cascadia Subduction zone, followed by a devastating sixty-foot tsunami was an everyday reality. Like many coastal residents, Noah had dutifully created an evacuation plan for his family, along with emergency food, water and first aid supplies. Soon Noah realized that security would also be an issue. Assuming his family survived the tsunami, it was likely that coastal communities would be isolated for several days if not weeks. There would be no police or fire units to respond to emergencies – or protection. He purchased his first firearm: a .22 lever action rifle – for shooting rabbits, he reasoned.

He soon added a shotgun, then a .380 Smith and Wesson Bodyguard, and finally a Glock 22. He applied for and received his concealed carry permit. He joined a few firearm forums on the internet, and even participated in some of the endless conversations about the "best caliber for home defense." With his stock of survival gear, emergency food, and a growing cache of guns and ammunition, Noah felt increasingly confident of his ability to protect and provide for his family in the event of "The Big One."

But inwardly, he never experienced a kinship with these communities. He found their patriotism simplistic. Based on their profile photos, most of the guys in these forums didn't look like they could run a mile much less survive an apocalypse. Over time, he tired of wading through the bravado and Hillary jokes to find substantive information. He found himself participating less and less. He felt sufficiently "ready," and his interest in emergency preparedness waned. The invitation to a weekend of para-military style training and all the accompanying macho posturing, wasn't necessarily something he was happy about. But the invitation came from a friend Noah admired, and he soon felt the familiar weight of obligation.

With the full blessing of his wife, Noah agreed to go. He e-mailed Dave, his ride and fellow attendee, and worked out the logistics. Dave was in his mid-fifties, older than Noah, with two grown children who had apparently moved out of the area. He'd been married twice. As expected, his politics leaned to the right. He liked his truck, his guns, and he pledged allegiance to his own independence and the US of A in that order. Noah had the unique ability to allow other people, particularly strong willed men, to be themselves. Noah had few hard edges of his own. With a chorus of "uh huhs" and "oh yeahs," Noah could exist around the largest egos and brashest personalities without the need to challenge them. To some degree, he'd leveraged this ability into moderate success in his corporate career in management. But in his darker moments, Noah wondered if he was simply weak or complacent rather than skilled with people.

The night before their road trip to Utah, he laid out his Gregory 55-liter backpack and attempted to list what he would need for the weekend. The focus of this training was living outdoors in your "bug out bag" – basically a backpack comprised of essential items needed for a "SHTF" scenario. The adventure had appeal to Noah, who had always wanted to plan an overnighter, taking only the emergency bag he kept in his vehicle. He worked in a small coastal town ten miles south of his home. In the event of a tsunami, the potential for having to hike home to his family and spend a night in the woods was real. Practicing made sense to him and eased his fears that the weekend would be a total waste of time.

But in reality, the pack Noah was putting together was nothing like the simplistic emergency pack that he kept in his vehicle. He was bringing a zero-degree down sleeping bag, sleeping pad, cook kit, freeze dried food, first aid kit, firearm – essentially what he would have brought on a backpacking trip. His emergency pack lacked many of these items, and that bothered him. However, he rationalized he would learn what he really needed to be "prepared," and wasn't that the whole point? Survive the weekend? The bug out bag could be fine-tuned later.

Dave pulled into Noah's driveway in a huge late model Ford pickup an hour late. No wonder he needed someone to split the cost of gas, Noah thought. Still, he was happy to see that at least he would be fairly comfortable in the big truck for the long drive. Dave shook Noah's hand firmly and seemed genuinely happy to meet him. Pleasantries exchanged, Dave lifted the hard top cover of the truck's bed, and nodded for Noah to load up his gear. With every-thing secured, Noah climbed into the passenger seat and Dave gunned the truck out of the quiet cul de sac, past the dewy mani-cured lawns of Noah's upper middle class neighborhood, beyond the salt air of the Oregon coast and out toward the dry high desert of Salt Lake City.

The ride was fairly uneventful. Dave had set up a satellite radio and favored conservative talk programs. Noah was fine with that. Politically conservative himself, Noah found the talk radio shows comfortable starting points for conversation. Occasionally Dave would veer off toward a darker, more extreme position, but Noah simply would go silent and let Dave run his mouth until he seemed satisfied. The only awkward moment was when Dave told a racially inappropriate joke, and Noah heard himself chuckle out of polite-ness. He immediately felt ashamed. Why did he care what Dave thought? Certainly it would have added to the uncomfortable nature of the drive to have corrected Dave but still... wasn't that the right thing to do? Noah mulled on this until he became aware that Dave had sensed his discomfort and changed the topic. Perhaps, Noah thought, he had still made his displeasure known. That was probably good enough.

By the end of the drive, Noah had come to find Dave enjoyable company. He came from an average home with all the average prob-lems. His father had owned a small feed company but was retired. His mom baked and was active in her church. He had two sisters who he rarely heard from and a younger brother who had died a week after he was born. His first ex-wife lived in Salem and had remarried. Surprisingly, Noah found they had more in common than expected. Dave was a wine enthusiast with a keen interest in wine making. They both played golf. As the miles passed, Noah relaxed and found himself enjoying the road trip and even the prospect of a weekend outdoors.

An hour outside of Salt Lake City, the country station broadcast on Dave's satellite radio was replaced with an odd tone that lasted three seconds. The sound immediately reminded Noah of the long signal that would precede a fire emergency call on his police radio. This time, however, the tone was followed by a long silence. Noah glanced over at Dave, who stared dully at the radio. What followed was an emergency alert. Reports of an explosive device. Los Angeles. Terrorism? The details were vague and difficult for Noah to understand or process. Had we been attacked?

Finally, Dave turned to Noah, his face breaking out slowly into a huge Cheshire cat grin. "HOOOOOOOLLLLLYYYSHHIIITTT!!!! It's on!" Dave slapped Noah's knee hard and knocked Noah back to that familiar place where he existed outside of his own experience, unable to join the moment, unwilling to believe.

MOVEMENT DREW Noah's attention from his thoughts about the trip, to getting back to his home in Oregon. A car raced toward the bridge and slowed to a stop a hundred yards from the blockade. The car sat there idling for a couple minutes, then slowly approached. Noah leaned forward and twisted the binoculars into clearer focus.

Pop. Pop. Pop.

Shots? The car abruptly came to a halt and spun back in reverse.

Pop. Poppoppoppopopopoppop.

The car stopped moving. Bits of glass exploded. The shooting stopped. Men approached the car slowly. One man stepped up and peered into the space where the windshield had been. *Pop. Pop.* Then nothing. No movement. The scene froze. The men began dragging bodies and items out of the car. Ten minutes later, they retreated to the shadows of the blockade. The ruined car steamed. The bodies lay still and mute. Noah sat silently for several minutes, absorbing the violence and steadying his breathing.

Shit. Shit. Shit. Shit.

He flipped the binoculars onto the passenger seat and consulted the map again.

Clearly, this bridge was not an option. There were at least three more opportunities to cross the river and get back to the interstate. After twenty minutes, he slowly backed the truck out and headed west down the empty blacktop.

Trying to keep aware, but not allow himself to stress about his situation, Noah thought about his trip to Utah. By the time Dave and he finally arrived at the compound for the training weekend, they had exhausted all conversational topics. The cab of the truck was littered with coffee cups and fast food wrappers. Dave parked the big Ford near a makeshift registration table. Noah was happy to step out of the truck and stretch his road-sore back and legs.

Two men in digicamo and Oakley sunglasses sat at the table with about a dozen blue folders. Each folder had the name of one of the weekend participants. One of the men had a live Fox News broadcast playing on his cell phone. "Early reports indicated possible casualties."

"Welcome, gentlemen!" Noah and Dave were greeted by a tall, extremely fit, friendly looking man with close cropped hair. "Scott Rails. This is Matt Drake." Matt remained seated and gave a curt but friendly nod. "Let's get you registered. Most of the guys are here already. First thing on the schedule is a meet and greet at 0900 hours. Tonight you'll set up camp on the main lawn. My contact info is in your packet if you need anything. Uh... you guys been following the news today?"

Dave and Noah nodded. Everyone smiled. A weekend of military/prepper/survival/fighting/woods/combat readiness training... all against the backdrop of real peril. Real threat. What could be better? *Hoorah!*

Noah was disappointed that his friend, Adam Shaw, had yet to make an appearance. Adam and Noah had known each other since grade school, and their lives had followed a loose but noticeable symmetry. They shared similar perspectives on life, family, religion, and politics. The main difference was Adam had made money. A lot. Exactly how much, Noah wasn't sure, but it was more than enough. Fortunately, the friendship had survived and the size of their wallets wasn't an issue.

When Adam finally appeared that first night, he took some time to greet each of the participants. Adam had funded most of the weekend, and the activities all took place on his expansive compound in the foothills above Salt Lake City. The tents, spread out on a dark green lawn, were within a couple hundred yards of Adam's massive home. Adam finally ambled over to give Noah a warm, sincere hug. "Good to see you, brother."

Noah noticed immediately that something was wrong. Despite his effort to be friendly, Adam was clearly distracted. Noah knew how important this training weekend was to Adam, so he could only surmise that something fairly urgent was occupying his mind. It had to be the news coming from Los Angeles. The attack was eerily similar to a scenario that Adam had described once to Noah during a Facebook conversation. The argument had been over how difficult it would be for society to collapse. Noah had argued that there were enough diversification and back up plans to prevent society from collapsing. The United States, Noah had argued, was too big to fail.

Adam, on the other hand, described a bloated culture that had grown soft and susceptible to a catastrophic failure. Society was more interested in consuming than producing. Selfishness had replaced virtue and compassion. Adam had argued that the food supply was surprisingly vulnerable. A targeted attack could set off a chain reaction that would lead to empty shelves and rioting within 48 hours. Fear and panic would finish the job – ensuring a total and complete meltdown of normal. Law and order would evaporate and modern society would take a thousand-year step backward into the dark ages.

Still, it was good to see Adam. Noah had few friends that were capable of luring him to an event so far outside his comfort zone and so clearly fraught with potential awkwardness and discomfort.

As the night wore on, a bonfire was started. Flasks appeared and laughter floated over the amber flames and out into an uncertain night. The news reports had become repetitive and were soon replaced with country western music. Adam had disappeared sometime during the evening, clearly preferring his ten thousand square foot mansion and massive king sized bed to the whiskey-fueled camaraderie and hard ground.

Dave had quickly bonded with several of the men who more closely shared his interests. Noah watched them from across the fire. Their faces aglow. Broad smiles and shoulders. Strong white teeth. A joke was told out of Noah's earshot. A pause and then each of the men erupted in laughter, their shoulders heaving. Dave slapped the shoulder of the man next to him. Noah smiled. Or was it a smirk? He didn't begrudge Dave his newfound friends. Nor did he begrudge this moment. It was what it was. And it had always been. Noah had never been the joke teller or the shoulder slapper. He was never in the moment. He was always off to the side. The observer.

Before he fell asleep in his small backpacker tent, Noah texted his wife. She was OK but was closely following the news and growing nervous. She asked when Noah expected to get back home. He told her they planned to leave as soon as the weekend's events concluded and drive straight home. Barring traffic, and the apocalypse, he promised to be home by very late Sunday night. He considered offering to come home early, but he wasn't sure how Dave would feel about missing any of the training.

Noah awoke to sirens. At first, it took a moment for him to figure out where he was. He pushed off his down sleeping bag and unzipped the tent fly. He peered out upon a strange landscape of tents and bivvy bags. The large bonfire lay black and cold. A camo clad shape lay huddled on the dewy grass, perhaps a casualty of the previous night's whisky. The siren resumed and Noah finally identified its origin. Adam had installed speakers surrounding the large lawn. His home was often used for weddings – which had necessitated the sound system. The sirens – probably recordings – were broadcast through the speakers. *Nice touch*, thought Noah.

Noah retrieved a schedule from his registration folder. Breakfast would be served in 30 minutes at 0700 followed by a morning briefing and day hike. Tonight the men would sleep alone in the forested property that encircled Adam's home. The point was to test your bug out bag, but like Noah, most men clearly came with more gear than would fit even the largest backpack. One guy even brought a heavy cast iron pan.

The day hike turned out to be a fun event. The weather was good and the activity and fresh air quickly made the men forget the previous day's alarming news. Noah took pride that he was in better shape than most of the guys – even the ones who claimed to be active military. A fairly aggressive regimen of working out and running 3 miles a day had clearly increased Noah's strength and endurance. Perhaps he did have what it took to make it in this group, after all? He thought he noticed several of the guys looking at him as they wheezed and huffed their way up the trail. "Who's the badass?" he imagined them thinking. Each man carried a small daypack that they'd been instructed to bring with a few required items: knife, flint, sack lunch, and para cord.

Once they reached a clearing in the oaks and scrub surrounding Adam's property, they were instructed to drop their packs and gather around. Noah was disappointed that Adam hadn't come on the hike. However, he understood that his friend was probably very busy both as the host of the weekend and as an active investor who ran multiple companies. Plus, he'd arranged for extremely competent guys with impressive pedigrees, including a Navy Seal and Army Ranger, to lead the activities. They were more than capable of running a group of wannabe survivalists through a few simulations and scenarios.

The first challenge was fire making. Each man was given one hour to gather kindling and start a fire without using matches. To be successful, the fire had to remain lit for at least 3 minutes without any assistance. Several of the men were adept at the task and able to quickly light handfuls of dry grass with showers of sparks from their flint, and blow them until they glowed, smoked and finally erupted in flames. At first Noah struggled to keep his fire lit, but he still managed to finish in the middle of the pack.

The men broke for lunch. Noah felt a growing sense of confidence and joined Dave and his newfound pack of buddies. Each sack lunch was identical: ham and cheese sandwich, mayo and mustard packets, small apple, granola bar and a water bottle. Noah carefully applied the mustard and mayo to his sandwich.

"Damn. You barely broke a sweat on that hike," exclaimed a large man with a massive beard and face still reddened from the day's activity. "Thanks," Noah replied. "I started running about a year ago when I found out I had high cholesterol. Turns out that running is not only good exercise but can boost your immune system and even prevent depression."

The red faced man stared back at Noah and smiled weakly, as if trying to understand Noah's words. He turned away and peered over at a companion's sack lunch. "What you got? Ham and cheese?"

The rest of the lunch was uneventful and no one engaged Noah further. Slightly rebuffed, he contented himself to nibble his sandwich and observe the scene. There were other men sitting alone. Some of them had an intensity that Noah found interesting. They seemed to be experiencing something different from the other weekend warriors. Every moment was more meaningful and important to them. They appeared disinterested in camaraderie and jokes. They rarely smiled. Their intensity bordered on impatience, as if they had only a limited amount of time to glean as much information as possible. They were lone observers like Noah, but still he felt no kinship.

THE GAS STATION sat dark and still. The night was clear and visibility good. Dull yellow light washed over the parking lot from three large sodium flood lights. Dave crouched a few feet in front of Noah, a five-gallon gas tank in each hand. Dave turned and nodded to Noah. He took a few hunched steps toward the closest pump and stopped. Leaving the gas tanks on the ground, Dave turned and crept back to where Noah knelt, partially concealed by a porta-potty, with the AR-15. Dave crept up close to Noah and silently reached toward the rifle, thumbing the safety selector to the "off" position. He exchanged an unsmiling look at Noah before turning to the gas cans.

Noah's job was to cover Dave while he filled the cans. They had spotted the card-lock gas station at sunset. After observing it for thirty minutes, Dave had determined it was unguarded. Still, he felt it was safer to wait until dark to grab the gas. The station had no actual attendants. Customers used a card to authorize and pump their own gas – typically for commercial businesses. Noah's card was issued to him by his employer, but he still felt some satisfaction that he was able to be of some help. Since leaving Adam's compound, the dynamic between Noah and Dave had changed dramatically. Dave was clearly in charge. His training and expertise was significantly greater than Noah's – not to mention it was Dave's truck they were driving. Dave was in charge and making the decisions. There was no disputing that fact.

The final morning of the survival training weekend had been a blur of confusion and growing apprehension. For once, all the major news outlets seemed to be on the same page: there had been a major attack on Los Angeles. Possibly nuclear. Power outages. Panic. Rioting. Lawlessness. Fires raged. Worst of all was the lack of information. In an age of almost instantaneous coverage of major events, there was disturbingly little coming out of Los Angeles. How does a city of over four million people go quiet? What in hell could be happening there?

As it turned out, while the men attending the survival weekend were vastly more prepared than the average person, their preparations had never taken into account that they might physically be hundreds of miles from their homes and families when the shit hit the fan. Such an oversight might be somewhat humbling at any other time, but at the moment, embarrassment was the least of their worries. Noah tried to call his wife several times but with no response. The only communication with her in the last forty-eight hours was a single text: "Please come home. I'm scared."

A third of the men disappeared Saturday night. Early Sunday morning, the men who remained began quickly packing up their gear. Hurried goodbyes were said. A small group of men gathered to pray. While never officially announced, the morning events were obviously cancelled. Noah had hoped to find Adam and say goodbye, but he was nowhere to be seen, and Dave was anxious to leave.

As they drove through Salt Lake City, all was calm and orderly. It was a clear, sunny Sunday morning. The parking lots of each Mormon church they passed were packed with cars. Two couples played doubles tennis in a neatly manicured city park. Traffic was sparse and unremarkable. The only sign of any apparent alarm was a crowd of people at Walmart, hurriedly loading their cars with groceries. Noah and Dave exchanged looks. Had they imagined the disaster? Was it a hoax or perhaps part of the survival weekend that had gone too far? Dave thumbed the power button on the radio in his truck and any optimism was quickly dispelled. The world had descended into chaos. Despite the veneer of normalcy that surrounded them, somehow both Noah and Dave knew that everything had changed, and nothing would ever again be as it was.

Traffic was light on Interstate 84, and they were making good time. Both men sat quietly, eyes focused on the horizon as they listened to the news on the radio. Dave reached forward and turned down the volume. "We have to swing by Olympia and check on my folks." Dave's voice was flat, steady, but lightly threatening. Noah tried to comprehend the statement and its implications. Olympia, Washington was only a few hours away from Seaside, Oregon, where Noah lived. Ordinarily, the detour would have added just four to five hours to their trip, depending on traffic. Ordinarily.

Dave's parents, as Noah recalled from their conversation on the drive to Utah, were in their eighties. They lived in the family home that Dave grew up in. Noah imagined they lived the kind of quiet life that people in their eighties usually did. Tending their small garden. Walking their little dog. Appointments with their doctors, followed by lunch at the little deli they both liked. The inconsequential routines and rewards of the twilight years of life.

Best case scenario, the drive from Utah back to his family was twelve hours. Twelve hours. Throw in traffic and an apocalypse and it was feasible it could take a full day to get home. Without the ability to communicate, Noah had no way to know if his family was safe. They lived in a good area with good neighbors. A comforting thought. But until Noah was reunited with them, every second felt like an eternity. His entire being was focused on returning to them. Every molecule in his body seemed to somehow align itself with this mission. Somewhere deep inside, a primal sub consciousness flipped on, and a strange clarity consumed him. There was only one thing in the universe that mattered: his family. Everyone and everything else that stood between him and his family was an obstacle that had to be overcome.

For the first time in his life, no inner voice second guessed

Noah's thoughts and intentions. He felt totally present. Totally engaged. The feeling was thrilling. He would take action. The detour to Olympia was unacceptable. The larger cities would be the first overrun with murder and mayhem. Dave's parents were either dead or would be soon. And if they were OK, then what? Would Dave be willing to leave them to take Noah home? It seemed unlikely. This wasn't a detour. This was a dead end. Noah sat silently. The magnetic pull towards his family pulsed within his brain. The sensation was physical. Overwhelming. He couldn't allow Dave to take him to Olympia. If necessary, he would kill Dave. Kill. Dave. The thought was so loud Noah glanced quickly at Dave to see if he had heard it. Dave's face remained grimly set on the road. Each man sat in silence. Equals in determination.

In the logic of the apocalypse, the decision was rational. If killing Dave allowed Noah to get home to his family sooner, it was worth it. If Noah's family was still alive, any sacrifice made was worth the cost. If they were dead, nothing mattered. Dave's death would be just one of countless others. Strangely, Noah felt little moral anguish about his decision to murder the man sitting next to him. Perhaps, morality was relative, he thought humorlessly. Whatever qualms his conscience may have, they were drown out by Noah's primeval compulsion to protect his wife and family.

NOAH GRIPPED the AR and slightly shifted his crouched position to stem off a leg cramp. Thirty yards away Dave filled the second gas can. Noah scanned the area. Suddenly the night exploded with the staccato of a large caliber semi-automatic rifle. With surprising quickness, Noah swung the barrel of the AR toward the muzzle flashes thirty yards to the right of Dave's position. He squeezed off five to seven quick shots, barely feeling the recoil or report. Peering through the darkness, he waited and watched for movement.

Nothing but a light tonal ringing in his unprotected ears. Though he'd given his position away, something inside instructed him to remain still. Minutes passed without any further movement or sound coming from the gas station.

Finally, he heard a soft groan coming from where Dave lay prone, his legs splayed awkwardly in the dim yellow light, his upper half concealed by shadows. Dave was alive but not moving. Noah scrolled through a variety of options in his head. Was the shooter dead? Were there more bad guys? Would the shots fired attract attention? Could he lift Dave into the truck?

The safest solution would be to retreat to where the truck was concealed, a hundred yards behind where Noah crouched. The problem was the gas. They desperately needed to refuel, and finding gas would only get more difficult. After almost twenty minutes without any discernible sound or motion, apart from Dave's one soft moan, Noah moved forward. His muscles were sore from crouching, and he almost lost balance. Without cover between Noah's position and Dave, he could only move slowly and pause – waiting for gunfire.

He had crossed half the distance between the porta-potty and the pumps where Dave lay, without any resistance. He picked up his pace and scurried, hunched over toward the gas pumps. He moved past Dave to the last pump and attempted to take a position that was concealed from whoever had ambushed them. Again, he waited several minutes.

Finally, Noah moved up slowly to where Dave lay on his back. Noah's nostrils filled with the acrid metallic odor of blood and gasoline. One of the gas cans had been punctured by a round about midway and was slowly leaking. As Noah's eyes adjusted to the dim light, he could see that Dave was still alive – his chest raising and lowering slightly. Noah set the AR down carefully and leaned over Dave until their faces were just inches apart. At first Dave's eyes moved back and forth erratically. Finally, they locked in on Noah with a desperate intensity. Dave tried to speak, but a low gurgle was all he could manage. Red bubbles formed in his open mouth.

The inability to speak seemed to intensify the emotion in his eyes. Frustration. Anger. Violence. His chest rose and fell more rapidly. Dave's head lolled slightly to one side, revealing a mass of gore where his left ear used to be. Skin and matted hair hung from the cavity left by the bullet. Blood oozed down his neck, soaking into his camo jacket.

Noah leaned in close to Dave's remaining ear, unsure if he could still hear. "Keys."

Dave's head twitched and his body shook slightly. His eyes, silently raging, betrayed him. A millisecond glance toward his right shirt pocket was enough. Noah reached in, unbuttoned the pocket, and retrieved the blood-stained set of keys. Dave groaned louder, trying in vain to command his ruined body. He tried to speak, but could only choke on the blood filling his mouth.

Noah pocketed the keys and retrieved the AR15. Momentarily unconcerned about an ambush, he stood on his feet. Dave's eyes closed, but his chest continued to move up and down. The pool of blood around him had doubled in size. Noah considered what to say. The dying man in front of him was not his friend or his enemy. He didn't even know his last name. He owed him nothing. Still, it felt wrong to leave without a word. Wrong. What did that word even mean anymore?

Noah grabbed the two tanks and moved off in a direction that kept the pump island between him and where the attacker had been in position. No one followed or shot at him. He had to move slowly to avoid sloshing gasoline. Following an indirect path, he was able to return to the truck without incident. He poured the gas from the damaged fuel can into the truck's tank and stored the full, undamaged tank in the bed. All he wanted was to leave the area as quickly as he could. He started up the truck and resisted the urge to punch the gas pedal. Leaving the lights off, Noah eased it onto a side street until he regained his bearings. The clock in the vehicle indicated only an hour had passed from the time they left the truck to grab the fuel. It felt like a lifetime.

Dave was dying or likely dead. Each mile put him farther in the distance. Noah didn't give it much thought. His focus was home and how to safely get back to his family. The moral reckoning of his actions would have to wait for another day. As he drove, the sky lightened in the east. He scanned the radio stations. Most had reverted to the Emergency Broadcast System. The news was all bad. He listened until the broadcast began to repeat itself. He scanned the other channels. The radio locked in, and the cab filled with the notes of a saxophone. Smooth jazz 103.3. Noah thought of his family. His shoulders convulsed and he began to sob. The truck weaved slightly, then regained its course toward Oregon.

A day later, Noah crossed into Oregon. After avoiding ambush at Walter's Ferry, he drove farther west to an unguarded bridge and was able to cross the Snake River without incident. Interstate 84 was a gamble. Easily the fastest way home, it was also the most dangerous. Noah saw abandoned vehicles and men, women, and children on the roadside, out of gas and luck. Some tried desperately to wave Noah down. Some even tried to block his car. Once, Noah felt the truck hit something as he gunned the engine and drove around a stranded motorist. He did not look back.

He gave up trying to call home. They never answered. He knew they would call if they could. Still, he checked the phone repeatedly, hoping for a text. He'd heard that texting would often work even when phone lines were down. He'd sent a number of texts to his wife, telling her he was on his way home. There was no response.

He thought about the men from the survival training weekend. How many had made it home? How many hadn't? How many of them had to make... tough choices like he had? Noah could not deny that on some level he felt a sense of pride. It was the apocalypse and he was surviving. He'd always felt underestimated in life. His strengths were the soft skills that went unappreciated: communication, empathy, observation, team building. But inwardly, he'd always felt like there was another side to him. A more dangerous side. A side he suppressed because society provided no outlet for it. Still, he had always known. He was a warrior. A survivor.

He wasn't a para-military poser or prepper wannabe. There was something inside that set him apart from the guys he'd spent the weekend with. He had it and they didn't. He could make the hard decisions. Maybe he didn't know the difference between a clove hitch and a bowline knot, but he possessed something they couldn't teach in the Boy Scouts: the will to live.

He thought of home. His family would be so happy to see him. More than any other time in his life. He had so much to tell them. His wife would be proud of him. Would he be able to tell her the sacrifices he had made to protect them? She would understand. Everything he had done had been for his family. What more could any woman want?

Noah felt a strange sense of elation. The weekend had been a success. He truly did feel prepared – not scared. He felt reborn. Fully alive. All the numbness and distractions of modern society had been stripped away. He could feel the blood in his veins. Every sense was heightened. His instincts, long ignored, were now his trusted advisor. When others had fallen, he had emerged unscathed. Every hesitant thought, every muted impulse, every inner doubt... all gone. Replaced by the delicious realization that in a world of wolves and sheep, he was a wolf.

When the windshield exploded, Noah instinctively raised his arms to shield his face. He heard loud thunking sounds as more rounds pierced the cab. His shoulder stung as if on fire and he ducked for cover. The truck swerved sharply and then was airborne. For a moment there was no sound, until it landed. Metal and bone crunched. The Ford rolled two times before finally skidding to a stop.

Noah hung upside down in his seatbelt, dazed. A trickle of blood poured from his mouth into his eyes. He squeezed them shut and blinked in a vain effort to clear his vision. He could hear shouting. He swallowed blood. The voices seemed to be approaching. Footsteps. A ringing in his ears replaced all sound or thought. His vision dimmed as all consciousness receded for the final time.

4

———

UNTETHERED

BY GEORGE GRIMM

*IF THE HISTORY Channel TV show **Alone** has taught us anything, it's that loneliness sucks the guts out of even the hardiest survivor. George Grimm spins this yarn about a young, war-addled veteran as he wanders the apocalypse trying to decide if surviving is even worth the ass pain. With death around every corner and his old Econoline as his chariot, Robert Malcolm does the Texas two-step with his indefatigable companion: manic depression. But as Robert crosses the border into the badlands of Utah, God cuts in on the dance. Without family and without a cause, what is the point? Robert is about to find out.*

George is a first-time fiction writer and Army veteran with a lot of good stuff to say about how life doesn't always go as planned.

-Jason Ross

THE NEVADA HEAT has cooked my ass for three days. I abandoned California in a mad rush.

I do have a plan, but I can't bring myself to my feet. I shouldn't feel this way, and I've left nothing behind of consequence, but here I am, high-centered like some kind of post-modern, belly-button-gazing Snowflake.

Snowflakes don't have a long shelf-life in the deserts of Nevada. These days, Snowflakes don't have a long shelf-life anywhere.

I've been awake since 2200 and I'm beyond exhausted. I almost drove off the road around four in the morning, so I pulled off––I can't remember the highway number, just another shitty two-lane strip of American infrastructure that probably won't be repaired again in my lifetime––and then I went catatonic without actually sleeping.

The sun's up now and it's back to doing its hateful work. The AC in my van's dead as disco, so no matter what happens next, the blazing sun and I will be getting up close and personal for the next thirteen hours. I look around, seeing the landscape in daylight for the first time. Essentially, there is gravel and two brands of tiny brush piles, each the size of a wadded-up newspaper page. One pile is the color of Maalox and the other is the color of vomit when dinner the night before came out of a bottle. Jesus was not having a good day when he created this corner of the world.

With a force of will roughly equivalent to storming the beach at Normandy, I roll off the back seat of the van and plant my feet on the floorboards. Then I crawl up to the driver's seat—the "captain's chair" as they called it when Ford made a flier about this long-forgotten model of van. I used to fondly refer to it as "the rapist van," but given the political climate in California, I had to put a stop to that. Humor dies as moral outrage flourishes.

My ass finds its depression in the captain's chair and I crank the ignition. With a herculean force of will, I'm "on the road again," in the immortal words of Willie Nelson. I feel exactly *none* of Willie's optimism.

I have nothing to lose, right? So, what's it going to take to push past my self-loathing? I hope I can get over myself soon because I have a family—a mom, dad and a brother--and they've got to be worrying about me. They're in Pennsylvania, and the pessimist inside my head keeps reminding me that Pennsylvania might as well be France, given this new, terrible version of America.

As the sun hits my face through the windshield, I realize that I am not a quitter. At least not yet.

The last week has been hell, and I'm not opposed to never seeing California again. Given the fact that overland travel is as dangerous as road tripping in Afghanistan, odds are good that I will never lay eyes on the ocean again. Fine by me.

I down a quart of water from my gallon jug and roll east toward Utah. Hopefully, my Utah friends are better humans than the friends I trusted in California. Friends don't rob and try to murder friends. I'm hoping that's a California thing and not a Utah thing. But in the end, I'm the one who saw the inside of that California dude's head, and he didn't get to see the inside of mine. I don't think I'll ever get that picture out of my internal slide show: a friend's brain. Never mind that he was a murdering asshole.

I only planned to hang out at his place until I could get past the blockade on the 580 freeway eastbound, but how bad do things have to get before a friend tries to kill you over a car? I can tell you exactly how bad: six days and four hours after a nuclear bomb detonates, things get that bad; even if the bomb goes off three hundred miles away. In fairness, again, maybe it was just a California thing. Maybe Californians are an order of magnitude more horrible than the rest of America. I watched an episode of *Keeping Up With The Kardashians* and it reset my whole framework about how horrible humans could be. Then again, I think that's New Jersey or thereabouts, so my theory on California being worse than America might not hold water.

I was lucky enough to grab a shortwave radio from that dead dude's home before I left, and it's been a godsend. The only channel

I can reliably get is a pirate broadcast from a drunk dude who calls himself a Drinkin' Bro. He's an alcoholic but at least he's honest.

I'm praying to make it to Utah in the next eight hours, but at the rate I'm going, I know it'll take longer. There's a deadline in my head, but it keeps getting moved out. Frankly, I didn't think I'd have the stones to survive the first couple days—when my mind started running down unfortunate side paths. I began to accept my place as another meat popsicle wandering the urban desolation that'd sprung up where society once bragged about how "God was dead." I've seen ten thousand such meat popsicles at this point.

Am I one too? That's been the big question rattling around in my brain bucket. Setting the big question aside, I focus on the here-and-now: can I survive the next eight hours? It's quite the mother-fucker to have your mind suddenly grow a "sell by" date, but that's the god's honest truth. I feel lost in a sea of sand, and I haven't been strong for a very long time, not even before the Black Autumn clus-terfuck. The nuclear bomb going off in Los Angeles made me wish I was in Los Angeles instead of in the Port of Oakland. But something kept pushing me past my first self-destructive thought. I tell myself it's my family that keeps me going, but that thought resonates more like a sales pitch than bedrock truth.

Is that the big win now? To survive? Or am I holding out to die another day in another way? Every time I close my eyes, I see that California asshole's brain matter blown across his kitchen cabinets and all over his Cuisinart.

Please get that picture out of my head, God. If you're still around, just do me this one solid.

───────────

IT'S BEEN five hours of driving and I'm approaching the Nevada/Utah border near Wendover. The place used to be a casino town, apparently. I lean forward and squint through the dirty windshield. There appears to be a row of bodies wired to the bridge over the freeway. I'm curious, but I don't slow down to figure out why a dozen corpses adorn the overpass. I stomp on the gas and the gutless van moans as it nudges the needle on the speedometer. Adrenaline fills my skin with biting ants, and I sail under the death show at a blistering seventy miles per hour. Then I cross the Utah state line with my undeserving hide intact.

Hallelujah.

I put as much distance as possible between myself and Wendover as I can, which means I keep up the seventy miles per hour even though I know it's not wise to push the van that hard.

A few dozen miles later, I spot a herd of elk rambling across the desert, and I pull over and stretch my legs. I grab my big rifle and double check the magazine for ammunition. I pull the charging handle back just enough to see a round in the chamber, then step onto the asphalt with my weapon at the ready. I have a vague idea that I'm supposed to kill animals to feed myself during the apocalypse, so I watch the elk through the scope of my .308.

"I really wish I wasn't alone," I speak out loud, which startles me. I haven't heard another voice, except for J.T. Taylor on the radio, for days. Somehow, watching the elk dip in and out of the folds of the desert reminds me of how much I would prefer to share this small miracle with another human being. I should've found a dog to fill the void, but it's entirely too late for that. Most of the dogs have been eaten, at least back in the big city.

I'm watching the elk through my optic. They're in no hurry, so I observe them without getting my panties in a wad. The desert's dead quiet and beginning to grow dark. The sun's near the horizon (thank you, Lord) and a cloud has materialized to cool things off even more. I sit down on the side of the road and rest my back against the van.

I perch my rifle on my knee and the scope steadies. Out from a hidden fold, a bull elk appears, maybe three hundred yards away. He looks directly at me through my scope and stands stock-still.

BOOM!

The rifle jumps in my hand. I don't remember making the decision to shoot. I don't even remember placing the crosshairs over his heart. When the gun bounces back from the recoil, I see a buck-skin-colored mound on the desert floor that wasn't there before. I suppose I must've aimed well because, as they say, results don't lie. I look again and the big body hasn't moved. The other elk trot away into the distance and they disappear down a wash.

As I stand and slowly work my way up to the dead bull elk, I'm frankly astonished. Something just happened that I don't understand. Survival just took an interesting turn, and I can't help feeling like a character in a western movie. The thought of what happened in California vanishes and my eyes swim. I thank God for whatever this was. The big animal, flipped on his side and no longer breathing, offers me sweet relief. Survival now has a name and that name is "honest work"—the honest work of breaking this big beast down and using him to harbor life. My life. The "sell by" date in my mind pushes out toward the horizon, maybe a long ways toward the horizon.

I quarter the elk with my folding knife and carry him to the van piece-by-piece. Not a single car drives by on the highway while I'm breaking down the animal, and that's good because I don't know if I could put my pack down and unsling my rifle fast enough to fight another man. It's not every day that someone takes an elk, let alone on the side of a highway. If someone comes along, chances are fifty-fifty that I'll have to fight to keep it.

I bag up everything I could possibly use from the animal. I wrap it in trash bags and load it into the back of my van, making trips out to the kill site until the sun's riding the line of the horizon. When I finally have everything stowed in the van, I stand back and regard my bounty.

At least I have this. I have this food and this moment. Back before the collapse, I could never stop thinking about the past and the future. I worried endlessly about what I'd done and what I'd do. Perhaps this is mental health: to just stand in the here and now, with a pile of copper-smelling, fresh meat and to know that it's enough. Tomorrow can take care of itself. Today, I have this.

The oranges and reds of late evening bounce off the mountains and reflect on the oasis effect of the still-warm salt flats. It's like looking out across a hundred thousand acre pond.

I'm still high from taking the elk, and my adrenaline is pumping from having to break him down in such a rush. Sticking around where I fired my weapon seems like a mistake, so I'm not going to eat any of the elk now. I haven't eaten in hours, but I can't hang out. Nobody has passed me in the forty-five minutes or so that I've been dealing with the elk, and that's been a minor miracle.

With my van full of meat, I have more than enough food for a while. I close the rear doors and continue driving along the freeway toward Salt Lake City. I stop when I get to an observation area looking out over the salt flats. The highway is still empty, and I don't want to take any chances, so I pull onto the salt flats and drive as close to the mountains as I can get, which ends up being more than five miles. Distances on the flats prove deceptive in the twilight. I step down from the van when I find a suitable camp-site. The fresh, salty air contrasts with the stink in the van. Even just clean meat and no guts, you could cut the ripeness in the van with a saw. I wonder how long that meat is going to last? Given how powerful the smell, I can picture ten trillion microscopic bacteria working that pile of meat like a massive army of tiny, evil zombies. They aren't going to rest for a second, particularly in this heat.

"God give me the strength to keep on keeping on," I pray as the sun disappears from view. Even in the shadow of my mountain of luck, I've found something to worry about.

"Well, I better eat something." I speak to myself out loud, which has become something of a new habit.

I open the side door and rummage through the bags of meat in search of a backstrap. I find a long cord of meat that's most likely a backstrap or tenderloin, and I lop off a six-inch section with my pocket knife and stuff the rest back in the bag. I wonder if the trash bags are holding in heat and accelerating the process of rot? Probably. When I was a Boy Scout, I went winter camping once. The scoutmaster had us bring trash bags to act as a "vapor barrier" around our sleeping bags to fend off the cold. I spent the night sliding that trash bag on and off as I alternated between freezing and sweating my balls off. It was a hellish night.

I'm going to need to spread the meat out in the back of the van the best I can before I go to sleep. I'm sure it'll take hours for the body heat of the elk to finally dissipate and reach room temperature, and I'd rest easier if the meat normalized with the chill of the desert night—ripe smelling or not.

I pull out my camp stove and a pan. When the bit of olive oil I add starts sizzling, I toss the meat on without salt. I was never someone to season a fresh piece of meat without cutting it into steaks. I flash-cook the heavy rope of meat to medium rare on the outside, then devour it like a starving man. I don't even use a fork or knife. I just pluck it out of the pan and gnaw off the ends. The inside of the muscle group tastes dead-raw, but that's really all the seasoning it needs. Just a bit of blood mixed with the slight char on the outside. I know that, technically, there's no good reason to even cook fresh elk, but it sure tastes fine with that coat of blackening.

There aren't a lot of calories in lean meat. I know it as a factoid, but I'm profoundly satisfied with the meal. It's just what my body needed. I sit back against the van tire and take in the night sky—the stars starting to show themselves in force. The Milky Way has just begun to take over the canopy, and for the second time in the same day, I find myself content.

"I should be safe here for the night," I say to myself, grabbing my rifle and steeling myself for the job of unpacking the elk meat. I check my mag, open the side door, take a big whiff and decide to sleep outside. The meat is a godsend, but three hundred pounds of raw elk smells like the armpit of a weightlifter.

I WAKE up to the sun glaring down on me. My vision's cloudy and I'm almost blind. The desert sand and salt's collected in the corners of my eyes, and they feel like rap music sounds. It takes a minute to figure out where I am and how I got here.

I remember the meat in my van and I panic, jumping up to check it. I swing open the door and take a deep smell. It still smells really strong, but I sense no appreciable rot. Undoubtedly, the bacteria has been cranking away at it all night, but it's still good. I lift up a big chunk and smell the underneath side. It's still better than anything I've smelled out of a package from the store.

"Shit. That was close."

I gather my belongings and toss them in the van, avoiding the meat-apocalypse back there. I hope to make it to a friend's house in Salt Lake today. Given my recent past experience with friends, a quote from James Mattis pops into my head.

Be polite, be professional, and have a plan to kill everybody you meet.

Slightly groggy, I open my bag of coffee and put a few espresso beans in my mouth to absorb the caffeine. No time for making a pot. I want to make Salt Lake by nightfall. I drive off the endless salt flats, following my tracks from the evening. But before I make the freeway, I spot smoke on the horizon where I estimate Salt Lake is located.

If I stay close to the mountains across the salt flats, I might avoid detection from whoever created the smoke. If I can see them, they can see me. I slow down, trying to figure out if the little ranch house is abandoned or not. Then I spot a horse tied to the fence outside. It's the horse that tips me over into approaching the dwelling. A man who owns a horse can't be all bad, I decide. In truth, I know it's just my loneliness getting the best of me.

I stop short of the horse, drawing my rifle as I exit my vehicle. I approach at the ready, horse or not.

"Is anyone in there? I am not here to fight. I'm just passing through," I yell from behind the rickety fence post.

A voice shouts back. " I'm coming out. Don't shoot."

An older man, probably nearing his seventies, steps slowly out onto the porch. He's limping and holding nothing in his hands. His face looks as though he's been rode hard and put away wet, which makes sense if he's been living on the edge of the salt flats. He focuses on my eyes and not the rifle.

"Son, you're not gonna need that gun here." It's like listening to your grandpa tell a story and I lower the rifle all the way. He turns around and walks back inside the ranch house. "Well, come inside. It's going to be a hot one."

I follow him inside. He heads straight for a chair and takes a seat, breathing heavy. He reaches into his pocket and pulls out a pack of cigarettes, sparking one up. His hands shake as he works the disposable lighter. He's wearing an old cavalry Stetson that's definitely seen better days.

"My name is Jim," he says, then takes a long slow drag from the cigarette. "What brings you to the middle of nowhere?"

I remove my sunglasses, mostly checking the cabin for possible hiding places—a trap. Nothing raises the slightest suspicion.

"My name's Robert. I'm just passing through. I didn't notice your cabin until it was right in front of me."

He takes another drag then puts out the cigarette in the already full ashtray on the table.

"I'm going to cut to the chase, son. I don't have much time left." He goes on to explain that he may only be alive for a short while because he was already battling cancer before this whole mess started. I'm looking at a dead man. I've seen hundreds of dead by this point in the collapse, so it shouldn't affect me—but it does. There's something about looking at a live person who will soon die that's profoundly inhuman. It reminds me of watching old newsreels of Nazi execution squads. You see those people marching in lines through the muck in tattered clothes toward the firing line and you realize: every last one of them is dead and they know it is coming. That moment before the executioner—the firing squad, the gas chamber, the ax man—it's a violation of all that is hopeful about the human race. Here I sit, across from a man staring down the long, dark hallway of death.

"I have been alone a long time, Robert, but I don't want to die alone."

I ask him if I can sit down and he agrees.

Looking him in the eye from across a cigarette-butt-covered coffee table, I ask how much time he has left. It seems like the right thing to ask—digging for any tiny bit of hope from this jacked-up situation. I'd rather be anywhere than on this couch. The room reeks of stale smoke. My hand drifts up to my face in a barely-subconscious attempt to cover the smell of the man's cancer-riddled body. I'm probably imagining things. There are so many bad smells in the house of a single, dying man, that cancer would probably be the last thing I'd notice. Still, I put my hand to my face and then all I can smell is the lingering tang of elk flesh. Maybe that was what I was smelling all along.

"I just don't want to hurt anymore. I think it's time to call it." The old man stands up from the chair and gestures that I should follow. He leads me to a back room where we find a bed perfectly made. I turned to him with eyebrows raised. Nothing about this spotless room looks like it belongs in the mess I've seen elsewhere in the ranch house.

"I want to die here, where Rosie and I slept." It dawns on me that Jim is asking me to take him out of this world. I'm not ready for that. Not right this minute. Not after California.

I turn and walk outside, away from the sick old man, wondering if God has led me here to help him die. After I slow the beating in my chest a bit, I head over to the van. The screen door screeches, then slams and the old man stands on the porch, watching me in silence.

I pull out a chunk of elk from the side door of the van--probably a piece of the rump. I could go digging for a better cut of meat, the backstrap or tenderloin, but I don't. It's his last meal, but a stranger is a stranger. I walk back in, rubbing the mane of the horse on the way. "When's the last time you had a steak?" I ask as I pass him on the porch.

"I don't know, but I'll take one if you're offering." The old man smiles and follows me back inside. I'd seen the big propane tank when I'd first pulled up, and I'm not surprised when the stove in the kitchen flicks to life as I turn the knob. There's already a greasy pan on the stove, and I slide it over to the blue flame.

I grab a can of beans from the cupboard, open it with a can opener that's laying on the counter between dirty dishes, and dump the beans into a saucepan, spilling some on the hot burner.

"Smells nice," the old man says. "A last meal."

I wish he hadn't said that.

After I finish cooking, we sit down at the table, and I watch him enjoy every bite. It should make me feel better, but it doesn't.

"So why now?" I'm hoping that he'll put this off until the next guy shows up on his porch.

He freezes, mid-bite. His shoulder's slump and he slowly finishes chewing.

"I have nothing to live for now and I think the cancer knows it."

I don't want to talk about his dead wife, and I'm relieved when he goes off, instead, on a litany of stories about his years of military service. He'd been career army. He gets up while he's still talking, goes to the kitchen, and comes back with a bottle of whiskey.

The whiskey sits on the table unopened while he finishes his meal. I eat my own steak and beans without much joy, still dreading what is to come.

"Will you pray with me?"

This thing keeps getting worse and worse. I nod my agreement and wolf down the rest of my steak while he grabs the bottle and heads into the living room. We sit down and he dives right in to talking with God. Lucky for me, the old man handles the praying part because I have no idea what to say to God about a dude dying from cancer. Until yesterday, God and I hadn't really had much to do with one another. I think maybe we only just met, and I'm far from certain that we're going to get along.

The old man prays for a few minutes and I glance up to see tears running down his face. I squirm in my seat on the ratty couch and I pray a little too—that this shitty situation will end before I freak the fuck out.

"Amen," he says, and I whisper the word too.

The old man cracks open the bottle, takes a swig, then passes it to me. I take a huge pull and the gasoline-like burn almost makes me cough. It's not good whiskey, but I'm not complaining. I've got an edge on me that would cut a rope.

"It's time," he says after he enjoys his mouthful of cheap booze.

I swallow and follow him into the back room. He lays on the perfectly-made bed and says, "One in the temple." Somehow, the cowboy sound of it makes me feel a little better. If I picture this as a John Wayne movie, maybe it won't feel like murder. Maybe it'll come off as a mano-y-mano, tough guy thing instead of being another friend I shoot in the brain pan. The old guy reaches over and pulls a pistol out of the tiny, pressboard nightstand. It's a revolver, which helps me spin this thing in my mind into an Old

West scene: one hard case man helping another hard case man ride off into the proverbial sunset.

Before I kill him—I think he said his name was Jim—I realize that I like this old man. I'd rather not see him leave this world. I'd rather amble on down the road with him in the passenger seat of my van. But, then again, there's the cancer. And the dead wife.

I look at the pistol in my hand and look at Jim. He's lying down now, with a grin that makes his forehead wrinkle up like a crumpled napkin. Before I lose my nerve, I cock the hammer, point it at his wrinkled-napkin forehead, and pull the trigger.

The gun goes off and I realize that I was braced for something much louder. I look at the revolver instead of Jim's ruined head. It's a .22 long rifle, I realize. They make just a little pop instead of a big bang. I focus on the revolver, turning it in my hands. Jim isn't moving. I can see that much without really focusing on him. There's a growing pool of dark on the pillow beneath his head, and that's not something I want to look at too closely. I set the revolver on the nightstand and walk out of the room. I wonder if the last thing Jim saw in this world was me wincing like a chickenshit schoolgirl as I blew his brains out.

———

STILL SWEATING PROFUSELY, I grab everything useful from the cabin and chuck it in the rapist van. I'm burning this ranch house down in a bit, driven by an indistinct notion that Jim deserves a funeral somewhere along the lines of a Viking warrior. I untie the horse and smack it on the rump, realizing too late that I didn't remove his saddle and reins. Oh well. If anyone finds him, they'll appreciate the tack.

I open the gas all the way up on all four burners of the stove, trot outside, dig around in the back of the van—it continues to smell like a blood-soaked locker room—find a road flare, light it, then chuck it toward the open door of the ranch house.

Nothing happens right away, which doesn't surprise me. I've never blown anything up before, much less a house. I get in the van and hightail it away from the ranch house and back out across the salt flats. Off in the distance, I see the horse trotting south.

Somehow, killing another man has made me less-than-eager to try my luck with my buddy in Salt Lake City. I guess I'd rather not find myself in another conflict, even though I have no reason to think my buddy will be a problem.

If I head south, I can make Arizona in a reasonable amount of time without dipping into the minor metropolis of Salt Lake. I have well over half a tank of gas, and I have the twenty gallons I stole from my dead friend in California—after he was dead, of course. That should get me far into the wastelands of the southwest, if I don't screw around too much. Losing myself in a desert sounded pretty good. *I need to find a dog.*

I check my rearview mirror and see a column of black smoke a few miles behind me. It appears old Jim got his Viking funeral. So, that's the plan? Avoid cities. Find a dog. Disappear into the desert. I know the plan has more holes than a bucket of whiffle balls, but it's the best I've got. I didn't wish for this and, Lord knows, I'm no survivalist. I was carrying a good rifle and a "get home bag" when it all went down. The gun turned out to be perfect for this "mission." It's the best California-legal gat I could find—a Springfield M14 in .308 with a decent scope. Even with ball ammo, it'd been enough to drop that elk.

The "get home bag" is a bit of a joke because I don't have a home on this side of the Mississippi. It's turned into a "wander around bag" and maybe a "flee into the desert bag" if the next couple days go well. Then there's my military experience, which is probably a mixed bag. I'm combat infantry. Or, I was combat infantry. I never killed anyone over there, but I came close to getting blown up twice. Some of my buddies weren't as lucky. I don't like to admit how the whole deal side-swiped me and jacked up my internal operating system—let's just say it rhymes with "PTSD." I came home and got a job as a union electrician doing solar installs for the Californians. The state government paid citizens big bucks to buy our solar systems, so the work was good and the money was even better. That's what landed me a million miles from home when the flag went up. So, yeah. I'm a combat vet. So fucking what.

I should drive straight to Salt Lake City and get in a gunfight with the next armed person I see. Probably do the world a favor.

I stop the van when I reach blacktop and I stare at the gauges. I remember my brother telling me he missed me when I called home a week ago. Then my mom got on the phone and told me how proud they were of me. She's still in "thank you for your service" mode, even though I've been home for three years. My old man didn't bother to talk to me, even though I heard him watching football.

I break down a little. The van rumbles and the meat stinks. I get misty, like a big snowflake again. That bastard didn't want to hit pause on the game. He probably didn't even know how. That was the closest we'd come to speaking in a year, and it would've been the last time we talked. Ever.

Humanity is far from a beautiful thing, contrary to sappy-happy liberals and gushing self-help gurus. Humanity is the nasty tumor that pops up wherever too many people live close to one another. Maybe the best I can hope for is a dog and some solitude. Maybe that's the best God has to offer me; a setting sun and an elk kill. But even the elk won't last. As I've been sitting in my captain's chair sniveling, the bacteria's been chewing away at the meat, turning something clean and pure into jellified nastiness that'll slop down into the nooks and crannies of my van forever. Maybe God doesn't sleep, but neither does the devil. And the devil is us.

THE SHADOWS GROW long and I've threaded a few dead and dying towns as I roll south through the west desert of Utah. I haven't checked a map since morning, but the setting sun doesn't lie—I'm heading in the right direction and I've totally avoided Salt Lake City.

I haven't had to speak to a soul, and it's a good thing because my wonder at the world the day before has gone sour. Rotting meat and killing a good man can have that effect.

A day in the hot van hasn't done the elk meat any favors. It's gone from smelling like a locker room to smelling like three-day-old, wet socks. It makes me want to turn toward the mountains to gain some elevation. It's cooler up there, but I'm less likely to get shot down here in the Utah drylands. I'll soon be far enough south to totally avoid the Wasatch Front, and the cities dotting the foothills of the mountain range that bisects Utah north-to-south.

I'm constantly second-guessing the smell in the van. Has it changed in the last hour? In the last twenty minutes? I keep picturing the bacteria. Feasting, feasting, feasting. Turning bounty into ruin.

I wish I knew a damn thing about wild game. Being in the army didn't teach me anything about hunting or meat preservation. Back in Pennsylvania, I'd been more the guy to Drink a Twelve Pack and Watch the Game instead of Wear Camo and Shoot A Whitetail on the weekends. It's not that I'd never hunted—I've shot four or five deer. It's just that I always dropped them off at Rick's Butchery in town instead of going through the rigmarole of getting bloody. Looking back, I see the error of my ways. I don't know shit about the process going on in the back of my van.

Do I have two hours to get this meat preserved or two days? How do I even preserve it without refrigeration?

These questions drive me to distraction. When I come around

the bend in the road, I'm actually leaning forward on my steering wheel and glaring out the windshield in agitation. I'm fretting about how bad I need to take a piss and how worried I am that my meat is spoiling. That's when I see the guys in camo shooting at a big barn just off the highway. I slam on my brakes and the rapist van howls like someone stepped on the dog. All eyes swivel to my van. The gun barrels follow.

"Oh shit!" I roll out the door and snag my M14 on the way out.

A half-dozen bullets punch spiders in my windshield, but the incoming fire is uncoordinated and thin. I scamper around to the back of my van, trying to put as much metal and meat as I can between me and the soldiers. I have no idea what I'm up against, but I know that camping out behind my van will eventually end with me getting shot.

Before I can get into a long conversation with myself, I bolt for the ditch at the side of the road. Again, a few bullets whiz by me, but nothing effective. I do a Pete Rose into the ditch, scramble toward the soldiers about fifty yards and slowly peek over the lip of the irrigation ditch. There's no water in the ditch, just moist mud cracked into black, square plates.

Nobody sends rounds my way. I don't think they had time to make sense of my arrival and get orders passed around. But why would soldiers be shooting at a farm house?

I spot a couple guys run up to what looks like a leader hunkered down behind a rusty combine. If they're U.S. Army, they should have comms.

Now that my suspicion's riding high, I notice that they all have the same camo, but some of it looks like it's been to hell and back. This Black Autumn thing has only been going on for two weeks. Why would a soldier *in Utah* have raggedly-ass camo?

Then they do the exact opposite of what I would've thought: they ignore my van and go back to shooting the farmhouse.

"What the fuck?" I whisper to my raging bladder.

Admittedly, I'm pissed off, aggravated and not doing my best thinking. There's something about these fake Army soldiers shooting at a house that makes my blood go hot as McDonald's coffee.

I'm on the edge of a big field, with the highway between me and the "soldiers." Unless someone is hiding out on my side of the road in a hole somewhere, I can crawl right up their tailpipe.

The field looks like harvested alfalfa, and other than the irrigation ditch, it's wide open. I decide not to piss my pants, hold it in for added intensity, and continue down the ditch.

Full disclosure: I'm not too worried about getting shot at this point. With my bladder yammering at me like a fishwife, and after spending an entire day agonizing over rotting meat, I'm about ready to throw in the towel. I might as well fuck some bad brothers up in the process.

By the time I pop back up to take a peek, I'm on the opposite side of the shooters from my van. None of those numb-nuts is covering their six and it adds to my conviction that they aren't army. With a gut-wrenching surge of the screw-its, I dash across the highway and slam to a stop behind a huge cottonwood. Amazingly, no bullets chase me. I peek around the cottonwood, and to my utter surprise, there's a young dude hunkered down not thirty feet from my tree. He's jacking around with his AR-15, apparently working out a type three malfunction with his car key.

I step around the cottonwood and speed-walk up to him in a crouch with my barrel covering his startled face. He can't be older than twenty-five years old. He's so scared he doesn't even whimper.

"I'm just a soldier," he blurts out too loud, as I step in back of the trash cans he's hiding behind.

I look for ID, dog tags, anything that'd mark him as a soldier. I want to believe him. I really do.

"What are your rules of engagement?"

The look on his face betrays him. He has no idea what rules of engagement are, and he has the rank of Staff Sergeant on his collar. He doesn't appear to have a handgun, and other than the car key, I don't see anything sharp.

I make the "shush" sound, then hold my finger like saying "hang on one second. I'll help you with that." I've got a big Glock Perfection knife on my belt, and I hand it to him with my support hand, pommel first.

At the last second, I flip it around and ram it through the middle of his throat.

His eyes go wide as goggles, and I kneel on his chest while I clamp my hand over his mouth. He goes a little squirrelly, and I'm forced to drop my rifle in order to keep his flailing, dying body under control.

One more on my list of murders, I remind myself as he stills, gurgling blood through my fingers. One more plank on my walk to hell. I check his pulse and catch the last little dribbles of his life.

If I go around these trash cans, I'm in it to win it. I'm certain enough that the guys in camo are douchebags. At the very least, they're lying about being Army. At worst, they're marauders trying to rob a family. I've heard a few rounds coming from the house, and to my ears they sound like shotgun rounds. I invent a picture of the Beverly Hillbillies bunkered up in their farmhouse, fighting for their lives: Pappy, Ma, Great Grandma, the dumbshit son and the hot daughter. I don't have a ton to live for, but saving that hot daughter...I could see that on my tombstone.

God, I need to piss.

I come around the trash can and there is Commander Big Belly behind the combine with another guy, his back turned toward me. I blast the guy in the center of the back and the round must go straight through because Commander Big Belly throws up his hands and his rifle goes flying. I put another .308 into his chest as the other guy slumps to the side. Rounds whoosh by my head and now I'm sprinting for that combine.

I slam into the front tire and immediately come around the huge lawn mower thing on the front and start shooting before I can find a target. But one appears, charging toward a chicken coop.

He makes the coop, but I just keep dumping my mag through the thin wood. When I run out, I pull the mag I've been keeping in my front pocket and change it out. That's all the ammo I have on me, but the guy doesn't reappear from around the chicken coop.

A man comes out of the house, the door slamming like another gunshot, and I drop back behind the combine, not interested in taking a handful of birdshot to the face. I hear four, five, then six blasts from the shotguns, and I make myself as small as I can— wedging under the combine as far as I can.

"I'm friendly! I'm friendly!" I scream between fusillades of twelve gauge. Turns out, I'm not so ready to die after all.

"Who are you?" A woman is pointing an over-and-under shotgun at my head. I'm not sure how she got around the combine without me seeing her.

"I'm a friendly, lady. I just shot those guys in the camo."

"So you say. Keep your hands where I can see them." I crawl out from under the combine without my Springfield. I can always come back and get it later.

"Where's your gun," she demands.

"It's under there. But if it's all the same to you, I really need to take a pee."

She turns away, slightly embarrassed. I take that as permission and I walk behind the cottonwood, holding my hands up in case her husband sees me.

Sweet, sweet relief.

"Come with us," the man orders.

When I come back around the tree, he's holding my M14 and his shotgun both. The lady is still looking away, apparently a little prissy about a strange man pissing behind a tree.

I dip my head at one of the dead men, still not entirely sure that I killed the right people.

"Who were they?"

"They're a militia from Salt Lake City," she answers me.

"And who are you?" I ask. She's still acting weird and I check my fly just to make sure.

"We live here," the husband stakes out his territory. "The neighbors would've come pretty soon. But thank you anyway."

I doubt that the neighbors would've come with assault rifles. Maybe hunting rifles.

We pass three other dead guys and one guy squirming and moaning on the grass. I think to ask about helping him, but he looks to have taken a full shotshell to the belly. He's got guts hanging out all over. That's another picture that's going to hang around my neck for a while. At least he wasn't a guy I killed. I'm never going to forget the sucking, rasping feel of pushing my Glock knife through that kid's throat. I think I may have left the knife in him. I can't remember, but it's not on my belt.

She talks about how they're all from the Mormon Church just down the road. The fake soldiers had been picking off farmhouses farther out from town. This was their first foray so close. I'm still not seeing any neighbors running toward the fray with hunting rifles, so I have to wonder how much this town is really prepared to risk for each other.

In this day and age, will men risk their lives for someone they see at church every Sunday?

Maybe they will if they're Mormons.

I'm at odds with my faith, and have been for some time. While I was deployed to Iraq, I would attend church every Sunday like clockwork, but as my friends began to leave this world, I questioned it all. I haven't been inside a church since I came home from Iraq.

I DRIVE my van over to the church and I meet the couple there. No sign of a hot daughter. The men in the church rush out with rifles at the ready.

Day late and a dollar short, I think to myself. But these men look like farmers and they're obviously no strangers to firearms. Sure enough, every one of them carries a wood stock deer rifle.

The woman holds out her arms and heads between me and the churchmen. "He's with us. He helped us with the militia."

"We were just coming," a young Mormon says to the lady, a little too loud. "We had to ... um, gear up."

Several of the men hold out their hands to shake mine, offering thanks, mostly. The farmhouse husband hands back my M14. I still don't know his name, but that's okay. It's been a messy afternoon.

"Thank you again for coming to help. That's a nice rifle. Is there anything we can do to, you know, pay you back?"

"I need to preserve the elk meat in my van. I could use some water, and maybe fuel if you have any to spare."

I'm not pushing my luck, but I did risk my life. Not that I cared about it in the moment. In retrospect, they definitely owe me. I don't want to stay any longer than I have to, but if I can get over my worry about the elk meat, it's worth hanging out with these Mormons for a bit.

They go to work figuring out the questions of preserving meat, but every other family sounds like they've killed and cold smoked a cow or two. While they're figuring it out, I wander back to the door to check on my van. Nobody appears to be jacking with it.

A man pulls me aside. "I can help you cure your meat. Drive your rig down the road four houses—the green one on the left—and pull around back."

If these guys want to bushwhack me, I figure they would've done it already. I follow his instructions and pull around to the back of the green house. Eight or ten men are standing around four old refrigerators with galvanized smokestacks sticking out of the tops.

They're poking and prodding inside the fridges, getting fires going. I quickly deduce the rural smoker tech: they've carved up old refrigerators to use as smokers.

I throw open the doors to the van and the men admire the heap of flesh.

"I'm not sure it's all still good," I try not to sound as clueless as I am.

"When did you kill it?"

"Two days back. Out in the desert."

"It's fine," the man of the house says. "You've got several more days before there'll be much of an issue. You generally want to season elk meat for a week or so, even if there's a bit of heat. Two weeks at least in the winter. Let's cut it up."

All the men join in and I borrow someone's knife. We go through the elk, cutting it into thin strips then laying them on the racks in the refrigerators. As we fill one, we close it up, adjust the dampers and move on to the next one. It's a long process, but not one of the Mormons leaves until the job is completely finished.

"This will take a while. Probably twenty-four hours," the man of the house, "Brother Stines," tells me as we wash our hands under the big spigot that pulls ice-cold well water. "You can stay with us in the spare room if you like."

THE SUN WENT down hours before and we've been working by lantern light.

"I'll hang here. Thank you," I say to him with a grin on my face. With the elk now "in the bag" as they say, I can finally breathe.

I have the bottle of whiskey in my pack from the dead old man's house. I grab it from the van and offer it to Brother Stines, even though I'm not dumb enough to think that Mormons drink. *An offer to be refused should never be missed,* my dad used to say. As expected Stines smiles and shakes his head.

I hope the Mormons don't hate me for it, but there's no way I'm moving on with my evening sober. I've killed more men in the last twenty-four hours than my entire platoon did in an entire deployment. I take a robust pull from the bottle and sit down on a fat stump in the backyard of the green house, enjoying the smell of elk and smoke.

A man appears from the dark on the gravel strip between the little, two story houses that make up this town. "Good evening. I'm Bishop Black. Thank you for helping the Tilletsons. I'm afraid we weren't at all prepared for that kind of trouble so soon." He shakes my hand. I wonder when they'd ever be ready if they weren't ready now.

"You're welcome."

I pass the bottle to him. He pauses. He swallows a mouthful.

"I haven't had a drink in 20 years, around the same time I found the church."

Did I just fuck something up?

He takes another pull and hands me back the bottle. "It's not your fault. It's been a long time and there's no chance of a relapse now, right? It's not like I'm going back to being an alcoholic." He laughs at the night sky. "I won't tell if you don't."

The bottle passes between us until it's empty. The bright orange light coming from around the refrigerator doors has begun to dim. The fires must be burning down, but the smoke will continue for hours, I figure.

I'M DRINKING my coffee with my legs dangling out of the side door of the van, sun on the rise. The little town glows, heralding a new day. The meat's ready to go, but I'm enjoying the early morning dew and the moments before the sun hits the town directly. The Wasatch Mountains hold back the morning for a solid half hour, drawing out the best part of the day—the time with coffee before the time with people. The elk'll hold me over until I can get deep, deep in the desert.

I begin bagging it up and the Bishop comes around the house with the lady from the shot-up farmhouse. The one I rescued.

"I knew you'd leave. I told them all you wouldn't stay," she says.

"I don't belong here, and my family will be expecting me," I lie.

I have no intention of trying for Pennsylvania, but I'm sure as hell not going to stay here among a community. I know how this goes. We start by trusting each other and then things get scarce. We find ways to screw each other out of this and that and the next thing you know, someone tries to steal and somebody gets killed. I have zero interest in being part of those dominoes.

"Well, thank you," she says, and walks away.

A few of the men wander in and help me carry the meat to the van. When I get in to leave, I notice that the fuel gauge shows full. There are a half-dozen five gallon jugs of water, all my meat, and someone has thrown in a case of bottled peaches. I motor down Main Street without looking back. It dawns on me that I never did ask the name of the town.

———

I DRIVE SOUTH, still trying to clear all the towns in the crook of flatland between the Wasatch and the lakes at the base of the mountain range. Salt Lake, Utah Lake, Mona Reservoir. The damned highways are forcing me to either bend to the west—back out to the Utah flatlands—or curl back in toward the small towns jammed against the mountains.

At some point, I need to get over those mountains and get to the big deserts beyond. I left the deserts of Nevada because I didn't have much to eat and I was thinking about my friend in Salt Lake. But I shit-canned that idea and now I'm committed to get past these hills and into the Great Nowhere in the American southwest. It just seems like the right place to run out of gas and to learn how to survive off the land.

I never imagined the apocalypse like this: endless open roads without traffic jams and zombie hoards. I think maybe I must've threaded the needle between the mass exoduses out of Las Vegas and Denver. By cutting across the middle of Nevada and the driest parts of Utah, I went east/west while everyone else went north/south. I'm in the dead, waterless space between two million abandoned cars piled up behind the Rockies and a hundred thousand cars jammed in the gorge of Saint George, Utah. I've passed hundreds of abandoned cars, but I haven't seen hardly anyone. The horrors that took place on these byways, probably no more than a week ago, are already fading into the past. Families suffering from thirst, agonizing over their wasted gasoline, dying from desperation —all that misery seems to have drizzled into the sand and sage. Those stories will never be told.

From the captain's seat of the rapist van, the apocalypse turns out to be surprisingly lonely. It's mid-morning, and the no-name town is hours behind me. I'm second-guessing my decision to leave when I spot something black and square across the road, shimmering in the distance. I stop and dig for my binoculars. They're a cheap pair of Bushnells, but they've been critical kit on this little adventure.

Sure enough, it's a roadblock, and I can see the shape of men with guns moving about like specters in the mirage off the asphalt. A truck's coming my way, so I ditch the binos on the front seat, grab my M14 and double-check the magazine. I can't remember when I topped it off. I don't have time now to pick through the box mag and I curse myself for the oversight.

It's a black Ford F-250, I can see now as it approaches my van.

I'm itching to roll around the back of the van to get more cover, but I also don't want to look like I'm going to war. It's likely someone from the town sent out to parlay. I split the difference and lean the rifle against the van and I keep the door between me and the truck—not that it'd stop a bullet.

The dirty, new truck pulls up and a man in a red California Angels hat climbs down. He doesn't seem to be armed, but he doesn't seem desperate, either. I remind myself: anyone who's not dead has a gun, somewhere, somehow.

"Stop" I shout.

"You're good, brother," he puts his hands up. "I'm just stopping to chat."

"What do you want?"

"I'm looking to trade. Is that cool?" he leans against the fender of his fancy truck.

"Maybe," I'm keeping my hands where he can see them too. There's no way I want to get in a fight that isn't necessary. "Are you from the town up ahead?"

Angels Fan looks over his shoulder toward the roadblock. "Those guys? No, I'm passing through. They let me drive through town. My name is Sal. Look, I'm just trying to get to my friend's place and could use some water, maybe food if you have some to spare," the man says.

"What do you have to trade?" I ask.

"Um, I've got some solar lanterns, three bottles of Jack Daniels, a couple extra ounces of weed, a bottle of Ibuprofen, half-used up, and a Coleman three man tent—three season. And, I can offer information about the road ahead."

I'd really like the three bottles of Jack, since I blew through my last whiskey with the Bishop. "Maybe we can work something out. Give me some info before I consider dealing with you, on good faith."

He thinks about it for a second and says, "Delta, Utah up ahead is a death trap. I had to shoot my way out of their road block." He nods at the bullet holes in the bed of his truck.

That's good info and I'm glad I had this conversation. I was going to pass through Delta this afternoon.

"I'll give you the water for nothing. I've got some freshly smoked elk. I'll give you three pounds in exchange for the Jack. I can spare another five pounds for the tent."

I'd love to sleep outside instead of curled up in the back of the van. I feel like anyone could ambush me in the van. I'd much rather sleep a short distance away from such an obvious target.

"You'll have to give me *ten* pounds of elk for *two* bottles of Jack. The tent's got a bad zipper, so I can part with it for another ten pounds of meat."

I have about a hundred and fifty pounds of dried elk. It lost a lot of weight when we smoked it. I picture myself parting with twenty pounds and it makes me wonder how much I really need that Jack.

"Do you need gas?" I ask, reluctant to give away so much of my elk.

"No, sorry. I just traded for all I need three towns south of here."

"I'll give you fifteen pounds of elk for the two bottles of Jack and the tent. I'm telling you, it was just smoked last night and it's primo." I dig around in the pocket of my windbreaker and pull out a slightly-linty piece of elk.

"Here. Try it."

Even though I can tell he's a wily horse trader, his eyes roll back a little when he takes a bite.

"Okay. The water and fifteen pounds of elk for two bottles of Jack and the tent." He and I shake on it and I open the side door, still watching him from the corner of my eye.

"Do you have a scale?" I ask, suddenly seeing a potential problem with the trade. Who in this world travels with a scale?

He doesn't have a scale, so we go back and forth, guessing at the weight of the elk meat. The smoky smell rolls out of the van in waves, greasing the wheels of our negotiation. He clearly would like to get this behind him and settle down to chow time. Like my dad used to say, "never shop on an empty stomach."

By my best guess, I've shorted him a couple pounds of meat and he eventually grows tired of dickering. We conclude the deal, he gives me the whiskey and the tent, shakes hands and drives north toward Salt Lake.

I grab a piece of smoked elk from the pile, chew it and I wonder if he didn't get the better of me in the deal. It's truly delicious. On the other hand, elk is just protein. Nobody gets fat eating game meat. Still, it's the best this brave, new world has to offer.

As I gnaw on my elk, I contemplate going any farther south. If I can't get through Delta, there's really no reason to continue on this road. I dig out the map from the old, dead cowboy's house, and I look for alternate routes. If I double back a bit, I can cross the Wasatch mountain range at a town called Levan and then work my way east on Interstate 70. If my theory on traveling east/west holds water, the 70 should be clear sailing. The plan requires a bit of backtracking, but thanks to the no-name town, I have plenty of gas.

I CAN SEE the roadblock outside Levan from a mile away. I'm pulled over to the side, watching the barricade through the scope of my M14, since it's got more magnification than my binos.

Unfortunately, the magnification doesn't buy me much. It's a standard issue road block: several trucks parked nose-to-nose, a half-dozen armed men and nobody else around. I'm on the shoulder of the big Interstate—the I-15—but I haven't seen a moving vehicle since Sal and his Ford F-250.

The Utah desert is truly immense. I could see the town of Levan from five miles out. It looks like there used to be a lake alongside the freeway, but it dried up in the long forgotten past. The sweeping landscape—miles and miles of sage and curly dock across a salt-blighted plain—gives me the heebie-jeebies. Nothing about Levan looks inviting, but I suppose that's just my paranoia running into high gear. I mash it down and decide to take my chances. All roads lead to Levan, so it's not like I have much of a choice.

I decide to take my chances, and head straight into town. Pulling up to the blockade, a man covers me with an AR-15 and walks up to my window.

"You have a lot of balls. We saw you eyeballing us with your rifle. You're lucky our sniper didn't put out your lights."

"I didn't mean anything by it. I'm just passing through." I say. At this point I'm regretting my decision to approach the roadblock.

Post-collapse roadblocks come in two flavors: "we've got our eyes on you while you pass through town," and "get out of the car and say goodbye to your shit."

"Get out with your hands where I can see them," he says.

Shit. Door Number Two, I guess.

I open my door and before I can even think about putting my feet on the ground, I'm grabbed by the collar and slammed to the ground.

Two men appear from behind the semi trailer and the RV that comprise the roadblock. The three drag me to a pick-up truck, toss me in head first, and nearly knock me unconscious when my head slams into the door on the far side. It's one of those head-first impact collisions that goes way beyond seeing stars. My spine feels like it's been crushed like an empty water bottle, and there's a shrill ache in the back of my head that might be with me for a while.

Still, the only chance to extricate myself from this bad decision —quite possibly my last—will be to pay attention. I hand-crawl up the inside of the door of the truck, my brain swimming, and I watch the road go by as the truck rumbles toward town.

We pull up to the police station, or should I say Zombie Apocalypse Headquarters of the town of Levan.

The police station used to be a sheriff's office, or maybe a highway patrol base, but it's not in the town proper. It's ringed with nearly an acre of parking lot, and that acre is almost full to capacity with a random assortment of vehicles, semi trucks, RVs, family campers, apocalypse monster trucks, Jeeps and even a big boat on a trailer. We're more than a mile short of town and the lack of witnesses has got me worried. I'm dragged out and thrown to the ground like a bag of fertilizer. One of the men grabs both my feet and drags me into the building. I try to keep my head from bouncing on the concrete steps with mixed success.

I'm screwed, I'm screwed, I'm screwed, I repeat to myself as I glide across the polished stone floor and am dumped unceremoniously in a jail cell. The man who'd drug me by the feet, locks the cell, clips the keys to his belt and heads back the way he came without saying a word. I scramble to my knees and then to my feet. I consider the other men in the cell—no women—and I see nothing but defeat written in their eyes.

Fat man, skinny man, Latin American man (probably), another fat man and a teenage boy. All dead men, by the sludgy look on their faces.

No van, No elk meat. Fucking nothing.

I wonder how long they've been here, but I don't bother to ask.

I REMEMBER when I got out of the Army and realized how isolated American civilians were from the world outside of the United States.

I thought I would be happy to leave the Army, and I was; until the nightmares and insomnia began. Then, out of nowhere, I got into a bar fight and almost choked a man to death. I didn't even realize I was doing it at the time.

I ended up in jail for three days. Luckily, some liar at the bar told the cops that I acted in self-defense, and also luckily, the man I'd been choking wasn't a citizen and his paperwork wasn't squared away. They were so busy deporting his ass that they didn't keep him around to testify against me. After three days, I walked.

Despite the fact that I'm pretty sure I started the fight, I remembered griping to anyone who'd listen about how little Americans respected its veterans.

Sitting in a jail cell once again, with America gone, with the Constitution gone, and with the last Slurpee that would ever exist a red stain on a sidewalk, I realize what a little bitch I've been. I'd thought things had sucked then—living in the mucky haze that comes with sleeping a couple hours a night. At least then I hadn't been just another lump of human chattel, tossed in a jail cell. At least then, I'd been afforded some human dignity.

Back in the sandbox, we used to joke around when something would go horribly wrong. There were no limits to how crude we'd take it—no over-the-line boundary with our insults and our humor. With a thrown-together group of brothers, we'd pile on the laughs and gut our way through any amount of heat, terror or loss.

Maybe that's what I'd really lost: brotherhood. I'd traded my cushy life as a half-spoiled American teenager for the horrifying and hilarious life of an American soldier. I came home a man, according to my father an hour after I arrived. He called me into his office to share a finger of Kentucky bourbon. *Man to man,* he said.

What they *didn't* tell you is that you'd never get that brotherhood back again. You survived the fucked up grind of war by clinging to that deeper-than-family bond with men you'd only known for a couple months. That'd become your lifeline in a new world where you face the reality that you could be blown up at any second from a rocket, mortar or IED.

Once that cat got out of the bag, it would probably never go back in. The looming specter of death was the gift that kept on giving.

Thank you very much, United States Army. And *brotherhood* was the oxycodone that made it survivable, even tolerable. Sometimes, even pleasant.

But brotherhood existed only in the sandbox, as far as I could tell. Since arriving home, the looming specter of death had barely dimmed, but the brotherhood had vanished like the ghost of Christmas past. And that was even before the boogaloo.

Now, the filthy war had come to the States, with all the attendant mayhem: the whistles and bells that clank, rattle and hum along to the Grand Circus of Human Depravity.

The looming specter of death was alive and well, good people of the Land of the Free and the Brave. A brother here, would be just as likely to slit your throat for a can of peaches. Praise Jesus and pass the fire roasted rat.

I WAKE UP CLOUDY, wedged in a corner.

Where am I?

At first, I believe I've been captured by Al Queda. *A blast from the past,* as they say. I'm actually disappointed to discover that my current reality is far shittier than that. SEAL Team Six will not be coming to rescue me from a jail cell in the back of the Juab County Sheriff's office. Not today. Not ever.

I've been taken prisoner by some kind of Mad Max warlord, and I have nothing more than the shirt on my back.

I could accept my fate, like the others.

Where are the others? I glance around the cell, but while there are other men and women in other cells, it's just me in this one. I must've been unconscious for them to have been dragged away without waking me. The blow to my head, yesterday, must've tripped a circuit breaker in my cranium.

The missing men in my cell is troubling, to be sure, but the unconscious "sleep" has done me good. Surprisingly, I feel like a million bucks.

So that's what a night's sleep feels like, I exult. It's been so long since I slept like a normal person, that I'd forgotten what it feels like to wake up refreshed. I have no idea how long I was out, maybe eight or ten hours. Maybe more. I'm ready to kick some ass, take some names and bang the prom queen.

One of the assholes from the roadblock saunters slowly past my cell and out the other side of the little cell block. There are three cells with men, two cells with women and children and my cell with just me. Yellow light floods the dim cell block as Dipshit Number One goes out the exit. One of the kids in the other cell whines when the light washes over us, but then goes silent as the door slams shut.

That's my way out.

The door swings again, another guy, Dipshit Number Two marches toward my cell, pistol drawn. He inserts the key, turns the lock, and hauls the door open.

"Come out. We have questions for you."

Still, he doesn't look me in the eyes. That's a bad sign. That look —the look that isn't really a "look"—says that they have no intention of considering me a human being. Apparently, the apocalypse got underway fast in Levan, Utah. I now know all I need to know about where my cellmates have gone: probably a shallow grave in back of the Juab County Sheriff's station.

He presses his handgun into my back, pushing me out the cell block, around a corner and into a small room. I haven't spoken a word. I'm making a concerted effort to shuffle and look at the floor. As potent as I feel, I try to signal defeat in my every move. But in my shoulders, my haunches and my gut, I'm coiled like a spring. When the moment is right, I'm going to release that stored energy. I suspect this is my one-and-only chance, and my timing must be perfect.

Another man, this one wearing a police uniform, waits for me in the little room. There's one chair in the middle and a shiny wet spot on the tiled floor. This guy's older and he was not one of the toughs at the roadblock. There's a cold surrounding him, as if his soul has vanished. I catch a whiff of urine and fecal matter. Someone mopped up, but the tiny bits of gas released when the last guy pissed himself and shit himself still float around the room.

That won't be me, motherfuckers.

The older cop hasn't taken his eyes off of me and is fiddling with a hand towel, twisting it like wringing the water out of it. His glare tries to cut me, as though his questions will be perfunctory. The Main Event for this guy will be my pain. My fear. I do my best to appear afraid.

With an iron hand, the old cop rams me into a chair. The other man tapes my ankles and my wrists to the metal tubing. The strength of old cop's hand sends a gadfly of concern skittering through my mind, but it changes nothing. My one, big play is coming up and it doesn't matter if he's the Incredible Fucking Hulk, I'm going to make it count.

"We don't like strangers, here," the man with the towel says. He paces the room, as though circling me. I hang my head. Out of the corner of my eye, I see the old cop nod and the other guy leaves the room.

His knuckles are beat up and raw. "Where did you come from?" He leers at me, clearly enjoying my helplessness.

"I just banged your mom. She asked me to give you a few pointers for next time, you know, so you're not such a shitty screw."

The words hang in the air. Such a stupid thing to say. I guess I woke up feeling like I was in my twenties, and my mouth got ahead of my brain.

"This is going to be fun," the man says. He punches me in the stomach and all the air goes out of me in a giant "*woof.*"

"The three others from your cell are hanging out back. You're next, jackass."

He hammers me in the jaw, and the room does a couple loop de loops. I'm losing my spunk with every punch, and my window for escape is closing. He hits me again, hard, in the gut while my head's still spinning.

I feel as though I am watching myself get beaten from the outside. Blood is running down my face. He's breathing heavy but continues with an uppercut to my jaw. Then he pauses to catch his wind.

I am a soldier. I never quit. Again, I see myself being tortured by AQ.

He puts his hands on his hips, faces away from me and does a little stretching routine.

The spring in me unleashes. I jam my hands and arms forward at the same time, levering up from the armrests like I learned in escape and evasion class. The balloon where I've been keeping my reserve energy cuts loose, and I launch from the chair. The explosive movement blows open one of the duct tape restraints around my ankles. I have both hands and one leg free of the chair. I'm standing and in a fighter's stance, dragging the chair like dog humping my leg.

He turns and charges me. I let him hit me mid-body and we go to the ground. I wrap my arms around his head and jam my thumbs into his eye sockets. I go deep--all the way to the second joint. His left eye pops free from the socket and the right goes flaccid.

Instantly, his body shifts from trying to hurt me to trying to save himself. He's pushing away now, scratching for the revolver at his hip. He manages to draw but I've removed my thumb from his skull and I force his weapon away from our bodies. I'm not strong enough to take it away, but I'm strong enough to deflect it. I grab his balls with my other hand. I twist and pull and he appears to give up on shooting me.

Both of his hands seize my handful of his dick and balls, but then all he can do is hold them steady. If he rips my hand away, his nuts will go too.

His shrieks fill the room. The other guy must've gone off to do something else, because nobody comes running. I've got his gun and I hit him hard in the throat with the barrel, chopping his scream into a gurgling mewl. It sounds like I've collapsed his trachea. His hands go from his balls to his throat.

I let go of his balls, aim the pistol just under his ear, and squeeze the trigger. The blast obliterates my hearing. A river of plasma pools in my lap.

Another bullet in another man's head.

The door slams open and the other asshole stands in the doorway with his gun drawn, trying to make sense of the scene. I'm lying on my back on the floor, one leg duct-taped to the chair. The old cop is lying on me, face down. I'm holding his revolver. The back of his head must look like a bowl of scrambled eggs and ketchup. The asshole fires on me before I can get the revolver pointed at him. I feel rounds going into the old cop, but he's a fat old bastard and nothing comes through.

I get two rounds off, and the left half of the asshole's face blows back into the hallway. He drops straight down in the doorway.

Another head shot.

I hear the *pat-pat-pat* of running feet in the hallway, and I shift the body of the dead man around so I can use it as cover and still shoot. This is not a shooting position I've ever practiced: fat, dead man covering me, prone, on my back, revolver with four bullets remaining.

One of the other assholes from the roadblock appears in the doorway, his jaw agape. He looks at his friend, half his face gone, to the dead cop, to me, to the cavernous barrel of the big revolver pointed at his face, then back to his dead friend in the doorway. I see now that he's really just a kid. Maybe twenty-three. His slack-jawed face reminds me of pictures of myself when I got out of boot.

I don't fire. "What the hell is happening here?" I ask the kid.

He doesn't answer. Instead, he vomits on his dead friend. A yellowish stomach liquid splashes and mixes into the blood already covering the floor. He hasn't touched the Beretta in the holster on his hip.

"It was his idea. He's the sheriff," he points at the fat cop laying, face-down, on top of me. His dead face rests on my chest. Whatever's left of his brain pan drains through my shirt, courses down my torso and fills the back of my pants. It feels like I've shit myself, which is entirely possible.

"I want my van back," I say.

The boy nods.

"Take me with you. I can't stay here. They'll kill me for this."

I have no idea who "they" are. It seems like I've killed King Psycho Badass, but apparently there are others involved. I don't care. I just want my elk, the van and some open road. The kid doesn't go for his gun and he doesn't move from the doorway. He can probably tell that I'm deliberating. I have no reason to take him anywhere.

He negotiates. "You won't make it out of here without me. I'm the best chance you have, and the rest of the town will have your head on a spike if they catch you. Just like those other guys, and the ones out back."

He's right, but I don't know if I want his company. He's certainly no brother and I'm not in the "joining up" mood. I consider shooting him and calling it a day. But, the kid still doesn't make a move toward his gun and he doesn't step out of the doorway, either. He's putting himself entirely at my mercy.

"All right," I say. "Get my van and get us out of this town. Pull it around back." I make no move to get out from under the dead sheriff. The kid nods and just stands in the doorway. "Go now, if you want to get out of this alive." He nods and then steps back from the body of his dead friend. He turns and disappears.

Pat-pat-pat, he hurries away.

I shimmy my way out from underneath the dead sheriff. I dig his multitool out of his leather belt pouch, slice through the duct tape that holds my ankle to the chair, and pocket the multitool. I stand up and all the blood and brain goop slides from my ass, down my leg and into my sock.

I go through both dead men's pockets and belts and come up with two more knives, some 9mm rounds for the dude's Beretta, two speed loaders for the sheriff's Colt .45, a can of pepper spray and a huge wad of cash that they undoubtedly stole from travelers. As confirmation of it, I find a gold and diamond wedding ring floating in the pocket of Dead Sheriff.

I step over the dead deputy in the doorway and head toward the back door, passing the jail cells. The remaining men, as well as the women and children stare at me with glazed eyes. One man stands up and holds the bars of the cells. I stop. My left foot squishes in blood and brain matter. I want nothing more than to be out of this place, but I turn around and return to the dead deputy.

I know where he's got the keys—front right pocket—I fish them out and go back to the cells. I give the keys to the guy at the bars.

"Go out that way." I point toward the front of the station. I don't want them pouring out the back and drawing attention to me and my van. The least they can do for me is to act as a diversion. And, if the kid doesn't show up with my van, at least these other prisoners will cover my flight through the desert.

I go out the back door, slamming it open, only to discover that day has turned to dusk since I went into the torture room. I see three men dangling from ropes around their necks over the dumpster. There's a leg hanging out of the blue, metal dumpster and the Juab County correctional institution's current procedure becomes obvious: beat the prisoners for fun and profit, hang them over the dumpster until dead, cut the rope and dump them into the bin, repeat until the stink gets too bad, then haul the dumpster away.

I can't see very well in the dusk light, but it looks like someone hauled a twenty foot piece of well pipe up to the flat roof of the sheriff's station and spanned the inside of the corner to make a hangman's gallows. There are so damn few trees in this part of Utah, that they had to make do, the evil bastards.

I'm so stoked on my victory, that I don't bother to agonize over the tragedy I find in the dumpster. Maybe a dozen or more dead men are knotted up with one another, arms twisted in and out of each other, eyes open, legs akimbo. I paw through them until I find a guy about my size wearing half-decent 5.11 jeans and a plaid shirt. I haul him out of the mess of bodies and flip him over.

Excellent. He didn't shit himself.

I drag him half out of the dumpster and wriggle his limp body out of his clothes. I cannot get this brain mess off me quick enough.

I take another guy's T-shirt—this one did shit himself—and wipe the mess off my naked body before putting on "clean" clothes. For a moment, I'm standing buck naked in the back parking lot of the sheriff's station scrubbing my ass crack with a dead man's T-shirt. It's a new low for me.

As I pull on the pants, lo and behold, my van trundles around the corner of the backyard with the kid at the wheel. He jumps out waving his arms around.

"We've gotta go! There are people running all around out there and the town's coming." On cue, gunfire begins popping off in front. I feel bad for a second for sending the captives around front instead around back. But then some of them would've seen their father's hanging from a noose or dead in a dumpster, I self-justify.

I look in the back of the van to make sure my elk is still there. Fortunately, they haven't gotten to it yet.

"Seriously, dude. We need to leave now," the kid's still waving his arms around and stamping his feet. I climb in the cab and check the gas. For some reason I fail to understand in the moment, someone has filled the tank.

"Go, go, go," the kid urges as he jumps in the passenger seat. He pounds the dash and then points straight ahead. "Go out that way. There are guys shooting back the way I came."

I point the sheriff's hand cannon at the kid. "If I die, you die."

"Yeah, yeah, yeah. I know. Drive!"

We whip around the building and find ourselves in the middle of chaos. People are running around like frightened rabbits; families, singletons, women, men. A few men have shown up, presumably from the town and they're shooting sporadically. They don't seem to know what's going on and who to shoot. In the melee, I shoot the gap and swerve onto the highway at full speed. The van rocks back and forth on its springs and we slowly pick up speed as we flee the dark town, heading back toward the interstate.

"You can cut back over the 89 on the south end of town. Turn here!" he shouts. He's still bobbing up and down in his seat.

"What the hell was going on back there?" I ask. We're only a few weeks into ZombieLand and I'm having a hard time believing that a town full of Mormons would go full barbarian in such a short amount of time.

"It started before the bomb even went off in Los Angeles. That sheriff was a cast iron sonofabitch. He'd been running a Gestapo for a while here, all in the name of law and order. When the nukes went off, he declared martial law, closed the highway and began taking all of the people who didn't live here prisoner. A few townspeople disagreed, and we found them in the canal with bullet holes in their heads. After that, nobody said anything. We're all stuck, even the people that want him gone."

I follow the kid's directions and we skirt town on ranch roads until we can rejoin the highway. By the time we're clear, it's full dark and my world has become whatever I can see in my headlights through the bullet-pocked windshield.

I look around the van as the kid rattles on about how horrible the last few weeks have been. I glance back in the depths of the van, see the dim shape of my elk meat along with what appears to be all of my camping gear. Miraculously, I've managed to leave the man trap with everything I brought plus a full tank of gas. I even have a couple extra handguns to show for my injuries.

When the kid finally stops yapping for a second, I lay the Colt across my lap with the barrel in his direction. I pull the van over to the shoulder and stop.

"Very slowly. Slide your handgun out of the holster and place it on the floorboard between us." I cock the forty-five. It makes a sound, *click-CLICK.*

His eyes go wide and he does as he's told.

Clunk.

He places the Beretta on the thin carpet of the van floor between us.

"Now. Tell me why I shouldn't leave you here beside the highway."

"Dude. Please." The kid holds up his hands.

"Fuck that shit," I answer. "I'm no Millennial and I'm not your mommy, so don't beg. Make me understand how you're anything but a drain on resources or get the hell out of my van right now."

Strangely, he smiles. He nods toward the back of the van and motions with one hand. "Mister, can I show you something?"

I nod. He twists and reaches behind the passenger seat by the sliding door. I hold the Colt now in both hands and put my finger on the trigger. He grunts, climbs out of his seat, wrestles with something heavy and turns back to me from the dark with an M249 belt-fed machine gun cradled in his hands. It's festooned with a long belt of 5.56. You could knock me over with a feather.

"I grabbed you some stuff from the storage yard." He smiles again. "A lot of stuff."

"Put it down," I order. He turns back to the dark and obeys. He comes back to his seat and buckles his seatbelt, as though the question of his value has been answered in full. Indeed, it has.

I pick up the Beretta and tuck it in my door pocket. I put the van in gear and bump back onto the highway.

"Tell me what else you got me for Christmas," I ask as we head south.

———

TWO HOURS LATER, I regret not leaving him beside the road.

He does not shut the hell up.

It starts to rain hard. "Wow. That's a lot of rain," he adds to his running commentary. I grunt. The rain in the high desert is no joke.

"Bro, you need to shut the hell up, or I'm going to drag you out of the van and drown you in the mud."

He stops talking. I'm being a little hard on him. After all, he'd been one of the d-bags who took me prisoner and meant to hang me. But he reminds me of my army buddy, Eric. That guy was one of the funniest guys I'd ever met. A brother. He was blown up in an IED blast in Iraq on our second deployment.

The kid is staring at me.

"What the hell are you looking at?" I ask.

"Nothing." He turns and regards the rain hammering the windshield.

It's entirely possible that I killed men in Iraq. It was too crazy to know for sure, the couple of times that we mixed it up. I'd pointed my rifle downrange and let the hot rocks fly. No question about that. Men downrange of our guns had died, but had it been my bullets, our belt-feds, the other guys' bullets? We never knew, even though we tried to take "credit" for this kill or that kill. It had been one of our favorite topics of argument: who killed whom. We were a truck crew, after all. We weren't ever going to mix it up like a Ranger battalion, or whatever.

We were hit a few times on the road, another time or two we were hit at base, and that'd been it. Maybe I'd killed men and maybe I hadn't. But the number of men I'd killed in the last three weeks, there was no question about that. I wouldn't be arguing with anyone about those kills. Shit, I probably wouldn't be *telling* anyone about those kills.

I dig around in the door pocket of the van and find a couple (or maybe a few) dust-pasted Xanax. I pop them and swallow them dry. I'm coming down off the high of last night's—or today's—good sleep. We drive for almost an hour without talking, but the kid's been fidgeting in his seat for the last ten minutes.

"What's your name?" the kid finally asks.

I haven't wanted him to know. He's not going to make it on his own. Trading names means less elk for me.

I stare straight ahead at the road and the rain. "I'm Robert." I'm not sure why I tell him, except that it's hard not to answer a direct question.

"I'm Andy," he replies. "Where're we going?"

"That way," I say, pointing at the windshield.

We go another hour without words. The rain has stopped. We've gone through three small burgs, all of which looked like ghost towns.

I feel myself starting to drift off after going out and around Sevier, Utah. The pills are hitting me hard, really hard. I slam on the brakes, throw the van into park, jump out and vomit on the pavement.

Andy hops out of the van to make sure I'm okay. I spit the remaining vomit from my mouth and push him away.

I dry heave, as though I am going to vomit again, but my stomach is empty. I lean against the side of the van and slide down into a squat.

"Get me some water," I order Andy. He hovers in the glow of the headlights, waiting for something to do, so I give it to him.

He gets my water bottle from the cab. I take a few sips, making sure not to make my stomach turn again.

"You're driving for a while." I stand up and walk around to the passenger door.

I get in, draw the hand cannon and lay it on my lap.

"Avoid the towns. If you see anyone, stop two hundred yards short and wake me up."

"Sure thing," he says.

I lean back the seat and close my eyes. I hope I can trust him, but my head's spinning either from the pills, getting slammed into the door of that truck or both.

As he begins rolling, the ceiling in the van starts to spin, and the need to vomit returns. I make him pull over and I ralph.

He comes around to check on me again.

"I think we should camp for the night," I say. "Pull the van off the road at the next two-track. We need to be far enough away from the 89 that we can't been seen from the highway. Set up our tent a good ways away from the van so we don't get ambushed."

"All right." He sounds like I'd told him I'm taking him to Disneyworld. Maybe camping off the road is a new high point in the "after."

I'm sitting in the passenger seat and one-eyeing the nighttime view through the windshield as we drive off-road for what seems like an hour. The world's stopped spinning and I count my blessings.

"This looks like a good spot to stop," I say. I'm trying to get to sleep soon so the pills don't wear off before morning.

"Sounds good to me." Andy pulls over.

He sets up my tent, and I give him a wool blanket. I'm taking my chances sleeping in the van.

"G'night," I say and head into the rear of the van. I put my back against the dried elk meat—the garbage bag pile has spread wider during the drive—and I shove the meat with the strength of my legs into a more-upright pile to give me room to lie down.

The peppery smell of the meat fills the van in a wave. I dig into a trash bag by my side and draw out a nice quarter pound chunk. I was getting a bit sick of the meat before my time in the slammer. Now I'm ready to chow down.

"Quarter pounder, no cheese, no onions, no bun, no pickle. Extra dry," I say to myself as I tear into the jerky. I hunt around until I find the shortwave I stole from the first man I killed. Well, the first man I killed in the States, at least.

I crank the radio, charging it up, and the reassuring tones of my favorite radio personality whisper from the small, silver box. I close my eyes and fall asleep to The Drinkin' Bro of the Apocalypse, rambling again about booze, coffee and loose women.

IT TAKES me and Andy two days to complete the two hour drive from Levan to the emptiest desert I can find on the map. We have a simple rule: *no roadblocks*. We do not approach them. We do not watch them. We do not drive anywhere near them. We do not like Green Eggs and Ham. We do not like them, Sam I am.

We have our PhD in how shitty roadblocks can be. We drove over some gigantic mountains to avoid what might have been a roadblock on the west end of Price, Utah. We've driven a hundred miles on dirt roads to circumnavigate undoubtedly charming, but potentially deadly burgs such as Mount Pleasant, Manti, and Marysvale.

We topped off the gas in the van from an abandoned skidsteer front end loader we found in a field. So far, we were batting a thousand on fuel. Still the strange, empty wasteland roads persisted. Probably because of the occasional roadblock, the highways and byways of this part of Old America were empty as a church after Carnival. We'd passed a grand total of six cars driving the opposite direction.

At this point I don't know what to do with Andrew. He's

annoying me and simultaneously growing on me. He's one of those types where you love them so long as they don't talk much. I still can't remember if he was the one to throw me across the backseat of a truck. Still, any man who shows up with a SAW as an apology gift can't be entirely bad.

We make it past Moab and we disappear into true nothingness. If the last hundred miles were wasteland, this is freaking Mars.

My eyes are burning from staring through the windshield and my hips are cramping. As we near the four corners—the four-way boundary between Utah, Colorado, Arizona and New Mexico—I pull over at a wide place in the shoulder.

Andy asks, "Do you want me to drive for a while?"

"Hell no." I'm being surly, but the pills have run out and I'm not my best self.

He raises his eyebrows but says nothing. We're probably both "Beta Males," I suppose. But I'm the Beta Male with the van and a hundred and thirty pounds of premium, dried elk meat. That makes me the Alpha. Anyway, this young Turk clearly doesn't want the job.

Like a chain smoker who can't quit, I grab a piece of elk from the small bag on the floorboard beside my captain chair.

"Do you mind if I have a piece of that?" Andrew asks quietly.

I freeze mid chew, then pull out a palm sized piece of elk and hand it to him. He devours it and then nods at me. I fight the urge to smile and I don't know why. Maybe because he'll talk more? Maybe because I'm not ready. Without my pills, frankly, I'm not sure where I'm going to land.

I climb out of the van and stretch my legs. I double-take. For the first time in days, I see people walking on the highway, maybe three hundred yards away. They're behind us. *How the hell did we drive past them and not see them?* I reach in the van and grab my AR.

"Andy," I call him, my voice laced with alarm.

"What?" he comes around the corner of the van with his Beretta drawn. He might make it after all.

"Visitors."

"Should we haul ass?" he asks.

Now a hundred and fifty yards out, I can see them limping and carrying one another. Maybe fifteen of them. They're wounded and they're young. They stumble up to us and one of the older boys, maybe thirteen years old, approaches. He eyeballs my AR, but apparently, whatever they're running from is scarier than my gun.

"Mister. We need help. Javier is shot."

He says "mister" like "meester." They're illegals for sure. I don't see any weapons.

"¿Que les paso?" Andy asks in what sounds like perfect Spanish to my uneducated ear. I give him a wide-eyed look of amazement.

"What? I was a Mormon missionary in Peru." Andy shrugs, obviously proud of himself. I fear I've underestimated him.

The boy rattles off a response in Spanish and one of the two girls begins to wail. Apparently, they've seen some shit.

Andy explains, "They were working in an apple orchard about fifteen miles back toward Moab and a few miles off the highway. Somebody hit the orchard and took out their parents and owners. They've been walking for two days. That dude's shot in the leg and another guy died crossing the desert."

"Where are they from?" I ask, already knowing it's a stupid question.

"I'll ask." Andy starts to yakety-yak again in Spanish.

"Stop," I interrupt. "It doesn't matter. Who hit them?"

He goes back to the taka-taka-taka. The shot kid answers this time.

"He says they don't know. He thinks maybe five or six men."

"How far along was the harvest?" I ask and they go back and forth in Spanish for a while.

IT'S the next afternoon Andy and I are hiding on a rock outcropping watching several men try to fix a broken tractor. I'm ninety-nine percent sure it's out of gas.

There's a trailer on the edge of the apple orchard, and it's full to the brim with apples. Apparently, Black Autumn caught the apple harvest in full swing here. The men are trying to haul the trailer away to wherever they came from. To me, they look like Mexicans, but I'm almost a thousand yards away.

"Those aren't the kids' parents?" I ask Andy.

"No. Their parents are up against the barn," he says, pointing with his finger while looking through my binos.

I swivel my AR around to the barn, look through the scope and realize that what I'd thought was a log pile is actually a body pile. I count six aggressors and no friendlies. The shot-up kid looks to be about right.

"Look," Andy shows me his iPhone. "OnX. Here's the boundaries of the farm." He runs his fingers along a map on the display. Then he expands the map with his fingers. "That's the Lukachukai Indian reservation bordering it to the south. Maybe that's who hit them."

I'd known the four corners would have a lot of Navajo, but I'd never heard of this particular tribe. I start to ask Andy why they'd raid the orchard, but the answer is obvious: food.

"Should we hit 'em back?" I ask Andy. He shrugs, his eyes wide. He's apparently shocked I'd consult with him. "How many rifles did you steal back at the sheriff's station?"

"Six, I think. Plus the big machine gun."

I wave him off our OP and we scurry back to the van and our new friends.

THE SUN SINKS into the earth and the umber rays glow wane in the distance. A few sparks fly from the fire, almost entirely sage brush. The kids gathered a ton of wood while Andy I and scouted.

I reach into my pocket and slip a piece of elk into my mouth and enjoy the flavor.

THE SPOKESPERSON KID from earlier walks around the fire and crouches beside me. "Mister. Thank you for helping us. I wish we had something to offer." He held out his hands.

I point at the rosary around his neck. "Maybe pray for me now and then."

I say it in jest, but his face draws tight. Serious. "I will, sir."

"Don't worry about it. I was joking. I'm just trying to do the right thing, kid."

He nods, turns and vanishes from the edges of the firelight.

I lay there, cozy in the warmth of the fire, staring at the stars and asking God what the hell I'm supposed to do now, even though I already know the answer. The stars in the sky glow brighter as the fire dies. My eyes grow heavy, I grab my sleeping bag from the van, burrow in and drift away.

I WAKE up with the sunrise. All the kids are asleep. I dig the med kit out of the van so I can tear into that kid's shot up leg when he wakes up. I already know it's a bad graze and probably fixable with my unimpressive first aid skills.

I watch them sleep as the sun works its way over the mountains to our east. They're really just babies, but if they're here, that means they've seen enough of the world to last a lifetime—crossing illegally into the United States is more "real life" than most American kids ever see.

I don't need to ask them to know: there's next to zero chance that any of them know how to handle firearms. Guns and ammo are too expensive in Latin America for kids to mess around with training and safety. Hell, guns are entirely illegal in Mexico, if I'm not mistaken. If I use these kids to go after the raiders at the farm— like I know I've got to do--they'll be cannon fodder, pure and simple.

Nobody gets out of this life alive, I suppose. I hear Andy stirring in the tent. A few minutes later he emerges and meanders over to me wringing the sand out of his eyes.

"Hey boss. You know these kids haven't eaten in a couple days, right?"

I didn't know that, actually. I hadn't even thought to ask.

"What am I supposed to do about it?" I hiss. "I can't feed the world."

He does me the courtesy of not even glancing toward the van, where we both know I have a hundred and thirty pounds of prime jerky.

"I just thought you'd want to know, is all." He picks up a stick and pokes around the fire. It's cold.

"Andy, I need you to stay here with the young ones this morning."

He turns back to me, the stick dangling by his side. "Why? Where are you going?"

"We're going to take down the orchard."

"With THEM?" he points the stick at the sleeping kids.

"Just the older boys." As though that makes it better. All the boys look to be between ten and thirteen years old. I'm hoping they're older than they look.

"Lord have mercy on us," he prays. "They're not going to be worth a crap."

I throw a rock into the dead fire pit. "They're worth more than you think." I'm remembering the local fighter kids in Iraq. They weren't much older, and they did just fine at pulling attention away from our guys as they made the serious raids.

I dig the belt-fed out of the van and grab the can of belted rounds. I gear up with my assault pack, my pistol, and I tank up my Camelback. The kids stir as I set my kit on the lip of the open van door.

The kid with the rosary from last night finishes pissing in a bush behind my van and comes around. "Mister, the kids haven't eaten in two days. Can we have food?"

It's a little direct—a little needy and demanding. Even though I know it's only a language barrier thing, it makes me feel better about what I say next.

"I'm glad you're hungry, *Paco*. Because you're going to have to fight for your food today."

He cocks his head. "My name is Juan Luis. Fight? *Luchar*?"

"*Combatir. Con armas,*" Andy explains. He nods as though he's a fighting man instead of the child of a migrant worker.

"Okay. I fight."

"All the boys twelve years and older will fight." I get up and sling the M249. "We're taking your orchard back."

While I'm taking a piss and gathering my nerve, Andy repeats what I just said in Spanish. Then he comes around the van and hits me up, as I knew he would.

"I'm worth ten of those squirts. Let me go with you and take their place."

"So now you're the tactician, huh, missionary boy?" He looks hurt. I know he's just trying to be the good guy, but I need him to stay with the young ones. If he dies, I'll never get the fuck away from these kids. So long as Andy's here, I can bail on them without spending the rest of my life feeling like a dirty sonofabitch.

"Seriously. Stay here. Let me do the shooting. You do the diaper changing."

It's a mean thing to say, but I'm grinding my teeth without the pills. Frankly, throwing myself at some bastards who shot up immigrant kids and their parents sounds like an excellent way to spend my morning. If I take a bullet or two, so much the better.

"Sorry. I'm in a bad mood," I try to soften the bite I took out of his ass. "Would you be a prince and get the kid with the injured leg. I'm going to patch him up before we go. He fights too. Then we head out."

SOME THINGS CAN'T BE EXPLAINED. They have to be *shown*. The ball shriveling mayhem of a belt-fed machine gun is one of those things —a "show me" kind of reality. I deliberate over whether to explain to the Native Americans why they should give the apple farm back to us, but I just don't think they'll believe it about the M249 SAW unless I show them.

The kids are filtering through the apple orchard from the east. We practiced staying on-line this morning for half an hour. I cajoled, berated and even whacked one young man in the back of the head to make my point. Finally, they learned to stay in one, long row—no more than two trees between each boy.

The apple trees make it easy to stay perfectly on-line and maintain a perfect interval. They're only a base of fire for me, and I hope that means they won't end up actually fighting the men who took their farm. Without the Xanax, I have zero hope of that outcome. I guess I didn't watch enough Disney as a kid.

Fuck it. Everyone earns their keep in the apocalypse, even baby face immigrant kids. I can't do this op without them. Those are the cards they've been dealt by the Grand Poobah on High. Today, they fight for their breakfast.

I'm set up in a sweet, little overwatch between granite boulders. The still-broken tractor is my focal point, and I've decided it's three hundred meters from my position. It's a bit far for the

5.56, I suppose, but what I lack in range, I'll make up for in volume.

Before I'm ready, the orchard begins to crackle with gunfire. One of the kids has touched off the fight early, which was to be expected. It's not like I can turn them into a Ranger squad in half an hour while they're three-quarters starved.

The Indians react like they know what they're doing, which makes my stomach flip sideways. I was hoping they'd panic.

I can only see four of the six men, but those guys grab nearby rifles and duck behind cover. One guy shouts out orders, and another man peels off back to the farmhouse, presumably to go get their buddies in the fight. If I had to guess, I'd say the guy giving orders is some kind of vet. He'll be my first target.

But first, I let the battlefield mature a bit. I'm way around to the west of the orchard, so I have a clear shot at the men barricaded behind a wood pile and the busted tractor. I hear a porch door slam, and the three remaining men run out of the farmhouse and loop around to the east.

No plan survives first contact, and this is very definitely NOT in my plan. If they'd made their flank around to the west—my side of the bucket—I would've been thanking the Lord Almighty. Well, we play the hand we're dealt, I remind myself again as I tuck the SAW into my shoulder and go full cyclic.

The beast roars and I walk the first string right onto the guy giving orders. From where I'm shooting, it looks like I take the top off his head, but it's hard to say for sure. He's down, and that's what counts.

I pause, let the barrel cool a second and roll to the guy behind the tractor. He tries to swivel around to the front of the machine, but there's two feet of ground clearance beneath the tires.

I send a rope of bullets under the tractor, and the ground under him explodes with frag. He goes down, probably hit in both legs.

The remaining guy is wise to my tricks, and he's put the woodpile between me and him—disregarding the ineffective fire from my kids in the orchard. The three flankers have paused behind some sort of outbuilding. I send a few rounds at the building just to hold them up. The corrugated metal goes *poing, poing, poing* with my incoming rounds.

The easy part is over and I can either run back the way I came to counter-flank—which is probably over a mile—or I can charge down off my castle, run around behind the farmhouse, and try and get at them from behind.

Now, they're looking at me, but as my kids fill the pause with sporadic fire, the Indians will re-evaluate their priorities. So far, not a single bullet has hit my position.

Fuck it.

I seize the carry handle of the SAW, grab the ammo can, jump up and book it down the hill. I'm running like an idiot, now *DEFINITELY* drawing fire, but none of it sounds like semi-auto.

Ping. Thunk. Whizzzzz.

Rounds hit rock, dirt and thin air in a halo around me as I run. I'm praying that there are six men and not seven or eight. If I gain the farmhouse and there's even so much as a greasy cook with a pellet gun in there, I'm screwed.

The good news about being downrange of my kids is that they can't hit anything, so I'm relatively safe. So I tell myself. I wonder how many of the rounds coming my way are theirs.

I reach the farmhouse without any additional holes in my body. Rather than do the obvious—keep running around to the side of the house—I do the unexpected. I charge through the first door I see, duck inside the farmhouse, and run up the first stairs I can find.

It's a two-story, so I'm hoping for the high ground. Sure enough, the first room I find has a perfect view of the orchard and even a small balcony. I hit the floorboards and low-crawl out on the little porch. The dude behind the woodpile is fully exposed to me and he's posted up, waiting for me to come around the far side of the building. I dump fifteen rounds on him from fifty meters and end his vigil.

I turn to the corrugated out building and see nothing. Either the three guys are hunkering down, or they've hauled ass for an even better flank on my boys in the orchard.

Or, they're coming for me in the farmhouse.

I look around frantically. Have I just out-flanked myself?

I slow my breathing and listen. I dig the foamies out of my ears. I put them in before the fight, and I've been running around listening to myself huff and puff. With the foamies out, I hear nothing but random gunfire from the orchard. The house doesn't creak, which settles my nerves a little. I draw my handgun just in case. Still nothing.

I peek out the balcony, and I see nothing moving, aside from the occasional kid shifting around in the orchard. As ordered, the eight boys I sent to fight are still on-line, except for one. There's a four tree hole in their skirmish line and I fear the worst.

There's no time for worry. I pivot the SAW on its bipod and cover the outbuilding. Still no sign of the three men who've disappeared.

I try to read the minds of my kids in the orchard. They're still shooting occasionally, but I can't tell where they're aiming. I conclude they don't know where the enemy is holed up either. The shooting slows and then stops. The battlefield quiets.

I hear a *scree* then a *thud*. It's the sound of metal on metal, like the outbuilding is groaning. Good enough for me. I dump half a belt on the outbuilding, panning left to right, then right to left. I've forgotten to put my foamies back in my ears, so now I'm in a roaring, ripping world of concussion and rage. When the last links chitter through the SAW, my gun goes quiet.

I wait and listen, but now I can't hear a damned thing because my ears are whining and ringing like the electric guitar at a Clapton concert.

Three minutes later, a white T-shirt pokes out from behind the outbuilding. I've reloaded another belt in the SAW and I consider ripping the corner of the building apart.

Apparently, the last three guys had, in fact, hunkered down behind the sketchy cover the outbuilding provided. It was the natural human reaction, in my experience: to hunker down and hug the ground. Only hardcore guys will bust a serious flank in the face of incoming fire. Luckily for us, these weren't hardcore guys, at least not after I ventilated their leader.

I don't know how to tell my immigrant kids to cease fire, so I don't even try. We hadn't gotten that far in training.

Two of the three native dudes sidle out from behind the outbuilding, waving their T-shirt. I don't see the third guy, and I hope that means I hit him and not that he's getting ready to bush-whack me in the farmhouse.

"Where's the other guy?" I shout at them. One of them points a finger back behind the outbuilding and yells something I can't understand. I assume he's saying, "my pal is on his back with one or more 5.56 rounds in him."

The kids have all stopped advancing in the orchard and they all appear to be hiding behind trees. That's good because I don't want to get shot by my own guys at this point in the fight. It looks like we've won the thing.

"Cover them," I yell to nobody as I holster my handgun and collect my SAW. I leave the ammo can on the balcony. It's still half-full.

I come around the farmhouse puffed up and feeling like ever-loving Rambo with the SAW at my hip with the belt swinging in the wind. I see now that I'm close up that the Native American fighters aren't much more than kids themselves. The barrel of my SAW has their full and undivided attention.

"Cease fire! Cease fire!" I yell to my "men" as I buffalo toward the surrendering kids. They've left their guns back behind the outbuilding. I pass them and check it. There's an Indian kid writhing around on the ground and three rifles—all three hunting rifles—laying on the ground beside him. I don't bother to collect them. That kid's not going to shoot anyone today and I don't have a free hand.

"You speak English?" I ask the Indian boys. Scared though they may be, they're still teenagers. "What other language do you think we talk?" one of them answers.

He's too scared to sneer, but he comes damn close.

"Smart ass, huh? Are you from the rez?" I ask.

They nod.

"Is that your truck around back of the farmhouse?" They nod again.

"Why did you attack the farmhouse?"

"That one," smartass Indian kid points to the guy whose head I cut in half. "That guy is an army guy, and he said we should take the apples and sell them to the Navajo over in Little Water. He said we could trade them for horses."

"The council didn't send you?" I'm thinking about the future at this point. If the grown-ups back at the tribal council want this farm, it'll only be a matter of time before we lose it again. In this helter skelter world of post-America, Native American tribes are some of the largest organized communities still standing. Maybe they don't know it yet, but the Navajo are probably the strongest force in the region.

Both boys shake their heads. I'll take that to mean they were acting on their own greed and not at the tribe's bidding.

We still have a problem. Even if these men were marauding on their own, the tribe's going to be pissed. I killed at least four of them.

"I'm a U.S. Army Ranger," I lie. "The United States sent me and my platoon to take back this farm. If you come again, we're going to hit the rez with tanks. You got that?"

The boys nod. I pray that my "platoon" stays put.

"Put the bodies and your wounded in the truck and leave. You hear me?"

The boys nod. "Go!" I wave the SAW toward the truck in back of the farmhouse. The boys drop the T-shirt and run toward the truck. I head for the apple orchard. I need to get my kids out of sight.

ONE OF MY boys is gut shot, damnit. It's the kid who was supposed to be praying for me. I show the other kids how to make a gurney out of two shirts and a pair of shovels, and we carry him out the back of the orchard. I can't afford to have the surviving rez kids see us.

As I hear the truck's engine race back at the farmhouse, I step out of the orchard and menace the departing Indians with my SAW. One of the boys gives me the middle finger out the window as they leave me in their dust. Maybe I should've sent them with the trailer full of apples as a peace offering. Maybe that would've emboldened another attack from the rez. Maybe it would've placated the council. Who knows?

I can no more guess what a tribal council will decide than I can guess what a house cat is thinking. With the aggressors gone, I can focus on my kids. I run to catch up to the gurney-carriers and I come alongside my wounded kid. He said his name was Juan Luis, or Jose Manuel. Fuck, I don't know. The rosary kid.

I sling the SAW and look down at the big bloody patch in the kid's flannel shirt. I lift the tail of the shirt and see a rifle-round size hole in his gut. To me, it looks like it went through his lower intestines, which might as well be his heart without an intensive trauma care facility.

A buddy of mine in Iraq got gut shot. He survived, but it took four surgeries to finally get the yuck and infection out of his belly.

He went from being a bull of a man to a little fawn during the three months he spent under the knife in Germany. We don't have medevac here, and we sure as hell don't have intensive trauma care. My young man beside me, is going to die. Plain and simple.

"How are you feeling?" I ask as we carry him back to the van. It's a stupid question, but anything more nuanced is going to be lost in translation.

"I hurts," he answers.

"You did good. You fought well. You're a hero," I try to comfort him.

He smiles through a mask of pain. "We did win. Now we have *un hogar*. Now we won't die from no food."

Well, I think to myself, the *rest* won't die. At least not right away. Before I ditch them, I'll make sure Andy knows how to bottle the apples, assuming we can find bottles. I imagine the apples will keep for a while packed in straw.

During the fight, I saw a few chickens and a couple pigs. If the Native Americans leave them alone, there's a chance they'll make it to spring.

We arrive at the van and Andy rushes up to the gurney. He looks under the shirttail and looks up at me. I give him a half-shake of my head. He lets the shirttail fall back in place.

"We've taken back the apple farm and it has everything you'll need to make it through to spring. The guys there were natives from the rez south of here. I'm hoping they won't come back, but..." I shrug.

"Where are you going? These kids need both of us," Andy argues.

"Maybe so, but I'm not the man you think I am. Little brother, I'm an untethered piece of work. If I were to stick around long enough, you'd all come to understand what I mean. I'm more of a liability than you think."

I'M PACKED TO LEAVE. The kids have been installed in the farmhouse and we found a stash of over a hundred canning jars. Praise Jesus and pass the applesauce.

As I load the SAW and the half-full ammo can into the back of the van, Andy approaches me.

"I get it that you gotta go, boss. But are you going to leave Juan Luis like that?"

"What the hell else am I going to do? I'm no lower GI surgeon. Hell, I barely know first aid. He's going to die, pure and simple."

"I know he's going to die, Robert. I just think he'd rather go to the Celestial Kingdom with his commanding officer by his side."

I don't know what a Celestial Kingdom is, but I close my eyes and breathe in the truth of what he's saying. My hand drifts down to my holstered handgun, checking that it's where it's supposed to be. I close the van door, sigh and lean my head against it.

"I'll be right up," I say. Andy turns and heads back into the house, and I contemplate jumping in my van and hauling ass down the dirt road. Instead, I head inside the farmhouse.

The boy has been laid in the master bedroom upstairs and I head up the stairs with a heavy heart. He sits up a little when I come into the room.

"Mister," he says. "Help me."

"I can't fix that," I point at the hasty bandage someone's taped over his mortal wound.

"Yes. I know. I will die. Please, you do it."

Mother Mary on the half-shell. It's this again. "Here," the boy points at his temple. He looks me in the eye and I know that I'm looking into the soul of a thirteen-year-old boy who is undoubtedly a man. He struggles to sit up a little and works the rosary around his neck and off over his head.

"This is for you." He hands it to me. If I'm being honest with myself, I've been crying since I started up the stairs. There's only two of us in the room, and only one of us is coming out, so lying about the hole this is digging in me doesn't accomplish a damn thing.

I'm so tired of doing God's dirty deeds. I'm so sick of this new world, where death buzzes around day and night, thick as flies on a dairy farm. I pocket the boy's rosary.

I draw my handgun, ignoring his request to shoot him in the temple. The bullet might skip around his skull, plus I don't know who's in the room below. These are the kinds of practical tidbits my mind mulls to distract itself from what actually matters.

I put the barrel under his chin, aiming through the wall and outside, and I pull the trigger. His head bucks back against the headboard and his brains paint a fan of wasted life on the old brick.

"Adios, little hermano," I say, trying to sound more John Wayne than I am.

This one's going to stick, I realize. One more dead man. One more shot through the head. Without the pills, I'm probably as terminal as this gut shot boy.

I holster the gun, wipe my watery nose with my shirtsleeve and stab my hand in my pocket. I feel the rosary beads. I have no idea how to pray the rosary, but I finger the beads while I ask God to care for this forfeit soul.

The kids are huddled in the big room when I tromp down the stairs. The older ones already know what the single pistol shot meant. The younger ones are probably afraid of me on general principle. Andy has a ten year old boy sitting on his lap. The boy cries into Andy's Kenny Chesney T-shirt. It's a new, clean shirt, so it must've come from the apple farm.

I motion with my chin for Andy to ditch the kid and talk with me. We meet at the side van door for the last time.

"This probably needs to be laid out on racks," I motion to the pile of trash bags filled with elk. "It's going to mold like this."

He looks at the elk jerky and then looks at me, perplexed.

"Help me unload it." I pull the bags of elk meat out of the van and set them on the gravel driveway. When it comes to the last bag, he looks at me again. I reach in, grab it and set it on the pile.

With all the elk out, the inside of the van looks almost tidy. I grab my AR and breach check it. I open the driver's door and lean it up against the dashboard. I realize how utterly "John Wayne" this looks to Andy, and what a loner badass I've become in his eyes. That'll last until he has to clean the blood and brains off the wall upstairs.

My head's swimming in the dull thrum of depression, and I need to get out of here before I drag them all down with me. I start to think of something cool to say to Andy as a goodbye, but I tousle his hair instead. I climb in the van, start the engine and roll down the road.

Why did I do that to his hair? I shake my head and hitch up in the captain's chair.

I'm still agonizing over the hair thing ten miles down the road, when I see a huge buck mule deer on the edge of a stream. He's nibbling on some willows and the sound of my van doesn't even cause him to lift his head. I roll to a stop and reach for my AR. I slide it out the window and slump down deeper into my seat, aligning the crosshairs on the big beast. I pause, grab a dirty pair of foamies from the divot on the console, stick them in my ears and settle in again.

BOOM!

The AR rocks into my shoulder. I re-center the crosshairs on the muley buck just in time to see him go down on his knees, then topple over on his side.

"Thank you, Lord," my heart whispers.

5

DEAD MAN WALKING

BY JEFF KIRKHAM

*IF YOU KNOW JEFF KIRKHAM, then you know that he's a man who can't visit the county jail without also figuring out how he would bust out. Jeff's a 28-year Green Beret and former DEA agent, so he hasn't spent any time in the slammer **per se**, but he has spent some time figuring out how to defeat construction materials with heat and friction. Some people do fantasy football. Jeff does prison breaks.*

What happens to the prisoners in the apocalypse, anyway? Do they rot or do they run free?

Dead Man Walking tells the tale of a man who finds himself in county jail after his third DUI, but it quickly becomes a death sentence after a series of terrorist attacks on the outside. Plunged into darkness, plagued by thirst and surrounded with the dregs of society, will Steve rediscover the relentless survivor in his heart that modern society had done its best to snuff out?

-Jason Ross

"Well I know I had it coming, I know I can't be free, but those people keep a-movin', and that's what tortures me."

- Johnny Cash, the Man in Black

FOR AN ETERNITY, the screams trilled through the hallway of the jail, more like a cat being gutted alive than a human. The shrieks hadn't stopped for more than ten minutes over the last thirty-six hours, and Steve's imagination ran wild with possible explanations, each more terrifying than the last.

He had no way of telling time, but it seemed like three days since the lights went out, and the twenty-four men of Pod Four had been locked in the community room—but it could've been twice that long. Or maybe half.

A red glow lit the edges of the two-inch thick Lexan between them and the hallway of the Utah County jail. The hallway connected six pods—some of which must have become the deepest environs of hell. Steve's imagination alighted upon the conclusion that the red glow came from an emergency exit sign deep inside the maze of the jail. It must've been in the visitor corridor, since nobody intentionally showed prisoners how and where to exit. Fleeing the building in an emergency was not in the cards for these men; not until *The System* was good and ready for them to exit.

Steve's mind gnawed at the question, *where the FUCK had The System gone?* He'd come to hate, despise, even piss on *The System*. When his whore of a wife started fucking his best friend and racking up the cost of their sexcapades on Steve's credit card, his education began in earnest on just how crooked *The System* could be. It could hand your slut ex-wife and your best friend everything you'd earned in twenty years. It could strip you of access to your kids. It could throw you in jail for drinking too much because, *God*

Forbid, you despaired over losing your life to a lying bitch and her asshole boyfriend.

But at this point, Steve would give his left nut to get *The System* back. If *The* Fucking *System* would please, *pretty please*, press a button and release the mag locks on Community Pod Four and let him have a drink of water, Steve would never touch another drop of booze so long as he lived. Three DUIs was not supposed to be a death sentence, of that he was certain. Not even on *The System's* worst day.

The screaming from the other pod warbled into a keening screech and Steve's imagination could not begin to explain the sound. What bend, break or jagged tear in the human body would produce a sound like that? He had no idea. A mechanical engineer wasn't trained in the arts of butchery.

The pounding began again. It'd taken a two-hour break, but now the vicious thumping resumed, laying down a bass rhythm to the shrieking sound of the human being disassembled.

Steve imagined the metal tube bench in another pod being used to ram the Lexan glass in an attempt to break out. Every third or fourth boom, he thought he could hear a tinny edge to the percussion, as though the end of one of the legs had impacted the bullet-proof glass. At least Steve hoped it was a bench frame and not a human body being battered against the impact-proof glass.

Steve peeled his tongue off the roof of his mouth. Food and water had stopped coming as soon as the power died. The water held out a little longer. Time had slowed to a thick, red crawl. He didn't know how long he had until he would die of thirst, but he'd heard men slurping out of the toilet tank attached to the community room hours ago, so the supply was definitely gone. Nobody in that room was going to be alive and kicking in another forty-eight hours, of that much he was certain.

He looked about his pod, the dingy red glow painting the men's faces. These were the non-violent offenders, which probably meant they would remain non-violent for a few hours longer than the other pods. Anyone would lose their shit given enough time in the dark without water. Lord knew Steve was close enough to the tattered edge himself. Maybe that's why he finally spoke up.

"I think I know how to get out," Steve said to the dark.

A few of the men had been talking in hushed tones, one of them blathering on to his cellie about how much he loved the *blue* Slurpee at Seven-Eleven. They'd been stuck together for God-knows-how-long, and Steve's outburst was the first time anyone had spoken to the group. It'd all been one-on-one complaining up until that moment. Nobody had the sauce to shout over the screams from down the hall.

The Slurpee guy shut up.

"What the fuck does that mean?" a big guy asked into the dark. Steve knew his name was Paul, but he'd never spoken to the man. It'd only been five days since Steve had been thrown in the pod and he only knew a few of these shitheads.

With Big Paul's half-witted question floating in the air like a Las Vegas fart, Steve could tell the entire history of *The System*—how idiots and malcontents had chipped away at society's patience to the point where the nannies of the world had built net after prissy net to entangle even men like Steve. Productive men. The Big Paul's of the world had landed Steve here in a room with twenty-four of Utah's most utter ne'er do wells with just one bathroom, where the toilet had stopped flushing and the shit had now almost entirely filled the bowl.

Steve figured he was already dead, so why not be honest for once?

"Hey, numbnuts. Do you want to ask stupid questions and die marinating in the smell of another dude's shit?"

Steve couldn't see the man stand, but he felt the air move. Big Paul must've stepped on someone in the dark because a disembodied voice hissed.

"Where are you, asshole?" Big Paul seethed.

"Are you that dumb? Do you really want to screw your only chance of getting out of here?" Steve found that he might care more than he thought at first about getting his face stove in. He'd quietly gotten up and slid around into a darker corner of the room.

"Just how you gonna get us out of this room? You some kind of rocket genius? You smarter than the prison builder?"

He could hear the other men huff and curse as Big Paul stepped on them while hunting his voice. Steve had good night vision—better than most—and he slid around the room ahead of the menace. Some of the time, he could tell where he was in the community room just by the power of the shit stink. Steve kept to the shadows.

"The prison was designed to be unbreakable *with prison guards watching*. Nobody ever thought we'd be left alone for days. Anyplace is breakable with enough time."

Big Paul stopped hunting him.

"We don't have much time before this thirst gets us, Little Einstein," Big Paul hissed, but his voice didn't sound half so violent as before.

"Then stop fucking with me and let's do something."

Now committed to action and fresh from salvation, Steve stood a little straighter in the dark. He was a far cry from clear as to how they would escape from this cinderblock and plastic box, but he did know this: high impact plastic may be ultra-tough, but it doesn't hold up against heat or friction forever. Steve wasn't entirely bullshitting Big Paul when he said he could figure a way out. There was a slim chance. It really depended on how long it took the human body to shut down from thirst. Steve had heard "two days," but that'd been in the context of a survivalist maxim. He didn't know if that meant "two days more-or-less" or "two days on-the-nose."

Steve couldn't hear Big Paul moving about anymore.

"What's it going to be, Big Guy? You want to die or do you want to get out?"

"I'll help. But after we get out, I'm going to crush your skull."

Steve was ninety-percent sure that it was a hollow threat, which beat the hell out of the odds of dying here. He pictured the room in the light of the sodium arc lamps, before the power had gone off, the deputies had vanished and the water had dribbled to a stop.

Steve groped a chair in the dark and found it unoccupied. He felt the skinny legs—thin-wall metal with a galvanized zinc coating. He cranked on a leg and felt it give a little. He bent it hard at the ninety-degree bend that'd been rolled into the tube at the factory and it gave more. He put some muscle into it, scissoring the other side of the chair between his knees and the chair leg folded. Once kinked, he bent it back and forth until it grew hot and floppy, loosened and popped free. Steve dropped the maimed body of the chair and ran his finger across the bent and broken end. It was sharp as a ragged pike.

The other twenty-three men had fallen silent as Steve worked the chair. "Hey man, what are you doing?" a disembodied voice whined.

"Shall I do or shall I tell?" Steve shot back as he picked his way toward the red glow filtering through the plastic pane. Does a mechanical guy say shall? A smart ass one, maybe.

"Just shut your hole," Big Paul ordered. "Let him work."

Steve leaned against the clear plastic and drew the jagged end of the metal leg across it. A wispy peel curled off the end of the chair leg and left a deep scratch. He plucked the plastic burr off the pane and rolled it between his fingers. Four thousand more like that and he'd be halfway through.

"Is it working?" Another man breathed on Steve, trying to get close enough to see what was going on in the almost non-existent light. Steve could smell death by thirst on his breath. Suddenly, the warm breath wasn't on his shoulder.

"Sit the fuck down," Big Paul snarled, now directing violence at anyone who got in Steve's way.

"Paul, I need their help. I need four men to bust off chair legs like this," Steve held up the leg in the red-tinted dark, "and score the glass with the sharp end. It's going to take hundreds or thousands of cuts before we have any chance of breaking through." As if to emphasize his point, one of the other pods began slamming the window again with their metal bench.

"How the hell am I supposed to break the leg off?" a voice complained from the dark.

"Here, look." Some other guy, apparently someone with an extra dozen IQ points, took over breaking the chairs. Steve scratched three more gouges—a square on the plastic window the rough width of a man's shoulders. He handed his chair leg to another man and stood back. The man dragged the tool down the first scratch Paul had started. Grunting and chair-banging rattled around the room as men torqued and busted the chair legs.

"How many of you worked with your hands on the outside?" Steve asked the room. He caught a little motion in the dark. "I can't see you raise your hands so you're going to have to say your names."

Four men mumbled their names.

"You four. We need tools to unbolt the bench from the floor."

"What the hell do we need a bench for?" a man carped from nearby. Even after only five days in the pod, Steve knew this douchebag by the sound of his voice. The guy's name was Kyle and he was in for embezzling fifty grand from his former boss. The only reason Steve knew this was because he'd overheard Kyle bragging about it at least a dozen times.

Fifty grand...fifty grand...fifty grand.

It was as though Kyle thought the financial magnitude of his theft meant he had more criminal street cred than the idiots who'd gotten busted stealing a generator off the back of a taco truck, or the morons like Steve, who'd been busted drinking and driving one too many times. As best Steve could tell, all Kyle had done was write himself a check that nobody was ever going to fail to notice.

"The bench is the heaviest thing in the room, and we're going to need a battering ram once we get the window ready."

"Yeah, right," Kyle sneered. "You're going to cut through that bullet-proof glass with chair legs. You may have these imbeciles fooled, but not me." Kyle pronounced "imbeciles" like "em-bee-siles" as though they'd just flown him in from Oxford to grace the Utah County jail with his higher education.

Steve snorted. "Don't help if you don't want to. I don't give a shit."

"You're going to cause us all to catch charges for attempted escape. I'm not going to prison for your idiot plan."

"Can someone shut him the fuck up? I need to think," Steve spoke into the dark.

He heard a *thunk* and a *woof* and Kyle went silent. Maybe it'd been Big Paul. Steve didn't know. He needed to focus on the bench. The sound of scraping at the plastic pane had become a steady *screech, screech, screech.* All the friction, and the removal of material, had to eventually compromise the toughness of the plastic pane. Steve hadn't worked much with impact-resistant plastic, but he knew metal and glass. Nothing could withstand a hundred hours of friction. But they didn't have a hundred hours. They'd be lucky to get thirty more hours before they dropped off to die in the corners of the community room. These weren't the strongest men when it came to willpower. Even for Steve, it was everything he could do to stay at the problem of escape. How long until they quit?

Steve wasn't much for people problems. Mechanical problems were more his thing. People problems ate his lunch.

He crouched down and sensed two other men beside him on the concrete, working the problem of the bench. They mumbled back and forth as they fingered the nuts on the threaded studs poking up from the concrete.

"You guys got this?" Steve asked the dark.

"Maybe," one man mumbled. "I'm thirsty as fuck. I don't know if I'm going to be able to work."

"We get this bench up or we die. That's all there is to it." Steve stood and his knees popped. He watched the scratching on the window pane and he knew in his gut that it wasn't going to be enough. Something about the corners of the scratches bothered him. Those corners would hold like a sonofabitch. They'd never give, no matter how deep the scratches and no matter how hard they hit it with a battering ram.

He needed to punch a hole in the glass on those corners—break the surface tension where the plastic would be strongest. It'd take friction and heat. And *TIME*--time they didn't have.

Quite intentionally, there was nothing in the community room that could be used to start a fire. Nothing whatsoever. But before he'd become a cuckold and a drunk, Steve had done a stint as a Scoutmaster. He'd gone to scout camp and even though he'd never tried it himself, he'd watched scouts struggle with a bow drill to start a fire. None ever succeeded, but he didn't need to start a fire in the pod. He needed heat and friction. He needed to wear a hole in the window pane.

He glanced at the scraping and noted the red shadow of Big Paul, taking a turn at gouging the window.

The System allowed pajamas in this pod, assuming that someone on the outside put money on an inmate's books. Steve's brother had stuck a hundred bucks on his books the moment the judge sentenced him to thirty days, so Steve had been wearing a brand new pair of prison pajamas when the lights went out. He'd purchased them right up front, worrying about the message it might send his cellmate if Steve slept in his underwear. He'd never been to jail before.

But, he needn't have worried about the sanctity of his butthole. His cellie hadn't said six words to him in the last five days. The twig-thin redhead had been busted for scamming cell phones to pay for his meth habit, and he'd been going through the worst days of withdrawal while in the pod. Steve was no bull of a man, by any stretch of the imagination, but he wasn't likely to be violated by a hundred and sixty-pound meth-head.

Still, Steve wasn't a man proficient in violence. He glanced at the window, because the scraping sound had dwindled. Big Paul was still at it, probably enjoying a moment of physical exercise, even though he had to be dying of thirst like everyone else.

"Hey, Big Man," Steve spoke softly as he stepped up to Paul.

"Yeah, asshole?" Paul didn't stop gouging.

"Um. Did you notice that you're the only one working? At this rate, we're going to die long before we get through this window. And I'm pretty sure it's not the only thing standing between us and fresh air. There's going to be more work after we get out of the pod. Maybe a lot more work."

"So what's your point, Genius?"

Steve ran his fingers through his hair. "Maybe you could motivate some of these guys to work?"

"I'm no leader," Paul said, still working the sharp end of the chair leg. A substantial pile of plastic shavings had accumulated on the edge of the window below the gouge. The other scratches in the plastic—roughly forming a man-sized square—weren't nearly so deep.

"Yeah, but maybe you could knock some heads?"

Big Paul stopped working. "Just point the way." Steve pictured Big Paul grinning.

"Listen up, folks. Paul here is now in charge of the work detail on the window. Form a line. Four men must be carving at all times."

"I'm so thirsty, I'm not doing it. Fuck you," someone in the dark said with menace.

"Form a line and anyone still sitting is going to get the open palm from Paul. How's that sound?" Steve turned to Big Paul. "Open palm for starters. Right?"

Big Paul clapped his hands together so hard it sounded like a gunshot. Everyone stood and shuffled into line. In the slight red light, Steve couldn't see anyone still seated. The four-part harmony of scraping resumed.

Steve went back to his dark search for parts that might make a bow drill. His mind drifted to thoughts about his ex-wife, Juliana. She'd been carping on him for years about being a man who let things happen rather than a man who made things happen. She took pleasure in comparing him to his brother and his best friend, both rich business owners.

Steve had worked as chief engineer, a glorified repairman, for a large hotel in Park City. His wife had taken every opportunity to size him up against men who made more money, no matter how big of a douchebag they might otherwise be.

Steve supposed that he'd even bought it. He'd believed her down-sized, disappointing version of himself. Now the erstwhile leader of twenty-four men with the only plan that could save them, it dawned on Steve that he might have been suckered into her game.

She'd set the chessboard, made up the rules and then fooled him into playing. He'd been feeling like shit as a husband and father for a long, long time, and it had everything to do with the size of his paycheck. Now playing a different game—this one against Death--Steve realized that he *liked* this version of himself. He liked being the guy who figured things out in the hardscrabble world of mechanical leverage and materials; *steels and plastics, tension, compression and shear.*

He hated the very *idea* of white collar work. His best friend had yapped endlessly about being a big swinging dick in business— before his best friend had pointed his big swinging dick to pounding on Steve's wife. Everything about that business life struck him as a living hell. Steve was happier finding practical solutions to practical problems. Fuck his ex if she didn't value in that. Sincerely, she could have her life with Big Swinging Dick Matt, and Steve would happily move on with his tools and his dirty fingernails. For the first time in a long time, a bottle of Black Velvet didn't sound like liquid salvation to Steve. Not that he wouldn't drink it. He was so fucking thirsty he'd gleefully drink horse piss.

Steve found a bigger chair behind the desk where a deputy once sat and monitored happenings in the common room. He felt the arcing shape of the armrest and liked it for the arm of a bow drill. He knelt on the seat of the chair and ripped the armrest away with a pop and a tinkle, which likely was the screw and washer tearing out of the pot metal of the frame and falling to the floor. Steve marked the location in case the hardware might come in handy later. For now, all he needed was the bow-shaped piece of metal tubing. He tore the padding away and ran his hands across the top and then the bottom of the armrest—quarter-round metal tubing with screw holes on each end, molded into a slight curve. Probably cheap pot metal, but otherwise perfect.

While Steve worried the string out of the waist of his pajama pants, he checked progress on the bench. Two men were still working it and they seemed to be making progress. Steve jostled the bench, and it jumped up two inches on one side. Two of the nuts had been successfully removed. In the red light, he could barely see the wrench the men had fashioned; it was like an oil filter wrench with wires from the television twisted around the nut and then torqued with a chunk of chair leg. Bits of wire lay all over the floor, so they must be busting wire by overtightening, but it was working, slowly but surely. Steve slapped one of the men on the back, the man looked up with a slack face, nodded at Steve's thumbs up and went back to working the bench nuts loose.

Steve stepped back to give the men space to work and fished the pajama string through the holes on the ends of his bow. The string felt like it was some sort of cotton/poly blend, and that worried him. Would it hold up to the friction of drilling? If the string parted, he had no idea where he'd get another three feet of line. The jail had eliminated anything that could possibly be used to hang oneself, so that left a pretty short list of cordage inside the pod. The copper wires from the deputy's computer and the TV weren't going to tolerate being flexed over and over again, of that he was certain. All their hopes hung on the pajama rope; that and about six other gut-read snapshots he was taking on applied physics.

With the bow complete, Steve grabbed one of the three-legged chairs and levered off a straight section of leg about eighteen inches long. He unscrewed the metal pivot-pad on the end and fingered the screw hole. The little hole—probably one-quarter, twenty thread—would be enough to disqualify the chunk of chair leg as a drill. The bolt hole would create a cavity in the plastic that wouldn't heat up or cut away. It'd plug up and stop the progress of the drill. This little hole in the chair leg, smaller than a pencil, would screw his plan.

But this is what Steve enjoyed about the mechanical world: he loved the uncompromising nature of problems and solutions. He loved that the chair leg didn't give a fuck if he lived or if he died. That quarter-twenty hole would be there till the end of time, forever ruining the bow drill until someone came along and put his hands on it and cut, welded or smashed it into being something else. There would be no swinging-dick best friend to talk the chair leg into being a secret enemy, there would be no lawyers to spin words around the quarter-twenty threaded hole and make it bigger or smaller, there would be no judge to believe a lying whore and redefine what a quarter-twenty hole really meant in a bow drill. The hole in the chair leg would forever remain, predictably and undeniably, what it was. The quarter-twenty hole was an honest reality in a world of liars.

"Watch your fingers," Steve warned the other men as he raised the end of the heavy bench and slid the tip of the chair leg into the gap. He slammed the bench down against the concrete and mashed the tip of the chair leg. There wasn't enough light to see the tip, but he could feel twin flats—one on each side of the rounded tip—where the bench cross bar had mashed one side, and the concrete floor had mashed the other. It was working.

Steve used the bench like a triphammer, slamming and crushing the tip of the chair leg until he mauled the end like a twisted plastic wrapper of hard candy that cheap houses gave kids on Halloween. The quarter-twenty hole had disappeared in the beaten mess of metal and what remained was ragged and sharp. He kept at it with the jerry-rigged triphammer, doing the best he could to smooth out the sharp, scraggly tooth on the end of the chair leg. He wanted it sharp and toothy, but not so sharp that it caused the drill to seize in the plastic. By the time the cutting end of the drill felt right, a bead of sweat rolled down his back, and his thirst had found a new universe of agony.

He'd been ignoring sounds of slapping and punching that'd been going on in the dark fringes of the pod. Big Paul came up behind him and interrupted his examination of the chair leg.

"Hey, Einstein. That one dude over there's dead, I think. He prolly died from thirst. Or maybe from getting the snot beat out of him for being a lazy piece of shit."

Steve looked up into the man's blacked-out face, the red glow making a halo of his hair.

"Okay. Maybe stop beating on people when they pass out from thirst, then."

"Half these worthless motherfuckers are sayin' that they're ready to pass out from thirst."

"I don't know, Paul. Use your best judgment. I'm kind of busy here trying to save our lives, you know? Don't kill them, okay? Dead men aren't good workers."

"Yeah, right. That's not much help, but okay. Oh. And the dead guy shit his pants and he's reeking up the pod," Paul reported.

"Jesus, Paul. Figure it out, please. Throw him next to the toilet, maybe."

"Okay," Big Paul sounded relieved. Maybe the work of thinking was actually harder for Paul than the work of carrying a shit-stinking dead body across the room. This made strange sense to Steve. For him, dealing with people and their idiotic ways was actually a lot harder than shaping chair legs into tools. He'd rather go up against steel than human emotion—any day of the week.

His thoughts had taken on a weird, slow spin. In a way, it felt more honest. What felt more honest? Slow spinning thoughts? Explain a bit, but in another way, it felt like slow death. Given the circumstances, slow death was the most likely explanation. As the blood thickens, the brain falters. Like bad gas gone to varnish, his blood had begun to foul his mental engine.

The drill end of the chair leg that he'd just beat into shape would probably work, but the other end--the butt end—that was still sharp as a glove full of glass. He'd need to put pressure on the butt end with a bearing block in order for the drill end to chew at the plastic. He needed the butt end to be smooth or it'd eat the bearing block just as fast as the drill ate the plastic window pane.

He needed to sit down anyway. The trip hammering had wiped him out and driven his thirst to epic levels. If he did much more work like that, he'd end up on the pile next to the toilet.

Steve slumped against the mag-locked steel door, now forever secured. As he scraped the ragged butt end of the chair leg across the concrete, slowly sanding it smooth, he imagined the mag lock. He had never seen the design or taken one apart, but he could picture the blocks of metal, the electrical solenoid and the electro-magnet. Working in concert, the components would employ the shear strength of steel together with a ninety-degree countervailing trigger mechanism, moved by a solenoid, that would unfailingly lock twenty-five men in a room for the next ten thousand years.

These mag locks failed *closed*. He thought about the chief engineer of this facility, a more grim but still parallel position to his own at the hotel, and he envisioned how the man would order mag locks from a catalogue when they needed replacement. For every mag lock that failed *closed*, like this one, there would be a hundred that were designed to fail *open*. He couldn't even think of another application for a fail-closed mag lock beside jails and prisons. There weren't many moments in the liability-obsessed world where people were to be kept *inside* during an emergency.

Steve didn't hate the mag lock for being itself. In its simplicity and mechanical nobility, he rather admired it.

More quickly than he would've liked, given his enjoyment of the tedium of sanding against the concrete, the end of the tubing went from being ragged and rough to straight and smooth. Even sanded, the butt end of the tubing would chew through a plastic bearing block almost as fast as the drill end would chew through the plastic window pane. The bearing block—the piece he would grip and press to transfer pressure to the drill—would have to be tougher than the metal of the chair leg or the leg would dig a ring straight through it. The sole of his shoe wasn't tough enough. The backs of the chairs were made of plastic and would fail quicker than the impact-resistant plastic window.

Steve hauled himself off the floor and wobbled over to the deputy's chair that he'd already robbed of one armrest. He felt around the adjustable backrest and discovered a large knob. He unscrewed it, held it up to the thin, red light, and saw what appeared to be a large, brass nut inset into the chunky plastic knob. Fatefully, the sanded end of the chair leg fit perfectly inside the brass nut. The brass wouldn't hold out as long as the metal chair leg, but it would hopefully hold out longer than the plastic window.

Steels and plastic, tension, compression and shear. Steve smiled. His bone-dry tongue again peeled away from the roof of his mouth with an audible *slat-schmap*. It was not lost on him that this was likely one of several phases in the process of the machine of his body failing for lack of water—saliva withdrawing into the all-important core machinery of life support. Steve rubbed his fingers together and the skin felt wrong, as though he'd put on skin gloves two sizes too small.

Even so, there was only one, narrow path to water—through the high impact plastic window and out to freedom. And maybe not even then. Steve hadn't paid much attention to the hallways of the jail when they'd tossed him in the pod. He'd been too busy spinning up his black-on-black fury against the DUI judge, his ex-wife and ex-best friend. If he could reach back to his past self and recoup that energy, that scrim of water his anger had consumed, he certainly would. He would admonish his past self, *"That shit don't matter, bro. Focus on the real world. The real world of tension, compression and shear. That asshole and that bitch don't matter. Worry about the things you can touch, the things you can hold in your hands and fix. You can't fix the evil in their hearts, but you can definitely set down that bottle of Black Velvet. And you can definitely call an Uber when you've been drinking too much at the biker bar, bro."*

While Steve contemplated the coming of a gravel-dry death, his hands had been busy. He looked down and examined the bow drill in the light of the unseen exit sign. The foot-and-a-half long drill had been twirled and twisted into the pajama string bow. The string had gone violin-tight, and the metal bow from the deputy's chair twanged with the tension when he rapped it against the wall.

He stepped up to the plastic window pane and wordlessly bumped aside two of the four men on scratch duty. It'd been six hours since they'd begun rasping the chair legs along deepening furrows in the plastic window. An uneven square shape, barely the width and height of a man's shoulders, had formed. The scratches —now more furrows than scratches--over-extended each other on the corners. The tac-tac-toe shape glowed bright red. For some reason, it reminded him that the emergency lighting wouldn't hold out forever. It was certainly battery-powered and probably not designed to last for more than a few days. At some point, very soon, they would be working in the dead-dark.

He let the worry go and returned to the plastic window pane. He pictured the big square and the point where the furrows crossed. Some part of his brain refused to imagine the square of plastic simply popping out into the hallway when they rammed it with the bench. His mechanical engineer's intuition stubbornly knew that the corners would hold, no matter how hard they hit it.

That was why he'd constructed the bow drill. With the corners drilled through and the surface tension of the plastic pane relieved, his mind's eye could feel the window pane become *willing* to break, at least on one or two of the furrowed sides.

He applied the toothy tip of the drill to the closest corner and slid the smooth end of the drill into the bronze-lined chair knob. He ran the bow to the left and then to the right. The drill spun, the tip buzzed and a poof of fine plastic chips drifted away like the wet, red breath of a demon. The men standing near gasped and mumbled their dim hope.

Steve added more pressure to the knob bearing block, and the red mist thickened. Actual chips of plastic fell away from the point of penetration. After a dozen melodious pulls of the bow, wisps of smoke tendrilled up from the drill. Suddenly, the work became ponderous and Steve could feel that the penetration had ceased. He pulled the drill away and felt the tip. It was gummy and hot. The melted plastic filled in all the burrs and tiny teeth in the ugly, hammered tip. He picked at the cooling plastic and cleared the sharp points. He would have to drill more patiently, allowing the bottom of the cut some time to cool so that the drill would cut rather than heat up and clog in a gummy mess.

Now working the drill more slowly and removing it every four strokes to cool, he could feel the millimeter-by-millimeter progress of the drill. The men gathered around him. Only those poised on the edge of death remained scattered around the pod. Steve hadn't thought to check on the number of the men succumbing. He thought about it while he waited for the drill bit to cool. In this new world, the world where drunk drivers and check kiters were left to die of thirst, he found that he couldn't afford to give a fresh shit about those men.

On the other side of that pane of glass were his four-year-old boy and his six-year-old girl, both somehow dependent on the wits and wiles of Whore Juliana and Big Swinging Dick Matt. Given that truth, he'd walk over the corpse of every man in this pod to make his way home to those two hapless little ones—their every breath reliant on the thin common sense of two adults who might be able to sway a dithering judge, but who would never comprehend the merciless world of steels and plastics; tension, compression and shear.

On his next set of careful pulls of the bows, the drill popped through to the opposite side of the plastic pane. He exhaled, almost feeling the drill bit's intrusion into the world of freedom. Steve twisted and pulled the leg free. The other men leaned in to inspect his work.

"Three more to go," Steve flexed his shoulders and flapped his arms to force the men to back away. He resumed drilling in a new corner.

Forty minutes later, he'd cut tidy, five-eighths holes in each of the four corners of the furrowed square. He had begun to doubt if it'd be enough. The holes felt small to him, and not a single groove looked like it had dug more than halfway through the plastic pane. Steve suspected that many of the men had been working their turn at the scraper just to keep from getting their heads bashed, and they hadn't been applying any real pressure. He closed his eyes and shook his head. It wasn't the first time he'd felt like he was the only man in the room who could actually get things done.

"Seriously, nobody has any water?" Steve complained to the sullen room. He already knew the answer. Two more men had died of thirst while he drilled the window pane. He thought about how they might extract water from the dead men's bodies, but that would be a question for a physician, not a mechanical engineer. All he could imagine was drinking their blood—blood that had to be as thick and sludgy as his own.

"Boss, the bench is ready. The last nut was a bitch. But it's done," one of the men croaked. "Imma go sit down for a while."

Steve nodded and shuffled over to Big Paul. He was one of the few silhouettes he could easily recognize in the hazy red light.

"Paul. Pick three other men and ram that bench into the square."

Steve guessed that there wasn't a man in the pod who was more than two hours away from fainting forever into a final sleep. This would be it. Either it would work or they would die. The simplicity of their reality felt strangely right to Steve. His anger with *The System* had vanished with the wispy smoke from his bow drill. This had always been reality. The physical world had waited like a gathering storm while men blabbed and negotiated with one another, falsely believing that they'd architected a new reality. But then the storm had come, knocked out the lights and returned them to honesty. And God bless it. Live or die.

Paul organized the ramming party while Steve slumped in a chair. Like Vikings ramming a castle gate, the men rocked the heavy bench back and forth at the hip, gaining momentum until Big Paul shouted out.

Three...two...one...*Hit it!*"

Thunk-crackle!

Steve could tell right away, by the resonance of the strike, that the pane was going to give way.

"Three, two, one, HIT IT!"

Thunk-snap!

"Three, two, one..."

Thunk-boom! *Wa, wa, wobble.*

"Hold on," Steve struggled to his feet and padded over to the pane. "You got it. Sit down."

The men backed away with the bench. Their body language betrayed their disappointment that more physical violence hadn't been required. Steve felt frankly surprised as well. On rare occasion, the whims of the storm went a man's way. Hopefully, their luck would hold.

He pushed on the square of high-impact plastic, and the two-foot section levered outward into the hall. Cool, clean air rushed through the gap into Steve's face. Incredibly, three of the four sides had cracked and busted loose. One stubborn side still held, but that wouldn't be a problem. He pushed and pulled, hinging the thick plastic section so a hot crease formed at the scratch line. After thirty or forty widening arcs, the window bent all the way into the hall, folded back flush against itself, snapped at the gouge and fell to the floor of the hallway.

"Lift me through," Steve ordered the men standing nearby. He sure-as-fuck wanted to be the first man outside of the pod. There wasn't a man inside who could be trusted not to fuck up any opportunity they might find there. In any case, nobody had the force of will to stop him.

Steve went through feet-first, and held himself balanced at the precipice of the opening. There was a precarious moment when he thought his back might break. Barely holding onto the top of the hole with his fingertips, he bent in a way that his back wasn't meant to bend. At the last moment of "oh shit" pain, his ass slid across the edge of the hole and he dropped to his feet in the hallway.

The air *tasted* like freedom. He'd apparently become accustomed to the heavy stank inside the pod because the air outside in the hallway felt like it had twice the oxygen. Men inside were scrambling and gesticulating, probably fighting to see who would go next. Before they could implore him to help someone else through, Steve took off down the hallway at a fast walk, gathering what little strength he could and focusing it on forward momentum.

He already knew there were at least four pods in the jail, and maybe another pod for women. Each of the pods formed a ring around an exercise yard that could be seen through a twelve inch-by-twelve-inch window at the back of each cell. The Utah County jail was a giant pentagon or hexagon, depending on how many pods there actually were. He didn't know, but he meant to find out fast.

Steve's legs locked up before he even knew what his eyes beheld. He skidded to a stop in the hallway just a few feet after the first corner. The exit sign that'd been supplying the wane light hung just over his shoulder, so the light here blazed almost bright by comparison. Yet, his mind struggled to understand what he was seeing. A black sludge had been basted, stippled, and poured across the window of this next pod.

Nothing moved inside. The greasy, dark sludge obscured the view. His inner beast screamed, *DANGER!*

Steve backed away from the window. *That had been their intention. They didn't want anyone to see what they were doing to each other.* He pressed forward, hugging the outside wall, as far from the dead pod as he could. He picked up speed in a shuffling gallop, driven by blind horror, lately sprouted at the back of his brain. The mindless reptile of instinct and self-preservation in his mind sat up. Its eyes went wide. Thirst be damned. Steve ran.

As he turned the next bend in the hallway, Steve shook his head like a dog shaking off a barking spree. The light from the exit sign dimmed and as Steve's eyes adjusted, a shot of adrenaline climbed up his back. He found himself looking into the dull eyes of a woman, hands against a window, trapped inside the women's pod. Even in the slight red glow, he could see her pleading gaze.

"Hawaap-uhs." Steve couldn't understand the words through the thick plastic.

Whaap!

She smacked the window pane with her hands. A half-dozen other women rose from the benches and the chairs and stumbled to the glass, adding their pleas and their claps against the plastic.

"Hawaap-uhs!" Help us. Steve understood. Half-dead from thirst and three-quarters devolved into a desperate animal, he felt a rush of cortisol so strong that it made his ears ring. Steve grabbed the handle of the steel door to the pod and yanked hard. It didn't give a millimeter. The mag lock pinioned the door to its frame.

He had to keep moving or the animals from his cage would get there first—wherever "there" might be. He had to leave the women.

You NEED the women, something primal screamed at the back of his brain. *They are YOUR women,* it howled. Steve ran his hands through his hair and forced his feet to continue.

As he drifted down the hall, picking up speed, the women slapped with greater urgency. Their pleas became shrieks. He ran his hand along the window pane, an impotent apology from a reservoir inside him that nearly swamped his sense of self-preservation.

Help these women! it yammered in ear. *Take these women!* it commanded him.

His eyes adjusted to the light and he could see deeper, behind the panicked females and into their pod. Bodies were strewn about like old laundry. His eyes jumped from one face to another at the glass and some deep part of his mind registered their suitability as mating partners.

The primordial animal, brought-forward in the endless hours of the struggle to escape—to survive--glanced from one woman to the next, seeking breeding. Looking to have them. Knowing it was insane, but seeking anyway.

After seventy? a hundred? hours of slowly dying in a sealed, plastic box, not one of the women was enough to stop his shuffling feet in their flight of self-preservation. But his feet considered it for the space of one or two confused flashes.

He left the women behind, wailing their failure to draw this man into their plight.

There was nothing he could do, some piece of his brain argued with the other. He would die of this damnable thirst long before he could drill even one hole in their window.

To drill. To penetrate.

But his seed... all those women. All his for the taking. All open to him, for the price of his workmanship. His manhood's investiture, his mating right.

Again, he shook his head like a dog. On some level, Steve knew the thickness of his thirst-sludged blood dragged at the function of his mind. He was a man, now only in the most-animal sense of the word.

He almost tripped and fell when he saw the carts haphazardly abandoned in the hall. His mind struggled to understand what they were, but the red light glinted off what could only be a water bottle. A dozen, maybe two dozen, water bottles.

Steve rushed to the carts, grappled with the cap of a bottle and gulped the sweet, sweet water. It cascaded down his open throat, rushing into the desiccated tissue along his trachea and his stomach, inflating the raisin-shriveled cells of his brain, his organs, his penis and balls. The water seemed to skip the bothersome delay of his digestive tract and flood directly into his tissue, reanimating him by gulps and gags as he pounded the plastic bottle and crushed it in his greedy hands.

He vomited on the linoleum—a thin, colorless puke. He leaned against the wall, snatched another bottle of water and drank it slower. He let the water slide down his throat, like a thin cord instead of a hawser of rope. He nursed the water into his gut and let it make its way through all the proper channels into his muscle and nerves.

"*Steve,*" the voice nearly caused him to jump out of his skin. His still-dry eyes attempted to focus in the murk. It was one of the men from the pod. He thought maybe the man's name was Rex. Men were catching up to him in the hallway.

"Give me some," Rex shouldered him aside and hammered back a water. Steve grabbed two more bottles and stuffed them in his pocket. He seized a third and set to drinking. As the third bottle vanished into the dry hollows of his body, his thoughts mustered.

Big Paul would be the next tool he would need to employ. Steve gathered two more bottles and went back the way he'd come down the hall. Two men shuffled toward the carts like zombies. With each passing man, the shrieks of the trapped women climbed, crested, then succumbed again to despondence. He felt the loss in the depths of his reptilian mind; the women he would now have to share.

They are dead women, his prefrontal cortex argued. *My two children are out there, which may be as ruined as in here,* his thinking mind protested. With water coursing through his veins, the clamor of his seed—the raw consciousness that lived in his mons pubis—withdrew to a subordinate chatter. His children were *out there* in the hands of fools. His seed already lived. His endowment—his kids-- needed him, urgently, above all else.

Steve picked up his pace, jogging back toward the pod. He passed another man staggering toward the carts. He passed the blood-caked window of the neighboring pod. He reached the square hole in his pod just as another man climbed through. Of course, nobody was helping on this side of the hallway.

"Paul," Steve shouted into the square hole past a man struggling to get through head-first.

"Yeah," Paul shoved up to the plastic pane. "I can't get myself up."

Steve couldn't reach past the stuck man, so he lifted the man's upper body as he shimmied through the hole and thunked down in the hall. Steve shoved another man back through the hole to reach inside to Big Paul.

"Drink these," Steve handed the bottles, one-at-a-time.

Two more men clambered through the hole while Big Paul drank.

"Hand me my bow drill and the bearing block," Steve shouted around a man's feet coming through the window. Paul gathered the parts of the tool and handed them through as a man cleared the gap and dropped to the floor.

Steve found that he could think, now. He could feel his brain coming back online, and he realized that he hadn't made the full circuit of the hallway circling the pods. The abandoned food carts had side-tracked him. While these men recovered their wits, he was first. He needed that advantage. His children might need that advantage.

He took off at a loping run with his two remaining water bottles bobbling in his pajama pockets. He ignored the other three pods— and whatever miscellaneous horrors they held--and checked each outside door, slamming into each with his shoulder, working the door handle until he knew their condition without doubt. Not one outer door gave even the slightest fraction of an inch.

As he made the round back to his own pod, he found men continuing to climb out and disappear into the red gloom toward the food carts. Just before the door to his pod, he discovered another door heading inward toward the center of the hexagon; a service access to the exercise yard, he reasoned. He'd never seen it before because he'd always entered the yard through the door at the back of the pod. When he slammed it with his shoulder, the door flew inward. It wasn't freedom, but it might lead to something that might lead to freedom.

Steve stepped into the passage and was enveloped in a sea of black. The light from the emergency exit sign hardly penetrated this passage and he had nothing to wedge the heavy, steel door open. He let the door slam shut behind him and jammed the parts of the bow drill in one of his pajama pockets alongside a water bottle. The bow and drill stuck out of the pocket a full foot. In bottomless darkness, he slid up the hallway with one hand on the wall and another hand protecting his face. Nothing stopped him and nothing snagged at his progress, just slick, endless wall. After an eternity in the dark, the hand in front of his face slapped into a door at the end of the hall. He shoved. Light exploded around him.

After blinking away the pain of a million starbursts, Steve looked out onto the exercise yard. This was a jail, not a prison, he reminded himself for the hundredth time. This was no exercise yard like any he'd seen on television. For one thing, there wasn't a single item of exercise equipment—no weight benches, pull-up bars or rusty, hulking dumbbells. In the Utah State jail, they kept you skinny, soft and undernourished. The only exercise that happened in the exercise yard was walking in a small circle, and even that required the prisoner have non-violent charges and a history of good behavior. He'd only been outside in the yard three times during his short stay at the Utah County Stoney Lonesome.

The exercise yard was only about a hundred and fifty feet across, hexagonal in shape and surrounded by eighteen-foot high, smooth plastic walls. The plastic was clear like the window pane in the pod, and it was set off from the cinder block wall four inches by what looked like cylindrical aluminum stand offs. For whatever reason, the engineers hadn't mounted the plastic plates directly to the cinderblock. Maybe mounting them to the wall would leave a cavity where moisture might collect, mold might flourish and the cinderblock could spall. Of course, that would never be an issue in the dry Utah climate, but engineers designed these products for nationwide use, not just for one climate. The stand-offs from the wall gave him an idea.

They would drill and cut footholds just like they'd done in the pod. The drill had worked better than he'd planned, and now with bellies full of water, anything seemed possible. They had a new lease on life. He fished out the bow drill snagged in his pajama pocket, and set it against the plastic wall of the yard. Like the walls of Jericho, patience and God-touched luck would defeat the Utah County jail.

But something wasn't quite right in the yard. Steve looked around and scratched his chin. Two of the small windows looking into the yard held the faces of damned men from other pods. One of them silently screamed at Steve behind two inches of plastic. Yet, it wasn't the disembodied faces of the trapped that gave Steve a sense of wrongness. It was something more fundamental, more obvious.

It was the color of the light. He hadn't been outside for a few (five or six?) days and he hadn't quite forgotten what "outside" should look like. He looked straight up, and it clicked: the sky was the wrong color. It made him feel sick to his stomach.

His children. Brittany and Ben.

Up above, it wasn't blue and it wasn't cloudy. It was amber and gray--the color of cheap honey if you whipped it with dirty dishwater. Nothing about the sky stood out, necessarily. There were no missile contrails or nuclear mushroom clouds hanging over the window of sky atop the exercise yard. The color was just *wrong*. His gut did a backflip when he considered his little ones out there, terrified under that weird sky.

He headed back into the black maw of the corridor, hurried toward the inner ring hallway and hit the door almost at a run. Time was running out. The sky told the story in a way that only a ruined heaven could.

As soon as he burst into the hall, he heard the sounds of battle and he understood instantly why. Steve paused, pulled his two water bottles out of his pocket, and secreted them behind the door in the dark hallway to the yard. He wasn't about to wade into a fight over food and water with two bottles of his own.

He closed the distance to the food carts and found half the men from his pod trying to kill the other half. He stood all the way back at the corner of the moon-faced women's pod until the melee slowed.

"Stop!" Steve shouted. "I've got a way out." The fighting abruptly ceased. His eyes danced around the scene. Big Paul was against a wall, eating what had to be a dangerously-old sandwich and surrounded by six bottles of water. He would not be required to fight for his share, apparently. The fifteen other men stood in various states of either trying to protect what they'd acquired or trying to relieve another man of what he'd acquired. The smart ones had hidden their spoils and backed away. Steve felt tempted to propose a sensible process of resource allocation, but realized that he couldn't care less.

"Come with me. There's still work to do." He turned and headed back toward the hallway out to the yard.

"What about these women?" Someone called out.

Without turning, Steve answered, "I don't care what you do with them. I'm going to find my kids."

Some number of the men followed him down the dark hallway, out to the exercise yard and under the malignant sky of the Black Autumn.

6

DEATH APPLES

BY CHRIS SERFUSTINI

THESE DAYS, Chris Serfustini runs social media plays for Florida hotels. Back in the day, he was a stone cold paintball killer for a factory team called Special Ops Paintball. Twenty years later, with a little less spring in his step but still handsome as the devil, Chris tried his hand at fiction.

It came as no surprise that Nick Orso, a dinged-up operator half-pickled in tequila, would spring from Chris' mind to wash up on a Yucatan beach in the first days of the apocalypse. This would be par for the course for "The Serf."

-Jason Ross

CHIQUILA, Mexico. October 15th

PLOP.
   Plop.
   Plop.

Nick Orso was dying. The sound of his blood dripping through the slatted wood into the water below echoed like a funeral bell. He clung to the shadows, not a hundred feet from the beach. He found himself in a hell of his own making.

Bodies were piled everywhere. The greasy smoke from trucks burning in the sand stung his eyes. He flinched as the camp cooked down to embers, the meaty bits popping like pork and the heat licking at his face. He turned away at the smell of diesel and gas as it tickled his nose and he dug deep for the patience not to scratch it— he needed both hands...one on the gaping wound in his shoulder, and the other on his thigh.

In a distinguished career of over twenty years as a top tier opera- tive, he couldn't believe he was going to lie here and bleed out alone, one hundred miles outside of some shithole Mexican town in the Yucatan.

Where was this place again? Chiquisa? Chiquita? Chiquila?

The name escaped him. All he knew was that he didn't want to die.

Not here, not yet.

Even though it was after five in the morning, it was hotter than a whore on nickel night. His body felt like it was steaming in a pres- sure cooker. He was soaked to the bone and unable to tell which was blood, sweat, or piss. He didn't care.

He'd known better than to come out of semi-retirement for this job. As an expat on the beach with a somewhat legitimate business and other streams of income, he was living in the lap of luxury in Mexico. Unfortunately, his taste in tequila was only exceeded by his taste in women, both growing more expensive the older he got. The money offered to him for this job was enough to set him up for the rest of his life, or at least a few months if he didn't pace himself.

Hell, he wasn't fooling himself. The money wasn't going to last a month.

None of that really mattered, bleeding out on some desolate dock in the middle of bumfuck Mexico nowhere.

The job was pretty straightforward. Simple recon and intelligence gathering on a local cartel operation. In and out without being seen or heard. No fuss, no muss. Not that he didn't like fuss and muss, but like the song said, 'he wasn't as good as he once was, but he was as good as he was, once.'

He had arched his eyebrows at the strange voice coming through the telephone when he'd answered the call yesterday, until he realized it was his contact at the pentagon. The stress in the voice of the caller strained Nick's ears like a bad song made worse by autotune.

His contact reported satellites showed strange activity going on with the Cartel De Golfo down on a deserted beach in the Yucatan. Sources said everything was about to evaporate, and the US needed eyes on it pronto.

Nick chuckled sourly. *He'd actually said pronto.*

His contact even played the "duty to his country" card and Nick had thrown up a little in his mouth. He'd almost slammed the phone down. Having an actual landline phone, it would have been more than satisfying.

He had his reasons for hanging up his guns and government-issued dark sunglasses and fleeing to Mexico so many years ago, and they were nothing to do with getting older. The thought of continuing to watch the good old U.S. of A. circle the toilet turned his stomach. America had become soft and repugnant like an over-bloated caricature of itself. Drunk on consumerism, fueled by narcissism, propelled by social media and the talking heads of the mainstream media, it had become a country both obsessed with and repulsed by itself at the same time.

It was all going down the drain and he didn't want to go with it.

First and foremost, Nick Orso was a survivor.

In the end he'd succumbed to his God-given American greed,

just like everybody else. The disgust with himself made him ill. He'd successfully escaped that life, but the lure of an obscene amount of fast money had caught back up with him, sealing a deal that just might cost him his life.

TWENTY-FOUR HOURS EARLIER.

Within an hour after ending the conversation Nick was on the road heading for Chiquilla.

The small town looked and felt like hundreds of others up and down the coasts of Mexico. The local economy was based almost exclusively on tourism. Tourists paid handsomely for water excursions ranging from fishing to whale-watching to paragliding. Unfortunately, the resort and tour companies kept the lion's share of that money and Chiquila looked like a town in a third world country with a pretty paint job. The locals led a simple but happy life, squeezing out a living from pennies in paradise.

He arrived around noon at the Hotel Puerta Del Sol. It was a brown two-story affair a few blocks from the Gulf of Mexico. It was no Ritz Carlton, but there was a shine to the well-worn floor that spoke of pride of ownership. He chuckled to himself as he took in the cheesy decor. Nick was constantly amused by the idea of what local Mexican businesses thought appealed to American *touristas*, but he had to admit that the mural of a whale and a dolphin frolicking amongst a backdrop of colorful sea life was a nice touch.

The front desk attendant gave a flirty smile to Nick as he approached, and his eyes wandered down to a generous sneak peek beneath her red-flowered top. She gave him a long moment before pulling his attention back to her eyes. "Welcome to Hotel Puerta Del Sol, Senor. Your name?"

"Dixon Cider," he answered, squashing down a laugh.

The pretty senorita missed the joke and pecked away at her

computer, eventually looking back up with the same smile pasted tight. "Do you have identification, Mr. Cider? And a credit card?"

"I prefer cash." He slid her some paper and winked. "Here's double to just leave my name off of that computer."

She winked back and discreetly slid half the cash into her pocket, stabbed at the keyboard again, and slid the key to his room across the counter.

He strolled through the open air lobby to his room. Once inside, he quickly laid out his gear and readied it for the night's foray into the unknown. Exhausted but on edge, he decided to catch some rack time. It had been forever since he'd played this younger man's game, and although it should be a walk in the park, he was going to bank every advantage.

Beep Beep Beep

Still groggy with sleep, he pried his eyes open to the sound of the alarm on his watch. His cheeks were warm from the sun as it dangled lazily, descending into the thick jungle to the west. Through the fog of semi-unconsciousness his mind skipped around, finally landing on one cognizant thought: *COFFEE.*

Out the door, he made his way through the lobby to the street. He jumped at the squeal of tires braking hard as the driver skidded to a stop and laid on the horn, trying to exit one of the *estacionamientos*--paid parking lots for the numerous tourists that made their way from the resorts.

"*Muévete del camino, pendeho!*" the driver shouted from the car, the middle finger salute telling Nick all he needed to know.

"*Besa mis culo.*" Nick grumpily shouted back as he returned the gesture, crossing in front of the car.

The heady, dark aroma of freshly brewed Columbian go juice drew his brain in like a homing missile, guiding him to the source.

He found the market and paid the equivalent of a quarter for a large cup of coffee and a homemade *concha*. He smiled at the sweetness of the delicious pastry melting in his mouth, his thoughts clearing as the caffeine burned away the fog of his mind like the sun on a summer morning.

Walking back to the hotel, his mind returned to his conversation with his contact at the Pentagon.

"What do you mean by strange activity?" he'd asked.

"We're getting some thermal readings, could be a power source. That and out of nowhere almost a hundred men with fifteen sailboats showed up," his contact had reported. "Unless the Mexican Olympic Sailing Team has an unscheduled regatta in the middle of nowhere, something's up."

The conversation went on to detail reports from the Middle East desk. Money was being transferred from Iran to the cartels. Two weeks ago a Turkish-flagged ship had been interdicted by the Mexican Navy carrying Muslim refugees. The Mexican government had detained them but on the third night after their arrival, they had vanished. Something was definitely up.

Nick returned to the hotel, navigating on autopilot while his mind churned the details of the conversation. He returned the friendly wave of the front desk attendant without even thinking about it. What did Muslim refugees, Iranian funding of the cartels, a power source in the jungle, and fifteen sailboats all have in common?

Whatever it was, he was going to find out.

NICK SLIPPED OUT of his room, gently closing the door as he stepped into the outdoor hallway. It was after eight o'clock in the evening, and the waning twilight had finally subsided. The soft rhythm of Mexican guitars floated through the air and Nick stopped to listen.

He heard the clinking of glasses, people laughing, and rapid-fire Spanish being spoken in the kitchen at the restaurant across the street. It was a typical night in a typical Mexican tourist town, but his gut flipped over a layer of acid that might've been his late-afternoon coffee. He didn't like it when his gut did that. Sometimes it knew something he didn't, and Nick hated being second-guessed.

Instead of passing through the lobby, he made a left and headed toward the courtyard at the rear of the hotel. He had to watch his step in the dark, the only light coming from the moon and the flickering of tiki torches lining the path. He passed a couple of drunk tourists that were more interested in each other than they were in him.

"You are the most beautiful woman I've ever seen, your smile so sweet, your eyes so deep, I could get lost in them forever," the man swooned while not actually looking at her.

Nick rolled *his* eyes.

Wow.

The woman turned from the man, but Nick saw her trying not to laugh, and she pulled farther away instead of moving closer, doubt crossing her face. As she pulled her hands free of him and crossed her arms, Nick noticed the tan line on her ring finger.

Hey, what happens in Mexico...

NICK'S back felt damp with sweat that pooled in the fabric of his black long sleeve T-shirt, and he reached into one of the cargo pockets of his pants to pull out a bandanna. He mopped the slickness from his face as he frowned, thinking about the gear needed for this mission. He dreaded putting on his battle rattle once he got to the jungle.

Exiting the courtyard, he walked to the corner of the hotel grounds to a gap between the fence and the adjoining property.

He'd noticed the gap when parking his Jeep earlier and had positioned it just on the other side.

The rusty fence scratched his arm as he squeezed through the gap, but he hardly noticed. Almost in a daze he climbed into the jeep. The only sound a slight *whoosh* and a comforting *click* as he shut the door. The hinges were well oiled, and he had disabled the interior lights.

Old habits die hard, he thought.

The hair on the back of his neck stood up. Something just didn't feel right. A veteran of hundreds of missions like this, he couldn't shake the feeling that this wasn't going to end well.

Suck it up, Buttercup. You're getting soft, he told himself. He turned the key and tapped the gas, the wheels rolling slowly. The soft crunching of the gravel went quiet as he turned out of the parking lot onto the blacktop, picking up speed until he was flying down the narrow road. Weaving and dodging potholes like a Formula One racer, barreling towards the unknown.

An hour passed in the blink of an eye as he drove down the desolate road. Approaching the turnoff that led to his target, every instinct screamed at him to just keep going straight, find a bar, drink copious amounts of tequila, and forget about all of this nonsense in the comfort of some young tourist.

Pulling off the road, the wheel jumped a bit in his hands. Slowly, the Jeep rolled to a stop as the dust caught up, playing across the headlights like a ghostly specter, the only sound the rhythmic purr of the engine. Closing his eyes he ran his mind through all of the reasons he shouldn't be doing this.

He made the turn anyway. "Fuck it." He'd never been known for his good decision making abilities anyway.

THE NEXT HOUR went on for days. The ruts shook his teeth as he drove down an overgrown trail leading deeper into the jungle. Parking the Jeep about five miles away from the beach, he stashed it in the thick growth just off the road. He fought his way through the jungle to the site on foot. Each step a new battle in a lonely war. Nearing his target, the blinding light forced him to shield his eyes so he wouldn't lose his night vision.

I bet it cost a fortune in bribes to the local Federales to keep this under wraps, he thought as he took in the spectacle of the camp. They'd made no effort to conceal it.

Nick slowed as he got closer—going for stealth over speed. Freezing in place out of instinct, he reached out with his senses. The faint odor of tobacco smoke aggravated his nose. After a few seconds of peering into the darkness, he made out the dim glow of the burning embers of a cigarette. The perimeter sentry was nestled in his hide, his vice betraying him.

Those things'll kill you. Well, cancer may not be an issue after tonight.

Without knowing the watch schedule, Nick decided it was better to detour around the man instead of taking him out. He didn't want to chance putting the camp on alert by discovering a dead or missing sentry. If he did his job right, no one would ever know he'd been here.

Recon mission, he reminded himself.

People milled around everywhere. From his vantage point in the trees overlooking the cove, Nick's mind skipped around as he tried to take in the extent of the full-blown smuggling operation.

The cartel had built a camp and a dock right into the large sandy beach of the natural bay. The dock stretched hundreds of feet into the water and the tents looked hastily constructed. The area was bustling with activity, reminding Nick of a hornet's nest—a hornet's nest that he definitely didn't want to kick.

Lung cancer might not kill that dude on sentry after all.

The bay was filled with a small fleet of sailboats ranging from thirty to fifty feet in length; catamarans and mono-hulls of different configurations. Some shiny and new, others had paint peeling, barnacles peeking up from the waterline, some even listing heavily to one side or the other.

Nick scowled at the flurry of activity on the beach. He was baffled as men yelled and horns honked all in disregard of concealment. He stifled a laugh when one of the loading trucks teetered precariously on two wheels, almost rolling from speeding and turning too sharply in the soft sand.

These guys are in a real hurry.

The diesel's signature *chug, chug, chug* filled the air as boats motored in. Nick winced as they cut power and coasted into the dock with a loud clunk that he could almost feel. They were loaded with cargo, and finally boarded by six middle-eastern looking men who immediately readied the boats, sailing out of the bay under the cover of night.

It was all very efficient and had the look of an operation carried out by highly-trained and motivated men.

Well, highly-trained other than their noise and light discipline...

In just the short time he had been watching, two boats had already gone through the process. Scratching his chin, he pondered the scene in front of him.

This doesn't make any sense.

The loaded boats still sat high in the water. The amount of cargo was much less than their capacity. If this were a drug smuggling operation, each boat would be loaded to the gills before casting off. There was also the matter of the men. Usually smuggling operations used the least amount of personnel required. These boats only needed two or three crew, not six.

The camera quietly whirred as Nick took pictures of everything, his steps not even a whisper as he made his way around the bay for a better angle, avoiding two more sentries. He stopped and turned, narrowing his eyes at a large tent on the west side of the camp. He saw tables and chairs as men entered and exited through the flap. The autofocus whined as it adjusted while he zoomed in, the image of pictures, maps, and writing covering the back wall of the tent becoming crisp through the camera's lens. This was definitely no drug operation.

I need to get closer.

Looking up from the camera, he saw multiple men in body armor patrolling the perimeter of the camp with AK-47 rifles.

Forget that, I need a drink.

In the end, his curiosity won out. To one side of the camp, near the open flap of the main tent, sat fifteen smaller tents that would be perfect to get a closer look and sit and observe the activities. He quietly crept toward one of the smaller tents, the jungle thinning out as it gave way to open space.

Pausing to look closer, the men guarding the camp appeared to be lazy and inattentive to their jobs. He concluded they were hired cartel muscle and not the 'true believers' he saw boarding the boats. Half the guys were just milling about, and the other half were working like their asses were on fire. Most of the Mexicans were chatting with each other, laughing and smoking, only intermittently walking their patrol routes.

Even with the lackadaisical behavior of the guards, twenty yards of brightly lit open space stood between Nick and the back wall of the smaller tent. Squinting at the bright light, he frowned. There was no way he'd cover that much ground without being seen.

The droning engine of a large cargo truck caught Nick's attention. It pulled up on the beach between him and the guards. The air brakes hissed as it rolled to a stop in front of one of the smaller tents. Spilling out the back of the truck, men quickly transferred crates to the truck from the smaller tent on the opposite side.

Now or never.

Nick raced from his hiding place, crouching low as he covered the ground to the nearest small tent. He stopped at the back wall and listened. Nothing but silence.

Ducking under the outer wall, he muffled a grunt as he bumped into the crates that nearly filled the tent. They ranged in size, stacked neatly in rows. This was the cargo he'd seen the men loading into the truck and then onto the boats.

The thumping in his chest calmed as he recovered from his short sprint. *I really need more exercise*, he thought, as he tried to slow his breathing to a normal rate while the autocorrect in his brain changed 'exercise' to 'tequila.'

Looking through the corner gap of the tent, he had a perfect view of the back wall of the larger tent. He saw pictures of shopping malls, hospitals, and government buildings. There were maps of American cities. The harsh staccato of Arabic grated his ears but he was too far away to make out the words given his rudimentary command of the language.

He moved closer, toward the next tent in the row. He peeked inside, nodding to himself as he discovered more crates. He slipped between the crates stacked within the tent, glancing left and right.

His heart stopped as he read the stenciling on the side of one of the crates: "CHARGE DEMOLITION M112." If all the tents held the same contents, there was enough C4 in them to create a crater a mile wide. The other crates were labeled, "30 GRENADE HAND FRAG| DELAY M67 W/FUZE M213."

Stored in the same tent... O.S.H.A. would not approve, he thought.

He paused to listen. Close enough to hear clearly now, the conversation seemed to be winding down.

"Adhhab mae Allah," (*go with God*) said a man sitting at a table in front of the back wall of the tent. He was flanked by two guards and dressed in typical Arab garb, sporting a long flowing beard.

Definitely an Imam, thought Nick.

The Imam handed a packet across the table to the man standing in front of him.

"*Allah 'akbar*" (*God is great*), the man replied. This man, although looking of middle-eastern descent, was clean shaven and decked out in high-end sailing gear, right down to his Sperry Topsider dock shoes. He looked like he was ready to hit the yacht club after the Sunday regatta.

Nick's body bristled as his mind put everything together. The crates of explosives, the maps, the pictures, the strike teams boarding the boats.

His blood ran cold. This was a no-bullshit recon mission with serious consequences. The cartwheels his stomach had been doing earlier made a lot more sense now.

The number of casualties would be *staggering*. This would be beyond anything the United States had ever experienced. This was Pearl Harbor-level shit. As he took it all in, the pure efficiency of the plan was almost something to be admired. The bitter taste of bile filled his mouth. He steeled his resolve and his training took over. The camera whirred again as he snapped pictures of the crates, the men at the table, the maps and the pictures hanging on the walls.

It was time to exfil back to civilization and warn his former homeland of the shit storm that was coming. He had to report his findings to his contact back in D.C. He was no fan of what the government of the United States had become, but the pure evil that was about to be unleashed in the country he almost loathed couldn't be allowed. It was still his home country after all. Even if he ran from it into the smooth arms of tequila, his blood would *always* run red, white and blue.

There was still time. Nick estimated it would take a week for these men to sail across the Gulf of Mexico. With his help, his former country was about to dodge one of the biggest bullets in history. He hoped.

Nick packed up his kit. Squeezing into his backpack he moved through the tent the way he had entered. In his haste to exit, he almost didn't hear the soft but distinctive click of the safety of an AK-47.

"*DATE LA VUELTA!*" said the man pointing death at Nick's back.

Nick slowly turned. The man holding the gun on him was short and pudgy, rubbing the sleep from his eyes. The sweat stains and grime on his shirt and pants had a permanent quality to them, and his filthy clothes looked one size too small. He had been dozing the whole time Nick had been in surveillance position.

"Manos arriba!" the man said, the slur of sleep still permeating his voice. Nick smelled the stale tequila on his breath and for a moment was jealous. Even if he hadn't been fluent in Spanish, the intent was clear by the gesture the sloppy little man was making with the gun, which was universal for "hands up."

Nick put on his best "'I'm in charge' face," and barked in flawless Spanish, "The boss is going to be pissed at you for sleeping on the job," he said with authority. "Tell me why I shouldn't report this immediately?" He moved toward the man, imperceptibly at first but gradually increasing his speed.

A confused look, followed by guilt, painted the man's face, frozen in place as Nick closed the distance. Like a wraith, almost too fast to see, Nick drew his knife and plunged it into the man's throat. He knocked the AK to the ground in one fluid movement. The gun made little noise as the soft sand absorbed it. Far noisier was the wet gurgling coming from the guard as Nick subdued him and lowered him to the ground.

The man's eyes flashed wide, and his expression flickered from guilt to bewilderment as he gawked at the knife handle sticking out from below his chin. Confusion became awareness as the pain rolled across his face. He slunk to the ground with a soft thud.

Nick's nose wrinkled at the metallic smell of blood mixed with the foul stench of other excretions. He knew the average human had about one and a half gallons of blood, and he was covered with every ounce. The syrupy mess was in his hair, underneath his nails, even in his mouth. So much for no fuss, no muss. He was in it up to his eyeballs.

He scooped up the AK and re-engaged the safety. Low-walking to the rear of the tent, he peeked out underneath the bottom edge. The truck that had covered his dash to the tent was gone, but everything else was as he'd left it.

Feeling on edge and a little shaky, he stumbled as the adrenaline of combat left his system. He retreated to the small tent closest to the edge of the jungle.

I'm going to need to lie on the beach for a week just to recover from this, he thought, smiling as he pictured his favorite waitress bringing him a bottle of expensive Anejo tequila and a bucket of beer to wash it down. With the money from this job, he'd lie on that beach for a long time. First though, he had to get the hell out of here in one piece.

Easy-peasy.

Well, except for twenty yards of open ground and thirty heavily-armed men. All he needed to do was make it to the jungle, circle around, avoiding the sentries outside the perimeter, and trek the five or so miles back to the Jeep. He was going to need a diversion.

Catching a distant flash in the sky, he looked up. The thunder rumbled in, the wind picked up, the air hinted at the smell of rain. A squall was coming from the gulf. They were common this time of year, and though they rarely lasted long, they made up for it in intensity. He didn't relish the thought of slogging through the jungle drenched to the bone, but he smiled anyway--the storm would cover his escape.

Backing quietly into the tent, he headed for one of the crates full of grenades. The lid creaked as he pried it open with his knife and surveyed the contents. He grinned as he studied the neat rows of "death apples." He didn't have a plan yet, but he was getting an idea.

When in doubt, go with grenades, he thought as his grin widened. He grabbed two and stuck them in pockets on his tactical vest. As he replaced the lid of the crate, he changed his mind and grabbed two more.

Four grenades are twice as good as two.

With the crate closed, he made his way back to the tent wall. He rubbed the scruff on his chin as the plan came together in his mind. It was simple: He'd throw one of the grenades across the camp toward the water. In the panic that followed he'd beat feet out of there, ricky-tick, while everyone's focus was in the other direction. If he needed to, he'd lob another grenade for effect, or maybe just for fun.

He ducked under the wall of the tent, a grenade in each hand. Using his teeth, he pulled the pin on each and spit them to the ground, the taste of metal lingering on his tongue.

Pure badass.

Two things happened at once.

Panicked shouts from behind him let him know that the guard he'd killed had been found. Men ran in his direction from all over camp—the hornet's nest had been kicked.

The brightness of a thousand flashbulbs painted the world white as lightning tore across the sky. Simultaneously, thunder cracked, deafening him. The concussion almost knocked him to the ground as the sky opened up and a torrential downpour engulfed the camp.

Time slowed to a crawl.

Nick felt the cold curved steel of the live grenade in each hand as the horde of men rushed him through the stubborn sand, each step taking forever to complete. They sluggishly raised their weapons. He saw each pore on their ruddy faces, twisted in anger. Their shouts came through low and unintelligible, like a record playing way too slow. He felt his heart beating, each beat seeming to thud forever. The smell of expended nitrogen was pungent as sparks and smoke hung in the air, lazily expanding out from the guns as they fired. He glanced to the sky as a massive horizontal ceiling of water dropped on him like a woman's wrath.

Nick flinched as the splinters from the wooden tent pole dug into his face. *That was a close one,* he thought. More shots kicked sand up in slow motion. The wave of water finally crashed to the ground with a giant clap. Time sped back to normal.

Nick sprang forward like a racehorse out of the gate. Running almost blind through the torrential downpour, he tossed one of the grenades in the direction of the men, and he took off in the other. He rolled the AK forward on the sling from his back and fired one-handed while he ran, spraying at anything that moved.

Nick sped through the camp not exactly sure which direction he was heading and barely able to see where he was going. Feeling, more than hearing the *whump* of the grenade, he checked his six without stopping.

All clear, he thought triumphantly, a split-second before he ran right through the back wall of the large tent, knocking all the maps and pictures to the ground. The tent wall gave way and rolled Nick up as he hit the ground. He grunted and flailed, struggling to break free from the canvas.

"Muh fuh fung ternt muh fuher," he shouted through the thick fabric, rolling around and flopping like a fish.

Like a party favor on New Year's Eve, he finally unrolled in the right direction and popped to his feet, spinning to face the shocked Imam and two armed men in the room, a live grenade in one hand, the AK in the other.

The wind and rain pelted through the opening in the tent, a blizzard of papers blowing around the room, knocking the lamps to the ground. Shadows played across the walls of the tent like a puppet show as the Imam recoiled in his chair. The guards raised their weapons, their faces painted with surprise.

"*Aloha snackbar!*" Nick shouted maniacally, pulling the trigger.

Click.

A flash of lightning lit up his face. He threw his head back and laughed like the devil himself. Confused even more, the men hesitated and gave him just enough time to lob the grenade at their feet. He dove through the gap in the canvas, back into the maelstrom.

The concussion from the grenade threw Nick even farther from the tent as a searing white hot pain coursed through his shoulder.

Great, shrapnel, add that to the list, he thought as he slid to a stop face-first in the cold wet sand. He rolled forward into a low crouch. The sand ground so loud between his molars that it blotted out the shouting.

Puh!

No plan survives first contact with the enemy, but he was amazed at how well this was going. He had evidence, he'd killed some men including, maybe, the Imam.

The rain stung his face and the wind rocked him back on his heels. Struggling to keep his balance as the storm intensified, he crab-walked away from the camp, trying to get his bearings. Still blinded by the squall, he crawled through the jungle, hoping it was toward the Jeep.

"*Uuuuuggh*"... he groaned as the sharp pain in his shoulder worsened, the warm, wet feeling of blood leaking down his back contrasted with the cold, wet rain. He was making good progress though, following the edge of the camp back around to the side he had come from. The twenty minutes it took to circle the camp took days in his mind. The storm abated by bits; the lightning drifted farther into the jungle. The rain tapered to a slow drizzle.

Shouts filled the forest behind him. Turning, he saw flashlights in the distance, flicking between the foliage, the shouts changing pitch as they picked up his trail.

Time to kick it up a notch

The earth felt wobbly under his feet as he stood, running deeper into the jungle, side-stepping as he heard the snap of a branch up ahead. Reflexively, he drew his gun from the drop holster on his thigh and the comforting grip of his Glock filled his hand. He yelped as his foot caught in a vine on the jungle floor. He went down hard in the mush, raising his pistol and firing blind. The stench of stale cigarettes filled his nose as his head exploded in a starburst of pain.

Darkness overcame him.

ALEJANDRO

Alejandro Rodriguez dove under his hasty shelter at the perimeter of the camp as the storm moved in, entwining his thin but muscular frame into the branches supporting his tarp. Thorns stabbed at his skin.

He hated the jungle: the smell of decay, the bugs, the snakes. At only seventeen, he was the youngest member of the Cartel de Golfo to reach the rank of *sicario*.

Orphaned by the cartel when he was eight, he and his younger sister Maria were "adopted" by them. While his sister grew up in the house of the local jefe, Alejandro was trained in the way of the cartel. At first this meant cleaning up after the men had partied all night, but he quickly progressed to lookout for a packaging house where his grandmother worked.

Despite the sour smell of chemicals, there he felt like he had purpose. He enjoyed his job as lookout, like a shepherd tending his flock as the old ladies weighed and wrapped packages.

He killed his first man when he was eight, at the beginning of the war with the Zetas cartel. A man barged in and killed every last soul at the packaging house. Alejandro was in the bathroom when the power went out and everything went dark. The screams and pleas for mercy echoed in the warehouse. Through the crack under the door the muzzle flashes lit the small bathroom like a photo booth. The *whoosh-click* of the suppressed .22 echoed softly as the killer worked.

After what seemed like an eternity, the power came back on, and the killer opened the bathroom door to rinse the blood and pieces of brain off his suit. The stench of death clung to him. Behind him was a scene straight from hell. Bloody bodies lay askew at odd angles. The eyes of the dead stared into the high corners of the room. Alejandro sat on the toilet, weeping.

His cheeks burned as the man laughed at him. Alejandro covered his private parts, his pants around his ankles. The killer smacked his head so hard that he flew sideways off the toilet and piled up between the toilet and the wall. The man washed his hands and checked his reflection in the mirror.

"You must be the lookout," he sneered. "Too small and too stupid to do any of the work. You couldn't even do that right. Pitiful."

Alejandro wept as the man dried his hands, taking his time to straighten the towel after he was finished.

Without warning the killer drew his leg back and lined up for Alejandro's stomach. The blood from the warehouse had spread under the door, and as the killer went for the kick, he slipped. The kick glanced off Alejandro's shoulder. Lurching to keep his balance, the killer fell to one knee and floundered between the toilet and wall.

Alejandro's mind came back into his body. He jumped to his feet and lifted the massive pipe wrench that had been propped behind the toilet. The cold steel of the wrench felt mighty in his small hand as he turned and brought it up, stretching as high as he could, then hammering it down on top of the man's head.

The man fell to the floor, dazed, but still conscious. Over and over, Alejandro lifted the wrench and let it fall. Now the man sounded like the people in the warehouse, screaming and pleading for his life as an eight-year-old bashed in his face, then his skull. The killer's brains spilled like soup from a bucket. All Alejandro saw was the cold dead stare of the people in the room. He imagined his grandma among them.

Word got out of the boy who had killed the killer. Alejandro's life improved, but he never smiled after that day. He flew up the ranks of the cartel and became a *sicario* by the time he was fifteen. He took contracts and made a name for himself by killing the enemies of the CDG and protecting their turf. The *soldados* of Los Zetas, Sinaloa, the Mexican army, even the agents of the United States fell before the slash of his blades and the blast of his guns.

Every time he killed, he saw the face of the man in the bathroom, mocking him for his failure to protect his flock. But each time the light would go out in his victim's eyes, that face faded a little.

Brilliantly ruthless and elegantly brutal, he soon became known as "*El Demonio*," the Demon. His skill with both guns and knives became legendary. His story travelled like wildfire, told among the members of other cartels like mothers scaring children with tales of the boogeyman.

He trained every hour that he wasn't stalking his prey. He became an expert in stealth and tracking. He studied meditation and learned English. He became a proficient medic, and treated his own wounds, which made sense since he always worked alone. Training until he bled or passed out from exhaustion, it never completely erased the memory of that day in the bathroom. He was the consummate killing machine, wrapped in the body of a lean teenager, driven by the cold rage of his secret shame.

Nobody knew of that shame except his sister, Maria. Maria was the only family he had left--the one shining spot in a world of soul sucking darkness. Her smile was brighter than the sun and her laugh sweeter than any music. His sister embodied everything that was right in the world, and his status allowed him to shelter her from the ugliness. She attended private school, and under his protection, sidestepped the ways the cartel used young girls.

He visited her on the weekends. Still, he never smiled. They told stories and comforted each other as they cried, remembering their parents. They dreamt of one day escaping together. Maria wanted to go to Europe and Alejandro dreamed of escaping to America and becoming a businessman. With her he almost felt whole.

Lightning snapped him back to the present. The storm raged around him, and he felt one with the tempest. As the rain beat down his face, he could almost taste the salt from the tears he had shed the day he'd found her nude in the ditch at the edge of town, splayed akimbo like a rag doll that'd been shaken and torn. He'd tortured three men—cartel brothers all--before he learned the truth: she'd been raped and murdered by their latest clients—the Muslims. Those unholy fucks.

Alejandro left that night, driving straight through until dawn; until he'd reached Chiquilla. He passed through the perimeter at the beach under the guise of a late arriving sentry. It'd be his last job for the CDG, and not a single man in or around the camp would be spared his blade. He couldn't care less what they were doing—but they would certainly die.

The muffled sounds of a battle startled him out of his thoughts. Men shouted frantically on the radio as all hell broke loose in the camp. There had been an intruder. He had no idea what that meant to his mission. There were no friendlies tonight. There would be no friendlies ever again.

The tarp slapped and stung against his face as the storm raged. Even so, he lit a smoke and delighted in the chaos and skin-deep pain. Movement, different from the wind, jostled the undergrowth not thirty feet away. He ground the butt under his heel, focusing his predatory sense.

The static from his earpiece startled him. "The Imam has been hit. Six casualties. Intruder still alive," the disembodied voice barked in his ear.

Alejandro must know if the Imam had been killed. Murdering that glossy-eyed piece of shit was his first priority. He prayed it'd be *his* knife to drain that dog, but a storm like this took who it would take.

Alejandro felt more than saw the man crawling through the jungle. Hot on his trail, less than fifty yards away, was a loud group of Middle Easterners, blathering in their nasal language. Their searchlights crisscrossed the jungle as they closed in on the intruder.

Alejandro let the man slither past—if he had to choose, he would definitely take the foreigners first. Whether the solo intruder was Zetas, CIA, DEA, Israeli or any one of the dozens of enemies of the Muslims, Alejandro didn't care. The interloper certainly hadn't been the one to violate his sister, which put him way down the list of targets of opportunity.

He grabbed his guns and slipped into the night, creeping through the jungle behind the man, biding his time and planning his ambush.

Nick

DARKNESS.

Swish, swish, swish
Dampness.
Swish, swish, swish
Pain.
Swish, swish, swish
Nick's head throbbed as he flitted in and out of consciousness.

His hands dangled, each bump and dip jostled him as a man dragged him through the jungle. Their wet fatigues swished the cadence of approaching death.

He concentrated on his leg, feeling the emptiness of where his Glock should be.

"Over here! I've got him!" his captor shouted in Spanish.

Nick was now fully conscious, his captor coming into focus. The man was thin, with dark hair. He wore black fatigue pants and a plaid shirt, open at the neck. Judging by the way he dragged him through the jungle, he was strong.

Up ahead, Nick heard multiple voices; hasty conversations in both Spanish and Arabic. Light danced across his eyes as the group closed on him. Nick's captor stopped abruptly, leaving Nick's body posed at an awkward angle. The group of men was still ten yards away and Nick played possum. He kept his eyes almost shut, hoping they would think he was still out. A voice in his head whispered, *grenades*.

A Hispanic man separated himself from the others and approached with authority. He was decked out in full cowboy attire with a straw hat and rodeo belt buckle. Not jungle warfare attire, but flamboyance was common among Mexican cartels.

"Was he alone?" he asked as he stopped in front of Nick, the turquoise and red diamond pattern of his cowboy boots staring Nick in the face.

Well howdy, Tex, Nick thought. Being almost dead did nothing to quiet his internal comedian.

"Yes. I found him heading south in the jungle, toward the road," the man standing over Nick replied.

"Our patrol just reported in. They found a Jeep five miles in that direction," Tex said as he smiled and pointed in the direction Nick had been heading. "They disabled it. It won't be driving anyone anywhere."

Fuck. Bad news. At least I was heading in the right direction, he thought.

Tex pointed at Nick and said, "The Imam wants to interrogate him."

Seriously? The Imam? This night just keeps getting worse and worse.

"You will be rewarded for this," said Tex, as he placed a hand on the shoulder of Nick's captor.

A look of realization came over his captor, quickly replaced by a scowl. "You have no idea," he said, his voice gravelly.

One second Nick was looking at the pattern on Tex's ridiculous boots, the next he was staring into Tex's eyes on the ground next to him, the light draining away. The moon cast a harsh shadow across the man's face. The metallic smell of blood flooded Nick's nose as it soaked into the ground, gurgling from a gash in his throat.

Then, the screaming started.

ALEJANDRO

The cartilage in the man's neck gave little resistance to the surgical sharpness of the blade as Alejandro swept it across his neck.

Chish chish chish, the blood sprayed like a sprinkler, the hot liquid splattered his face and cascaded down his clothes. He snatched the man's flashlight before it hit the ground, switching it off. The cowboy hat teetered for a moment and fell away. The man folded to the ground with a soft thud next to the American.

At least he thought the man was American. He'd mumbled garbled English as Alejandro checked his pulse after whacking him with the butt of his pistol. The man kept murmuring about death apples. He hadn't wanted to hurt him, but had no choice when the idiot tripped and went down firing his gun. The old man was a menace, but not necessarily an enemy.

Thirty feet away, emerging from the jungle, four men chattered in Arabic, their hands making wild gestures as they spoke. Flashlights were tucked into their armpits, pointing at the ground. They were oblivious to the demon stalking them.

One of the men looked up. "What happened to the Mexican?" he asked in Arabic.

"He's mine now," the darkness replied. The night came alive with a glint of steel. Alejandro sliced the first man from waist to sternum, exhaling as he claimed his soul. The entrails spewed out like candy from a piñata. The man fell screaming as he slipped on the intestines of his friend.

Alejandro leapt high and came down with both feet on the man's face, pushing his teeth through the back of his neck as blood and brains gushed with a loud *pop*.

Pirouetting on one leg like a dancer, he kicked the man opposite from him squarely in the chest, the *whoosh* of his breath exploded from his lungs as it replaced his frantic scream. Launched backward by the kick, he flew into his fleeing friend, and both landed on the ground in a tangled heap.

Alejandro pounced, a blade in each hand stabbing both men through the heart at the same moment. He paused, closed his eyes and listened for their last breaths. Not five seconds had passed since the first cut.

Alejandro stood up and wiped his blades on his pants, his blood ringing in his ears like a freight train. He replaced the blades in the kydex scabbards on his back with a soft *click*. He knelt to collect his thoughts. His breathing slowed. Calm washed over him as he went through his mental exercise. He looked toward the lights of the camp, and then back to where the American lay, still unconscious.

Who was he? What was he doing here? Alejandro wondered if, somehow, this was his chance to escape this life. Soon the question was replaced with the image of Maria, her decomposed corpse festering in the sun. The blood of the Imam called to him.

The American was on his own.

Nick

NICK GROANED from the pain in his back as he sat up, alone in the jungle. Not precisely alone. He was surrounded by the life-impaired. His knees creaked and he scowled in the dark.

I'm getting too old for this shit, he thought for the millionth time.

He cocked his head and listened intently. He heard only the noise of the jungle and the muted sounds of the camp in the distance. He was dying of thirst, his mouth dry and gritty. His saliva felt like paste as he ran his tongue over his teeth. Thank God he still had his pack. He opened it and the camera seemed remarkably no worse for wear. It had been chosen for jacked up missions like this. He found his canteen and shook it, frowning as he stuck his fingers into the thirty caliber holes in its side, the plastic rough and jagged.

He turned and faced the dead cowboy. "Hey Tex, nice to meet you." He leaned down and searched the denim pants. Turning the dead man on his side he smiled. "Ooooh wee!" he exclaimed, coming up with a chrome plated 1911 with pearl inlays in the grip. "That's some 'rootin tootin' hardware ya got yerself, don't mind if I do." He slipped the pistol in the back of his waistband. Looking down at Tex he tipped his non-existent hat and grinned. "Yippee ki-yay, motherfucker."

He waded through the jungle, throwing his arms out to catch his balance as he nearly slipped on another body. He picked up one of the discarded flashlights and shined it around, marveling at the horror and carnage created by the dude who'd beat him up only twenty minutes prior. Nick gingerly side-stepped something he was pretty sure was a liver.

"Holy shit!" he whispered as he surveyed the scene. "You're one bad hombre, but I like your style. Especially the part where you let me live." He picked up one of the AK's and wiped the blood and chunks of grey matter off of it, disentangling an eyeball hanging by the optic nerve from the barrel shroud. He checked the magazine and picked up a few more spares off the bodies around him.

What the hell am I going to do now? he thought. His brow furrowed as he wrapped his head around what seemed to have happened. *Why had the sentry in the jungle knocked him out instead of killing him? Why had one of their own taken out Tex and four of the Arabs?* He definitely didn't have the whole picture.

For sure, he wasn't driving out in his Jeep. Walking out would be iffy at best. He was at least thirty-five miles from the paved road, and he guessed another seventy back into town. He had no food or water, was injured, and there was at least one roving patrol out there somewhere.

No bueno.

Stealing one of the trucks from the camp was an option. He'd still have to worry about the roving patrol. With a little luck he'd be back in town by noon, transmitting his data and warning his contact at the pentagon. He could be drunk by sundown.

He made one last sweep of the area and *whoop whooped* under his breath when he shifted one of the dead Arabs and came up with a canteen half full of water. He grinned as he gulped it down, pretending it was tequila.

"Ahhh!" he mumbled, wiping the water from his chin. His hands were smeared with blood, none of it his.

There's still some fight left in this dog, he thought as he jogged back toward the camp. The aches in his stiff muscles loosened as he rambled through the dense undergrowth.

He stopped at the edge of the jungle. The storm had moved on just as fast as it had arrived and a half moon lit the scene. The large tent was half flattened in the sand, knocked over from the storm after he had punched through the wall and detonated a grenade inside. Half the small tents were knocked over. The warm breeze whisked his face. The flaps of the tents still standing blew back and forth like forgotten flags. All the tents were empty, and he saw only two boats left in the bay. A forty foot sloop was at the dock, the Imam's men loaded it frantically. The shrill staccato of the Imam's voice carried on the wind. The last boat, a fifty-foot catamaran, was anchored two-hundred yards away in the bay, just past the gentle break of the surf.

Nick rubbed his chin. He didn't see any cartel thugs.

Wonder what that's all about? He scanned the scene again and came up empty. His shoulder still ached where the shrapnel had hacked into it. It was now more of a dull throb and the bleeding had stopped. Dried blood glued his shirt to his skin.

His eyes landed on a cargo truck parked within rock-throwing distance. He caught the low rumble of the diesel as it idled. It was unattended, except for the dead guy covered in blood, his pants around his ankles, leaning against the front tire....

Wait a minute... that doesn't belong, he thought just as the truck exploded with a *whump,* followed by a giant fireball rising slowly into the night sky. The heat from the blast singed the hair on his skin and tossed him on his back.

ALEJANDRO

The driver had stopped to take a leak, leaving his truck idling. He'd dropped his pants and held his piss in mid-stream at the sight of a blood-covered demon exploding from the jungle. Alejandro flicked his throwing knife into the gaping maw of the man's open mouth, severing his spinal cord from his brain stem. It bought him the split-second he needed to cover the distance and palm-thrust his Boker through the driver's heart.

Alejandro smelled the ammonia as the man's bladder released in death, resuming its stream as he lowered him to the ground and leaned him against the front tire. Alejandro recovered his knives and wiped them on the man's shirt.

He scanned the camp, not seeing any of the men from the cartel. Trucks were missing and he guessed they had fled as soon as the storm ended. Most of them had been locals and weren't full-time cartel. Even if they were, this was a client's camp. Nobody was paid enough to risk death for foreigners. As soon as shots were fired and the grenades went off, he pictured the local help scattering like cockroaches at the first opportunity. The Imam's hardened fighters would be a different story.

Exactly as he'd hoped.

Across the camp a boat idled up to the dock. The Imam's remaining men unloaded cargo from a truck and readied it on the dock to transfer to the boat. The Imam stood on the dock and directed them with frantic gestures. They didn't seem to want to finish the fight.

Alejandro's pulse quickened. He would burn this place to the ground and kill every soul. He would annihilate them.

He walked to the back of the truck and yanked crates out, throwing them to the ground. The contents flew across the sand. He pawed through grenades and bricks of C4 until he found what he was looking for: the detonators.

He grabbed a grenade and shoved it in his pocket. His eyes widened as comprehension rolled over him, the words of the American echoing in his head.

Manzanas de la muerte...death apples.

Snatching up a brick of C4, he plunged the detonator into it and set the timer for five minutes. He pushed the button and slapped the brick under the fuel tank. He slipped into the jungle and skirted the camp, looping toward the Imam and his men.

Minutes later, he stepped out of the jungle just up the beach from the dock. The water was cool as he slipped into the ocean, cleansing his body and soul of the sins of the night. He silently swam toward the men. His strokes were graceful, barely causing a ripple on the gentle surf.

As they finished loading the boat, half the men jumped on board and it inched away from the dock, leaving only six men and the Imam. Across the camp, the truck finally exploded. The Imam and his men raced down the dock toward the beach. Their faces belied their panic. The fire painted the ocean in reds and yellows as the demon surfaced, seemingly baptizing himself in flame. He climbed onto the dock behind them, a gun in each hand. As he got his knees under him, the two pistols spit death. They rocked his hands gently back and forth as he cut the men down from behind.

The Imam turned to face him. The slides on both guns locked back empty. Spent brass casings tinkled to the dock and reflected the flame.

Behind the Imam, Alejandro watched a truck speed into camp. Dirt flew up from the front of the truck and it flipped, spilling men from the bed onto the sand. Gunshots rang out as they dove for cover, returning fire into the jungle, away from him. *Probably the American;* the gadfly thought buzzed past Alejandro as he took his time with his prey.

The Imam had nowhere to run. He pulled a curved dagger from his hip and charged Alejandro. His empty guns clattered to the dock. Alejandro pulled the grenade from his pocket and popped the pin as he allowed the dagger to pierce his skin at the waist. He wrapped the Imam in a bear hug and the force of his charge threw them both into the flickering water.

The water enveloped Alejandro like a warm blanket, and he let the Imam kick and flail, pulling him closer with each movement. He watched the bubbles of their breath circle upward as they sank. Het let go of the Imam and peace flowed over him. His hand holding the grenade was empty, the pocket of the Imam's robe was not.

The explosion filled the water with a cloud of bone and blood. The last image Alejandro saw before the world went entirely black wasn't the Imam, but of his sister's smile. The demon who never smiled, smiled back.

Nick

The fireball climbed higher in the sky as flames on the ground licked at the jungle in front of him. Rubbing the knot on his head, he watched a truck round the corner and charge through the sand straight for him. He raised his AK and went to work.

He saw the look of surprise on the driver's face turn to determination as he zeroed in on him. It took one smooth movement for Nick to reach into his pocket, pull out his last grenade, yank the pin and toss it in front of the speeding truck. The truck rolled over it at the perfect moment. The tire exploded and the truck careened sideways. The sandy pit ate the back tire and sent the men in the bed flying through the air.

Diving to the side, Nick opened up with the remainder of his mag. Invisible ropes of death coursed into the cartel patrol as they scrambled for cover. He levered the empty mag out and replaced it with one from his pocket.

The two remaining men returned fire. One of the rounds hit home, ripping through the front of his thigh and exited out the other side, barely missing his femur and femoral artery. It felt like his leg had been hit by a bat, the muscle contracting into a knot the size of a softball. Blood pumped out of both wounds in perfect time with his heartbeat.

Another bullet tore through two of the fingers of his left hand, splintering the wooden foregrip of the AK.

Worthless Russian garbage. He tossed it aside.

He struggled into a half-crouch and pulled Tex's fancy 1911 from his waistband. Resting the pistol across his injured forearm, he took careful aim, releasing half a breath as he squeezed the trigger and nailed the men to the ground with perfect double-taps to center mass.

Wahoo! Nick yelled in triumph. He had to give it to himself: his shot placement—particularly given the handgun—had been *fucking amazing*, particularly given that he was likely dying.

He scanned the dock for the man in black and the Imam. He didn't see either of them. He dragged his leg across the sand, using the AK as a cane. The barrel was still red hot from the gunfight, and he blistered his one hand that still worked. His other, blown apart hand struggled to stop the bleeding in his leg while managing its own mangled fingers.

He collapsed on the unforgiving planks of the dock. The wound on his shoulder reopened and the blood flowed down his back once more. Nick thought about screaming, but his throat was too dry to make the effort.

What he needed right now was a tequila. Rather, a double.

He crawled the last few feet. He stopped to rest. His head spun like a top. The world went dark and came back again. He resumed crawling, making it another ten feet.

Plop.

Plop.

Plop.

He was dying.

The sound of his blood dripping through the slatted wood onto the water beneath became his world as he clung to life.

He would never make it back to town.

He would never warn his country

He would never drink tequila again.

Ouch, that last part hurt. Darkness overcame him.

ALEJANDRO GASPED for breath as he came to consciousness on the beach, water pooling in his ear, waves lapping at his feet. He rolled over and gazed in wonder at a sky filled with a tapestry of stars. His whole body ached and spasmed with pain as he rolled onto his hands and knees and vomited, giving the saltwater back to the ocean.

The body of the Imam had absorbed most of the blast. He thanked God for his life.

He put a finger beside one nostril, then the next, and blew salt-water, snot, and blood onto the sand. He half choked on the acrid smoke in the air as the fires on the beach burned themselves out and not a soul moved.

He limped back to the dock, finding only bodies. He spied a dark lump halfway to the end of the dock and his eyes went wide with recognition.

"No way," he whispered only to the corpses. "Fucking Americans..."

He hurried over to find the American bleeding, unconscious, and with barely a pulse, but still alive. He took pity on him, unable to kill anymore tonight. Besides, this man wasn't his enemy.

He scanned the beach and saw only destruction, every vehicle either burning or burnt to the ground. Desperation washed over him as he searched for a way out of this hell. His eyes fell on the last boat in the bay, loafing just past the surf. A glorious gleaming white catamaran.

Jumping into the dinghy tied to the dock, he dragged the dead weight of the American after him, the body rocked the boat as it landed with a loud *thunk*. He moved forward and pulled hard on the rope on top of the outboard motor, each pull agonizing in its effort. On the fourth pull, the little motor coughed to life, sputtering as he engaged the gear.

He motored toward the boat, the sky growing lighter in the twilight of pre-dawn. As he approached, he read the word, "Wayfinder," painted across the bow. He smiled at the irony of the name.

Tying the dinghy off to the stern cleat, he climbed the sugar scoop of the starboard hull, gently pulling the American into the cockpit of the large boat. The wide smudged trail of blood leading off the deck on the other side answered the question of what had happened to the previous owner.

He barely felt the American's thready pulse through his fingertips. Alejandro smiled wryly as he located a first aid kit inside the large box on the deck stenciled with a big red cross on its side. He cleansed the many wounds on his patient, dousing them with alcohol before applying the dressings impregnated with *Qwik-clot* and wrapping them tight.

He just might make it.

He struggled with the anchor, creasing his brow until he found the right combination of buttons and levers. Pleased as he found the key in the ignition, he turned it and the diesels quickly caught and purred to life. Nudging it into gear, the boat gracefully crept forward, the sun peaking over the horizon as he motored out of the bay.

He had never sailed a boat before, but he whooped and hollered, realizing he was finally going to America to find his way.

7

OUT OF THE FRYING PAN

by **R. Chris Yates**

When the shit hits the proverbial fan, luck will be the fickle mistress of every man. For each dude with a bulging bug out bag and a fully-stocked survival retreat, there will be ten thousand wanderers going "all in" hoping Lady Luck throws them an inside straight.

R. Chris Yates, the author of The Swamp and Homesick, plays out a desperate gamble as Jim and Jane find themselves flat-footed and dangling in the wind at a food truck owners' convention when it all goes to hell. Will luck and grit be enough, or will they see the light of a new day?

-Jason Ross

Another day stuck in the bed and breakfast wore on Jim's nerves. He scanned the living room where most of the stranded guests had gathered. Several board games lay strewn around, along with packs of playing cards, books and magazines - anything to help pass the long hours while everyone waited for the crisis to end.

The streets had become increasingly dangerous since power

had gone out. As a result, no one had ventured outside for days. The bed and breakfast bore the smell of sweat, stale nicotine, and spoiling food in the kitchen. The board games and magazines had long lost their distraction. Trying not to worry had become their full-time occupation. Still, they tried to make the best of it.

Jim looked down at the cards in his hand and wondered if the pair of nines was worth risking his few remaining coins. He glanced up at Jane, who sat across the table from him. Her expressionless face gave away nothing. Her eyes bore into his. She could always read him like a book. Averting his gaze, he glanced over at the other two players. They look bored.

Jim contemplated going all in. Why not? What did he have to lose? Jane shifted slightly and caught his eye. Looking up, he saw she was staring intently at him. A faint smile curled the corner of her mouth, and she gave him a double wink with her right eye. He knew her well enough to know what that meant and dropped his cards to the table. "I fold."

Jim sat back in his chair and watched his wife take the pot with a full house. He was glad that the hand was over and that his wife had mercifully not cleaned him out.

"Well," Jim said, pushing his chair slowly back from the table, "that's enough for me. I am going to leave with what little change and pride I have left."

Jane stood also. "I think I am done as well. Night everyone."

Jim took her hand and led her up the stairs to their room, slipped into their light sleepwear and crawled into bed in the darkness. Jim reached over for his wife and she drew herself closer to him.

"What should I do with my winnings?" Jane joked.

"You better save them. You married a terrible poker player." In the dim room Jim could just make out the familiar smile lines in Jane's face.

"Hopefully tomorrow..." Jane's voice grew soft and hesitant, "we'll find out something. It's gone on so long."

Jim thought about what to say. He searched for encouraging words but found none. He pulled Jane closer and they held each other in silence until drifting off to sleep.

Loud voices woke Jim. He automatically sat up in bed. From years of habit, he reached over and felt for Jane. Finding her still beside him answered his first immediate panic, and he felt himself relax slightly. He'd always had an irrational fear that she would disappear while he slept. Feeling her warmth beside him had always been comforting.

A piercing shriek from the street below triggered his heart to skip a beat. Under his hand he felt Jane's body tense, as she too jerked awake.

"What was that?" she gasped, closing her fingers over his. The tightness of her grip betrayed her growing sense of fear.

Jim reached his free hand over and pulled the curtain aside. Still dazed, he strained to make sense of what he saw.

"There's a bunch of guys outside, one of them with an air horn."

"Is it the police?" she asked hopefully. "Is it someone coming to help?"

Jim glanced at the alarm clock on the dresser. Of course the clock was dark. The power was still out. Electricity had been the first to go. Then the internet and cellular networks. Initially, Jim had been relieved. The media coverage of the crisis put everyone on overload.

Everywhere you turned someone was watching news reports on televisions, phones and tablets about the nukes that had been going off. He liked to stay up on what was going on, but eventually it was the same information being repeated over and over. The lack of new information, along with the over analysis of the media was infuriating.

After a decade of marriage, Jane could sense what he wanted, and looked at the watch she wore. "it's just after one a.m...." she told him, holding up her Apple watch for him to see.

One of the men outside started calling out to the people inside. "Wakey Wakey!" He triggered the horn again, holding the button down for several seconds. "Who's in charge? You have some... things in there we want!"

Jim pulled the edge of the curtain aside and peered out again. A group of what looked to be young men in their late teens and early twenties gathered on the street facing the bed and breakfast. Each was dressed in stereotypical gang-style clothes: loose, baggy jeans and sports team jerseys. All had weapons. A few had rifles.

"Stay away from the window," he said in the calmest voice he could manage, "and get dressed."

Jim felt Jane's hand release and the bed shift as she slowly moved to find her clothes in the darkness. "What's going on?" she asked in a low voice.

He glanced back at her, just able to see her form in the dim moonlight filtering through the thin curtains. "There're some guys out there. I don't like the look of them," he answered, watching as the men began to spread out around the building.

Jim climbed out of the bed and moved to stand beside her. Jane handed him a set of clothes. Even in the darkness of the room, he knew it would be his jeans and one of his work shirts: a navy-blue polo with the company logo, a winged pig, and the name of his food truck "Oink and Cluck."

They had come to town for a weekend conference with a small business group he'd recently joined. Meetings and conferences were not really his thing, but he had joined for the health insurance discount offered to group members. Jane had talked him into coming out for the event in hopes of making contacts for his small but growing business of food trucks.

The closure of the airport and all public transportation had left them stranded at the bed and breakfast for an extra four days.

"I am sure the guard has already radioed for help," he reassured her, "the police will be here shortly."

"Do you think they'll come?" she asked as she anchored her hair in a bun with chopsticks. Even now Jim found himself amazed how women could make something so complicated look so easy.

He considered the question before answering. "Yes, they will."

For the last two days, they'd only seen one cop. The officer stopped by and said they were shorthanded, but that they were still around. Jim sensed that the policeman had understated the problems, but when no other police had stopped by, he began to expect the worst.

As he pulled on his shirt, Jim and Jane made their way down the stairs to join the group trickling into the front room. He looked around for the guard but couldn't find him. The owner of the bed and breakfast, a retired attorney, stood by the entrance talking to one of the men from outside. Through the open door, Jim could see the other gang members gathered behind their apparent leader.

"What's going on?" Jim asked a man reeking of gin standing nearby. The guy staggered slightly.

"The guard took a look at this group and handed his guns to them and they let him run off," he answered, disgust weighing heavily on his face. "Bill, the owner, is asking them to leave us alone."

Jane spoke up, "Did anyone get in touch with the police before he left?"

Another person nearby answered, "No. We couldn't reach anyone."

Jane stepped closer to Jim and gripped his arm tightly. He knew she only did that when she was truly scared, which was not often. A big part of his initial attraction to her had been her fearlessness.

Jim turned his attention back to the conversation at the door, trying to make out what was said over the murmurs of the group in the crowded lobby. But when the manager suddenly slammed and locked the heavy wooden door, he knew it hadn't gone well.

The slam of the door caused a collective gasp from those gathered into the tight space. Jim felt a change in the crowd as their fear began to rise. He knew they would soon panic if someone didn't speak to them.

"Everyone stay calm," the owner urged, "I've asked them to leave us alone. Hopefully they will."

As if on cue, something heavy slammed into the door. A woman screamed. A second impact. The gang outside was trying to break down the door.

The drunk man Jim had spoken with yelled, "They're coming in!" causing the crowd to press back away from the entrance. Pushed along by the surging bodies, it was all Jim could do to reach for Jane's arm and keep her close to him.

The door shuddered under impact but held firm. Jim allowed himself to believe the thick oaken barrier would be enough to keep them safe.

Jane's nails dug into his skin, and she gasped. "Jim, what do we do?"

"Help me find a weapon, a club or something," he answered, "and get ready."

Jim looked around the room. His eyes fell on an unlit lamp. He grabbed it and snatched its cord free from the wall. He hefted the lamp in his hand, feeling its weight. It wasn't ideal but better than nothing. Pulling off the linen shade, he considered himself armed.

The window beside the front door exploded in as a flowerpot from the porch flew through it. Shortly after a leg appeared through the window followed by a head, as one of the gangbangers climbed into the room. Jim released his grip on Jane's arm and rushed toward the intruder. He smashed the lamp down hard on the man's head.

The base of the lamp made a sickening sound as it struck skull bone, and Jim felt pain as the impact reverberated up his shoulder and stung his muscles. The intruder collapsed at his feet. Jim stared down at the blood-covered lamp, fighting back nausea.

The angry, raised voices outside reacted at seeing one of their own go down, and several gunshots rang out in the night. Bullets punctured the walls, and one of the men, huddled inside, fell silently to the ground, a red hole appearing in his cheek.

The room erupted into panic as people tried to rush in several directions at once, toward whatever their brains perceived as safety. In the rush, several people were knocked to the ground and trampled.

"JANE!" Jim yelled as he hurried to where he'd left her.

From outside, a voice yelled out "LIGHT 'EM UP!" Jim tensed.

Jane pressed herself tightly against a wall to avoid the milling rush as people moved back and forth across the tight space.

Somewhere behind them, breaking glass caught his attention. The panicked cry of "FIRE" sounded through the house. Seconds later the shrill screech of a fire alarm added to the clamor.

Jim yelled to Jane, "Hold on..." as the crowd around them surged toward the door the manager hurriedly unlocked. In seconds, they were pushed out the door and into the range of the gangbanger's swinging clubs and slashing knives.

Jim realized he'd dropped his improvised weapon when he rushed back to find Jane. Unarmed, he faced the furious gang. In a flash, a man rushed up and swung a bat at him. He felt it connect, but was out before he hit the ground.

THE DARKNESS slowly receded as Jim's mind struggled to swim up the inky wash of unconsciousness. Above him, the swirl of nothingness resolved into the shape of rooflines and a patchwork of stars.

He felt for the throbbing spot at the base of his skull, and his hand came away wet and sticky. He examined his crimson stained fingers in the thin light and concluded it could only be blood. The memory of the punk with the bat rushed back to him and a surge of adrenaline helped clear his mental fog.

"JANE!" he yelled into the night, though the volume of his own voice drove the frozen pain of a spearpoint through his skull. Every movement caused a rush of nausea, and he retched onto the pavement. Only when his stomach emptied was he able to regain his senses.

Struggling to lift his beaten frame off the ground and to his feet, he noticed the carnage around him. The yard and street were littered with the bodies and belongings of the others in his group. The structure and roof of the bed and breakfast was still burning vigorously, so he knew he hadn't been unconscious for long.

"JANE!" he yelled again as he began searching for her.

He turned to the lifeless form next to him and recoiled. He barely recognized the man from the business convention. His skull had been reduced to a flattened mass of bone and blood-matted hair.

He stepped over the man to the next body, splayed awkwardly on the grass. Aside from funerals, Jim had never seen a dead body before. Here were two. Both brutally beaten almost beyond recognition. Jim struggled to comprehend how this savagery could exist in civilized society.

His mind raced back to a week before. The Independent Business Owners of America conference. The break-out sessions. The meet and greets. Drinks and appetizers. It all seemed like another world now. Then, a nuclear attack in the Middle East. Next Los Angeles. Then the power grid fell and the descent into hell began. It took far less time for the truly violent to shake off the restraints of civility than Jim could have ever imagined. It had all felt surreal until this had happened tonight.

"How could it have all gone downhill so fast?' he thought as he checked the dead around him.

Jim distracted himself from the mental trauma of turning over the dead in search of his wife and anyone he could help, by letting his anger at the guard fill his head. Claiming to be an ex-cop, the man had talked a big game about offering protection. Instead, despite taking almost all their cash on hand, he abandoned them.

"Fucking Bastard!" Jim thought to himself as he bent down to check another pulse.

This one, a heavy-set man of middle age, was still alive. His eyes opened as Jim touched his neck to check for a pulse. The man groaned in pain as he came awake, and tried to sit up, eyes casting around in fear.

"It's okay," Jim said quickly, "they seem to be gone."

Jim checked the man over; a large wound gaped open on his forehead. The sagging skin revealed his skull bone. The front of his shirt was soaked with blood from the wound. Ripping the sleeve from his own shirt, Jim pressed the cloth against the wound, trying to force the two ends of the ragged slit together.

"Have you seen the woman I was with?" Jim asked, his voice cracking.

"They took all the women," the man answered weakly. "I saw them leading them away before I passed out."

"Where did they go?" Jim demanded, desperate for any information about his wife.

"They headed off that way," the injured man answered, pointing a bloody finger at the road leading north. "They took all the women they didn't kill. There were three of them."

"Can you walk?" Jim asked. "We have to go after them!"

Jim helped the man to his feet, but when the he grunted and collapsed back down, Jim knew it wasn't going to work.

"Sorry man, outside of my capability," he said, pointing at his left leg. "Something's wrong."

Jim looked down at the man's lower half and noticed his knee was bent at an odd angle and the joint swollen tight against the fabric of his jeans. His mind filled with the image of broken bones, torn cartilage and ligaments.

"We have to get you off the road," Jim told him. "Somewhere safe while I go find the women."

"No," responded the man, "Just go get them. I can drag myself over to that alley."

"Keep pressure on this," Jim ordered and placed the man's hand onto the cloth on his forehead.

"I got it. Go save your lady. I'll be fine!"

Jim started to protest, but before he could speak, he heard an airhorn shriek off in the distance.

Without thinking, he rushed toward the sound. After only a few feet, he glanced back, but the man was already dragging himself toward the shadowed alleyway. It would be slow progress but at least he was moving.

The fairly close, maybe just a few blocks away, scream of the airhorn sounded again. Jim hurried his steps despite the ache in his head with each footfall.

Feeling the back of his head, the blood felt both tacky and slick, indicating a mixture of drying blood and active bleeding. One finger found the actual wound and another one slid into the gap. The best he could tell, the split in his skin was at least two inches long by half an inch wide. He would need stitches, but that would have to wait.

He heard shouting ahead. Even without understanding the words, he knew the gang leader was repeating demands he'd made at the bed and breakfast. Jim slowed his pace, sensing the scene was just around the next corner.

Forcing himself to slow down to a walk, he did his best to take in the situation. The worst thing he could do was rush headlong into the group. Getting himself killed would accomplish nothing. People depended on him. Jim had never served in the military or been in actual combat. He had no experience to fall back on. He hoped his survival instincts would kick in. Somewhere, deep within, a part of him not necessary for civilized life, needed to wake up NOW! Especially the part that knew how to kill.

Jim peered around the corner of a building to see what was going on. The men he pursued were arranged in a semi-circle in front of what seemed to be another small hotel.

Beyond the standing crescent of thugs, he could make out movement from within the house. Shadows cast on the curtains from the candles or lanterns waved about. He could see more than one person inside. A sick, sour taste rose in Jim's throat as he recalled the panic in the bed and breakfast just prior to the attack.

He tried to remember the number of gang members earlier in the night and cursed himself for not counting them. With a sudden surge of panic that some of them might be behind him, he looked over his shoulder before settling himself to count his adversaries.

In front of the building, nine stood in the group now demanding that those inside come out unarmed. Jim made a mental note that the tallest man dressed in an oversized shirt and baggy pants, doing all the talking, must be the leader. It did not escape his notice that the man carried an aluminum baseball bat. The sight of it made Jim's head throb again.

Every member of the group carried a firearm, either slung over their shoulder, tucked into their waistband or held ready in hand. Many were armed with bats and even a few machetes.

Glancing subconsciously at his empty hands, Jim wished for a gun, or even a good solid pipe. He and Jane had decided it was faster to fly to the convention rather than drive. Due to airport security, he didn't even have the pocketknife he normally carried. He thought of all the knives and pans that filled his food truck back home, but scolded himself for the wasted mental effort.

Jim slunk around the corner to a shadowed area. Here he had a better view of the street and could scan the area, hoping to discover where other members of the gang may be hiding.

Commonsense told him some attackers would be around the back of the building, watching for anyone inside trying to escape. The Molotov cocktail that had started the fire at the bed and breakfast had come from the back. It made sense that the group would use the same method again. Before he could safely rescue Jane, he would need to know where all the bad guys were hiding or risk making himself an easy target.

Jim's eyes moved from shadow to shadow, until he caught a glimpse of movement at the other end of the block. Lifting himself slightly out of the darkness of the stairs, he could make out two men standing at the other corner of the same building he hid by. They stood watching the events unfolding as the gang leader made ever-increasing threats to those inside.

He focused on a man standing at the shadow's edge. Behind him there appeared to be several smaller figures. They seemed to be kneeling and huddled together. It was probably the captive women!

Jim fought the impulse to call out and rush forward toward Jane. Instead he forced himself to shrink back into his hiding place and think of a more effective plan. He couldn't afford to make a mistake.

Staying low, he skulked back around the corner and quietly worked his way down the block to station himself behind the men, still unsure of what he would do when he reached them. He cast his eyes around desperately for a weapon, anything he could use. The clean street provided nothing. He considered searching a few of the cars he was using to conceal his movements. Even if one was unlocked, the interior light coming on would be like a searchlight in the unpowered city and draw the bad guys down on him.

Jim glided around the last of the three corners and was now directly behind the men guarding the captives. He forced himself to slow down and place his feet carefully. With each step, he expected to be discovered. Fortunately, the men kept their backs to him, all their attention being held by the yelling between the people inside and the gang leader.

As he grew closer, the details began to clarify. He could make out the shapes of the two men and three women. One was clearly Jane, her head raised defiantly, glaring at the back of the men who held her captive. Another of the women was slumped low, shoulders moving in a quiet sob.

Jim's heart ached at the sight. A need to defend the women bloomed deep within his soul and it galvanized him into action.

Forcing himself to remain stealthy, he stepped slowly forward, across the thin strip of grass that bordered the building he had circled. As he approached the men, he finally saw his weapon.

Someone had tried to brighten the dull commercial building's small yard with a birdfeeder mounted on a shepherd's hook. The hook stuck into the ground and now leaned at a precarious angle.

Jane had bought a similar birdfeeder for their backyard, and Jim knew the ground end was a sharpened point. It would be unwieldy but he could make it work.

He carefully lifted the feeder from its hook and slowly placed it on the ground. He kept his grip on the feeder until he was assured it would not tip over. Then he firmly gripped the pole and pulled up with steady pressure. It resisted at first, but with a slight jerk it came free.

Not taking his eyes off the men, he felt for the tip of his weapon. The end was indeed sharp--created by cutting the pole at a 45-degree angle. Less than a foot from the bottom, a second prong protruded out and straight down. The second prong was also sharp.

Holding the pole like a spear, Jim began to move forward again with every bit of stealth he could muster. An icy feeling spread in his chest as he closed the distance. He worked up the nerve to do what had to be done.

He could hear the nearby confrontation escalating. On one

hand, the drama helped him as it held the attention of the guards. On the other, Jim knew he didn't have much time. Violence would erupt soon. To reach the guards, Jim had to move out into the open. If any of the gang members surrounding the hotel turned their heads in his direction, they would spot him.

He'd closed to within ten feet of the nearest guard and was about to make his move when a gunshot blasted across the night. Jim instinctively jerked back and ducked.

The report sent the men surrounding the building retreating behind the cars along the street. The two guards stepped back deeper into the shadows.

"Did you really just take a shot at me?!" yelled the leader angrily from behind the truck he had chosen as his cover.

A voice inside answered, "I will do it again!" The speaker's voice cracked as he spoke, likely from the stress and fear he'd been trying to hide.

"STUPID... FUCKING... MOVE..." the leader shouted back. "I might have let you live if you hadn't decided to be a DUMB ASS!" He placed a strong emphasis on the last word.

The man inside the house answered, "Get out of here while you can!" After a few seconds, he added, "We've called the police. They're on the way!"

The thugs outside chuckled, including the two nearest to Jim.

"No more police, asshole," the leader answered, a laugh evident in his voice, "didn't you hear?"

The sound of a baby's cry came from inside the hotel. Remembering the fire that had been set when his own group refused to give up, a cold chill ran up his spine. He knew they wouldn't wait much longer.

With this, the leader shouted a command. "Teach 'em a lesson!" At the same time, he raised his gun and fired several shots into the hotel. A window shattered.

Before he knew what was happening, Jim raised his improvised weapon and rushed toward the man closest to him. He drove the two sharpened ends firmly into the back of the guard's exposed neck. The sensation of piercing through flesh and sinew transitioned up through the pole into Jim's hands.

He pulled his weapon back sharply, freeing it from his victim, but the man didn't fall. Instead he turned slightly, as if to glance over his shoulder. As he twisted, a pulsating geyser of blood erupted from his throat. His face contorted as if to scream, but all that came out was a wet gurgle. He swayed and lost his balance. Jim turned to the other man and rushed forward. His quarry, a few feet away, had just spun toward the death rattle of his partner when the spear punctured his rib cage.

Using his momentum, Jim shoved the man against the wall behind him. The steel pole vibrated as the points struck and embedded into the mortar. The force of the impact stung Jim's hands and shoulders. The shock of his own capacity for brutality stunned him.

As Jim's hands fell away, the criminal reached up to grasp at the shaft. His eyes moved back and forth from the pole pinning him to the wall to Jim's own eyes. The look of disbelief gave way to anger and hatred. He opened his mouth to speak, but a thick gout of blood silenced him.

Jim held the man's gaze as the guard's eyes lost focus and his head and body went slack. The improvised spear kept the man upright and pinned to the wall. Jim heard a wet thump behind him and turned to find the first man had fallen and now lay motionless.

Jim turned to the huddled captives. Each woman was bound and gagged tightly. As he worked at the knots, the nearby gunfire tapered off. Glancing up, he was relieved to see all the gangbangers were still focused on the hotel. The sound of the shooting had concealed the noise of his attack.

"Stay quiet!" he ordered the women in a whisper as he removed their gags. The knots binding their wrists were too tight to untie in the dim light. Jim rushed back to where the dead guard was pinned to the wall and pulled a knife from the man's belt.

He returned to the captives and cut them loose as quickly as he could. Jane enfolded him in her arms in a fierce hug and began to sob. Jim held her tightly in return, but freed himself with a quick "I love you, but we have to get going."

He held still and scanned the group of killers surrounding the hotel. They were focused on their task at hand and none were looking in their direction. He felt himself release a breath he hadn't been aware he'd been holding.

"This is your last chance," the gang leader called to those he had under siege, "Shut that kid up. Give us your shit. Give us your women, or you all die!"

Jim could hear the infant still crying inside, and the sound made up his mind. Turning to Jane, he ordered, "Take the other women and go back to the hotel. Find someplace safe to hide. "

"What?" she protested. "Aren't you coming with us?"

He nodded toward the now bullet-ridden structure. "There's a baby in there..." he said simply.

She wrapped her arms around him again and laid a kiss on his cheek. "I love you," she said.

"I love you, too," he answered. "Now get going. I'll be along shortly. Don't come out for anyone but me. If I'm not back in an hour, try to get to safety."

Nothing further needed to be said or explained. Both knew that if Jim was not back in an hour, he would never be coming back.

Jane hesitated.

"Go!" Jim whispered firmly.

She moved away, pulling the other women along with clasped hands. Jim watched them fade into the darkness and disappear before he risked moving. He worried that any movement by him would draw the attention of the gang and limit the time the women had to escape.

Jim stayed low and gathered up what he could from the gang members he had just killed. He came up with one knife, a revolver, and a chrome semi-automatic pistol. He chided himself for his lack of firearm knowledge, wishing he'd taken all those offers from friends to learn to shoot more seriously

Studying the weapons, his eyes caught the sheen of blood covering his hands. He didn't know if it was his or someone else's, but the emotions of what he had done rushed up on him. He had taken the lives of at least two people tonight, and maybe a third. The contrast of his life one week ago sprang into his mind and he fought back tears. He spotted a dark corner in the building in front of him, and hunkered down while he waited to be sure the women didn't cry out, or that he heard gunfire in their direction. The tender moment with his wife brought his mind back to better days.

Jim had met Jane while working at the same restaurant. Jim worked as a cook and Jane was waitressing part-time while attending college. She was easily the smartest, strongest, most beautiful woman Jim had ever met. He couldn't believe she would be interested in him. Some days it still surprised him. For whatever reason, Jane saw everything good in Jim and it helped him be a better man. After endless dead-end cooking jobs, it was Jane that encouraged Jim to chase his dream and open his own food truck business. It wasn't easy, but together they made it happen. Jim worked night and day, but he had never been happier. After several years, the hard work had paid off and they were able to buy a home.

A discount on health insurance wasn't the only reason Jim joined the small business association. Truthfully, he hoped to learn some tips on how to grow his business. He envisioned several food trucks bearing the Oink and Cluck logo. Always the mind reader, Jane had suggested they come to this conference together. Initially Jim balked. Conferences and socializing weren't his cup of tea. But Jane could be persuasive, and soon they registered for the conference and purchased their flights.

The odd thought pushed into Jim's brain that if they hadn't come to the conference, their lives would probably still be normal. He'd be getting up at 5 a.m. to prep the food truck for the lunch rush. Jane would be dressing and heading to her job as vice principal for the local junior high. If they had just stayed home, everything would've been fine. Jim smiled wryly at his own illogical thinking. The crisis wasn't restricted to this one neighborhood. It was probably everywhere. Perhaps across the country. Perhaps, even global. Still, he couldn't shake the feeling that his old life was waiting for him if he could just somehow find his way home.

Forcing his mind back to the task at hand, he examined the two firearms. He couldn't find a safety on the revolver, so he assumed it didn't have one. He hoped it was just point and shoot. Flicking the safety off on the semi auto, he drew back the slide to make sure it had a round ready to go and thanked all the cop dramas and action movies he'd watched for showing him how to do that.

He flipped the safety on and tucked the gun into the back of his pants. The man he had taken it from kept it tucked under his belt buckle, but Jim didn't like the idea of where it pointed. He felt foolish for that paranoia but couldn't help it. Apocalypse or not, he preferred to keep his dick intact.

A sudden flair of light caught his attention. Looking up, he saw one of the bad guys had lit a piece of cloth that stuck from the end of a liquor bottle, and it now burned brightly. The leader called out from his hiding place behind the vehicle. "Throw the guns out the window and come out with your hands up or we burn this mother fucker down."

Jim took a deep breath and positioned himself at what he hoped was a good shooter's stance, sighting down the barrel at the man holding the makeshift incendiary device. He squeezed off three shots. The man spun and fell. The flaming bottle smashed against the ground and erupted into a bloom of flame which quickly engulfed the injured man. Screaming in agony, the man writhed and contorted as the inferno grew until the brightness hurt Jim's eyes.

Jim felt an eerie sense of calm as he turned the pistol toward the next target. He took aim and squeezed, feeling the recoil. Another man dropped. He saw movement and took aim.

Miss.

Second shot. Hit.

The man staggered but stayed on his feet. Jim pulled the trigger again. *Click.*

It surprised him that he was out of ammunition already. He thought he had counted carefully and still had at least one round. The sound of bullets striking the wall behind him spurred him into a run. He dove behind the nearest car as the windshield exploded into a shower of gummy safety glass.

Jim stuffed the revolver in a pocket and reached into his waistband for the semi-automatic. From his position, he could see underneath the car for approaching feet. He felt a bit of pride as he remembered to flick off the safety. Soon, he saw several pairs of feet running toward him.

Gunfire rang out and two of the approaching bad guys dropped. One went down in a heap, but the other rolled around crying out in pain. Jim realized the shots had come from the direction of the hotel. Whoever was inside was still in the fight. A flicker of much needed hope surged inside Jim.

He watched as the other feet heading toward him scrambled in several directions, seeking cover from the ambush. Two gang-bangers rushed behind a short wall. Unfortunately for them, their position was still visible to Jim.

Jim remembered a TV show he'd watched where someone said the secret to shooting was to "control your breathing." Not totally sure what that meant, Jim breathed out and slowly lifted the pistol until he could line up the sights on one of the bad guys.

Breathe. Aim. Squeeze. Breathe. Aim. Squeeze.

The man jerked as the bullets tore through him, painting the wall in chips of brick and sprays of blood, before he fell and lay still.

Jim stayed there panting for several minutes, listening to the sporadic exchange of gunfire between the gang and whoever was holed up in the hotel. He knew that several of the bad guys were now out of the fight, but not knowing how many were left, he was unsure how to proceed. Now that the rush of adrenaline was receding, indecisiveness took hold.

He'd heard nothing from the direction the girls had gone, so he assumed they'd gotten away safely. He would need to start moving in that direction soon if he hoped to catch up with them. He figured he should allow himself at least fifteen minutes to reach them.

On the other hand, he wasn't sure if it was safe to leave yet. Bad guys were still out there, and he didn't know where. He held no illusions they could not be sneaking up on him right now. Hadn't he done the same thing to them? Twice?

Forcing himself into action, Jim crawled forward toward the front bumper of the car and peeked around to survey the street. It appeared empty. The fire had gone out. Even though nothing was moving, Jim knew there could be enemies out there hunkered down like he was.

He fumbled around on the gun until he found the button that ejected the magazine, and using the cutout window down its side, he determined he had four shots left. Not many, but it would have to do. He rose to his feet slowly and peered over the hood of the vehicle, again watching for movement, but seeing none.

The street was quiet. The firing from the siege had petered out, and now no shouts or angry noises came from that direction. The only sound was the baby, still crying. Jim cocked his ear. Singing? A woman's voice? His heart leapt. The baby was still alive and someone was comforting it.

Using whatever concealment the shadows afforded, he made his way back to where he had freed the women. His hope was that the bad guys had scattered after being fired on from both directions, and they possibly left behind weapons and ammo.

From the shadows of his new hiding place, he again scanned the area. The fire had indeed gone out on its own, leaving only a charred corpse. From here he could see two other bodies in the street. The only movement was an occasional shift in the curtains covering the faintly lit windows across the street.

Jim decided the bad guys had cleared out and decided to risk communication with those inside.

"HEY!" he yelled out. "YOU GUYS SAFE IN THERE?"

He cocked his ears to hear an answer while straining his eyes for any movement in the dark. It took a full minute before he got an answer.

"YOU THE GUY THAT SHOWED UP AND HELPED US?" A male voice yelled from the direction of the hotel.

Jim followed the voice and could make out a man standing on the roof, barely visible over the half wall that lined it. "YEAH! YOU ALL GOOD?"

"YES," The man shouted back, "YOU WANNA COME IN? DO YOU NEED A PLACE TO STAY?"

"NO, I NEED TO GET BACK TO MY FAMILY," Jim answered.

"WELL... THANK YOU," the man said sincerely. "WE ARE GETTING OUT OF TOWN IN THE MORNING. I'D SUGGEST YOU DO THE SAME. NOW SHUT UP BEFORE YOU GIVE YOUR POSITION AWAY."

Jim waved and scampered away from the alcove into the street to search the bodies. The first body had a pistol but no ammo. Searching the second dead gang member, Jim found a switchblade tucked into the man's pocket, and transferred it to his own.

Glancing to the burned heap on the sidewalk, he decided to skip a search. Anything valuable would have been ruined by the flames.

With his scavenging complete, and knowing the people inside

the hotel were safe, Jim could finally make his way back to Jane and get the hell out of this town. The man inside had said they were clearing out in the morning, and the idea sounded good to Jim. Getting out into the countryside had to be better than this.

He started back toward the direction the women had run. As he jogged, he made a mental list of all the things they would need to find on his way out of town.

Food, blankets, ammunition... His thoughts were consumed with what hasty preparations he could make.

In a matter minutes, he found himself back in front of the burned-out bed and breakfast. He looked around for the women, but seeing no sign of movement, he decided to call out for them.

Cupping his hands to his mouth to amplify his voice, he took a breath to yell for Jane. Before his throat could form the word, he felt a spear of fire in his lower leg. Jim collapsed to the ground, face first into the pavement.

Shaking off the ground's impact, Jim forced himself to roll toward the concealment of a bus stop. Blood streamed down his leg and he used the remaining sleeve of his T-shirt to blot at the wound. He searched the shadows for whoever had shot him. Nothing moved or stood out.

Hastily he rolled up his pants leg. His calf showed an angry furrow of missing flesh where the bullet had grazed him and torn the skin away. It radiated a stinging agony, and the amount of blood flowing out was concerning. Jim pulled his shirt over his head and tied it around the wound as tightly as he could. The pain increased, but he hoped it would control the bleeding.

He reached back to draw the firearm, mentally scolding himself for not doing it earlier. He felt a cold lump form in his chest when his hand came away empty. The gun was gone. In a panic, he started slapping and feeling around for it.

"Looking for this?"

Jim felt the cold lump in his chest double in size as he looked up into the face of the gang leader. The man had one hand holding the crotch of his pants, keeping the saggy pants from falling. The other hand held the silver pistol, leveled at Jim's head.

A second man appeared at the gang leader's side, his gun held sideways pointed at Jim. Jim raised his empty hands and leaned back against the seat of the bench behind him. Despite the pain surging through his leg, he made a conscious effort to stay as still as possible.

"Yo, you that one that shot up my boys?" the leader asked.

"You took my wife," Jim responded.

"No reason for you to bust a cap at us," he answered. "No one fucks with the Belleview Posse. We take what we want, when we want." As he said the last part, he stepped forward and pushed the barrel of the gun against a fresh abrasion on Jim's head.

The pain seared from the force of the gun, but Jim resolved not to let the kid see him wince, and locked his face into a mask of anger. He used the chance to take in the pair standing in front of him.

Both were dressed like something from a Spike Lee movie, but Jim had noticed the absence of any visible scars or tattoos. In fact, both looked like actors playing a part. The hand that held the gun against his forehead was not calloused, and the nails showed the shine of being professionally buffed.

Seeing that he refused to respond to his torture, the young gang leader drew the gun back and slammed it into the side of Jim's head. Jim fell, struggling to retain his grip on consciousness. The kid drew his foot back and delivered a quick kick to Jim's gut.

The blow left him gasping, and he cradled his stomach, fearing another kick.

"Don't mess him up too bad, T-Red," the other captor cautioned, "he has to show us where the women are."

"You'd better just kill me then, Tread," Jim spoke between gasps.

The gang leader's face grew red, and he lashed out with his foot again, striking Jim in the face. "That's T-Red, fool!"

Jim's head snapped back and he tasted blood flooding into his mouth as something broke. Despite the pain, he coughed out a loud laugh. "If you're Tread, is he Traction?"

The other gang member reacted and brought his foot into Jim's stomach. "Call me AK, fucker!"

Spitting a mouth full of blood to the pavement, Jim shot back, "Ok, AK Fucker."

Blows fell on his body for what felt like an eternity. Jim recognized he should have felt more concern for the pain and damage being inflicted on him, but with each strike against his flesh, something shifted in his mind.

His tormentors had gone from objects of fear, transforming into objects of pity. He barely noticed when they stopped beating him and lifted him to his feet. The two dragged him into the center of the road and dropped him.

"So where are they, old man?" T-red asked as he loomed over him.

"Not a chance Tread," Jim spat. "You better just go ahead and kill me now."

The thug drew back his foot as if to kick again but held the movement. "Nah fool. If I don't get those girls I'm gonna do much worse."

As he spoke, he reached into his belt and drew a folding knife from a case. He glared down at Jim as he pulled the blade open, brandishing the knife's blade in Jim's face.

Jim felt another wave of laughter building up inside but forced himself to stifle it. Several angry retorts flashed through his mind, but he settled on one last try at reason. "There is nothing you can do to make me tell you where my wife is."

"We'll see about that," T-Red said as he brought his sneakers down on the wound on the back of Jim's calf.

This time Jim couldn't suppress the scream of pain, and it escaped his mouth as a bellow of agony. Instinctively reaching to grab the man's shoe and push it off the wound, he left a bloody smear on the immaculate white leather.

"JANE!" Jim yelled as loud as he could, ignoring the aching pain radiating through him. "Don't come out! Run away!"

T-Red snatched his foot back from Jim's hand and caught his balance as he stumbled. "Fucker got blood on my Kicks!" he exclaimed as he wiped his foot with the handkerchief from his head.

"If he is yelling to her," AK said, "she must be close..."

"Fucking ruined!" T-red complained. The white material on the toe showed a pink smear from where the blood had not come off completely. He abandoned the cleaning and turned his attention back to the man he had just been torturing. "You're gonna pay for that!"

The youth lifted the blade he held and drove it into Jim's calf several inches. The pain again raced up Jim's leg, traveling along his spine before nesting in his brain. A scream exploded from deep in his chest.

"Yo Jane," T-Red called out as he stood, "you hear that girl? Your man ain't doing so good. Better come out before he gets a whole lot worse."

"Don't do it, Jane!" Jim grunted as loud as he could through the pain as he clutched the wound. The makeshift tourniquet had fallen off while they had dragged him, and the blade had opened the wound even worse than before. A spreading pool of blood formed rapidly beneath his leg.

"Shut up, old man," AK ordered from where he stood near Jim's shoulders. "I am not gonna tell you again."

"Why are you doing this?" Jim asked. "The world's gone to shit; you should be trying to get somewhere safe..."

T-Red answered, "That's why we are doing this, fool. No cops. No rules. No more holding us back!"

"Yeah!" added AK. "We are claiming our turf! Everything around here is ours now. The food, the buildings, the cars and the pussy!"

The two men exchanged a high five to celebrate their new situation.

"You two are a joke," Jim said. "You may be tough ass punks here in the Bed and Breakfast district, but there's always bigger fish."

"What are you talking about, asshole?" AK demanded.

Jim smiled up at them. "The world's gone to shit in case you hadn't noticed," he said, "and in only a few days, most of your gang of homeys is already gone."

"Yo," T-red snapped back, "that's cuz you and those other dudes smoked 'em."

"Exactly," Jim said. "Mean ass thugs like yourselves, and all it took was a cook and a couple of tourists to wipe you out."

As he spoke, his mind raced frantically for what to do. Injured as he was, he doubted he could overcome the two men in hand to hand combat. He briefly considered grabbing for the gun or the knife, but he knew that wouldn't be as easy as it was depicted on TV. The risk of him being shot or knifed was too high. The only other option was to try to provoke the gangbangers to kill him. If that happened, Jane and the other two would have no reason to come out of hiding, and they could just wait for an opportunity to get away.

"In case you didn't notice," T-Red said. "You are the one laying on the ground bleeding."

"Yeah!" added AK.

"Lucky shot," Jim said calmly. "Why don't you toss down that gun and get rid of your blade? Tell your boy to stay out of it, and you and I can handle this like men."

T- Red drew the pistol from his waistband and stepped closer, pushing the barrel of the gun against Jim's temple.

From the corner of his eye, Jim saw the young man's finger tighten on the trigger. Jim closed his eyes tight, waiting for the end.

The next second stretched for what felt like an eternity, and Jim wondered if he would hear the explosion, or if it would suddenly just be over. Instead, it was a voice that made him open his eyes.

"STOP!" Jane shouted, "Don't shoot him!"

There was a panicked tone in her voice that Jim had never heard before, and it made his heart sink. She appeared out of the shadows of the building next to the ruins of the bed and breakfast and stopped at the edge of the moonlight, allowing herself be seen.

T-Red kept the gun against Jim's temple, but the pressure he'd been applying lessened, and his finger relaxed on the trigger. Jim forced himself to take several slow, deep breaths. The situation had changed, and he needed to keep his head. As slowly as he could, Jim moved his hand to feel for the lump in his pocket that was the knife he had taken from the dead man earlier. He found it where he had left it, a cold and heavy shape under the fabric on his right thigh. He slid his hand gently up the denim and down into his pocket, saying a silent prayer that the two thugs would have all their attention focused on his wife.

"It's about damn time, Bitch!" T-Red said scornfully. "Lift that shirt up and turn around slowly so I can see that you don't have no weapons…"

Jane did as she was told. Her pink bra glowed against her tan skin as she turned slowly. When she finished, she let the shirt fall to cover her midriff and stared at the two, awaiting their next command.

"Where are the other two chicks?" asked AK.

"They left," she explained. "We ran back here, and I stopped to wait for him. They kept going."

"Bullshit!" T-Red exclaimed, "They got nowhere to go. You better not be pulling nothing!"

As he spoke, he glanced around nervously, as if expecting to see one of the other females sneaking up behind him. When he saw nothing, he returned his attention to Jane.

"They were scared," she said.

"AK," T-red commanded. "Go tie the bitch up."

AK took a step toward her, but she stepped back.

"No," she said and pointed to Jim. "Let him go first."

"You got me all kinds of fucked up, ho!" T-Red said back. "I'm in charge here, you do what I say. AK, I said tie her up."

AK started forward again, and this time Jane let him close the distance, locking her hands together behind her head. He tucked the pistol he carried into the front of his pants before reaching into his back pocket and producing a length of white cord that Jim recognized as clothesline. He held it up as he approached.

Jane turned her head and locked eyes with Jim, ignoring AK. Jim was aware that the movement was very deliberate and not just a casual glance. She winked with her right eye twice in quick succession as a thin smile curved one corner of her mouth, and Jim caught the meaning instantly.

Glancing up past the barrel of the handgun into T-red's face, he saw that the gang leader was watching the woman with all his attention. Looking back to Jane, he mouthed the words 'On three' hoping that the man above wouldn't pick that instant to look down.

Jim felt down the length of the knife to find the button that would flip the blade out to the ready position and closed his hand around the handle.

"One..." he mouthed silently.

AK began patting Jane down.

"Two..."

Jim gripped the stiletto firmly in his hand, ready to thumb the release and thrust it upward into the gunman's abdomen.

He saw Jane take a deep breath as AK's hands lingered over her breasts in his supposed search for weapons. Still watching, T-Red licked his lips and let out a whoop.

"Three!"

Jim formed the shape of the word with his lips, counted half a heartbeat, and sprang into action. Pulling the knife from his pocket and driving it upwards as he hit the button to flip the blade out. The steel arced out in a silver blur and snapped into place just milliseconds before the point dug into flesh. At the same instant, Jim windmilled his other arm, knocking wildly at the firearm against his head hoping to dislodge it just enough to cause the inevitable shot to miss his brain.

Across the road, Jane moved at the same moment. Pulling her hands from behind her head, she produced two long items, one in each hand, previously hidden in her hair, and drove them into the sides of AK's neck with all the force she could muster. Jim suddenly remembered the chopsticks she had in her hair.

As if of a single voice, the two gang members let out screams of pain. AK fell to his knees and clutched at the thin sticks embedded into his throat. T-Red dropped his knife and gun and reached for the knife embedded in his stomach.

Jim wasted no time and scrambled for the discarded firearm as T-red staggered backward. Finding the gun, Jim stumbled into a shooting position with the gun pointed in the direction of the injured, stumbling T-Red.

The sight of T-Red's terrified face and blood-soaked pants made Jim hold his fire. He glanced over toward Jane to see she had pulled AK's gun from his pants and now had it trained on its former owner. AK collapsed to the ground and convulsed. Jane looked up at Jim, shock spreading across her face.

Jim returned his attention to the sole remaining threat. T-Red was now several steps away, and still trying to back away, both of his hands on the blade still protruding from his abdomen. Two more steps and T-Red would reach the bus stop where Jim had taken refuge earlier.

Jane rushed to Jim's side and kneeled beside him. "Are you okay?" she asked.

"My leg is messed up," he said. "But I will be okay. Help me up."

Jane called over her shoulder into the darkness. "Come help me!"

The other two women stepped out of the darkness that Jane had appeared from earlier. One was supporting the form of the heavyset man Jim had helped earlier that night. The other rushed over to help Jane lift Jim to his feet. The entire time, Jane kept the gangster covered with her pistol. As they got him to his feet, T-Red reached the bus stop and collapsed backward onto the bench, half seated, but leaning heavily to the side.

The small group moved in unison to stand in front of the slumped young man. A spreading puddle of blood was forming under the bench, and Jim noted that soon it would intersect the puddle he'd left there only a few minutes before.

"What should we do with him?" Jane asked.

T-Red came out of his stupor and looked up at them, "Call me an ambulance... help me..." he pleaded weakly.

Jim sighed heavily. "Sorry kid, nothing we can do," he said. "Phones don't work and no one to call."

"You gotta do something!" T-Red protested. "I'm gonna die!"

Jane leaned forward and grabbed the handle of the knife tightly. "This is the only help you deserve!" she said bitterly and twisted the blade before wrenching the knife upward.

T-red gasped as his skin tore under the edge of the knife and blood splashed out, covering her hand and splattering onto the pavement between his feet. As she withdrew the blade, the thug went limp and slid down the rest of the way onto the bench.

Turning to Jim, she said, "Let's move you over to those cars and get that leg taken care of."

Jim followed her numbly. He couldn't fault her for what she'd just done, but the cold manner with which she had done it had shaken him. It seemed to be an entirely different Jane than he had known less than twenty-four hours ago.

The five of them made their way to a pick-up truck parked against the curb, and Jane lowered the tailgate for Jim and the other man to sit on. She used the switchblade to slit the pant leg of Jim's jeans up to the knee and examined the wound.

"It's not as bad as it looks," she declared. "But it probably hurts like hell. We'll wrap it up to stop the bleeding, but I don't think either one of you will be ready to do much walking any time soon."

Jim looked to the other man and saw that the women had already attended to his injuries. His leg was straight again and braced with what looked like duct tape and pieces of a pallet. His abdomen was wrapped in a heavy cloth that reminded him of curtains. Some blood had seeped through the fabric, but it seemed, to his untrained eye, that the bleeding had stopped.

"We have to get out of town," Jim said to the group. "Find somewhere safe."

"Where can we go?" one of the women asked.

Jim realized he didn't know her name and felt embarrassed about that after all that they had been through tonight but figured now wasn't the time to ask.

"Somewhere rural. Someplace with fewer people." Jim paused. "It's going to get worse here." He thought back to his conversation with the gangbangers about bigger fish. T-Red and AK were bad, but worse were sure to come. Much worse.

"We can't walk out of here. And we have no vehicle," Jane observed.

The man beside Jim in the truck dug into his pocket and produced a set of keys. "Maybe I can help? These are the keys to my truck." He smiled and gave them a quick jingle.

They piled into the large Ford truck. The three women had

climbed into the cab with Jane behind the wheel. Jim and the other man rode in the bed where there was room to stretch out.

As the vehicle roared to life and began to move forward, Jim noticed the sun cresting over the buildings behind them. The long night was coming to an end. As they made their way out toward the country, Jim wondered about what they would do. Truthfully, he had no plan and that scared him.

But he was with Jane, and in the end that was all that mattered. All he had to do was keep her. He couldn't prevent the collapse of society. All he could do was try to piece together some semblance of safety. Perhaps the worst would be over soon. A week? A month?

No matter how long it takes, thought Jim, *I will keep her safe. And keep her by my side.*

8

FINDING HIS HEART

ONE COULD ARGUE that no one has worked harder to build the prepper fiction genre than L.L. Akers. She's the undisputed queen of the prepper novel and penned the mighty SHTF Series, among other literary lovelies. For a vision of hardy (and sexy) women who carry more than their own weight in the apocalypse, look no further than Fight Like a Man.

The next two short stories in our anthology push the Black Autumn story years into the future when the Chinese come en masse to "help" the United States recover from its bottomless collapse. As one might anticipate, the help offered is not the help wanted—and things go downhill steeply from there.

Finding His Heart introduces us to the next generation of freedom fighters; kids who barely remember the America that once was.

-Jason Ross

WAR WAS HELL.

Sherman said that, after the Civil War.

He was addressing a group of cadets.

IF I COULD, I'd tell our own cadets the same.

DAVID, the leader of a teenage Freedom Fighter team of six kids, sighed heavily. His new recruits were down in the dumps. Some were hungry. Some were tired. Some were terrified.

All were missing their families.

Some of their parents had been executed for one ridiculous crime or another, and some had been taken prisoner, by their new Chinese overlords. Some were still at home, forging ahead in their new version of reality, one nightmarish day at a time, hoping one day that their family might be reunited.

The Chinese had come months ago, invading America in the dead of the night, beating on every door, kicking them in when they weren't answered quick enough, and dragging out all the children they could find—screaming for their mothers the whole way— carting them off to child labor camps beneath a tsunami of tears.

The children were also used as pawns to keep the Americans in line. Bars and chains weren't necessary when faced with threats, bribes, and promises of their children, running freely from the lying tongues of their enemies. Bribes promising visits with their kids in exchange for turning in their fellow man for hoarding so much as a biscuit or a slice of bread over their assigned rations, or for violation of any other crazy law, or even to squeal about a possible pregnancy, which would result in the 'Chinese OutReach Program' escorting the mother-to-be to an undisclosed location for 'special care,' where the baby would unfortunately not survive childbirth for some unexplained reason.

Veiled threats about their children worked to squash insurgency too. One cross look toward a 'supervisor' as the Chinese were called, and a clipboard was quickly produced, checking the name of the American's child so they could be sure to use it for maximum shock and affect in their taunts. No one wanted to hear their own child's name upon the tongue of these devils.

When the Chinese had invaded the American homes, they'd split up the children. Any child under the age of thirteen went one way, and thirteen and over went the other way. Even solace betwixt siblings was banned by the heartless monsters—their enemy.

David looked out over his team.

The new recruit stood strong and ready with a look of determined, but contained rage on her face. She removed her dark sunglasses and met his eyes with a steely gaze.

Brooklyn.

She looked like she was a force to be reckoned with her almost-white blonde hair, a ramrod stiff back, balled up fists, and the lightest blue eyes he'd ever seen, that were filled with fire. Her fury made her five foot five frame look ten foot tall and bulletproof. At sixteen years old, Brooklyn had the determination of someone three times her age.

Her anger was for the loss of her parents. They'd refused to give her up, as she'd squatted—hidden—in the middle of a round-bale of hay, hastily thrown together around her, listening to their screams from the back yard.

Earlier, when they heard the Chinese making their way down their street, answered by screams and cries of her neighbors, her mother had begged, and received, Brooklyn's promise *not* to show herself, no matter what.

Brooklyn had told her story to David, sobbing on her knees, when she'd finally found her way to the Freedom Fighters, and asked to join their fight for her own revenge.

He'd swallowed down a knot in his throat as she told him she'd known exactly when the interrogation was over, and when the

Chinese had given up on getting her whereabouts from her parents...she'd known at that moment that the camp would not be her parents' new home, as was their hope when the Chinese had come a'knocking. The punishment for not producing a known child in a residence was swift and sure, so they knew in their hearts it would be dealt, even if they'd harbored hope for a reprieve to the concentration camp.

But she'd heard the finality in the Chinese supervisor's voice, when he offered *one last chance* to give her up.

Deadpan.

Angry.

Committed.

In that moment, she'd forgotten her promise, and jumped from the hay bale, running swift-footed toward the house, ready to give herself up at the last second to save her mother and father. How bad could it be, where they'd send her? At least there would still be *a chance* to be together if they were still alive, one day. Her friends would probably be there anyway. She wouldn't be totally alone.

But she'd been too late.

Before she could reach the stoop, she saw them through the glass door. On their knees, looking out at the yard, holding hands. Their faces wore identical countenances of peace. They'd made their decision.

Her eyes had met her mother's, as the supervisor held a gun to the back of her head, and Brooklyn had clearly seen the goodbye painted on her face and the reminder of her promise reflecting back at her through her mother's silent tears. It was what she'd truly wanted. She'd made Brooklyn swear it on a Bible, over and over...

She'd dropped to her own knees in the dewy grass, one hand over her aching heart and one over her mouth, smothering a scream... and she'd silently nodded her goodbye, and then kissed her own hand, weakly throwing the kiss to her mother, hoping she could somehow feel the love it contained.

Her mother had given a slight nod back, not able to return the kiss for fear of giving Brooklyn away to the supervisor.

The gunshot had split the air, nearly stopping Brooklyn's heart too. But she'd forced herself to repeat her goodbye to her father, watching one lone tear trail down his face as he'd given her his special wink, one last time, nearly choking on his own grief through his bravery.

His hand had still grasped the lifeless fingers of his dead wife, who lay face-down beside him on the floor, as he'd struggled to stay upright on his own knees. His eyes had said 'go,' and she'd blown him a kiss, too, and then dragged herself up as quick as she could, running like the hounds of hell were after her, hoping to outrun the sound of his life being extinguished.

Now she stared back at David, her new Chief.

David almost cringed under her stare. He was only one year older than her at seventeen, but she gave him full respect as her superior and mentor, in her father's absence. It was a heady feeling, to hold her life—and those of the other four kids—in his hands. He hoped he was ready.

He could see in Brooklyn's eyes that *she* was ready for her first mission. She was ready for blood.

He hoped she wouldn't be disappointed to find out it didn't involve spying or killing, or setting traps for the Chinese demons.

Not this time.

This time, they were doing something dangerous and disgusting, but necessary.

They were returning honor to a man who'd served his country, but came home only to ultimately find himself wandering lost, and homeless.

A man who'd had *everything* stripped from him, even before the collapse and the invasion.

A man who'd lived on the streets like a pauper—a homeless veteran left to his own devices after sacrificing so much to serve his country, even earning a medal, but not so much as a room or board when it was over—yet a man who was still a hero who treated his fellow brothers and sisters like queens and kings, providing them food and shelter as well as he could, when the Chinese refused to do so.

A man who'd been shot down for it, like a dog in the dirt.

David squeezed his fist, feeling a sharp poke to his palm, needing to feel a small measure of the same pain that this special man had endured.

They were to brave the Ditch of the Dead—a place of their worst nightmares—where they would look upon their family, their friends, their neighbors. They would sort through the piles and stacks of empty shells of their people until they found him.

He opened his hand and gazed at the Purple Heart, flipping it over and memorizing the number, and then stepped over and pinned it to Brooklyn's shirt. She stared down at it, running a finger over its edges.

David cleared his throat. "This is our mission, and Brooklyn is the keeper of the heart."

All eyes turned to Brooklyn.

He nodded solemnly at her. "Wear it well, soldier, with as much bravery as its rightful owner did, until we can return it to him."

He looked around at his young, tired team. "Let's move out."

While America still had heart—so would this man they sought.

Their mission was to return Archie's honor to him: his Purple Heart.

SPECIAL FORCES VETERAN, Sgt. First Class McNight, grumpily brewed his chicory roots over the open fire, wishing once again, as he did every morning, for a cup of real joe.

His dog lay stretched out beside him, his nose on his paws,

giving him a sad look, hoping for something more than the two deer jerky strips he'd already scarfed down. McNight shook his head no, and held his hands up in the air, feeling like the world's worst blackjack dealer, and received an almost-human guilty look in return, followed by a long whine—and not from the dog's mouth.

The dog had broken wind.

McNight chuckled and reprimanded him. "Dammit, Shithead, I know you did that on purpose. I can't give you food anytime you beg, boy. Just be happy I saved you from *becoming* food."

The Chinese had taken so much from America.

Life.

Guns.

Freedom.

Food.

Family.

Pets.

And so much more.

Most of their reasons for living, actually. But to McNight, a lone-wolf of a man who didn't need what most did, the loss of his coffee was what perturbed him to no end. It ranked up near the top of his list, and it pissed him off that the enemy kept him from it.

He didn't miss his car, or his house. Or his big-screen TV. He could live without his queen-size bed and a fluffy blanket, and definitely that damn spying smartphone. He'd tossed that aside within minutes. No, it was the simple things that he missed the most.

His coffee.

Clean socks.

And good healthy dog food that didn't make his dog fart.

When the collapse came, McNight had topped off his bug-out bag, adjusted his rig, grabbed his M14, and hauled off on foot without hesitation, his loyal dog alongside him. He'd already been in war-torn countries, he'd soldiered through economic collapses, too. He and his team had been right in the thick of it, and dealt with the after-effects, as well. They'd torn down cities, and rebuilt cities. They'd mowed down humans, and saved humans.

He'd seen bad things.

Lots of them.

He'd *done* bad things—but all under orders.

He had worn the uniform, followed their orders, broken down his body, and had served his country well with every fiber of his being, sacrificing almost everything, until it'd nearly broken him.

But he'd survived.

He wanted no part of it again.

McNight had made his mind up long ago, if and when the balloon when up—any balloon—he'd live his life out in peace, alone.

Well, almost alone.

No more fighting for him.

Having been counting his days to retire from his *second* career, after first retiring from the armed services, he'd almost welcomed the shit hitting the fan.

Finally, a do-over.

The country had gone cuckoo-banana-pants, in his opinion, and so far over to crazy-town that only a re-set of this magnitude would ever set it back to balance. He'd almost been waiting on it... let the economic collapse come. He didn't need money to live. He'd be fine.

He'd relished the thought of stepping off into the woods, away from the rat-race, and living off the land awhile. It would be an extended vacation for him and his dog.

Or so he'd thought.

But what he hadn't counted on was the invasion that followed the collapse. Soon, hordes of the skinny little bastards were surrounding every American, with not enough warning to fight them off, due to the first crippling blow that had been dealt.

The old quote of *behind every blade of grass* had been turned on its head... because behind every blade of grass *now* was a damn Chinese.

He'd watched in horror from his sniper rifle scope as one small town after another was taken. Families divided, men beaten, women treated as slaves—and worse. There was no way he'd wear their ridiculous jumpsuits, their prison-style-shoes, or do their menial jobs for a slice of bread, topped with green cheese and paper-thin meat, and a freaking rotten apple, if he was lucky.

And he was only one man. He couldn't fight them alone.

No.

Their home was here.

It was there.

It was everywhere, now.

They stayed in one place until the hunting was no good, or the danger was too close, and then they moved on; and they usually ate like kings while they did it, foraging off the land and killing small game. McNight enjoyed the nomadic life, the solitude, the open spaces. Especially after hearing the tinny screams traveling on the wind most every night; screams of victimized Americans.

Sometimes he wondered if they were even real... or just stuck on repeat in his head, echoing through his ears—a phantom call for help.

He shook his head hard.

Nope.

Not his circus.

Not his monkeys.

He was *not* getting involved.

His hero days were over.

McNight shook off his thoughts and got back to his own breakfast. Liquid only for him today, and then he'd gather and hunt more food for later. Using a bandana, he strained the dark brew and took his first sip of the day, cringing at the bitterness, and mumbling another string of curse words under his breath.

A branch snapped faintly and he and his dog both froze, listening.

"Shithead, hide," he commanded. The dog immediately rose up and crept silently into the woods, behind the first big tree he found and lay down with all four paws tucked beneath him, his ears pricked and his eyes watchful, waiting for his master to follow.

Quietly, McNight dumped his brew over the small fire, gathered his backpack and gun, and melted back into the woods behind him, silent as a ghost.

Within a moment, a small party of teenagers came into his field of vision. They were stealthy—for kids. Other than the one tell of the twig that gave him the warning, a sound so faint, most would never have heard it, they were a sneaky bunch.

He watched in admiration as their young leader used hand signals to move his troops, because that was what they surely were: a band of soldiers, albeit a *young* band of soldiers. Six of them in all. Four boys and two girls, ranging in age from probably fifteen to eighteen, at his guess.

The kids had weapons even. He smiled at that.

To hell with the enemy. Go ahead, take our guns... you'll still see the American spirit fight back in the young and the old. *Take that, assholes.*

The young women—the younger one surprisingly wearing a Black Hawk tactical vest with a morale patch reading: DD12—were downright pretty and were also armed. In collection, they had a ball-bat with nails protruding, wrapped in barbed wire. A few spears, a homemade bow and arrow, a slingshot, and a tomahawk.

Each one of them had a nice sized fixed-blade knife strapped to their side, too.

McNight relaxed and slid down from his squat into a sitting position, leaning against the tree. He'd let them pass and go on their way. They'd survived this long, so they didn't need him. They seemed to be focused on something and doing fine. He wouldn't spook them.

As they moved, one by one, into the stand of trees, he lost sight of them. They blended in and disappeared easily.

"At ease, Shithead," he mumbled low.

He sent a prayer up for the kids and stretched, considering a nap, when shithead let out a low growl. McNight turned to look at the dog.

Shithead wasn't at ease.

McNight hopped back up to his haunches and gripped his gun. Something caught his eye coming from the same direction the kids had come.

Chinese.

Two of them, even stealthier than the teenagers had been.

The damn kids were leaving a trail somewhere, and the Chinese had sniffed them out, like dogs on rabbits. It would only be moments before they were caught.

McNight violently shook his head, sucking in his lips.

Dammit.

He knew *exactly* what would happen, as if it'd already played out.

He'd seen it before.

The Chinese wouldn't drag all these kids into camp. They had plenty of men and boys to order around now. It would just be four more hungry mouths to feed.

Maybe he was wrong—maybe they *would* attempt to take them all. But he'd seen the determined look on these kid's faces. They wouldn't go easily. There would be a fight. Americans that were brave enough to stand up, even if they had to hide to do it, were Americans that followed the old ways of protecting their women. These sorts of traditional Americans would respect their women, and give them equal treatment, but when the rubber hit the road, they wouldn't stand for what those girls were about to endure. They'd fight to the death and sacrifice themselves first.

Real men would.

And these boys looked as though they were well on their way to being real men.

But they couldn't win against speeding bullets.

Someone was going to die today.

DAVID STOPPED, holding his fist in the air.

His team stopped behind him.

Was that a noise?

Sounded like a dog...

He signaled his team down and they all knelt in the brush a moment, listening. He didn't hear anything else now; must've been a trick of the wind.

He put eyeballs on each of his five men—and women—noting they already looked tired. They'd need to take a break soon, but he had a bad feeling about this spot. Giving one more look around, he stood and signaled them forward again, when suddenly, shots rang out.

The team scattered, taking cover.

All except Jackie, who had been bringing up the rear.

Jackie screamed and crashed to the ground.

David's heart jumped into high gear as he watched his friend try to get up and run, then fall again, grab his leg, and drag himself to concealment, his leg blooming a bright cherry red.

"Jackie!" David yelled. "You hit?"

That was a stupid question, David thought. Of course, Jackie was hit. He'd seen the blood with his own eyes, hadn't he? He silently cursed his stupidity. They would all think he was an idiot. *No one will follow an idiot.*

His confidence was crumbling.

One man down and he didn't even know which way the shooting was coming from. How could he lead a team? Maybe he wasn't ready for this after all? Panic crept in.

Before David could make a decision on what to do, he heard two more pops, and then silence.

Again, he couldn't make sense of where the shooter was.

His head swiveled, and he turned completely around, eyes peeled. He saw nothing. When he turned back to where he'd started, one lone man and a dog stood twenty feet in front of him, holding a long gun.

David gasped.

An American?

Jackie got shot by an American?

He gripped his tomahawk tightly, ready to fight, but scared to death at the stern-faced man in front of him, and the dog that growled at his movements. *But...an American?* He still couldn't believe one of their own people had just shot Jackie.

Crime between Americans had dropped to negative zero since the invasion. Especially with guns. If someone was lucky enough to have a gun and ammo, they hoarded it to turn on the enemy, not each other.

David gripped his tomahawk tightly and took a stance. "Everybody stay where you are," he yelled to his team.

McNight scoffed. "At ease, Soldier. I didn't shoot your buddy. I just saved his ass. Yours too." He ignored David's threatening stance and commanded Shithead at ease too, then hurried over to Jackie. "Let me see it," he ordered.

"Then who shot him?" David demanded, looking around, still unsure if McNight was a friend or enemy.

McNight spared him a few words. "Chinese on your tail. They're dead. But you nearly all got smoked."

Jackie grit his teeth as McNight squatted down and pulled his

Kabar knife out. He split the leg of the boy's pants open, getting a good look at the wound. He whistled through his teeth, and looked up at David. "You got any medical supplies?"

David shook off his fear and slid his backpack off. "I've got some alcohol swabs, and a bottle of water," he mumbled, digging through it. "I have a shirt we can rip up, but it's not clean. Ummm...."

McNight shook his head and removed his own pack. "Don't bother. I got this."

Quickly, he ripped out his own first aid kit, and waved David in closer. "The rest of y'all get in here too. If you already know how to do this, it won't hurt you to watch it again," he instructed. "No use wasting a GSW lesson on just two kids, especially since your buddy here probably won't remember a damn thing I'm about to show him, if he even sees it." He motioned at Jackie, who by now didn't care who was in front of him, or what they were saying. His eyes were squeezed tightly together in agony.

One by one, the other kids showed themselves, moving in to watch McNight closely. The girls each took one of Jackie's hands, squeezing tightly, as he did his best to suck it up and put on a brave face for them.

McNight's eyes slid right past the girls. He was sure they'd both caught their share of looks and leers, and he had no intention of making them feel uncomfortable in his presence. Besides, his focus was on Jackie, and what was going on around them.

"You," he pointed at David. "Watch our six while I take care of this."

David hurried away, leaving the other two boys with McNight.

McNight hurriedly cleaned the wound and then asked the kids who had the cleanest knife. One was handed to him and he sterilized it, then finished the job, causing Jackie to lose his fight with bravery and let out a girlish scream.

"Man up, Soldier," McNight barked at him. "You ain't even close to dying yet. It barely grazed you. You're lucky your shooter was a bad shot," he said as he wrapped the wound in his only clean T-shirt.

He stood up and called David back. "Y'all kids find me a long, sturdy stick. We need to make him a crutch."

While he instructed Jackie on how to clean his wound and re-dress it, and lectured him on what would happen if he didn't, the other five kids stepped away and hunted for a stick, finding the two dead Chinese.

They stood over the bodies with big eyes and open mouths.

"Holy shit. He killed them with one center shot to back of the head," Egghead mumbled. The rest of the group hurried over with big eyes and open mouths.

"Who do you think that man is?" Hailey wondered aloud, a grimace on her face as she stared at the dead. Hailey was a tough cookie, for a thirteen-year-old, but a hole in the head made her queasy.

Egghead poked his sliding glasses back up his nose. "I think he's a *real* soldier," he answered. "We need this dude, David. Ask him to go with us. He's got a gun."

"Yeah," Brooklyn whispered. "And he's a helluva shot."

"Shut up," David whispered back. "Don't let him hear you. We don't know this guy. Let's just get the stick and get the hell outta here."

David looked around. Scoop had disappeared again. The kid had a knack for it and he had to keep his eyes on him all the time, or lose him. "Keep looking for a solid, long stick, and if you see Scoop, tell him to stop taking off alone," he told Egghead.

Egghead tried to hurry away from the dead bodies, dropping his too-big glasses twice as he looked on the ground for the perfect limb, but nearly ran straight into McNight.

McNight gave him the dirty eyeball. "Hey," he said. "What's your name?"

"Egghead, Sir."

McNight stifled a chuckle. "What's wrong with your glasses?"

Self-conscious now, Egghead gave them another push, sliding them up his nose yet again. "They're too big, sir. They weren't mine. I lost my own."

"Lesson number two. Never waste anything. Scavenge everything." McNight stomped over to one of the dead Chinese, ripped his glasses off his face and tossed them at Egghead. "Here. Rinse 'em off and give 'em a try. You got a small head, kid."

Egghead caught the glasses and held them out with two skinny fingers. He shrugged. He stole a glance at the girls, and then wandered off to rinse off the glasses with a bottle of water, his boyish face crimson.

McNight stripped the Chinese supervisors of their side-arms, too, and handed them both to David, who in turn kept one and handed the other to Brooklyn.

"What are you kids doing out here?" McNight finally asked.

David straightened up to his full height, his face serious. "We're not kids. I'm nearly a legal adult. We're Freedom Fighters," he announced proudly. "We're on our first mission."

McNight scoffed. "Any of you ever had any training as soldiers?"

"No, sir. No time for that."

"Any of you ever killed anybody?"

"No, sir."

"Anyone ever been shot at before?"

"No, sir."

McNight blew out a breath and looked at Shithead, who was comically tilting his head from first his master, then to David, and back again, as though he too were following the questioning and very interested in the answers. "Let's go, Shithead."

David let out a big breath of his own, and looked around at his troops. His face didn't show much confidence, as McNight made his way back out of the woods.

"Y'all be careful out here," McNight muttered as he walked

away, his heart heavy. These kids weren't ready to be out here alone. The Chinese weren't some benevolent overlords. They were killers, and he doubted these kids stood a chance against them. *Must.Not.Get.Involved,* McNight thought, pushing other thoughts out of his mind.

The sixth kid had wandered off alone, but finally reemerged carrying a handful of mushrooms just as McNight was leaving. He cringed as the kid made to pass him, and he saw the kid had written something on the left breast of his shirt with a black sharpie: "Scoop."

He hoped that wasn't his name; but it looked like it. *Never give up your name to the enemy,* he thought. He shook his head.

"Look at these," Scoop said, proudly showing off his mushrooms. "Anybody want one?"

McNight slapped them out of his hand as he walked by. "Eat that shit and you'll wish you were dead," he grunted.

He walked away, guilt pinching his conscience. He wasn't sure what asshat had set these kids out on a mission, but they weren't ready. Nowhere *near* ready. They weren't even prepared with food. They probably wouldn't be making it home—whatever sort of home they had—alive. His eyes filled up. So many lives lost in this war, without even a chance to fight. These would probably be six more.

It was a damn shame.

But not my circus, not my monkeys, he reminded himself, walking faster.

Behind him, he heard David speak to his troops. "Look, we'll find something to eat after we get that purple heart pinned back on," There was a pause. "Let's move out," he ordered his team.

McNight stopped in his tracks. "What did you say? What *is* this mission of yours?" he called out over his shoulder.

David hesitated in his answer.

McNight held stock-still, still giving them his back. "Answer me now, Soldier, or find your head up your ass in two point four seconds."

⸻

RELUCTANTLY, McNight turned around.

Hearing Archie's story was all that he'd needed. It was one thing to look away from the rest of the world... but to walk away from a mission of returning a Purple Heart—returning honor—to a brave, fallen brother? A mission that was doomed to fail from the get-go without him or someone else leading these kids?

He couldn't do it. Not to his brother.

He stomped back into the clearing and ordered the kids to line up, making sure they were all facing the sun beating down on them.

Thankfully, they listened. They passed his first test.

"I'll ask for your name and age. Tell me, but know I can't remember names for shit. If I say, 'hey you,' then you better answer me quick. I'm not babysitting a bunch of snot-nosed kids out here, and I'm not wiping your asses. Sounds to me like you asked for this mission. If I stick around to help ya, then you need to give me your undivided attention all the time."

The six kids all straightened up to their full height—all but one who, not surprisingly, struggled to remain standing after just getting grazed by a bullet.

McNight walked back and forth, a scowl on his face in front of the kids, giving them each a long study. They wiggled uncomfortably under his inspection. Except for Shithead, who took a spot at the end of the line. When he stopped in front of Shithead, the dog stared straight through his legs, frozen like a statue, for a long moment, until he couldn't stand it anymore.

His big brown eyes began to slide up, looking his master in the face, hoping for approval.

"Good boy," McNight said under his breath, trying not to crack a smile, and then started back toward the beginning of the line.

Shithead wagged his tail.

"Name and age," he snapped at the first kid in line.

"David. Seventeen."

McNight didn't spend much time on David, a stout boy packed with muscle; it was clear he was the leader of the bunch and probably the one he'd worry least about. He moved to the next in line.

"Name and age," he asked.

Egghead pushed his newly acquired glasses up his nose. These were too big too. The kid really did have a small head. Small everything, actually. At probably six foot tall, he couldn't have weighed more than one-forty. He needed some meat on his bones worse than any of them. "I told you, sir. It's Egghead. I'm seventeen, too."

"*Real* name, soldier. I know your mama didn't name you after a damn egg!" he barked at the gangly kid, who visibly cringed in response.

"Egbert," he answered quickly, and kept going in a nervous explosion of words, "I'm named after King Egbert. Long time ago, he ruled the West Saxons and formed a powerful kingdom that eventually achieved political unification in England," he sucked in a huge breath and continued, "...and my dad nicknamed me egghead cuz my head used to be huge. I grew into it—and I guess out of it. But the nickname stuck." His eyes went to the ground, and then back up again. "Sir," he finished.

McNight nodded, fighting down the urge to scream TMI at the brainiac. But, he wanted to toughen them up, not scare them to death. He nodded and then took one step to the right, stopping in front of a tall, athletic-built African American kid. "Name and age?"

"Maximillian, sir. But I go by Scoop. I'm sixteen," he answered easily.

"Basketball player?" McNight asked.

Scoop rolled his eyes. "No, dude. Just cuz I'm black and tall and named Scoop don't mean I'm a basketball player. Racist much?"

"I didn't know *basketball* was racist. Thought it was *American*," McNight stressed the word American, leaning in to within an inch from Scoop's nose. "Now eat some *shut the hell up*, kid, because I don't give a shit if you're red, black, green or blue. When *I* fought for my country, we *all* bled the same color. I was asking because your name is *Scoop* and I can't see someone tagging you with a name like that cuz you like ice cream."

McNight finished his tirade and took another step to the right, but Scoop tried to correct his mistake. "Sorry sir, they call me Scoop because—"

"—Save it," McNight interrupted. "My give-a-shit don't give a shit anymore."

Next up was the kid on a make-shift crutch, and McNight was impressed to see the boy standing beside his team, using the stick to lean on. He'd seen some men in battle not pull it together as quick as this kid had after being grazed by a bullet. While it wasn't life-threatening, usually, it did mess with your mind a bit.

He studied his face. Chinese eyes stared back at him, with no malice. Their Chinese invaders didn't discriminate against Americans. They hated them all. Even the ones who looked like they themselves did.

"Name and age?" McNight asked, not as harsh as he'd been with the other boys.

"Jackie. Seventeen," he answered through gritted teeth, but still managed a half smile behind it. The boy had no accent at all. He was American through and through.

"Your parents born here?" McNight asked, curious.

"No, sir. They're legal Americans though."

"What side are they on in this war?" McNight had frequently exchanged tidbits of information with others like him, people passing through trying to hide from the Chinese and live their life alone, on the go. He'd heard of some Chinese Americans trying to play both sides of the field.

"They're on our side, sir," Jackie answered.

That was enough of an answer for McNight. The boy clearly said, '*our* side.' He took another step to the right and came face to face with what had to be the youngest of the bunch. He raised his eyebrows at her. What the hell was this kid doing out here?

"Hailey. Age thirteen, sir!" she said enthusiastically, yet with a small voice. Torn up jeans were topped by an American Eagle T-shirt and a Black Hawk tactical vest. The black and white morale patch on the breast said, 'DD12.'

McNight sucked in a deep breath, staring at Hailey, and then let it out with a sigh. He turned and walked back to the beginning of the line to stand in front of David.

"What the hell is that girl doing out here? She's thirteen. What're ya thinking, son?"

David ran his hands over his face. "Sir, she would've followed us. She was adamant she wanted to be a Freedom Fighter and other than hog-tying her and devoting someone to watch her every minute, there was nothing we could do to make her stay. We tried. She's young, but she's scary-smart and feisty. She has a mission of her own and is waiting for someone to go with her. She wanted to prove she could do this... to everyone... to hopefully find a traveling partner."

McNight nodded. He understood stubborn females. Understood that you could never understand them, that is. He'd tangled with his share and even a hardened soldier knew once a woman made her mind up about something, it was more trouble than it was worth to try to change it. He walked back to stand in front of Hailey.

"What's after this for you, Hailey? What is your *personal* mission?"

Hailey's eyes filled with tears, but she roughly swiped them away and swallowed hard. "I want to make it back to the Tennessee mountains, to my Pawpaw and Grandma's homestead. That's where my mom and dad are, too. I'm sure they need my help. I've got to get home."

"How'd you get stuck all the way out here?"

"Came with a friend and her parents to get a few books signed from one of the DD12 authors, sir." She tapped her morale patch on her vest.

"And that is...*what*?"

"It was a Facebook group of twelve authors, the Dirty Dozen Post Apoc Army, but some were having an in-person meet-up when things went sideways."

"So, they have an army? For the apocalypse? If there was ever a *post* apocalypse, it'd be now. Shit has definitely hit the fan. Where is this *army*?"

"They're spread out everywhere. We all stayed connected online. It was a book group of readers who love post-apocalypse fiction; mostly preppers, homesteaders, LEO, and military. But with the internet and phones disabled, the only way to reach them now is by HAM radio," she answered, gloomily. "But my pawpaw is probably in touch with them through the DD12 CommsConnect, if the Chinese hasn't shut them down yet."

This girl's devotion to her family touched McNight's heart. He hoped she'd find her family again. Maybe this would be his next mission, too. He'd always thought Tennessee was pretty country. He could always help her get there and then step off and live off the mountains for a while. Why not? It was as good a place to hide from everybody as any, maybe even better.

He moved on to the last kid in line.

Fast as a snake, the girl ripped her sunglasses off her face. Lucky for her, as McNight was just about to pluck them off himself, and comment about the lack of respect. She pushed her white-blonde hair over her shoulder and stood at attention.

"Brooklyn. Age sixteen," she blurted out in perfect English, not waiting to be prompted. She squinted hard against the blinding sun.

This was the first time McNight had been close to her. Through her squinted Chinese eyes, he saw they were very light blue. She was an albino, and from what he could tell, the sun was painful for her.

He stared at her a moment, measuring her grit. The sun was shining right into her face, yet she tried her hardest not to blink, causing her eyes to water terribly. "Put your glasses back on," he gently told her, and moved to the last in line.

Shithead perked up and sat tall on his haunches.

McNight almost laughed at the still serious look on his dog's face. "On your feet, soldier," he barked at the dog, who had been patiently sitting in line for more instruction, shouldered up to the last kid in line.

Shithead stood up on all fours and held his head high.

"Sit."

Shithead sat again.

"Play dead."

Shithead fell to the ground, his tongue hanging out the side of his mouth.

All the kids laughed, still standing at attention.

McNight had only been trying to teach Shithead a funny trick when they'd practiced this before the invasion, but it'd already came in handy once. They'd been caught unawares and McNight had to quickly shimmy up a tree with his backpack to avoid detection, leaving Shithead to fend for himself. He'd commanded Shithead to play dead and *stay* dead, which meant until he released him.

The Chinese had either been too full, or too lazy to bother with what they'd believed was a dead dog they'd walked past, and they'd both lived to see another day. Since then, McNight practiced that trick, and many others, daily with Shithead.

McNight jerked his head toward the shade. "At ease, soldiers. Let's get these Chinese into their birthday suits and then re-evaluate your plan for the Ditch of the Dead."

He walked away, with Shithead loping happily beside him.

———

MCNIGHT SPENT the entire next three days training the kids, and teaching them survival skills.

The first two days, he showed them how to feed and shelter themselves, and how to best use their weapons. They didn't waste any bullets, as they'd only found two full magazines on the dead Chinese men, plus the fully-loaded guns. McNight trained them as well as he could without actually allowing them to fire.

There was food all around them, they just needed to know how to find it, and he kept them going from dawn 'til dusk teaching them one thing after another.

He taught them to harvest and cook chicory roots for coffee.

He showed them the best way to gather dandelions and dig dandelion roots, and several ways to cook them and eat them, including hot or cold. He pointed out the good mushrooms versus the bad mushrooms. He taught them how to pick and cook Prickly Pear Cactus pads and fruit, without ending up like porcupines themselves, and how to use them to stay hydrated. The kids were amazed when they discovered the cactus pads tasted like green beans when cooked, and the flowers had a refreshing fruity taste.

He showed them how to tap a tree for water when they ran out, and how to make sure they didn't leave the tree to die; and how to make a homemade filter to utilize the water from any creeks and streams they found. He showed them how to light a fire without a lighter, and how to build a one-log fire, even if your one log was wet.

He taught them to build an underground cook-fire, to avoid smoke detection as much as possible, and the kids were now proficient at building a small, natural shelter, too. They could break ground and have cover in thirty minutes flat, sometimes less, after careful study of McNight's techniques.

By the time McNight was through, not only had they broke through his tough exterior and took to calling him Uncle Mick—usually behind his back—but they all now knew how to set a simple snare, use the bow and arrow, in case one was injured and they had to pass the weapon, and how to spear a fish.

Scoop in particular aced the snares and traps, and he was a dead-on shot with the bow and arrow, as well as the slingshot. Soon, Shithead was retrieving the arrows that hit low enough, and bringing them back, again and again for the team, and bringing Scoop rock after rock to add to the leather pouch for ammunition, earning a pat on the head or a rub between the ears.

Everybody took a turn with every weapon, but they'd all found the jobs they were good at, too. Even Shithead.

As expected, Brooklyn was deadly with the ball bat. She was also very accurate with the slingshot, if only they could find heavy enough natural ammo to be of use.

Egghead was amazing with the spear, for fighting, throwing, and eating. He pulled out more than a dozen small fish from the creek. McNight taught them how to make mushroom and fish soup, with a few onions and herbs they also foraged, and they ate well for dinner both nights. Egghead became the camp cook.

David was exceptionally good at almost everything, but McNight was able to give him some pointers on tomahawk throwing, and he found Hailey also had a knack for that, as well as the slingshot. She was a smart kid who learned quickly.

He showed them all how to sharpen their knives on river rocks, and he made sure they kept them honed sharp.

Next, he taught them to fight.

He had to get the group to straighten up and get serious for a while as he and David danced around in a mock knife-fight. Hand-to-hand combat with a knife could end very quickly, and very badly. Not for the first time, he wished they had more than two guns. Knife-fighting was a skill not easily taught, especially in a few hours, but he did the best he could with the time he had, and he hoped they'd not have to test their shoddy training.

McNight was a sniper, and planned to use his own skills in protecting these kids with his M14, if it was at all possible. The training on the weapons was hopefully for *after* they parted ways.

After the knife lessons, it was time to learn to fight without their weapons.

He was more than a little surprised to find out Jackie was a black belt in several mixed martial arts. His parents had migrated from China, and his namesake, Jackie Chan, the movie star born in their country, was a hero to them. Their first-borne was named for him and he'd eventually grown into the name, with a little push. He'd attended martial arts lessons since he'd learned to walk.

In spite of his leg wound, Jackie still managed to take McNight down a few times, bringing the entire group to laughter; even McNight, who'd lightened up, seeming to enjoy having something important to do once again, although he denied it and tried to grab back his gruff countenance as much as possible.

Shithead couldn't have been happier. He ran 'round and 'round, helping the young women when they were 'under attack,' by pulling at the pant legs of the boys and giving a ferocious playful growl.

When Jackie had taken McNight down, Shithead landed with a thud on his chest, nearly knocking his breath out, and covered his face with slobber, as he had done each of the kids who hit the ground.

At night, Shithead cheated on him, snuggling up between the two girls in their shelter, until the wee hours of the morning, just before breakfast, when he'd crawl out and relocate to McNight's side, knowing who the keeper of the jerky was.

Traitor.

He knew he and Shithead would be leaving these kids after this, and going their own way. His only mission was watching that Purple Heart be pinned back onto a fallen hero, where it belonged.

These weren't his kids, and he and Shithead couldn't get attached to them.

Especially to Hailey and Brooklyn.

Against his will, all the kids had grown on him, but especially the girls. They'd already wiggled their way into that dark place that kept his heart sleepy and unawares, and shined unwanted light in there. They'd also cracked his smile back open—a smile that was hard to find since he'd left Special Forces and all that happened *over there* behind.

He'd chosen a solitary life for a reason. He'd chose to not marry or have children; to live his life mostly alone. He liked it that way...*didn't he?*

But, between Hailey's own sweet smile looking up to him with the twinkle in her eyes, and her unending optimism that she *would* get home to her family, combined with Brooklyn's raw determination to fight like a man and bring vengeance upon the Chinese for her parents—which he found incredibly brave and admirable—he was having a tough fight with his need to keep everybody at arm's length.

But he had to admit, if only to himself, that these kids had taught *him* more than he could ever teach *them*. They'd taught him that just because he'd been there and done that, and wasn't *active* military anymore, a veteran was still an asset to this country. He could pass on what he'd learned to the younger generation. He could teach them to survive, and to fight. And he'd barely touched the tip of the iceberg with them on what all he knew. The longer he stayed with them, the better trained they'd be.

If only he could round up more veterans. They could train these youngsters, and even their parents; teach them everything they knew, and then... they could take their country back.

If only...

McNight took a break, leaning against a tree to catch his breath, deep in thought. If he *had* a daughter, he'd be hard pressed to choose which she would be like: Brooklyn or Hailey.

"Hey, Uncle Mick," Jackie dared to call him. "Want to wake up from your nap, old-timer? See what Hailey can do now?"

McNight wasn't an old timer...not by a stretch, but he was feeling quite ancient watching these kids with their never-ending energy. His head popped up, to see Jackie on the ground, with Hailey's foot atop his chest. With her hands on her hips, the thirteen-year-old beamed with pride at having put the much larger boy on his back.

Jackie stuck his tongue out and played dead, imitating Shithead's trick. The boy was a ham, always being silly or making a joke, but he was also the most dangerous out of the bunch. Between the two of them, he and McNight taught the other five kids as much as they could in one day in self-defense, evasion, and even how to incapacitate or kill their opponent.

By the sixth day, McNight was ready to move on their mission.

McNight RAISED HIS FIST, and the kids all stopped as one, squatting down low. He dropped to the ground and crawled up the hill, looking down into a valley.

He took a long look and then unfolded the map.

This appeared to be the right road. The crude hand-drawn map only showed the barn that Archie was last believed to live in, which was ten miles past this spot, and an "X" with *Ditch of Dead* scribbled beside it. This place must've just been on the way; some sort of camp or outpost—but this was not the Ditch of the Dead.

They probably either just assumed that it was, or didn't know about this place on the way to Ditch of the Dead. It certainly wasn't on purpose, McNight thought. The adults were probably given wrong information, or not enough. The fact was, no Americans returned from the Ditch of the Dead to talk about it; it was a one-way ticket to hell: the eternal dirt-nap.

So, it was only a guess that it was out here, based on seeing the Chinese heading this way with prisoners; some dead, and some alive, but never *returning* with them.

But no dead bodies could be seen—or smelled—as far as he could see.

McNight waved the kids up, and they all shimmied the hill on their bellies, lining up beside him to peek over as well.

For the next four hours, McNight and the kids rotated two teams. One team watching behind them, and the other team watching two small, squatty rectangular buildings at the bottom of the hill, seeing nothing but two plump, old Chinese women going in and out.

There were no bars on the windows, so it was doubtful it was a prison, but to further confuse them, four guards were posted at different corners of the buildings. At the top of the hour, the guards changed, and the previous guards would hit the latrine, and then step into a round, canopied hut, where they'd hear dishware clattering.

After the third guard change, McNight waved the team down off the hill to formulate their plan.

"YOU SURE YOU CAN DO THIS?" McNight asked Brooklyn, for the third time.

"*Yes, Uncle Mick,*" she answered sarcastically, while tucking her hair up into a hat. "Why aren't you asking Jackie the same question? Is it because he's a guy?"

She checked her weapon once more, like McNight had taught her, and slid it into the holster she'd stolen from the dead owner of the gun.

McNight's original plan was for them all to keep on walking. It was his belief the Ditch of the Dead was still this way, just further down the road.

But the kids didn't agree with him. They wanted to take a look-see.

It scalded his ass that they were ready to break off from him, even under threat of him abandoning their mission altogether, because they believed the younger children *might* be in one of those buildings.

He'd even promised the kids that once they secured Archie's Purple Heart back to him, he'd return alone and find out. And he meant it. He didn't want these kids taking any more risk than they had to, and he also didn't want to risk that medal not being returned to its rightful owner either.

But, all but Brooklyn and Hailey might have sisters or brothers that they'd been separated from in there, and if there was a chance, they wanted to free them.

Or at least *see* them.

So, it was onto Plan B.

Jackie and Brooklyn, the two Chinese Americans, donned the uniforms, and the guns, of the dead Chinese supervisors that McNight had killed six days earlier.

They were to sneak up behind the squat building, incapacitate the guards, and peek into the windows.

Whatever they saw, they were to return to the bluff and report to McNight for further instructions. They were *not* to enter the building, and were not to use their firearms unless their lives were in danger.

If they *were* seen, it was McNight's hopes that with their ethnicity and the uniforms of the enemy, they might just walk on by without being questioned.

Meanwhile, McNight would be on the top of the hill, lying prone with his M14.

It was a fat chance.

But it was a chance.

BROOKLYN'S HEART RACED.

They'd scoped out the camp from every direction and so far, they'd only seen four armed guards, three old Chinese women, and a goat that was tied up in a shed, lying on a pile of hay, with a stack of metal buckets beside it.

Sneaking like bandits, and then running like their tails were on fire, they'd snuck between the two buildings into a small alley, and waited for the guards to walk around as they'd seen them do earlier.

The uniforms the kids wore caught the guards by surprise, up close and personal, leading them to unanswered questions, but lending them a small window of opportunity to dispatch the two men before they were fired upon.

The first building they'd peeked into was a medical facility of some sort. A metal rolling tray had an assortment of surgery tools next to a dirty gurney, covered in blood-spattered white cloth. It had an adjustable spotlight hanging over it that swung spookily in the empty building, casting a bouncing light on the inside wall that was lined with blood-spattered ice coolers... weirdly, it was the best American coolers on the market: Yeti and other top brands.

Each cooler was marked with a red sharpie in Chinese letters; thus, they couldn't read it.

On the other wall an ice machine stood alone, with a metal scoop hanging from a nail on the wall beside it.

An apothecary cabinet was the only other thing in the room. Behind two glass doors, it was filled to the brim with bottles and jars of what appeared to be medicine, and stacks of gauze, tape, and white cloth.

There was one door with a padlock hanging from it. From the position of where that room should be, and where they were outside, they could see there was no window. The padlock had the key in it and was hanging loose and open.

She jumped down from Jackie's back, who had knelt on the ground to give her a lift up, and stared at the two Chinese guards, leaned up against the wall of the other building, checking to be sure they were still out cold. She wondered how long they'd be out. One was directly under the window of the other building she needed to look in.

"Can you move him without waking him up?"

Jackie easily dragged the man away from the window.

Brooklyn still couldn't believe she'd managed to knock out a full-grown man with only one day of training. Jackie had handled his much faster, but they'd both gone down, and Jackie had easily dragged his man over to Brooklyn's.

Jackie leaned them up together against the wall, side by side and then reached down and clasped one's right hand with the other's left hand, and pushed their heads together, turning them to face one another just a breath away. He stepped back and pointed at them, mimicking a Chinese woman's voice and saying, "Me love you long time, yes?"

He smothered a laugh.

"Stop it," Brooklyn whispered loudly at him. "Do you want to get dead?!"

Jackie took in a deep breath and let it out. "Sorry. I goof around when I'm under stress. Come on," he said, and motioned her to the window.

He got on all fours and waited.

Brooklyn climbed up, using him as a step, grabbing the sill of the window to balance herself.

She peeked in for a long moment and gasped. "Holy crap."

"What's in that one?" Jackie whispered.

"Babies!" Brooklyn whispered back. "The sign in there says, 'Chinese OutReach Program.' Those lying pigs..."

The Chinese OutReach Program was supposedly a program for Americans, provided by their generous overlords, that helped pregnant women. The American's didn't want it, but they got it anyway.

The Chinese said it was years and years of poor nutrition that caused the American's to now lose nearly every child born. They blamed fast-food habits, junk food, loose women, and use of dangerous pharmaceutical medicines. If they even heard a whisper of a pregnancy, the Chinese OutReach team immediately arrived to extract them from their husbands and homes, and take them somewhere where they'd supposedly get fed better, and taken care of, with little to no hard work until time for them to give birth.

The only problem was, each time the mothers returned *without* their babies; if they returned at all. They were not conscious for the births, and when they awoke, they were told their babies did not survive.

They were told their babies were *dead*.

No one believed this.

Brooklyn was now looking their lie in the face.

In *four* faces.

While the babies' eyes were covered with bandages for some reason, Brooklyn could clearly see the babies were *not* Chinese. These were American babies; two were African American with darker skin and thick, tight black curls atop their heads, and two were Caucasian—milky white skin-toned; one with curly blond hair and one with bright red hair.

The babies were laying in crude excuses for cribs on bare, dirty mats. Their hands were covered with layers of socks, and she imagined that was to keep their fingers out of their eyes. She wondered what had happened to them.

There were no toys, no fuzzy blankets, no musical aquariums.

Clothed only in small, short-sleeve T-shirts, and what appeared to be a ripped-up piece of sheet pinned with a cold, sharp safety pin, their bottoms were wet, and worse. She could see the children desperately needed fresh diapers.

The babies were laying in their own filth, and shivering without even a blanket to keep them warm.

She couldn't hear their cries through the concrete walls and thick glass, but she could see all of their mouths open wide, each making a dark little anguished 'O.' They were all either terribly hungry, uncomfortable, and scared, or missing their mothers.

Probably all of the above.

A tear ran down Brooklyn's face.

She missed her own mother.

"Hurry up," Jackie whispered loudly, struggling to hold Brooklyn up so long.

Brooklyn quietly hopped off. "*Shhh...*" she said. "Here comes someone."

They both squatted down, staying quiet.

After a moment, they heard the door click shut. Brooklyn motioned Jackie to help her up again, and he moved to get on his knees, on all fours. She climbed up.

She slowly raised her head to look in the window. A chubby old Chinese woman came in with four bottles filled with milk.

Brooklyn watched as she stuck the first bottle into the red-headed baby's mouth, while the baby waved its arms around, frantically trying to grab at the food—or for human interaction—while she meanly swatted its tiny hands away. The baby sucked long and hard for only a moment before the woman snatched it out of its mouth and moved to the next crib, repeating the process.

"Omigod," Brooklyn muttered. Her heart clinched. These innocent babies were clearly starving and the brusque old woman wasn't giving them a chance to drink much.

She finished two bottles between four babies, left them all red-faced and screaming for more, and then ignoring their needs to burp or be changed, she took the other two bottles to a rocking chair in the corner.

She fluffed up the pillow, sat down and removed the nipples, and drank them herself.

Brooklyn was livid.

She hopped down, noticing the guards were starting to stir.

"Hurry," she said, running for the woods that led them to the hill where McNight lay on watch.

Jackie ran behind her, only showing a slight limp from his injured leg.

McNight listened to their report and then quickly led the team back down the hill, approaching the two downed guards just as they were coming to. He knocked them out again with one strong tap against their temple with the butt of his rifle.

David and Scoop each grabbed one man under the arms, dragging them into the empty building behind McNight, who cleared the rooms first, and then ordered the kids to put the Chinese behind the door with the padlock.

Brooklyn passed her gun to Egghead, who stayed outside, watching their six, and followed David and Scoop.

The door with the padlock was a storage room, filled with rice, blankets, baby clothes, and ammo, and to the kid's sheer bliss: Pop Tarts.

Seems the Chinese weren't immune to the pull of *all* American junk food after all. *Someone* had a hankering for these flat American delights, filled with artificial flavors and sugar.

Shoving them into their pockets, while McNight bit his tongue and watched the door, listening for any warning from Egghead, the other kids quietly fussed and argued over the flavors: blueberry, s'mores, strawberry, until McNight hissed at them to *come on*, locking the padlock behind them, and leaving the guards behind and secure.

Before moving to the next building, he examined the blood-spattered coolers and the ice machine, and then looked at the metal cart with the surgical tools, and the bloody gurney under the light.

He had a suspicion he knew what was going on.

Careful to avoid the other two guards, he peeked out the door, and waved the kids behind him.

He tossed Egghead several packs of the Pop Tarts, receiving huge eyes and a smile in return, and then they moved onto the next building.

The door creaked open and he quickly cleared the one-room building, finding it empty, other than the babies.

He hurried over to the first child and lifted its shirt.

The child flinched at his touch.

Rage filled his head, and he moved to the next, and the next and the next, his body vibrating with anger.

His suspicions were correct.

These children's *parts* were being harvested. A bandage covered a spot on each of them where a kidney had been removed, then probably put on ice, and auctioned off for a million bucks and flown to some rich asshole with more money than ethics for his own loved one, or himself.

He was afraid to look under the bandages across where their eyes should be. He didn't know that he could keep it together if he found two black empty holes staring back at him from these infants. He ignored those for now.

McNight pushed his rifle to hang behind him, and spoke to David. "Keep your eyes open," he said gruffly, and picked up the last baby in line, holding it close. His nose wrinkled in disgust, but the disgust wasn't for the baby or the stench, it was for the people who weren't taking care of it.

Sadness stabbed him like a knife, for the mothers and fathers caught up in this unfought war, who hadn't been able to hold their own children, but especially for the children who were missing the warm, loving feeling of being held and cherished by their parents; who missed the skin to skin contact, and all the spoiling and love a newborn child—any child—should have.

Squeezing his eyes together against the smell, he checked its nappy; it was full. And it was a boy... McNight's heart clinched as he brought the baby close to him again, ignoring the stench of unwashed skin, feces and urine. He softly cooed to the baby boy, and rubbed his soft, dark curls, kissing the top of his head.

Animals.

That's what these Chinese were.

Heartless animals.

McNight looked up to see Jackie watching him hold the baby, tears filling his own eyes. Jackie swallowed hard and cleared his throat. "How can they do this?" he said, knowing exactly what McNight knew. "I mean, my family is Chinese. We come from China originally. How can people be of the same origin, with possibly the same blood somewhere down the line, but be so different? So inhumane? I'm *ashamed* to be Chinese."

McNight shook his head. "Don't be. You're not like them, and they're not like us. Blood doesn't make you family. *Heart* does. Look around you. Here's your family now, boy. Suck it up. Gather some things, we're not leaving them here."

Jackie hung his head low. "I would never do this, McNight, not to *any* human, even if they were our enemy."

"No shit, man. We know you're not one of them. You've got nothing to prove. Brooklyn is Chinese too; being like them in DNA doesn't make y'all *like* them. You're both one of us: *Americans*. Now get your head straight and your shit together."

A flurry of activity ensued. Brooklyn grabbed a rolling cart from the corner and she and Hailey filled it with blankets, clothes, bottles and whatever they could find. While they did that, the boys watched the windows and the door.

McNight turned and looked at the cart. There was a wire shelf with a lip on it directly underneath. Room for more stuff. It would make it heavy, but hell, David was built like an ox anyway. "Hey, Scoop. Run to the other building and grab as much rice as you can carry. Stack the bags under the cart on that shelf. Find a carry-bag or something in there and grab as much of the medical stuff in that cabinet as you can, too. Diaper cream, antibiotics, whatever they have. But don't get seen," McNight ordered. "Hurry! I've got one more thing to do before we go."

He turned to his task and very quickly changed four tiny diapers, not able to fathom leaving the children in soiled cloths one moment longer; he was careful to fold the top of the diaper over the cold, sharp safety pin so that it didn't touch their skin.

He looked over his shoulder to make sure he wasn't being watched before kissing each tiny head, speaking quietly to them, and gently rubbed their too-skinny arms and legs before placing them in the cart, atop the bundle of blankets. The babies had quieted at his voice and now-dry bottoms, even blindly reaching out to him again for his touch, their tiny limbs waving frantically in the air.

They were starved for more than just milk.

Jackie stepped over to the cart with his arms crossed, staring at the malnourished, bandaged babies once again. His jaw was clenched. He was stuck in his own head, doing nothing to help.

McNight gave him a light slap against the noggin. "Wake up. Let's go."

He took the lead after giving orders. "David, push the cart

straight back up that hill to where we were. Egghead, you trail David. Shithead is waiting for us. We'll all rendezvous there and two of us will take the babies to the barn that was on the map, while the rest of us go find Archie to complete your mission."

The babies began to cry. His head swiveled left to right and back again. "Scoop, you get that goat, and Jackie, you're with him. Watch his six. We'll need the goat for milk. Hailey and Brooklyn, with me."

Brooklyn was fidgeting with the babies. "Omigod. *Look* at this!"

One of the baby's bandages had slipped off of its eyes to reveal it still *had* eyes, but they weren't typical American eyes. Tiny stitches revealed recent surgery, re-shaping the eyes to look like their captors.

The baby looked around in wide-eyed wonder and then screamed in fright at the shocked eyes staring back at it.

Egghead cringed. "Dude. That's messed up."

They gathered around the cart and removed the remaining bandages. All four babies had been altered.

McNight looked around at the horrified faces. He'd seen worse done to prisoners of war, but not to *babies*. Not live babies anyway. Before he completely lost his shit and went to find every Chinese he could find, throwing lead at them and possibly risking the lives of all these children, he needed to refocus.

He waved the girls behind him and took off, assuming his orders were being followed as given, when suddenly Scoop yelled out for Jackie.

Before he could react, Jackie had taken off back toward the buildings.

"Dammit, Jackie!" he yelled. "Meet us at the barn then."

He had an idea he knew where Jackie was going.

McNight let him go without a fight; Jackie had demons of his own to purge, and something to prove to himself. This was his choice, and he was choosing to become a man—a real Freedom Fighter—or fail trying.

McNight mopped his sweaty brow with his forearm and then cringed at the smell. His head was pounding. His heart was thumping.

But it wasn't the sea of dead bodies around him that was bothering him. For the first time in many, many decades, he felt something unfamiliar to him.

Sheer panic.

And it wasn't the fear of being caught in this God forsaken place of death, surrounded by a sea of faces frozen in horror... it wasn't fear at all.

He'd faced walking into villages as the point of first contact, shirt off and arms spread wide, unarmed, and possibly facing his own death. He'd jumped out of perfectly good birds. He'd ambushed parties that had him outnumbered ten to one, and rarely blinked an eye.

He'd eventually slept like the dead in war-torn countries with blood and bullets flying all around him, not even fretting whether he would, or would not, wake upon the dawn. He'd learned to squash his feelings, burying them so deep he'd forgotten what they felt like.

So this... this *thing* he was feeling, it was unusual for him. *Foreign.*

Worry.

Was it possible that in less than six short days they'd unknowingly broken down the walls around his heart, and made him actually *feel* something again?

Something like... *love?*

He looked over at David and Brooklyn, who were also knee deep in rotting flesh, pulling, lifting, sorting, as though they were at the GoodWill looking for a pair of cool worn-out jeans.

But this was no bargain basement.

The strength these kids were showing, possibly looking into faces they'd known; now-blank faces that may have been related to them in some way, or friends, or neighbors, was amazing.

He was *proud* of them; another new feeling to him.

Despite the ugliness, despite the smell, the two kids stoically pursued their prize.

Archie.

He watched them with pride as they dug in, not shying away from the dirty work, and probably the hardest thing they'd ever had to do, looking for a hero.

When all along, *they* were the heroes.

McNight took in a deep breath and coughed it back out. He was glad Scoop had confiscated a jar of Vicks when he'd robbed the apothecary cabinet. They each had a generous smear of it under their noses and even so, the stench was stomach-curling. Without it, it may have been unbearable.

But yeah, watching those two kids right now, his heart swelled with all sorts of foreign feelings...topped with worry.

His worry: the group had split.

He'd sent Hailey and Egghead, with the babies, on toward the barn that was marked on the map. It was the group's understanding that Archie had once lived at that barn. Since he'd been captured and killed in town, it was possible the barn was still secure.

When the team arrived at the top of the hill, Shithead had met them, his happiness at being reunited with his master and the kids unbridled. He'd hopped around, barking and spinning in glee, and then curiously sniffed the cart that held the babies, jumping back when one let out a cry.

After that, Shithead promoted himself to *Protector of the Little Humans.* For a moment, when McNight, with Brooklyn and David, split paths from the babies, pushed by Egghead and Hailey, it was as though Shithead had to think hard about which way he wanted to go.

McNight had breathed a sigh of relief when Shithead eventually fell in step beside him.

But Jackie hadn't returned to the hill. And Scoop didn't stay...

Within moments of their return, the team had heard a *pop, pop, pop*, and they'd all froze.

But whatever had happened, it was too late.

McNight now had a mission of his own.

To get the majority of the kids, and the babies, to safety.

If he had to drag his feet through a swamp of blood and guts and empty stares to complete his mission, he'd do it. But he wouldn't sacrifice another one of them. He'd made a decision to go on without Jackie.

Scoop didn't like that decision—he'd turned tail and ran back down the hill after his buddy.

Very admirable, but it didn't change McNight's mind. The numbers didn't lie. Six lives weighed heavier than two. They all took off, him hurrying both parties along, and hoped to see Scoop and Jackie again, one day, but praying for their souls in case he didn't.

Brooklyn gave a low whistle, rousing McNight from his musings, and he and David turned in alarm.

The American worker that they'd bribed with a bag of rice to give them three orange jumpsuits and turn his head, was coming back.

And he wasn't alone.

Luckily it was just another American worker with him. The Chinese didn't get their hands dirty here. According to the first man, who more than happily traded the rice for allowing them to look through the dead, they rarely ever saw their Chinese bosses. There wasn't anything here to eat or steal... so they left them unattended to tend to the dead; to unload any new bodies that were brought in, and throw them into the ditch each morning.

Funerals and burials were a thing of the past in the *new* America. The Chinese considered this a waste of time and money if it was just an American life that was lost. Once a month, the men in orange suits would burn the stacks of bodies and when that had burned down and the smoke cleared, they'd continue to pile them on, as they were told.

The two men approached them. The new man, elderly and frail, scratched his bald head, tufts of white hair blowing in the wind around his ears. "What in tarnation are y'all doing in there?" he asked, with an incredulous look.

McNight's hand hovered over the sidearm he was hiding; one re-confiscated from the kids. David had the other one and McNight gave him a slight nod to be on the ready, before he answered, "We're looking for someone."

"Why would you need to find them? We check those bodies before we dump 'em. There ain't no valuables on 'em."

"We aim to fix that," McNight said. "Show him, Brooklyn."

Brooklyn turned to the men and unzipped her jumpsuit, showing them Archie's Purple Heart. "We came to pin this on Archie, and if it's possible, we'd like to take him with us and give him a proper burial."

The old man spread his mouth, showing off no more than a handful of teeth, and laughed. "*Archie*? Archie the homeless veteran that helped feed so many of us? *That's* who you're looking for in the Ditch of the Dead?"

He slapped his hand on his legs, with a huge belly laugh. His friend laughed along with him.

McNight didn't find it humorous.

He pulled the sidearm, and pointed it at the two. "Not sure what you find funny, mister, but I'll ask you leave us to it. This is a serious mission for these kids. They aim to give that hero back an honor he earned."

The men held their hands up, palms out. "Wait a minute," Toothless said. "You should've mentioned his name when you showed up. You won't find Archie buried in that mess. You head out to the old barn where he used to live, and you'll be able to re-pin that medal."

The other man nodded his agreement. "Can we keep the rice anyway?"

―――――

"He's coming!" Brooklyn yelled to the others.

The kids all ran outside the barn, each holding a squirming baby, their hope and anticipation tingling through the air. The goat followed them out, adding its own loud racket to the excitement. They'd been waiting on McNight—having full confidence that he'd return—for three days.

After the news from the men in orange, McNight had sent Brooklyn and David to the barn to meet up with Hailey and Egghead and the babies, while he headed back alone, to the Chinese outpost to see what had happened to Jackie and Scoop.

He just couldn't leave those kids behind.

Dead or alive, he *needed* to see if there was anything he could do once he felt the rest were somewhat safe.

Shithead came rocketing down the dirt road first, which was what had given Brooklyn the head's up that McNight would soon be following. She'd been sitting outside watching almost since their arrival, barely sleeping or eating.

The dog made his rounds, jumping up and greeting everyone, and getting rubs and scratches and pats on the head in return.

His master's head then topped the hill, carrying something across his shoulders. He walked heavy and slow under his burden, with Scoop trailing behind. He squinted his eyes as he approached the kids, his heart swelling to see all four of them, with all four of the babies, all in one piece.

Scoop ran ahead to his friends, hugging them in turn, and then ran back to meet McNight again, with David in tow.

David took McNight's heavy burden, giving him a much-needed rest as he finished his journey, and after suffering through the rest of them wrapping their arms around him in a huge hug that watered his eyes, McNight followed him inside the barn, with the whole crew behind them.

Gently, David laid Jackie on a blanket atop a pile of hay and then stood back, looking at his injured friend. He was alive, and that was all that mattered, but now in addition to a scar on one leg, he'd have another piercing his other leg.

"Did you get 'em?" David asked a weak Jackie.

Jackie nodded and smiled. "Every one of them, but not before they got me. Lucky for me though, the Chinese are terrible shots."

He held up a weak fist, and David fist-bumped him and turned to Scoop. "How 'bout you? Any injuries?"

Scoop shook his head. "Only my pride that this old man is stronger than me," he said loudly, hoping McNight heard him. "Took me hours to drag Jackie's ass up that hill...then y'all were gone. Uncle Mick carried him the whole way here and barely broke a sweat."

They both looked at McNight, who was currently sitting on the hard-packed dirt floor, four babies squeezed onto his lap. They gathered around him.

Embarrassed to be caught out in such a moment, McNight swiped at his eyes and cleared his throat. "So, did you find him?" He looked around, wondering if the man had been buried under this very floor where he sat.

"Yup," Brooklyn answered, with a smile. "Archie!" she yelled.

A grouchy, old voice answered. "What?" and then Archie came wobbling through the back door, wiping his hands on his dirty apron. He wore a clean bandage mostly covered with a bandana around his own head.

McNight gently handed the babies to the kids, and then stood up to meet the man with a salute. "Well, shit. You're alive," he said in surprise. "The men at the Ditch of the Dead didn't say *that*. They just said we'd find you here."

Archie laughed. "Loyal bunch they are. They're the two that pulled me out of that ditch. Saw I wasn't quite yet dead yet and patched me up. I owe them my life; what's left of it, anyway."

He noticed Archie wasn't wearing his Purple Heart. "And your heart?"

Archie shrugged. "No worse for wear. It acts up every now and again. Flops around like a fish in there until I sit down and rest a spell."

"I meant your Purple Heart. That's what the mission was. To return your Purple Heart to you. It's really important to these kids to see that pinned to your chest," McNight explained.

Archie reached into his pocket and took out the medal. He stepped up to McNight, pinning the shirt of the younger man. "Here's where I'm gonna have to pull rank on you, soldier. And the kids agree with me... you're the hero here."

IF YOU ENJOYED this short story from L.L. Akers, check out her full novels in *The SHTF Series*, and be sure to hit the Follow button.

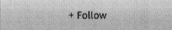

9

FINDING HIS HEART II

Finding His Heart, *cont.*

Author of over two dozen post-apocalyptic novels, Boyd Craven III takes us deeper into the Chinese invasion of America and the guerrilla war to stop them. As with all wars that grind on too long, children pick up guns and fight. And like all such wars, innocents suffer.

If you enjoy this story, you'll love Boyd's <u>Still Surviving</u> *series. As the big cities convulse, the rural South ambles toward the meltdown of society. Westley Flagg, a poacher, moonshiner and an all-around country boy does what he must to protect his family and his small town from the predations of a big city government and the small town evils that arise in the shadow of apocalypse.*

In this short story, Boyd picks up where L.L. Akers leaves off, and introduces us to a bad ass Irishwoman—a long way from home--who takes a very dim view of being raped.

-Jason Ross

"Who wants to do it?" McNight asked.

"I will," Brooklyn said, pushing her way through.

"No way," Egghead told her. "You're not —"

"It can't be any of the younger kids. The only adults working there are sympathizers and nobody else is old enough or smart enough to get the distraction we need so we're not mowed down."

"Nobody's going to get mowed down," McNight commented, lying on his stomach in the tall grass, looking at the work camp below them with a set of binoculars held to his eyes.

Their guerrilla war against the CTS had started picking up steam, and as the resistance grew, so did their numbers. There were just as many kids, as well as parents, hopeful of being reunited with their loved ones; some, they hoped, were inside.

Foster homes had been found for the few babies that had been liberated in the past, as the group moved on. Their advance wasn't nearly as well-known as A.R.C.H.I.E., and the stories surrounding it, but it moved with them and grew. McNight could feel it pressing against him as he lay prone watching.

"Trucks are coming up," Brooklyn said. "Time for me to go and—"

"I'll do it," Egghead interjected, a tremor in his voice. "I'm old enough, I'm big enough and I'm ... I'm smart and I can figure out how to get this diversion done. If you go in, Brooklyn, I'm worried that ..." His words fell off and both kids shuddered at the unspoken thoughts.

"It won't be safe in there," McNight said, rolling on his side before sitting up. "And you're not as good with your fists as she is," he added, nodding his head toward Brooklyn.

"If I do this right, no fighting will be needed," Egghead told him, his hands shaking.

Brooklyn looked at him, her head cocked.

"Why is it so important to you that I not go?" she asked him gently.

Egghead shrugged his shoulders and mumbled something unintelligible.

Brooklyn let out a dramatic sigh. McNight looked between the two and saw both of them were scared. Hell, he was scared for whoever ended up going. He did think Egbert had the right idea though. He was smart and pretty clever, but he didn't have the same killer instincts that the girl had. Then he had a thought.

"Here," he said, pulling Archie's Purple Heart out of his inner breast pocket and pushing it into the boy's hand. "Hold onto this until we come get you tomorrow night."

Egghead gulped, then nodded, something in his gaze changing, hardening.

"I'll keep it safe," he said, his voice almost a whisper.

"You do that. Remember, the meetup spot is by those fuel tanks, but if you don't hurry, those trucks down there are going to pass you by."

Egghead got up and hugged Brooklyn quickly, blushing, then shook McNight's hand and took off down the hill towards the main road. Brooklyn and McNight sat down, neither of them feeling good about what they had just done.

"It should have been me going," Brooklyn said, breaking the silence as Egghead made it to the roadside, the convoy of trucks still half a mile out.

"This might be the place," McNight said gruffly.

"Where they're experimenting on ...?" She didn't finish the thought.

"Yes," McNight said softly. "We won't know until we get the files. I figure that's why Egbert didn't want you going. You being the way you are ..." His words trailed off as he took in her pale skin. "You might be put right into the breeding program."

"I carry the albino genes," she said quietly. "In their eyes, is that a good thing, or a bad thing?"

Both went silent as Egghead started waving his hands over his head in an X shape and then out wide in a Y, over and over until they could hear the brakes and air cylinders compressing as the column stopped. Several soldiers hopped off the back, guns out and ready. Egbert was roughly frisked, then led to the back of the transport truck at gunpoint and pushed in. The brakes were released, then the trucks drove to the gate of the facility and entered one by one.

"I hope we did the right thing," McNight said softly, wishing his dog was with him, instead of back with the main group.

"I can always head to the gates and tell them I'm looking for a friend and they'll—"

"No, we're not going to let you get caught, too. If something happens to me, I'll need somebody I trust to carry on ... and keep Shithead fed."

Brooklyn was wiping her eye; the wind probably having blown some debris into it. McNight had the same issue, but he was already lying on his stomach. Using kids to fight a guerrilla war? He prayed none of them would be hurt.

"What happens if this is the breeding facility?" Brooklyn asked after a moment.

McNight's words were cold, spoken through clenched teeth. "No prisoners."

MANDY'S HANDS were sore and chapped, old blisters now healing and forming the basis for new calluses. She'd been in the re-education and work camp since the invasion.

"Faster, more efficient. Work better!" the overseer said, snarling the words at her.

She knew soon he was going to make up a bullshit excuse to have a private lesson with her. She'd heard about it from the other young women here. After a while, some went willingly. Their quotas would be lessened, and they were provided with more food and newer clothing that wasn't in tatters or smelled like the dead bodies they'd been stripped from.

"I'm winding these motors as fast as me poor hands can allow, lad," Mandy, or Andy her friends back in Dublin called her, said.

"You no make quota, three days in row. Today four day. You make quota, or you no eat!" The overseer was a swarthy Chinese man who was nearly as tall as Mandy's chin and was easily one hundred and fifty pounds, half of it lard. He'd been eyeballing her for a week now.

She shuddered at the mental image of his nude body on top of hers, but only showed a rolling of her eyes at the nearly screamed words.

"I always make my quota, you fecking muppet, why don't you go pester the lasses who like short, fat, dumpy men, humping them with their wee peckers?"

His face turned beet red, but Mandy was working hard and winding the electrical motor with the copper wire. She knew she shouldn't have needled the man, but her plan was simple, and she'd finally gotten enough materials hidden away in the small locker she was allowed, to affect an escape.

The blow was savage. Even being shorter, Overseer Chau snapped her head back with a chop to the chin that left her head spinning.

"You make quota, or else."

Mandy focused as her head swam from the blow, but she knew not to fight back, not here.

It was one thing to fight one man, and she knew she was perfectly capable of killing this one by hand, but it was the seventeen guards that rotated through this section of the adhoc factory she'd have to worry about. She'd be shot down in a heartbeat, and being dead was not on her immediate plan of things to do.

"I'll make your fecking quota," Mandy said, spitting the blood taste out of her mouth at her feet, and turning back to her work.

"Better, or tonight ..." Chau let the words hang there, his eyes locked on her with a hunger that normally would have creeped her out; instead, it filled her with a barely contained rage that her old boyfriend in Tennessee, Jax, would have blamed on her red hair.

"Quit slowing me down. Move your tub so I can wrap these motors," she said, pretending to be cowed.

Overseer Chau leered, then turned and walked away. Inside, Mandy seethed. She'd gotten another pencil, making her small stash of them six now. Waiting until nobody was watching her – even the quality control guy across the aisle from her was bored and talking to his co-worker – did she take the chance and pull her stash out. She'd gotten six small stubs of pencils.

Putting three together, she wrapped a small loop of copper wire over each end, twisting them tight before snipping it off. She repeated this until she had two triangular stacks of pencils about ten centimeters long. Then she pulled about fifty centimeters more of copper wire and dropped it in front of her, along with other scraps. Almost nothing was thrown away and, if questioned, she would claim it was the end of a roll to be put in the recycling.

She was able to quickly catch up and get ahead of her quotas, forming another blister on her left hand, in the pad below her index finger. She made sure that if the overseer of this camp's CTS work and re-education center claimed she'd missed quota again, she'd have witnesses.

"Mandy, what's the rush?" Sarah, the nearly eighteen-year-old who'd been in her left position all week asked, suddenly getting swamped with Mandy's parts.

"I kinna let the swarthy bastard say I never hit me quota," Mandy said, figuring some of the truth wouldn't hurt.

"But you've been hitting it daily. If you didn't, there would be no way I could." Her words rang true, but Mandy had been suspicious of her since they moved her to take the bolter's job down the assembly line from her.

"It doesn't make any sense to me, but it's not your ass that's on the line," she told Sarah truthfully. "Unless it really is."

"What do you mean?" Sarah asked, her mouth twitching.

"Yer too slick by far, too well fed. Ye claim yer about to hit eighteen, but you're much too mature for ya age, lass. So, who are you really working for?" Andy wasn't sure if it was her nature as a redhead, or the Irish getting up her blood, because she shouldn't have said that.

A look of anger crossed Sarah's face and she opened and closed her mouth a few times, before shaking her head and rolling her eyes.

THE END of shift hadn't been the end of things. Both ladies and lads were led out separate doors and to opposite sides of the compound. The ladies disrobed and showered quickly. Sexual assault wasn't common in the shower rooms, but it had happened. None of the young ladies wanted to be nude in front of their guards any longer than they had to. Each was required to quickly wash in cold water before heading to a thin supper.

Mandy hurried, barely getting wet. She knew Chau would be coming for her tonight. What she'd spirited out of the factory was hid easily in one hand, and none of the birds she was showering with gave two shies, nor cared. Talking was discouraged and most of them had been forced to deal with Chau one way or another. She wondered if the chairman fancied the boys the same way and shuddered at another unfortunate mental image. She quickly dressed in fresh overalls, her loot in her left pocket, before heading to supper.

Nobody talked to Mandy much, though she had long since quit trying to make friends here. Something about her made the ladies either avoid her or made them snarl at her. She was slightly taller than many of the lasses in her group at 178 centimeters tall, or about five foot ten inches in the complicated American system of measure. Her fiery red hair had a natural loose curl to it, and her mop was usually controlled with a black bandanna, if nothing else to keep it out of her face.

"Is this seat taken?" a boy's question startled her from her thoughts of escape.

"My feet are there, bugger off."

"There's nowhere else to sit." His words were soft, so Mandy rolled her eyes and pulled her legs back in front of her.

Other than the factory work, this was the only time the two sexes were allowed to mingle, and only for an hour. Mandy usually had her food eaten in five minutes and then just relaxed, or soaked her sore, bruised and blistered hands in the cold water of the lavatory.

"Thanks," the tall young man said, sitting down across from her.

She looked up. His head was a tad smallish, his glasses a bit big, but he wasn't staring at her the way other boys usually did. She wasn't on this boy's menu apparently. Maybe he'd be a good buffer, as long as she could get him to stay sitting there. It would be better than the parade of man boys who thought she'd appreciate their attention. Little gobshites.

"Your accent is... are you from England?"

Mandy dropped her spoon on the tray and looked up. "Are ye fecking kidding me, or are you taking the piss to me, lad?"

"Irish?" He was shifting in his seat uncomfortably.

"Next you're going to call me a Jackeen?" Mandy asked, her blood temperature rising again.

"I ... I don't even know what that means. Sorry, I'm Egghead, Egbert. I didn't mean to—"

"Aye Eggy, and I'm Mandy," she said, letting out a sigh and

trying to cool down, she didn't want to run this one off, not yet anyway.

Mandy had always looked at American citizens with skepticism. The news back home made the USA sound at one point like it was an armed camp, waiting for a civil war, or to fend off any invasion. What she'd seen while she had been here had been anything but. The fall of the country had come as a surprise to them as much as it had to her. Still, Mandy found the young lad's lack of guile amusing and he was keeping the spot filled so the muppets that usually tried to talk her up would move on.

"Sorry, it's just... were you born here?" he asked suddenly.

"Oh, you're a bold one," Mandy said grinning and pointed at his plate, "You going to eat those chips?"

"Chips?"

Mandy had been given a mixture of rice, vegetables and fish. The boy across from her though ...

"Hey, those are my fries!" Egghead said as she snatched a few off his plate.

"Not anymore, mate," she said shoving them in her mouth.

The boy didn't look put off; rather, a smile tugged at the corner of his mouth.

"So, what are you in for?" he asked her.

"Being born, what about you?" Mandy asked in return, without pausing to swallow her mouthful.

"Got caught on purpose," he said taking a big bite from his fish as Mandy's jaw dropped open.

"It's not that desperate out there, is it?" she asked.

"Judging by the newly formed bruise on the side of your face, arms and what I can see of your neck, you've been beaten?"

She shook her head at the sudden change in subject. "Naw, I take shite from no man or woman. Now why the feck would ye get caught on purpose?" she asked him.

He just smiled and slid his tray to her. "Oh don't worry, I don't plan on being here long."

She watched as he got up and wandered away. Looking at the two trays in front of her, the girl sitting kitty corner reached for the tray. Food rations had been getting shorter and shorter lately. Mandy saw the hand and waited, then lashed out, slapping her on the knuckles with her spoon.

"I'll gob smack the shite out of your fool head you touch my chips again," Mandy said, before dumping the tray on hers, then pushed the empty one back at the girl.

"Bitch," was the reply she got.

Mandy smiled, knowing she'd angered the lass. No matter, hopefully tonight she'd be breaking out of here. All she had to do was wait for the perfect opportunity. She ate in a hurry, oblivious to the angry stares of those around her as she devoured two portions of food. She ignored them. Given the opportunity, these lads and lasses would have done the same.

The five-minute bell rang, and the gymnasium-sized room started to empty out. Mandy waited her turn in line with the other ladies, as they would have one more class before their night's sleep. She was only half paying attention, tapping her pocket to feel the coil of wire when she realized her turn to file through would happen and there was double the compliment of guards.

"You, step aside," a short man said pointing to her when she went to pass through, as two of the five guards stepped in front of the doorway, their Type-95 bullpup rifles aimed at her midsection.

Mandy slowly put her hands up. "I take it ya lads aren't here to buy me a pint of the Black Stuff?"

"You come with," the first man said, pointing.

He turned, and Mandy followed, seeing in dismay that the two that had leveled rifles at her had turned to follow her, their guns out at the low and ready. Mandy mentally cursed and wondered if the overseer had found her preparations in the cleaning closet.

"Did I do something wrong, or are ya slagging me?"

"I speak English, why can't this American dog?" a man's voice said from behind her in a heavy Chinese accent.

"Because I'm not an American, lad."

The two men behind her started jabbering in Mandarin, their words undecipherable to Mandy as she followed the third. She broke out into a fine sweat as she realized she was being taken to the overseer's office. If this failed, it was going to be her arse, literally. Failure wasn't an option now that she was sure what Chau had planned. What she was counting on was the moment the two of them were alone.

All the slaps, the chops, the rough hands gripping her arms, spinning her; his foul breath breathing down the back of her neck while he creeped on her and tried to look down her shirt. Either it would all end today and she'd be free, or she'd be dead, with the overseer's tendencies making the plan possible. She'd only briefly entertained going to him willingly, getting him more comfortable with her, but it was a brief moment of madness not to be repeated.

"You no American, why here?" the guard in front of her asked.

The two chattering lads behind her paused, waiting for her answer. Mandy decided on honesty again, as the men escorting her were newer and she'd never seen them abuse anybody.

"I was here studying abroad when you lads came in. I was on the lam with my boyfriend actually."

"Engrish?" he asked, barely looking over his shoulder.

"Irish, Northern Ireland. I was an exchange student."

"You look too old to exchange study," a man behind her said.

They had walked back into the factory portion, where a night shift of young men was working. These were people who could come and go, being trusted party members of the CTS or sympathizers. Many eyes paused their work to admire the redheaded beauty being led down the aisleway. Mandy hated the attention and hated wolf whistles more than anything she could imagine, but this lot knew she wasn't being paraded through the factory for their benefit.

"Aye, it was my senior year, then I was headed to the Uni," Mandy told him.

They walked until Mandy could see the metal steps on the back wall that led up to a mezzanine level, where the Overseer had an office walled off. The rumor was that he slept up there. Mandy had only heard about it second and third hand, but the sight of him opening his door, looking down at her and smiling – that look chilled her, making her arms break out in goosebumps.

It was that moment that the guard in front looked over at her. "I sorry, miss. I do what overseer tells me. No choice."

"Don't let it worry you, lad. You fellows going inside with me?" Mandy asked as they all started up the stairs.

"No. Orders to wait here," he said, stopping outside the door.

The two behind her that had been jabbering in Mandarin had gone silent as she reached the mezzanine landing. The office itself looked to have been stick constructed with metal sheeting covering the walls. The floors outside of it were gridwork metal. She glanced a look down and almost went dizzy at the twenty feet of empty space and parts for the factory directly below her. If things went wrong and she had to, it was enough of a fall to ... she shook her head and stood up straight. She had to remind herself not to touch her pocket, assuring herself that her surprise was still hidden.

"Please," the nice guard said, opening the door for her.

Surprised by his manners and kind tone, she stepped inside.

"PLEASE, SIT," Overseer Chau said, then looked at his guard who had remained at the door and jerked his head to the side, indicating he wanted him to leave.

Mandy looked around. She was sitting on the edge of an overstuffed couch across from a desk Chau was sitting behind. His chair must have been on the highest elevation, because he was at eye level with Mandy. The office on the inside was wood paneled with papers and certificates put on the wall in a language Mandy had no idea what it was but suspected a Chinese dialect.

"Here we are," Chau said formally.

She slid her hand into her pocket and let her fingers curl around one bundle of pencil stubs. She could feel the lightly braided copper wire. If one strand broke, there were two more. Her only worry was that it was too stiff to use properly when the time came. She didn't think so, but the worry was still there.

"I made my production, Overseer," Mandy said, remembering to use his title and not to call him a muppet again.

"No, still behind. We talk; you want to eat, you make more parts. Lots."

"I can't go any faster than I am, you think I'm acting the maggot?" Mandy asked, biting back a more cutting retort, "And what of everyone downline from me? If I am not hitting production, they cannot themselves. Eh?"

"I don't think you understand how this works," he said in surprisingly clear English.

That made her sit up straight. He could speak perfect English without an accent? He was holding back that tidbit. If he was holding that back, what else was he hiding? Mandy chanced a glance out the door's window, seeing the guards had retreated down the mezzanine, probably not wanting to listen to her rape. She almost wondered if she called for help, would the lead guard come to her aid? She doubted it.

"I know exactly how this works, you fecking miscreant," Mandy hissed. "Ya won't be getting me out of my pants over some fake cooked up paperwork. I'm not selling my arse so cheap."

Overseer Chau's eyebrows went up and he stroked the thin beard on his chin.

"Who said I wanted your arse?" he said mimicking her accent.

Mandy stood up, rolling her shoulders, getting on the balls of her feet.

"Ah, a fighter, good. I like breaking you American sluts. When I'm done with you, you'll beg for it. You'll be willing and even eager."

"For a pecker the size of my wee little finger?" she asked, putting a mocking note in her voice and holding her hand up, showing him her small hand, pinky extended.

The taunt worked. Chau turned red, high in his cheeks and ears.

"It is no matter," he said standing, starting to come around the desk. "The guards know you will be difficult. I have standing orders to take you to either the hospital ward or isolation depending on your condition after I'm done with you."

"You're a disgusting boyo, not worth the spit of a slug. You disgust me. You make buzzards puke."

He moved fast, closing the distance. Mandy saw the movement and had time to pull the garrote out of her pocket. Chau was watching her face and missed her movement, thinking she was turning for the door. She wasn't doing any of that, but he swung so fast she didn't see the blow coming until it was too late to dodge. She turned her head slightly, taking a punch to the side of the head.

Despite being taller than him and nearly the same weight as the short tub of shite, the blow rocked Mandy. She bounced off the couch, her back smacking into the left wall the couch had rested on next to the door. Chau was still looking at her eyes, drinking in the look of pain and the brief look of real fear that washed over her face. Seeing her rocked, he straddled her knees, pushed her right hand back and tore at the top of her overalls.

It was the opening Mandy had been waiting for. She shook the garrote out with her left hand and swung it. The wire was stiff, but still had the partial shape of the coil to help it out. It wrapped around his neck as he was pulling at the front of her bra. He paused for a second as Mandy pistoned her knee upwards, one leg no longer trapped. She caught him by surprise and as he started expelling air, she brought her other hand around and grabbed the loose end of the garrote and pulled it across his throat. Tight.

Suddenly realizing what was going on, his hands had gone to his throat, pulling at the wire. Mandy had planned on doing this from behind him if at all possible, but she didn't have much of a choice now. He clawed at her hands until she took a chance and head butted him. The blow dazed both of them, but she was able to make enough room between them that he pulled his head back.

Desperation filled Chau's face, and he threw a quick and sloppy right-hand punch. Mandy tried to dodge but holding the garret with both hands she didn't have anywhere to go. The blow caught her right in the nose, immediately sending a spray of blood. She screamed, her voice high-pitched. She didn't have to pretend that it hurt – it really did hurt. That momentary lapse of attention gave Chau a chance to grab her right wrist with both of his hands and start pulling. Rivulets of blood ran down the side of his neck as the copper wire bit into his flesh.

"Not bloody likely, you fecking muppet," Mandy snarled, spraying his face with the blood that was running across her lips.

She used her knee as a piston once again and when it connected, Chau's face went white with pain. The half a breath he had gotten when he had pulled her wrist was immediately cut off. Without thinking, Chau put both hands to his throat and tried pulling the wire away again. Mandy had been ready for this and started twisting the wire hand over hand. Chau's right hand was trapped at the base of his throat, but Mandy kept twisting and tying, giving him no room to pull the garret free.

"You will not be touching another lass, nor another lass's arse, you piece a shite," Mandy told him as she watched his movements start to slow.

She watched as his eyes bugged out and then shoved him as

hard as she could with her open palms. He started slumping and gravity was working against Mandy. She wasn't able to push him backward, so she slid to her right, able to leverage him just enough so that he fell face forward, his head hitting the wall.

"No, I don't want to, you can't make me!" Mandy started screaming in a high-pitched voice as she walked around the office, saying it for the benefit of the guards if they had stayed where they were supposed to be.

She had to work fast and went to the only other door in the room which was behind his desk. She walked back there and opened it up. Filing cabinets lined two of the four walls, but the other two were taken up by a large king-sized bed, a small dresser, and a mini fridge. She noted there was no bathroom up here in his quarters, and wondered if the rumors were true, that he never bathed. He sure smelled like he never did.

Mandy let out another high-pitched scream and started kicking and stomping at the floor. What she was really doing though, was opening up the file cabinets and looking through them. They all appeared to be dossiers, including pictures. In the third file cabinet from the right she found her file. When she opened it up it had her picture, their estimated age of her, which was wrong, and what they knew about her health history.

She scanned through it and noted they also had her blood type and ancestry marked down. That puzzled her and worried her a little bit at the same time. There was a check mark about fertility. This was stranger and stranger. Mandy saw that they were screening men and women here for something medical but didn't know what.

She went to another filing cabinet, one that had the lock popped out on the front. She pulled the first drawer open and sitting right on top were two files that had not been properly put away. They were sitting on top of everything else in the drawer.

Mandy could see that one of them was not in alphabetical order like the other files.

"Egbert," she said, as she opened the file, seeing his name in black felt marker.

Sure enough, it had a picture of a bird in there but much of the data in the file was still blank or missing. There was a pink sticky note on the front of the folder that she ignored at first. She flipped it back closed and read the note: *connection to Archie.*

"Archie?" Mandy said, then let out another high-pitched scream and started pretending to beg and repeat no, over and over and over.

She opened the other file that had been placed on top and saw right away what it was. Archie was a veteran that the CTS had captured and had been believed to have been executed. There was a new note in the file that said, despite photographic evidence, Archie had survived the gunshot to the head. He had been linked to a resistance movement.

She quickly scanned through the notes they had on this resistance movement – some guy name McNight, along with a list of other names, Egbert being one of them.

"So ya got caught on purpose, ay buddy?" she asked no one. "Looks like these blokes might've been hip to you from the start."

Dark red drops started falling on the files. With a start, Mandy realized that she'd been dripping blood all over the place. She was pretty sure her nose was broken but it'd started off as a gush and had slowed rapidly. To make this ruse work she would need to keep the guards out of here long enough to go to the hospital ward. She had a plan if they took her to the isolation/lockup instead, but the hospital ward put her right next to the supply closet she'd stored her stuff in.

She hurried into the other room and put her hands under Chau's armpits and slowly dragged him off the couch. His body hitting the floor had one of the guards look up just as Mandy noticed his movement from outside the door. She crouched down and started yanking him as hard as she could toward the back door.

"Overseer Chau?" a guard's voice rang out behind the steel door, just as Mandy slammed the door behind her and the overseer's corpse.

"No, I don't want to, it hurts, it hurts!" she screamed as she used all her of her core body strength to push the overseer onto the bed.

She screamed again as there was a knocking at the steel door in the outer office. She hoped she was convincing enough, otherwise they might beat her to death before she had a chance to make her escape. What the guards would do in the next thirty seconds might change the outcome of her entire plan.

There was a lot riding on this. She pulled the blankets over the overseer, and then looked down to see her overalls covered in blood, the top ripped open, her black bra and chest covered in her own blood. She unzipped her overalls down to near her waistline and made sure the blood was smeared all over her hands, her face, her chest, and her stomach.

She heard the outer office door burst open and two voices call out in Chinese. She opened the door to the office and slid out slamming the file room/bedroom door behind her. She screamed as if she was in fear and ran to the first guard that had been kind to her while leaving her up here.

"No more, no more, no more! Please?" she asked, falling to her knees in front of him as if in supplication.

"How bad you hurt?" the kind guard asked her, offering an arm to help her stand up.

"My nose doesn't hurt as bad as ..." She let the words trail off and then shot a long glance at the closed door where the overseer's body was tucked in neatly.

One of the guards that had been behind her joined the nice guard in the doorway and smiled, poking him in the ribs. The nice guard kind of shoved him back, either making more room or showing his disgust.

"You come, we will take you to doctor. They fix nose. They give you ... after morning pill. Morning after ... whatever."

Mandy didn't say anything as the nice guard pushed past the other two, closing the office door behind them. They led her back down the mezzanine staircase toward the factory floor. Men would look up as they walked through, but seeing her condition and her attempts to hold her bloodstained overalls closed, they quickly looked away.

She hadn't planned on getting hurt or busted up at all, but if she had the chance, she was going to let the doctor set her nose. Then the real shenanigans could begin. The kind guard looked back to make sure she was following close, and she gave him a shy grin. The sight of her bloodied teeth made him shudder and he turned back around, walking a little bit faster, trying not to run. Her plan was working. So far, so good.

MANDY DIDN'T SEE the doctor right away, but she was given two generic pain pills and another one she figured was their birth control. She rinsed her mouth out from the drinking fountain, making sure there was no blood, then swallowed the pills, knowing she didn't need the Plan B pill, but taking it anyway. Things in the back were unusually busy with people running in and out of the room.

The front of the hospital ward was heavily guarded, but she was mostly alone in her room. She'd left the front of her overalls open as if they'd been ripped from her, with her blood drying to a crust on her chest and stomach. She'd wiped up her face as much as she could after swallowing the pills, but without a bathroom mirror she didn't know how bad it looked.

"Mandy O'Hanson," a woman's voice called before knocking on the door and entering the small room Mandy had been put in to wait.

She understood why they didn't want to keep her in public, even though she wasn't very hurt to begin with. She looked exactly like how she wanted to look, a survivor of a sexual assault. She was using everyone's squeamishness to divert attention and hopefully allow her a chance to make it to the woman's restroom alone.

"Aye, that's me." Her words were quiet, but she made herself sound more pained and less confident than she actually was.

A woman in her mid-forties came in, her hair pulled up into a severe-looking bun. Her gray hair seemed to be pinned in place with two sharpened pencils, which Mandy noted as a potential sharp object to acquire and use if necessary. She was wearing a white doctor's coat, and beneath that a set of blue scrubs. She had those rubberized orthopedic shoes that walking billboards for abstinence showed.

"Mandy, it says here you're almost nineteen years old. Exchange student from Ireland, originally from the Dublin area. You have all the required immunizations that were up-to-date until ..." The woman broke off her words and looked at Mandy, her features American, then she looked in the direction the guards were standing and scowled, "and you're here today because some asshole broke your nose and I see they've already given you the Plan B pill."

"Aye, the overseer, the sorry bastard, though he'd manufactured a reason to get him a piece of me arse," Mandy said coldly, wondering why this lady was working with the Chinese when she clearly hated them.

"Are you in any pain?" she asked. "I can help, but they won't let me prescribe – "

"How many lasses have you treated? How many rapes do you allow to happen under your roof, and how many aborted babies do ye kill on average?"

The Irish was rising in Mandy again, and she wasn't very happy. Truth was the only thing that hurt was her nose, but to see someone semi-willingly working with the Chinese and not fighting back? That made her all kinds of pissed off, and when Mandy O'Hanson got pissed off people understood why redheads had a fierce reputation.

The doctor had a name tag that said *Fikes* on her white lab coat. Mandy took in the rest of her features. She looked like she'd once been slender but now gentle curves filled out her frame. Then she did a double-take – the doctor was not nearly as old as Mandy had originally thought; rather she was working under tremendous strain.

"I have absolutely no choice in the matter," she said, tears threatening to spill down her cheeks. "They have my husband and my daughter locked up here. I'm good at healing people, even if I'm doing it after the monsters hurt the innocent. Can you blame me for trying to do my best for you?"

"I just ..." Mandy's anger fizzled at that moment, and she realized the doctor was right. She was working here of her own free will, but she was doing everything she could to counter the mess the Chinese had brought to the American shores.

"I'm sorry, Doc," Mandy said rubbing the bridge of her nose where she felt a large bloodied knot. "I'm angry at the whole fucking world right now and my nose is hurting." She leaned forward and in a softer tone said, "And I'm hoping to get me arse out of this joint soon. I don't suppose you all wouldn't love to do the same?"

Dr. Fikes walked closer to Mandy and put her right hand on the young woman's face, then she put her left hand on the other side, cradling her face and pulled her closer. In a quiet voice the doctor said, "Don't we all?" Then her thumbs pushed to the sides of Mandy's nose and pulled.

A bolt of pain shot through Mandy's head, and then she jerked out of the doctor's reach. New drips of blood fell down her front, but Mandy had felt the moment her nose had been set straight. It was not something she bloody likely ever wanted to feel again. She held one hand under her nose while Dr. Fikes reached into her lab coat pocket and tore open some gauze. She handed the gauze to Mandy and left the room.

Mandy wondered if she'd said too much, but Dr. Fikes was back a moment later with a handful of supplies. The first thing she did was punch a chemical ice pack, knead it, and hand it over to Mandy. Pinching her nose with the gauze, Mandy put the ice pack over her face.

"Your nose set pretty easy, there's a possibility you'll have a small bump or a scar where it broke, but without proper supplies it's the best I can do." Then she leaned in with a quieter voice again, "and if you have some sort of plan, keep it to yourself. You can trust me but some of my nurses are collaborators, just like some of the people that work on the floor in the factory."

Mandy pulled the ice pack back to study her and nodded. "I've had to learn quick who I can trust and who isn't worth the shite the Lord scraped off his shoes. If you could tape me up and then let me use the bathroom, I'll be out of your hair superfast."

"Part of the Ray protocol the Chinese have forced on us is to always have a guard nearby when someone is using the restroom. I don't let them come inside the bathroom because there's no point. There are no windows; one door in and one door out. You can have your privacy if you need to cry. But I can't have you doing anything stupid in there."

"Do something stupid? Do you think I'm gonna try to off myself like some crying fucking violet?" Mandy asked her with a little laugh at the end.

Dr. Fikes was ready and taped her nose and advised her to put the cold pack back on top. Mandy held it there barely able to see the short doctor over it.

"You know, cut your wrists, jump out a window, hang yourself, all that stuff's been tried before, and the guards know to look for it."

"I know what you fucking mean," Mandy said testily. "I'm not a suicide case. I just want to wash my arse. I told you, I'm getting out of here."

"And how are you doing that?" the doctor asked her.

"I've a feeling all hell's about to break loose, so if I were you I would be ready when the time comes."

Dr. Fikes shook her head and reached in her pocket and pulled out a small, plain white pill bottle. She handed it to Mandy and walked out of the room letting the door swing closed behind her with a bang.

"Bloody hell, she's either the bravest woman in here, or a complete nutter."

The door banged open and a Chinese guard was there, the nice one from earlier. Mandy quickly tried to cover herself with her overalls, but he was already turning away, his face red.

"Doctor say you need chaperone. I am ... it was unfortunate ... I offered to do it myself in case other guard not so kind."

Mandy pulled her overalls closed as much as she could with one hand and stood up. She was half a head taller than the guard and when she tried to meet his eyes, he turned his face.

"You dunna have to be ashamed for me, lad," she said softly, realizing he was only a handful of years older. "I'm still alive and ye've not done nothing to impinge upon your own honor. Ye've been kindest of all and I appreciate your offer to be the chaperone."

She did, but she also felt bad, because it was almost time to make her escape and she was worried that if she failed, he'd be blamed and punished. He was the only decent Chinese guard she'd run across to date. He nodded at her words and motioned with his hand for her to follow him before turning and holding the door open with his other hand behind him.

Mandy followed, and when she pushed the door with her

shoulder, he let it go. She dumped the ice pack into the first bin she saw. It would have to be enough, and she prayed it was. She knew she was going to have two black eyes, but she also worried about one of them swelling shut. So far it hadn't happened, but the night was early, and the overseer's body hadn't been found yet.

"If you wait, I have washcloth and new cover," he said, pointing to her overalls, "coming from laundry. You wash up, put on clean clothes. Use bathroom first, then come back here and I have things ready."

Mandy was surprised at that and nodded. She'd go along with it until she had clean overalls. She didn't want to make a spectacle of herself being blood-stained, but sometimes the Lord provided, and he was smiling down upon her right now. She promised herself she was parking her arse in the next bloody Catholic church she saw when she got out of this bolloxed shit box of an institution.

"Where's the loo?" she asked, following him.

"Through," he replied, still leading.

She followed him through a doorway where there had been a mass of people coming in and out earlier. It was a triage area, with four beds lined up in a hallway section beyond the door. One of them held a figure in bloodied sheets, moaning softly. Mandy hoped it wasn't another lass, coming from having the worst moment of her life. Then the sheet moved, and she let out a gasp, recognizing the boy's face.

"Wait," Mandy called to her guard. "Eggy, is that you?" she asked, walking to the bed.

"Mandy?" he replied quietly.

"Aye, lad. What are ye doing in here? Fighting the world?"

"Sort of," he said, looking at the guard warily. "Getting caught on purpose might not have been such a good idea after all," he added, still eying the guard. "I think they busted a few teeth out and my ribs feel bruised. Are you okay?" he asked her, taking in the blood-stained clothing and puffy face.

"Sort of," she shot back at him, admiring how the beating he'd taken that had put him in a hospital bed hadn't broken his spirit. "The fecking overseer busted me nose."

"She need go now," the nice guard told him and gently pulled on Mandy's arm. She let him do it, knowing she could have broken his arm in three places before he had a chance to react or call out an alarm. Knowing that and not acting was making her twitchy.

"Let me talk to the lad a moment more, will ye? I've taken a shine to this one and ... I have things to tell him."

She batted her eyelashes, but not to flirt, but in what she hoped looked like mock shame. It worked, and he gave her a quick nod, then backed up to the doorway. Mandy put her hands together and gave him a mock bow and smile, then turned back to Egghead.

"So, you've taken a shine to me, eh? Did the overseer ... did he ... take advantage of you? Are you okay?"

The words were a vocal diarrhea of sorts, and she suddenly saw he was absolutely terrified and scared. It was infectious; either that, or Mandy was starting to think about the cooling body of Chau upstairs.

"Sort of. You're an interesting lad. No, the overseer just busted me nose. I'll be okay, but he won't be," she said smiling.

"He won't be ..." When the realization hit, it was like watching a light bulb turn on behind his eyes and Mandy nodded to him when he got it.

"So, I won't be here long, lad, and there's something you should know. They know all about you, some guy named Archie and McNight and a ragtag army of kids. Bloody wolverines or some shite like that. How bad are you really hurt?"

The last was whispered, as Mandy leaned forward so they were almost face to face. She looked back and saw the guard watching. He looked away quickly.

"I hurt, but not as bad as I make it seem," he admitted. "Why? How soon are things going to get crazy?"

"I'm going to the loo. When you hear the gates of hell kicked in, you make yourself scarce, and stay away from the smoke and fire. I have a feeling they're going to have to let the people outside to the gates before long. I just pray nobody is hurt."

"What are you going to do?" Eggy asked.

She brushed aside the hair on his forehead and leaned down, pressing her lips against it in what she hoped would be taken as a gesture of affection by the watching guard, and now nurse who had joined him in the doorway, their brows furrowed as she whispered to him.

"I'm going to blow the fecking bastards into bloody bits."

"You're IRA, aren't you?" Eggy asked suddenly.

"No, ya silly boyo, I watched too much YouTube growing up!" She snickered and stood.

Egghead touched his forehead where her lips had made contact. His face was turning red around the purple areas. Mandy gave him a little wave and then nodded her head to the nice guard. He came forward.

"Now I gotta go before I piss myself," she said to both.

The guard pointed at a door with his finger, his lips pinched at her vulgarity. She grinned and followed him as he opened it, showing a single stall bathroom, a sink hanging off the wall, with a heavy-duty toilet against the adjoining wall, and a stainless-steel grab bar on the left side of the porcelain throne.

"Thank ya mate, I think I got it here," she told him, closing the door.

"No locking," the guard called back.

"Not bloody likely," Mandy whispered to the door.

SHE IMMEDIATELY TURNED on the water and turned the lock slowly until she heard it click. She hoped the water would be enough to mask the sound, but she doubted the guard would be outside the door in case she was doing something like dropping a load, let alone piss loudly. Mandy almost snickered. That guard was the best of the lot, but he seemed very naïve or very, very shy. She hoped it was shy. She turned the water off, then walked over to the toilet. Everything in this room was white: the fecking walls, the tile on the floor and the drop ceiling with its white fecking gridwork.

Mandy stood on the toilet, then put one foot up on the grab bar, leveraging herself high enough to push one of the ceiling tiles up. She slid it aside and boosted herself up on the partitioning wall. She'd already mapped this and knew she'd had the luck of the Irish. That had made her grin like none other. She didn't have far to crawl through the utility access points. She replaced the ceiling tile and lifted the tile in the adjoining space and tossed it aside. She wouldn't be coming back this way.

The strong smell of chemicals wafted to her as she lowered herself halfway through the opening. It made her smile. She made sure to grab the box on top of the wall divider before getting all the way down. Using the utility closets shelf as a ladder, she made it to the floor soundlessly. That's when Mandy cracked open the box. Inside she'd smuggled a few things, mostly the metal containers and discarded cans from the mess hall that she'd rinsed out. It wasn't as reactive when she had been mixing and experimenting.

"If this works, ya little boyos are going to get you a big surprise," she said, her grin almost a rictus of pain from her broken nose.

"Where she go?" she heard somebody yelling in the distance.

"Time to make the donuts, lads," Mandy said, opening the door.

She'd gone to another wing of the entire place by just crawling a few feet across another wall. She'd discovered the dead space that the utilities and heating and cooling systems had occupied above the drop ceiling and had been squirreling supplies away, and then she'd made the TATP.

It's right dangerous stuff, but the Chinese were shipping everything over and it must have been cheaper to ship the concentrated hydrogen peroxide rather than the diluted stuff. She'd found a lot of it in the cleaning closet of all places, but did people clean with that shite? Mandy didn't know, she hoped to figure life out someday, when she wasn't locked up.

"I hope this bloody works." She pulled a cloth satchel out of her metallic box and packed the five containers she'd prepped and wrapped with rags, so they didn't knock together, then opened the door.

Pounding feet had her looking to the right, seeing guards running toward the corner where the hospital wing was separated from the rest of the area. She was between the manufacturing plant and the public restrooms. She grinned. It wouldn't take long to find where she'd gone and how she got out. She had to move fast. Communications was her first order of business. She wanted it cut off if at all possible, but first she had to do something right here.

"Hey, you!" A shout had her turning to look back to her right. Two guards were running at her.

"Hope this works," she said putting a can down and, using a Bic lighter she'd stashed, lit the shoelace she'd spent hours cutting in half and twisting.

It started burning and Mandy took off running toward the manufacturing side.

"Stop, we shoot!" another voice yelled from behind her.

Mandy was running full stride, her long legs giving her an enormous advantage over the shorter, and consequently shorter legged, pursuers. She knew that they weren't joking though, they would shoot. No matter how fast she could run, she couldn't outrun their AK's. She hit the polished tile, sliding like a runner would in baseball just as two things happened. The wall next to her erupted from a gunshot, followed half a second later by a small roaring explosion.

She glanced back seeing the hallway filled with smoke, chunks of pink and red things splattering as gravity finally took over, or they dripped off the ceiling.

"Good, now we know it works," she said with a grin.

Regaining her feet, Mandy almost flinched as the sirens went off and the sprinklers doused the entire hallway with water.

"Oh shit, I dinna think o' that," Mandy cursed herself, now running and trying not to fall across the slick surface of the tile.

Her plan was to gain the door just inside the manufacturing plant, run down that hallway to the communications room, disable it with one of her bombs, and then out the set of double doors that one of the guards had shown her when she'd first moved from janitorial to the production floor. He had ideas of romance, but when she spurned his advances, she was reassigned.

She knew that it led to the fuel depot outside. If she put one of her fuses there, she might blow half the north fence out, as well as the wall. She also might fry herself to a crisp, but she'd promised herself that she'd get out no matter what.

"What's going on?" a man in coveralls asked, screaming from the doorway to the manufacturing side, to be joined a second later with a guard looking around his shoulder.

"Some arse wipes blew something up down by the hospital!" Mandy yelled, running right at them. "The chem closet is going to blow!"

They stood there staring at her. Mandy's feet were making a slapping sound, and she felt a breeze. She looked down to see her blood covered chest and stomach once again, though the water was washing the red away. Feck, she didn't change and had hardly wiped herself up. The man started to run but the guard shouted something at him as he was yanked back in the doors by multiple arms.

Mandy hadn't entirely lied, she knew what was in that closet, but she wasn't running from an explosion, she was running from two chemicals mixing together. She was pretty sure the explosion had knocked over the bleach she'd put in a paint can with a loose lid. It was mixing with another can of ammonia. The smell would hit soon if it had happened, creating a noxious cloud that would cut off pursuers from that side of the building, cutting down the guards by two thirds.

"Out of my way!" Mandy yelled as three guards' faces filled the doorway, their words lost over the wailing of the siren and the low roar of the sprinklers dumping water.

At the last second, one of them recognized her and brought his rifle up. Not able to stop, Mandy once again decided to go low in a baseball slide, holding the cloth bag to her stomach. Now that the tiled floor was slick from water, she had a lot more momentum going. Ten feet. Five. A gun tracked her, and a shot rang out just as her lifted leg impacted the shooters knee. She heard a sickening snap as the guard fell, his screams drowning out the din of noise from the alarms.

She bounded to her feet, but shoes still wet, she slipped. One of the three guards tried to make a grab for her, but she pulled back at the last second and snapped a kick out, catching him high in the ribs. The blow pushed him into the other guard, knocking both of them to the ground next to the man rolling around, holding his leg to his stomach.

"What's going on?" the man who'd been pulled back in screamed, pulling on Mandy's shoulder.

The fabric of her open overalls had more give than he expected, and when Mandy spun, he also wasn't expecting the solid right-hand chop that took him in the side of the throat. He made a quick choking sound, letting go, hands going to his waist as he bent over to breathe.

"Sorry, bubba boyo," she said to him breathlessly. "Didn't know who ye was at first. Pro tip, don't grab a lass unless she gives you permission, got it?"

He fell to the ground as well, on all fours, finally taking in big deep gasping breaths. Mandy was aware of the volatile substances in the bag, the slide, and the fighting. It all could have been enough to blown her to hell and back, but she'd been generous with the padding and her prayers were heard that she hadn't been hit with—

"Smell?" one of the guards barked, regaining his feet and pulling at his partner, coughing.

Mandy ran. They could follow her, they could shoot her, but suddenly the acrid smell of chemicals was almost overpowering. She had to hurry, or her window of opportunity would close. She ran for all she was worth, her right hand cradling the satchel, the lighter in her other hand. The communications room materialized and she almost slid past it. She looked inside and saw a panicked guard. She burst in the door.

"Get out! Somebody's attacking us with chemical weapons! We must flee!"

"What? How you get here? You no supposed—"

"The bloody arseholes down the hallway sent me. We must evacuate, so hurry!"

She didn't want to hurt him if she didn't have to but was more than willing to give this a shot before she resorted to violence again. Her hand she chopped the man with was sore and she didn't want to bust herself up fighting everyone, wearing herself out when what she really should be doing is running.

"You come," he said getting to his feet and motioning to her.

"Ye lead," she panted out to him.

That's when he saw the cloth sack and the lighter in her hand. His panicked face took in Mandy's gaze. When he went for the radio, she was already in motion. He'd knelt to press the button to talk, to alert the whole fecking facility. Mandy had other plans. Her foot shot out, kicking him in the elbow, throwing his entire arm upwards. She held the bag tight and shot out her leg again as he started to yell, her foot impacting with his temple. He dropped like the sack of shit he was.

Mandy looked around, and seeing no one else, dragged him backwards by his shoulders outside into the hallway. If the poison gas got to him, she didn't mind. None of the Chinese here deserved any better, and unless those in the manufacturing side got trapped by something stupid, they should be running outside the other set of doors on the opposite side of the property any second now.

Mandy turned the deadbolts on the big doors, then looked around the communications room. She went to the radio and yanked the handset out, the cords ripping free. She thought about picking up the chair and smashing it, but then looked back at the file cabinets and what she saw on top of it. An old iPod, really old.

"Now the bastard's got my curiosity piqued," Mandy muttered and snatched it up.

She started scrolling through the songs, seeing it had probably belonged to a lady before it was confiscated by the guards here. It was a lot of girl bands, but one in particular stuck out to her, and she was glad she hadn't damaged the PA system yet.

"Patti, you'd love this song, girl," she muttered, remembering a dear friend from Ireland. She ran to the controls.

The microphone jack plugged into the iPod and she hit play and repeat. *In This Moment* started booming as the song *Blood*'s opening intro started blaring.

"This is some good music to open the dance, don't ye think?" she called to the doorway she'd taken the guard out through.

Mandy's gaze then went to the double doors. Outside. Freedom. Almost. Then the lyrics got heavy, the words of the song booming all over the entire facility. Goosebumps covered Mandy's arms as she pushed through the double doors and went outside.

It was dark now, and although she had the harsh chemical smell of the chlorine gas in her nose, she could also smell something burning, and saw a streamer of smoke along the edge of the building. Grinning, she looked straight ahead to the motor pool. Men were running and in half a heartbeat, she saw what looked like a short-bus version of a firetruck headed in the direction of the smoke.

"Almost too easy—"

Gunfire raked the building near her, and a spotlight came on, pinning her in place. The shots had been warning shots. She slid to a stop and put her arms up.

"Mandy, go!" She recognized that voice and took off at a sprint.

There were three large tanks above the ground parked near a couple of trucks. She headed that way until a figure stood up, making her slide to a stop, almost pitching her ass over teakettle.

"Mandy, over here!" Egbert screamed, holding his side, where he'd broken his ribs.

"You muppet!" she yelled back as the gunfire went silent. "What the bloody hell are you doing?"

"My friends are here," he said, grinning. "They took care of the guys shooting at you. They're also about to blow the fence."

"Well then, let's give them a bloody hand," Mandy said, pulling out a soup can, then putting the entire bag down under the fuel tanks.

"What are ..."

"It's TATP. It's still sorta wet, so it's not quite as dangerous as it could be. Now I'm going to light this fecking satchel and you run like the devil's nipping at your girly bits."

"Girly bits?"

Mandy chuckled as she lit the fuse, knowing the explosion or burning cloth bag would ignite the rest of the bombs. Egghead looked at her in a strange light, then realized what she'd done. She stood, yanking his shoulder, almost pulling him off his feet.

"Which way do we go?" he screamed.

Mandy was already moving. The skinny lanky man-child wasn't moving fast enough from being injured, and being a fit lass, she put the bomb in his hand and then took him in a fireman's carry. Gunfire peppered the ground, though she wasn't sure who was shooting at whom. When she'd mentally counted to eight ... nine ... ten ... she dropped to the ground, rolling on top of a screaming Egghead behind a parked military vehicle of some sort, opening her mouth, trying to tell him to do the same while covering him and the last bomb.

The explosion earlier was nothing in comparison to the thunderous boom behind her. The ground seemed to tremble, then open up. Glass shattered for half a mile. An angry avenging god had dropped the hammer. A dozen different anecdotes for the sound went through her head, but the one thing she could say without a doubt – it was the biggest sound ever.

Feeling like all the air had been sucked out of her lungs, Mandy looked around. Something flaming crashed into the armored vehicle they had slid behind. A second set of explosions rocked the night, though Mandy and Egghead were deafened from being so close to the first set. Mandy rolled off Egbert, pulling the bomb out of his hands, before trying to pull him to his feet.

"Look, there they are!" Egghead yelled, but she was reading his lips.

She followed his hand as dozens of figures rushed through the breach in the fence. Two of them broke off, pointing at Mandy and Egbert, who was trying to wave them down with the arm that wasn't holding the muppets guts in from his busted ribs.

"Who are they?" Mandy hollered, not knowing if he could hear her or not.

"My friends. My family," he told her, though this time she could hear him.

Screams from the work camp were almost nonstop now, mostly shouting to coordinate firefighting efforts in two languages. Gunfire rang out from all around the fence. Mandy pulled Eggy with her toward the breach, but he yanked his hand back as a lass with dark glasses and a tall thin man in camo clothing, a dog following along behind them, approached. All were heavily armed, right out of a

Soldier of Fortune magazine: side arms, what looked like the same rifles the Chinese had been using...

"How bad are you hurt?" the man said without pause to Egbert.

"Busted ribs," he replied, then they all hit the ground as rounds started hitting over their head. "Who're your friends?" he screamed to the two newcomers.

"Locals who have family locked up in here. Sorry it took us so long," the pale skinned woman said, brushing the side of his face. "You've got blood coming out of your ears."

They were now all prone behind the armored vehicle, an APC of sorts as gunfire rang out around them. Mandy crawled on her hands and knees as she saw civilians running through the fencing, some coming, some going. Chinese soldiers were trying to stop a massive escape from happening, trying to fight a fire, and fighting off the people who were assisting in the escape all at the same time.

"There's not enough of the CTS to put up much of a fight," the man said rising to his knees and firing his rifle in neat sounding three round bursts.

"There's enough of the bloody fecking bastards to take the piss right out of my plans," Mandy snarked back at him, ducking as bullets rang out on the bumper she was trying to look around. "Shit," she swore.

She then remembered the bomb in her right hand and grinned. She could see the pocket of CTS firing from behind the burning hulk of a transport truck. That's when she realized her left hand was empty.

"What are you looking for?" the pale woman in dark glasses asked her.

"I need a lighter," she said, patting the pockets of her overalls.

The man who'd been firing pulled something out of a breast pouch in his vest and tossed it to her. A Zippo. Mandy caught it on the fly and lit the fuse. The flame flickered but caught. Her hands shook as she put the fuse and flame together.

"Cover me!" she screamed.

Both the man and pale woman stood and started firing.

Mandy had learned to love American softball while she was an exchange student. She'd been a top athlete and had scholarships awaiting her at the Uni if she ever got out of the country. Running, pole vaulting – her parents had even hoped one day she might have been interested in the Olympics of all the fecking bloody ridiculous things. The running she did willingly, but her entire life, she had fallen in love with the martial arts and had been practicing Krav Maga since middle school. Still, the softball bug had bit her hard, and she'd been an excellent pitcher.

She wound up and tossed the burning can underhanded, going more for accuracy than speed. The flame of the can made it easy for her to track its progress in the dark. She stayed up half a second too long and when the ground erupted all around, something hot and sharp cut into her side before she dropped to the ground. She rubbed her cheek, her hand coming back with a red smear as another explosion rocked the night and the gunfire coming at them ceased.

"You got them!" the man said, his gun falling silent.

Mandy wanted to run, but suddenly her limbs felt like jelly, her inner bits wobbly and nauseous. She leaned against the APC's big tire and listened as the explosions and gunfire tapered off to nothing. She watched as civilians fled the area around them, some running all the way around the fence, calling names she didn't know.

"How bad are you hit?" Egghead asked, pulling something from his pocket and holding it against Mandy's cheek.

"I'm not hit!" she shot back.

"Cut from a ricochet," the man told Eggy.

"Well shit, my Ma and Pa always said Americans were a funny lot, liked to worry me to death about getting shot and now ..."

They shook their heads, Egghead rolling his eyes.

"You three stay here. I've got to link up with the local resistance and I'll have the medic that came in yesterday come check on you all. It sounds like things here are wrapping up."

Mandy looked at the man as he tapped his ear. An earpiece was connected to a clip on the vest. He must have been listening to the radio chatter.

"Is it safe?" Egghead asked. "Or should we get the girls out of here first?"

Both Mandy and the pale girl turned to look at him. Mandy knew she was rolling her eyes, but she couldn't see the pale girl's. Shades? Wearing them in the bloody dusk of day?

"I carried your arse once, don't make me conk ya and carry ye wee bones outta here again, boyo," Mandy said, pulling his hand back from her cheek.

"I ... I mean ... you are ... just that I—"

Mandy leaned forward and kissed him on the forehead, rendering him mute.

"That works?" the pale girl asked.

"Seems to," Mandy told her. "Mandy," she said holding out her hand.

"Brooklyn," the pale girl said, shaking her hand. "The tall dude is McNight, and it looks like you've met our Egghead here."

"Yeah, we've become a little acquainted in a short period of time, yeah?"

"Yeah," Egghead said, still three shades of red underneath the bruising.

THEY STAYED THERE AN HOUR, listening as the odd gunshot rang out. They were mostly in cover, but Brooklyn watched over things while Egghead and Mandy took turns cleaning each other's bumps and bruises from a kit she had. Mandy had long ago fixed her coverall situation and now that the fabric was drying, it was starting to stink and stick to her.

"Here's McNight," Brooklyn said to them.

They struggled to their feet to see the smiling face of the tall man making his way toward them.

"We're all clear. All the CTS have been captured or... you know."

"I've done my fair share of killing them," Mandy told him.

"I know you have, but the others?" he shot back.

"I've got my own count, I'm sure," Mandy shot back. "Now if you blokes don't mind, I'm going to get my arse out of here. I have an island to return to, somehow."

"Going back to Dublin?" Egghead asked her suddenly.

"If I can make it," Mandy told him, then reached over and straightened his glasses.

He took it well, though everyone could see his ribs were hurting him. Finally, he leaned against the APC to take the weight off.

"McNight, I almost forgot," Egbert said, pulling something from his pocket.

"What the bloody hell is that?" Mandy asked.

"Something that was earned because of a bloody hell. Given to me by the man who earned it, which I then loaned to Egbert. It's a purple heart," McNight said softly, holding his hand out as a medal was placed in his hand.

"Where did ye hide that from the guards?" Mandy asked Egbert, blurting the question out.

McNight looked at the medal then back at the young man. "I'm going to need to use some *Purell* on my hands, aren't I?"

"No..." Egghead stammered.

"Let's get out of here kids," McNight said standing up. "Ma'am, you're welcome to join us."

"Maybe I will for a time," Mandy said, getting under Egbert's shoulder on his hurt side. "But I've got places to be, and I want to make sure none of the CTS here lives."

"How bad was it?" Brooklyn asked.

"If you were a woman in there ..." She let the words trail off. "They were doing medical things. Something about fertility. I worry they were breeding the lasses here."

McNight whispered something into the microphone on his vest. Gunshots started ringing out behind the building again. The air was thick with the stench of burning chemicals, burning buildings, burning bodies. Mandy saw him motion for them to start walking. She prayed no innocents were hurt in this breakout, but she was a realist. In every war, there were innocent lives lost. She'd done her best to send the CTS to hell. She just prayed she could find her way to a ship, a plane, some way back home.

"You could always stay here," Egghead told her softly as they walked.

"Maybe I will," she replied, grinning. "We'll see."

Together, they walked into the darkness, toward a rise of land where a group was waiting for them.

———

IF YOU ENJOYED this short story, check out Boyd Craven's collection of full novels on Amazon, and be sure to hit the Follow Button.

+ Follow

10

GETTING OUT OF JERSEY

BY ARTHUR DORST

WE ARE GETTING OLDER, whether we like it or not. Will the relentlessly declining trend line of our physical age cross the rising risk line of a collapse before or after we're able to defend our families?

New author, Art Dorst, takes on the best case scenario in a worst case world. Jake and Kate are sixty-something year-old retirees who have maintained their fitness and prepared to the maximum extent allowed by common sense.

Even so, can they pop enough Ibuprofen and leverage their wisdom far enough to escape the dark gravity of a deadly version of New Jersey? Will they leave behind their dreams of Florida, retirement and Social Security soon enough to rescue their children?

In the twilight of human society, even a river you've crossed a thousand times can mean life or death.

-Jason Ross

BOOM, Boom, Boom.

The windshield spider webbed, showering Jake and Kate with glass. The car yanked hard to the left, slamming into the curb, bouncing up over it, coming to a stop. Jake shook his head and looked over at Kate. Blood trickled down her face from a dozen small cuts, but her eyes were open and she was alive. Jake touched his own face; his hand coming away with blood.

"Move, move," yelled Jake as he heard voices and caught movement off to his right. He pushed the car door open and braced his foot against it. He attempted to roll out of the car until he realized he had not unbuckled his seatbelt. He glanced over at Kate.

"Kate, your seatbelt!" he said. Kate stared back at him with blank eyes, her hands not moving.

"KATE, snap out of it!" Jake yelled into her face. Kate blinked and moved her hands, releasing her seatbelt.

"Fuck. Thanks," she replied, her seatbelt clicking open as she began sliding low across the seat toward Jake.

"Keep down," he hissed. With the Mini-14 in his hands, he scanned the street just as another blast struck the car. He instinctively ducked and urged Kate to move out of the vehicle. Jake rose up, shouldered the Mini-14 and squeezed the trigger. Nothing. He rotated the rifle to the left and stared down at it, realizing that in the excitement he had forgotten to take off the safety. Two more blasts hit the car, forcing them both to duck.

"Forgot the safety," Jake muttered.

"Dumbass," replied Kate, back to her old self.

"Grab the bags. I'll cover you," Jake said.

Kate snaked her hands through the bag straps and looked up at Jake, waiting for his go.

"Now."

Jake rose up just as a man in camo with a pistol grip shotgun came running across the street toward them. The man stopped frozen in his tracks, his eyes widening with the realization he had moved out too quickly. For what felt like seconds the two men stood, staring into each other's eyes. Camo man lifted the shotgun and wheeled around as if to simultaneously attack and retreat. The shotgun belched flame, but the shot was high and right. Jake squeezed off two shots, knocking the attacker to the pavement. Jake returned to the cover of their vehicle where Kate waited with their backpacks and go-bag.

She leaned in close to Jake, her face pale and trembling. Her eyes searched his. "What now?"

Jake swapped out magazines. "I think there're only a couple of them. One is down." Jake paused for a moment, considering what he'd just said. He exhaled and scanned the neighborhood.

"I think if we cut between the houses behind us, we might be able to lose them. Hopefully they're having second thoughts about whatever the hell they'd been planning."

"Better than staying here and getting shot," she whispered.

They shrugged into their packs. Jake grabbed the heavier go-bag with their extra ammo.

Fuck, this stuff weighs a ton. I'm in better shape than most guys at sixty-two, but definitely not ready for guerilla warfare. I should be applying for Social Security and heading to Florida for the winter.

"Okay, you move first. I'll cover you," Jake said. "Wait for my go."

Kate nodded. She kept a brave face, but the violence and surging adrenaline rattled her.

Jake gave her a nod and she took off, bent at the waist, moving quickly for someone unaccustomed to demanding physical activity. Jake peered over the car but saw no movement. He counted off five seconds and turned to follow Kate. Running between two houses, he saw the flash of a face and curtains being pulled tight.

Thank God there aren't any fences between these houses. The last thing I need is a broken leg or heart attack trying to climb over.

They jogged between the two houses until shortness of breath and weary legs forced them to slow to a rapid walk. It was obvious that most of the homes had been broken into and looted.

Some were burned and still smoldering. Discarded clothing, furniture, and household goods were strewn across the yards, including an occasional body. The air hung heavy with the stench of death.

They continued walking for a few minutes, but were soon out of breath and sweating when Jake said, "Hold up. Let's find someplace to catch our breath and figure out what to do next."

It would be dark soon. They walked slowly through a few more yards, watching for any signs of life until they came to a ransacked house with an open shed in the back. The shed contained standard yard tools, but other than those it was empty. They looked around for any movement, seeing none, they entered, closing the doors behind them.

They sat on the floor breathing hard for a few minutes, saying nothing, each lost in their own thoughts, occasionally glancing at each other.

"We've only traveled about six miles from home and it took us over four hours," Jake said to Kate wearily.

Exhaustion was written in heavy lines across her face.

Jake grunted. "I didn't expect the streets and roads to be this fucked up so soon."

He thought back two weeks to the first news reports about dirty bombs going off, the stock market crashing and power blackouts. *All it took was a few days before we are killing each other in the streets.* An image of the camo man's body jerking with the impact of each gunshot flashed through Jake's mind. Kate glanced at him, as if reading his thoughts. He looked away.

"What now?" Kate asked, graciously steering the conversation forward. Jake didn't respond. She let him wrestle with his thoughts.

After a few minutes of silence, Jake said, "Hell if I know. It'll be getting dark in a couple hours. As long as no one comes sniffing around, I say we hunker down for the night and figure out a plan in the morning."

"Works for me," Kate said, rubbing her shoulders while stifling a yawn.

Kate was forty-seven, fifteen years younger than Jake. But Jake was fit and active, thanks to years in the military and law enforcement. They had met while working a labor strike in Illinois two years earlier. Jake was in semi-retirement as a security contractor, and Kate was a dispatcher/EMT on the jobsite. They hit it off immediately, and despite her being from Nebraska and him from New Jersey, they had much in common. Both were divorced and not currently dating. They shared a pragmatic, no-nonsense view of life.

For a while they tried the long distance off and on dating relationship until Kate decided to make the move to New Jersey. She reasoned she wasn't getting any younger, and despite the age difference and occasional "get off my lawn" moment, she had never met a man that made her feel as comfortable as Jake. Uncomplicated and straightforward, he loved her in a way that made her feel secure. Plus, he looked good in jeans. Kate smiled to herself, thinking about their relationship. Finding your soulmate this late in life was a blessing and a surprise. If only the world hadn't gone to hell when she had finally met her prince charming.

Jake rubbed his throbbing forehead. The adrenaline spike brought a massive headache with it. It'd been a long time since he'd been in a gunfight. The moves were still there, but emotionally he wasn't the warrior he'd once been. Pulling a Nalgene bottle from his pack, he took a long swig of water. Almost as an afterthought, he retrieved a packet of low-dose aspirin from his pocket and grimly chewed on them, for once the bitter aftertaste seemed bearable.

"Water?" Jake said, holding the bottle out to Kate.

"Yeah... I feel like I've been hit by a train." She took the water bottle, two long draws and handed it back to Jake. Their eyes met and exchanged unspoken reassurances. Their entire world was now this dark, empty garage ... and each other. But for now, it was enough.

———

KATE WOKE WITH A START, her body jolting upright. It was still dark outside. She was chilled. They'd been too tired to change out of their sweat-drenched clothes before they fell asleep.

"Did you hear something?" she asked, nudging the snoring Jake.

"Huh, what?"

"A crashing sound, like glass breaking."

"No, I didn't hear anything."

"Listen."

Jake closed his eyes and slowly moved his head, like radar listening for any sounds beyond the wind. Then he heard it off in the distance: a crashing, glass breaking sound, followed by loud voices and gunshots.

Kate immediately began gathering and repacking her gear. Jake reached into his pocket and grabbed the Ziploc bag full of low dose aspirin and put a couple in his mouth, stuffing the bag back into his pocket without her seeing him.

He turned to his gear and mentally ran through what he had. He checked the chamber of his Mini-14.

"You have anything besides the Glock 26 with you?" Jake asked.

"Yeah, I've got the Mossberg Sidewinder. It was strapped to the side of my pack. Do you think we should go back to the car and see if it's drivable or if there's anything we can salvage?"

"No, I don't think so, we were lucky to get out of that mess. When we head out, stay close and watch for anything that moves. It will be light in a couple hours. We need to get to the marina within twenty-four hours or we'll miss our window."

"Shit," Kate said, "I almost forgot about that."

"Ready?"

Kate nodded.

"Okay on three. One, two, three."

He pushed the shed door open and rushed out.

Kate followed a few paces behind. They stayed low and quiet, looking and listening for any movement. Seeing nothing, Jake turned to Kate, "Looks clear. We've got at least eight miles to go."

Kate nodded.

Jake stood, wobbling slightly.

"You okay, babe?" Kate whispered.

"Yeah, I'm good. Just loaded up like a pack mule."

"You sure? I can take some of that shit. You know you always overpack."

"No. I've got it," he said.

"Okay, tough guy." Kate let out a sigh. Jake was the worst liar she'd ever met. It was one of the qualities she loved about him. She knew he was trying not to let on that he wasn't the badass he was twenty years ago. She'd have to keep an eye on him from here on out. Kate knew he would push himself until he dropped dead to protect her. She felt her eyes rim with tears. She had to keep this man alive. He meant too much to her.

They moved forward in the darkness. Progress was slow, but fortunately they seemed to be the only ones out this early in the morning. With each step, Jake breathed easier. He pulled on the load lifters of his Gregory pack and cinched the thick belt tighter to keep the weight on his hips. Despite his efforts to concentrate on any potential threats, his thoughts returned to before everything changed.

Summer cook-outs. Beers to drink, and burgers and brats on the grill. Laughter. Good memories. At first, planning for a SHTF situation had just been an opportunity to get to know his son-in-law, Max, better. Max had no military experience, but he had a solid head on his shoulders and respected Jake's expertise. After finishing off their burgers, Jake and Max would grab their beers and seclude themselves in Jake's garage while Kate and her daughter, Jen, sipped wine and visited.

Max's analytical mind complemented Jake's direct, forceful approach. Together they listed a variety of potential scenarios and ran through the options available to them. Despite the difference in age, both men believed that society had grown unsustainably soft and weak. Entitlement had replaced responsibility. Convenience had replaced self-reliance. A collapse felt more inevitable than just a remote possibility. They drew up a SHTF plan over several weeks. In a sense, it had been fun.

Both Jake and Max acknowledged that living in a large urban area like New Jersey was a significant problem. When the shit went sideways, the heavily populated areas would fall apart fastest. Even in better times, violence always simmered just beneath the surface of America's troubled inner cities. Once the rule of law was gone, urban areas would become literal hells on earth. Getting out of South Jersey was their first priority. Their plan was fairly simple, at least it had seemed that way back then.

Pooling their resources, the men purchased a Zodiac raft and motor, which they kept in a marina storage unit. They agreed on a 72-hour deadline for meeting up at the marina. Once reunited, they would retrieve the raft and cross the bay to a safe house near Woodland Beach in Delaware. The safe house was really just a summer cabin that had been in Jake's family for generations. Over the last year, they had transported several large caches of emergency food, water, first aid kits, clothing, and hundreds of rounds of ammunition to the cabin.

From his home to the marina to the cabin was only a distance of about twelve miles. When they made the plan, the distance seemed reasonable. But looking back, they had failed to imagine the speed at which the violence would start. Jake had also failed to account for the hesitancy of leaving his home. Normally a decisive man, he had waited at least twelve hours too long before initiating their evacuation. He realized now that their plan had lacked some critical details, including exactly when the 72-hour clock would start ticking.

Cell service had gone down almost immediately, so there had been no way to contact Max. Jake thought back grimly to the discussions about purchasing expensive satellite phones. Instead, they bought identical portable ham radios and promised they would learn how to use them. But the apocalypse came sooner than expected, and the ham radios sat untouched in their packaging. Hopefully, Max and Jen were on the move and would be waiting for them at the marina. If not, after the deadline passed, they would be forced to cross over alone.

Jake's leg buckled and he fell to the ground.

"Mother fucker," he swore under his breath.

Kate knelt at his side, "Hey, babe. How about we take a break?" she asked.

"I'm good. Let's keep going," he said as he slowly struggled back to his feet, his thoughts still focused on the deadline.

"Well, I need a break. Let's take five and drink some water," Kate said.

"Okay. Five minutes, no more." Jake wriggled out of his pack and set it on the ground. It felt good to have the weight off his back. He sat down stiffly and reached for the water bottle in his pack. He took several long sips and washed down a couple more tablets of aspirin.

"We have to pace ourselves. We still have eighteen hours to get there. We'll make it in plenty of time," Kate said reassuringly. She leaned over and started gently rubbing out his calves.

"I know. I'm just worried about Jen and Max and the kids. He's never had any military type training, and all they have are a couple pistols."

Kate pushed back on the fear in her own thoughts. Crawling through this nightmare was hard enough for her and Jake. She couldn't imagine having small children with them. She thought back to vacations and long car rides with Jen in the back seat keeping herself occupied with made up songs. Jen was always self-reliant and independent. She would make the best of this. She was strong.

Kate sat quietly for several minutes and then stood. "You ready?"

"Yeah. Let's get in another couple hours of walking and then we'll stop for a food and rest break." As he shouldered his pack, Jake looked directly at Kate. "Thanks for uh... looking out for me."

"Somebody has too." Kate smiled and kissed Jake on his cheek. "Now move your ass."

JAKE AND KATE were making good time and covering more ground than they had earlier. Jake noticed they'd fallen into an easy symmetry: he moved forward and cleared the area, while Kate remained ten to fifteen yards behind watching their six. Kate moved efficiently and was attentive to the slightest motion or sound. She moved when Jake moved and stopped when Jake stopped. With each step, Jake's pride and confidence in Kate swelled. He wasn't the sharpest guy in the world, but he'd been smart enough to recognize that Kate was one hell of a woman.

For several hours they followed a simple pattern, stopping after about a mile for rest or water. Jake's leg still throbbed but hadn't given out on him again. In many ways, he felt some of his old energy returning. If he had any vanity, it was his physical fitness. He enjoyed working out and keeping in shape. When he turned sixty, he ran a half-marathon. The signs of age were there, but Jake prided himself on keeping pace with much younger men. For once, vanity had an upside.

Within a mile of the marina, they stopped for their last rest break in an empty machine shop. The faded sign read "Precision Watercraft – Custom Engines." The rear entry door had been jimmied open. Jake went in first and cleared the area before going back for Kate. They were well ahead of the seventy-two-hour deadline, at least in Jake's estimation. Kate suggested they each nap while the other remained on lookout. Jake agreed, dumping his pack and lowering himself to the cool concrete floor. Laying his head on his pack, he was out within seconds.

Jake woke to a hand shaking his shoulder. For a moment, he felt like he was rising up from the deep back to consciousness. He'd dreamed that when they'd arrived at the marina, all that remained was a burned-out hulk. He had picked his way through the smoldering rubble to where his storage unit was. A blistered slab of charred rubber was all that remained of the raft. The MREs were gone – perhaps looted before the fire was set. The smoke stung at Jake's eyes. Just beyond a blackened pile of boxes, huddled in a corner, lay a pile of ashen corpses still clinging to each other. Max, Jen, the kids... Jake screamed and fell to his knees.

"Jake... Jake!" Kate shook him more forcefully and he gradually completed his slow ascent to the surface. Shaking off the sleep, Jake looked at Kate and glanced around the warehouse. Dust mites floated in the fading light that streamed through the remaining unbroken windows.

"Max and Jen... the kids..." Jake fought to regain consciousness. Kate put a hand to his cheek.

"They're ok. You're ok," she said gently. "You must have had a bad dream." Kate pulled Jake in and held him. His shoulders shuddered and he began to sob. As the shaking subsided, Kate closed her eyes and kissed the top of his head. "I thought they were gone," Jake whispered. Kate had never seen Jake cry before. He rubbed his face against her jacket and wiped a sleeve across his nose, laughing.

"Look at me. I'm blubbering like a baby," Jake sniffed. Gazing at her, he caught her eyes. Clear, blue, with no judgment. Jake decided then who the strong one really was in their relationship.

"It's your turn to nap," he said finally.

"I'm good. We should keep going."

Jake didn't feel like arguing. The residue of his nightmare still remained at the edge of his consciousness. The vision of the burned bodies still felt real to him. The sooner they got to the marina, the better.

Before leaving the warehouse, Jake refocused on the challenge ahead. This was no time to miss a detail or walk into a trap. The rest had actually helped. He was energized and ready to roll. Kate handed him his water bottle and an energy bar. He looked for a trashcan, but finding none, let the wrapper fall spiraling to the floor. Before the collapse, Jake had always been zealous about not littering. He kept his home and yard immaculate. On walks, he'd take a small plastic baggie for picking up litter. He glanced at the curling plastic wrapper. Fuck it.

He stood and shouldered his pack, reached for the Mini-14 and exhaled. Looking at Kate, he flashed a grim smile. "Let's go."

NEARING THE MARINA AREA, their progress slowed. They noticed signs of activity. Even back before the chaos, the marina wasn't exactly the safest part of the city – especially at night. Most of the shipping industry had moved to larger ports that could accommodate bigger cargo ships. Smaller marinas like this one had fallen on hard times. Crime and neglect had taken their toll. Gone were the gleaming watercraft and cheerful weekend sailors, replaced by broken windows, drug deals, and homeless encampments. Of course, that was why the rent was so cheap.

He turned and motioned for Kate to move up to his position behind a low concrete wall. He scanned the area and then turned to her. "We're getting close. Chances are we aren't going to be alone. Stay low and be alert."

Kate nodded. "Sounds good. How far are we from..." Kate went quiet as the whine of a truck engine approached from behind them. They both crouched to avoid being seen. Exchanging glances with Kate, Jake focused on the sound of the engine. The high whining was strangely familiar. He had heard it many times before: a rotary engine. Shifting on his knees slightly, Jake peered over the wall. A copper-colored truck about two hundred yards away approached slowly.

Jake ducked backed down and caught Kate's eyes. She nodded her head as a quick smile of recognition crossed her face. When they had met, Jake's daily driver was his beloved 1993 Mazda B2000. In the early days of their relationship, zipping around with Jake in the little truck had made Kate feel like a teenager again. The truck had an odd habit of not starting whenever they were parked anywhere remote and romantic. Kate couldn't resist a smile, thinking back to the number of times they fogged up the little truck's windows.

The truck slowed and then revved up slightly, the distinctive skittering of the rotary engine screeching ominously on the empty roadway. It was clear now that whoever was in the truck wasn't simply driving somewhere, they were searching for something. Slowing at anything of interest, the men were either scavenging or worse. Jake's gut signaled instinctively that trouble was coming.

By now, the truck was too close for Jake and Kate to move to a better position. Any movement by them would have been noticed instantly, likely resulting in a hail of bullets. Their only option was to huddle as close to the ground as possible and hope the low wall was enough to conceal them. Jake pushed his chest to the pavement, praying that his large pack wasn't visible. He desperately wanted to shift to his side and get his bulky pack into a lower position, but he knew it was too risky. Worse, he couldn't see Kate. All he could do was remain still and pray.

The truck approached and slowed. Approached and slowed. Whatever their intent, they were methodical. Skitter and pop. Jake remembered how much he loved the unique sound of the Mazda's rotary engine. But now, as he pressed his face into the pavement, it sounded alive, like a massive prehistoric cockroach inching across the floor toward him. The truck slowed... Jake squeezed his eyes shut, wishing himself invisible. A man's voice rang out from inside the cab, "¿Cualquier cosa?" A younger male voice responded, "Nada."

The moment stretched on. All Jake could hear was the thumping of his heart and the low ticking of the truck's idling engine. From the sound of the voices, Jake estimated that the truck was less than fifteen feet away. If the young man was sitting up in the bed of the truck and looked in their direction... would he see Jake's pack? The concrete wall was only about three feet high. Was it enough?

"¿Puedo conducir?" the younger man's voice rang out plaintively.

"No, gilipollas, sigue mirando."

The younger man muttered something and the truck lurched forward. Jake held his breath, the pebbles embedded in his cheek began to sting. A shard of glass, perhaps? The truck whined its rhythmic pattern down the street. Accelerating and slowing, as if in heavy traffic. Jake knew it was stupid, but he couldn't resist taking a peek. He lifted his head slowly, inching over the rough concrete horizon. The truck was roughly one hundred yards away and idling motionless. A male figure crouched in the bed of the truck. As he turned to scan the street, Jake could make out the familiar bulky outline of an assault rifle, probably an AK.

He slowly lowered his head and exhaled. That had been close. Clearly, the streets were growing increasingly dangerous. It had only taken a few days for Jersey to feel like Mogadishu. The sooner they got to the marina and across the water, the better. They had been lucky this time. How long would their luck last?

Jake sat up and whispered, "Kate!" Kate was still lying motionless on the pavement. She looked up, her eyes rimmed red and wet.

"Why are we whispering?" Kate whispered back, breaking into a crooked smile. The emotion of the moment finally broke like a wave sending them both into each other's arms. Jake could feel Kate shaking, sobbing. This time, it was his turn to offer consolation. Pulling Kate closer, Jake cursed whoever was responsible for the attack. It struck him for the first time that he didn't even know what foreign nation or rogue terrorist cell had attacked the United States. It didn't even matter.

Kate sucked in a deep breath and wiped the back of her hand over her face. A glistening string of snot stretched out upon her cheek. Jake laughed and Kate slugged him. Wiping her cheek on her sleeve, Kate finally joined in the laughter. Their chests heaving, they relaxed in each other's embrace, momentarily forgetting the world on fire around them. Jake leaned in and kissed Kate softly on her forehead. He could taste the tang of sweat on her skin. God, he loved this woman.

They sat there for what felt like a long time. Each unwilling to move. Jake breathed out, aware that he had released something but unable to describe exactly what. He felt lighter somehow, unburdened. He had always been an uncomplicated man in an increasingly complicated world. Strangely, he felt at home in this new world. He had clarity. Survive or die. Nothing else mattered. Complete clarity.

"Let's get moving." Jake's tone was more direct and forceful than he had intended. Kate didn't seem to notice. She struggled to her feet and pulled on her pack, tugging tight on the chest belt and load lifters.

"Yes, sir!" she smiled.

Maybe she had noticed, thought Jake.

They covered several blocks of row homes quickly, occasionally catching the flash of a face in a window. They stopped frequently, looking and listening back to back. Jake would scan the area with a small pair of binoculars for anything that seemed out of place. He had a keen eye for small details; years of security work had given him the ability to notice things that didn't fit into the landscape. He called it the "flow of a place" - how things looked, people moved, all the little details that make up the picture.

They kept moving until they were just a few blocks from the marina storage yard. As they crept past a warehouse, they heard voices and the rattle of wheels coming from around the corner. Jake raised his left hand in a fist and brought the Mini-14 up with his right. He moved into a crouch, and Kate followed his example. They were stuck in the middle of a stretch of street that offered no available concealment. Whatever was coming was sure to see them.

A moment later a haggard family pushing a shopping cart full of supplies scurried by, trying not to be seen or heard. The man, in his early thirties, and a tired-looking woman roughly the same age, walked at his side. In the shopping cart was a huddle of blankets and the form of what appeared to be a sleeping child. As they passed where Jake and Kate remained crouched, the man and woman locked eyes with Jake. Their faces betrayed unmistakable fear as they considered the barrel of the Mini-14 tracing their movement.

Jake nodded at the man as he pushed the grocery cart down the street. The man regripped the handle of the baseball bat straddled across the cart and picked up the pace. The tired looking woman clutched what looked like a large kitchen knife and lowered her head, resigned to whatever fate lay ahead for her. Jake and Kate remained motionless, shifting only their gaze to follow the little family down the street until they turned a corner and the rattle of the cart faded into the dimming afternoon.

Jake and Kate exchanged glances. Rising to his feet, Jake felt his leg give and he lost his balance. The weight of his pack pulled him to the right and he awkwardly careened into the outer wall of the warehouse. Catching himself with an arm, he looked back at Kate.

"You ok?" she asked, real concern spreading over her face.

"Yeah, just stood up too quick," Jake admitted.

"Have some water."

"Good idea," he said, pulling the Nalgene from the side of his pack. He dug into his pockets and slipped out a couple more low-dose aspirins. Chugging down the water and aspirins, he gave Kate a wink and a broad smile. She smiled back but kept a watchful eye on him. He couldn't tell her he felt light-headed and dizzy. Old habits were hard to change. Jake kept his own counsel and was not one to complain. It didn't matter anyway. Kate always knew what he was thinking.

The shadow of the warehouse stretched out across the empty street. Jake checked his watch and squinted at the rapidly setting afternoon sun.

"We're losing daylight. Let's keep going. We're almost there."

They strode forward into the uncertain late afternoon. Fortunately, they reached the marina without incident. As the sun set, the streetlights twitched to life, indicating the electrical grid was still at least partially working in this part of town.

Jake and Kate hunkered down in a looted storefront across the street from the marina storage yard. A few sodium lights along the perimeter cast a weak, yellow glow. A streak of marine fog crept in from off the water, cloaking the marina in a growing gloom.

Jake scanned the storage yard with binoculars. The square yard was organized into three rows of 10 x 10 storage units and a fourth row of larger 14 x 14 units. Altogether there were forty-eight units. Jake's unit was in the row of larger ones and was stocked with cases of water, MRE's, ammo, medical supplies, clothes, and most important, the inflatable Zodiac raft with engine and fuel tanks.

Jake and Max had spent almost ten grand prepping for a SHTF scenario. The raft itself was almost six thousand dollars. At the time, Jake felt slightly embarrassed by the purchase. Had he joined the tinfoil hat crowd? Sure, the signs that society was discontent and ripe for trouble were there, but was he simply suffering from an overactive imagination? He wondered if Kate would try to slow his roll, but she simply said, "It's a nice raft. If we need it, we'll be glad we have it. If we don't, we'll take the grandkids out on the lake." She had a point. You can only prepare in advance. You can't wait until the need arises.

Something caught Jake's eye. About twenty yards from the entrance to the marina was a truck. It was difficult to say for sure, but he was fairly confident it was the copper-colored Mazda that had passed them earlier. He scanned the street, but the driver and the younger man were nowhere to be seen.

"How does it look?" Kate whispered.

Jake considered not telling Kate about the truck and decided against it. This was no time to withhold information.

"No movement. There's a truck parked that could be the one that passed us earlier," Jake said, handing the binoculars to her.

Something about the lack of activity bothered him. Even the rundown marina storage was certain to have things of value. Either the looting had already finished or it hadn't started. Neither of those scenarios sounded quite right to him.

Kate glassed the area and returned the binoculars to Jake. His view of the storage units was on an angle and he counted down to theirs. The large roll-up door appeared to be open. Jake and Max had agreed that whoever arrived first in the 72-hour window would check the unit, lock it back up and take a position from where they could protect it from looters. They had portable radios that they would use to signal each other to clear entry. Either Max had arrived and was breaking protocol by staying in the unit and keeping the door open, or the unit had been compromised.

Jake took the small radio out of his jacket pocket and switched it on. As he fiddled with it to send a transmission to Max, he noticed movement by the storage unit. Quickly glassing the area, he could make out the figure of a man relieving himself just outside of the unit door. He squinted and adjusted the focus, but in the low light it was difficult to see if that was Max.

"The storage unit looks compromised," Jake said. "I just saw a male come out and take a piss and go back in. I'm pretty sure it wasn't Max."

"Fuck," Kate said. "What should we do?"

"Nothing yet. Let's watch for a bit. Once we know for sure what's going on, we can figure out what to do."

It wasn't much of a plan, but Kate nodded in agreement. She trusted Jake, knowing he had been in some shitty situations in the military. In their relationship, he had only shown her gentleness, but she knew he had a harder side. She'd never seen it until the last couple days. Glimpses of his violent side were both disconcerting and comforting. She knew Jake would do whatever it took to protect her. She just wasn't sure what exactly that might mean. Or what it would do to him.

Jake kept watch through the binoculars, looking for any movement. After about ten minutes he said, "Could you keep an eye on things for a bit? My eyes need a break."

"Sure," she said, taking the binoculars.

Jake rubbed his eyes and settled down with his back to the wall. Reaching into his jacket, he grabbed the baggie of aspirin and chased a couple down with a swig from his water bottle. For whatever reason, Jake thought about the whiskey they had cached at the cabin for "medicinal purposes." He could use a swig right then. He closed his eyes and dozed off almost immediately, snoring lightly.

Kate whispered, "Two guys just came out of the unit. They're outside right now, smoking."

Jake sat up and took the binoculars. There were two men

standing outside the storage unit. Light spilled out from inside. He couldn't say for sure, but one of them looked like the younger male from the truck with the rifle. It had to be.

Jake lowered the binoculars and took a deep breath. In his mind he ran several scenarios, none of them good. It was unlikely the two men in the truck had just stumbled upon the storage unit. It was more likely they had followed Max and Jen and gotten the jump on them. Hopefully all they wanted was money or supplies. Jake's mind raced to several darker scenarios.

"Jake? What's happening?" Kate demanded, knowing something was wrong.

"I think Max and Jen may be in trouble. We need to go find out for sure." Jake gave Kate a few moments to let the meaning of his words sink in. She opened her mouth but no words came out. Finally, she pursed her lips and exhaled.

Kate reached for the shotgun secured to the side of her pack.

Jake grabbed her wrist. "You OK? You good?" As much as Jake loved her passion, he couldn't afford to go into a potential combat situation with an emotionally off-balance partner. Too much hung in the balance.

An intensity flashed across Kate's face that Jake had never seen before, something between anger and determination. She shook Jake's hand off.

"I'm good. Let's go."

THEY LOW CRAWLED into a position about twenty yards from the entrance of the storage unit. The grass was overgrown here and provided concealment. A six-foot security fence topped with barb wire surrounded the entire perimeter of the storage yard. Fortunately, during previous trips to the storage yard, Jake had taken time to walk the entire perimeter and noted two sections where the fence had been cut. He doubted anyone had made repairs since then.

Jake scanned the unit with the binoculars, but the men had gone back inside.

"Mother fucker," he said below his breath. "How the fuck did this happen? God damn it."

"What?" asked Kate as he passed the binoculars to her, "What do you see?"

"I have to get closer," Jake whispered. Leaning on his elbows, Jake edged in close to Kate. He could feel her breath on his cheeks. "Stay here. Shoot anything you see. If I'm not back in five minutes... I don't know, come after me if you can. Or clear out of here. Just stay safe, whatever you do."

Jake hesitated. Kate rolled her eyes.

"I'm not leaving you here, asshole. Get going!"

Jake thumbed the safety off on the Mini-14 and handed it to Kate. With a wink, he low rolled into the darkness. Kate watched him, wondering if she would ever see him alive again. She pushed down the growing lump in her throat and raised the binoculars to her face. Shifting slightly for a better view, she focused on the storage unit and whispered heart-felt prayers.

Jake moved quickly, low crawling to the nearest hole in the security fence, he pulled himself through, taking care not to snag or make noise. He racked the slide on his Glock 22. He'd made enough trips to the storage yard over the last year to have a good mental map of the layout. He knew roughly what route he could take without being seen.

Before he made any move, he needed to get a good look inside. To do so, he would need to climb on the roof of the strip of units just in front of his. No other vantage point would offer him a sufficient view inside. Fortunately, each storage unit had a built-in steel ladder providing access to the roof.

Locating a ladder, Jake slowly began to climb. At the top, he paused. The roof was the sprayed-on PVC type. Moving carefully, he took a few low crawling steps and listened. Nothing. He continued on until he heard voices.

He crawled to a point just ten feet short of the edge of the roof. Carefully lowering himself into an "army crawl" position. Twice he scuffed the roof loudly and froze in place. Fortunately, the ambient noise of the marina seemed to muffle the sound. He could hear the two men conversing loudly in Spanish. He couldn't understand what they were saying, but they both sounded like they had been drinking.

Jake pulled himself up to the edge of the roof, aware that the light flooding out of the storage unit would likely illuminate his face if he wasn't careful.

Looking down, he could see into the building. Two men, engaged in an animated conversation, paced back and forth. Jake winced. Max and Jen were sitting on the floor, their hands tied behind their backs. Dried blood covered the side of Max's face. Jen kept her head down. The two children huddled close but were unbound. Jake could hear their soft whimpers.

The young man from the back of the truck prowled the storage unit like a caged tiger. An AK-47 hung around his shoulders on a sling. A nickel-plated pistol was jammed in his waistband. The second man was older and kept rubbing his hands over his face, as if unsure what to do. He appeared unarmed.

"Podemos tomar su mierda y salir!" the younger man said, waving his arms.

The older man remained silent, as if formulating a plan. He nodded, considering their options.

"Pueden valer más que esta basura. ¿Pensaste en eso?" exclaimed the older man, finally.

The younger man looked down at Jen. He pushed the barrel of his rifle into her face. She turned away, pressing her face into Max's shoulder. The young man scowled.

Jake had seen enough. He crawled back to the ladder and carefully lowered himself over the edge, descending to the ground.

He paused, trying to formulate something close to a plan. The layout of the storage units gave him little options beyond a direct approach. He could wait until they took another smoke break, but he wasn't sure if he could take that chance. The younger man seemed jumpy, and that made Jake nervous. He ruled out waiting as an option.

The only plan he could think of was "1. Kill the bad guys 2. Rescue your family."

Works for me, Jake thought. Taking a deep breath, he stepped around the corner and moved quickly toward the building.

With each step, more of the storage unit opened up. He could see the kids. Jen. Max.

"Que mierda?" The young man stepped out from storage unit, reaching for the AK, his eyes flaring with a mix of surprise and anger. Jake lined up the Glock's night site and fired three shots into his chest, dropping him instantly. The AK-47 clattered to the floor. He stepped sideways with the Glock held in front of him until the older man came into view. He was standing still, incomprehensibly looking down at the younger man splayed out in front of him.

"Hermano?"

He looked up at Jake quizzically, his eyes locking on Jake's. His lips parted as if to speak just as Jake squeezed off two shots. The man spun and fell into a pile of boxed rations.

Jake stayed in a shooting stance, moving the Glock back and forth between the two downed men, his ears ringing from the close quarter gunfire. He edged toward the closer body, the younger man, and kicked away the AK-47 with his foot.

After several moments, satisfied the bad guys were no longer a threat, Jake pulled a knife from the sheath on his belt and sliced the ropes on Max's wrists.

Once free, Max rubbed out his wrists and took the knife from

Jake to free Jen. She quickly covered the children with her body, shielding them from the carnage.

Jake stared at the two unmoving bodies. The younger man was even younger than he previously thought, maybe just seventeen. Chances were these two had not been actual criminals in their prior life. The temptation of opportunity may have just gotten the better of them. Jake wondered where they had obtained the AK? He checked both for a pulse, frisked them quickly, finding a knife, a cheap.380 pistol and a wad of cash. Neither carried identification, which was just fine from Jake's perspective. He didn't want to know their names.

A growing nausea pushed up his throat.

Jake holstered his Glock and noticed that for the second time in as many days, his hands shook. A sudden exhaustion overtook him, and he sat down on a box of freeze-dried food. He glanced over at Max and Jen, but they were preoccupied calming their crying children. The ringing in his ears continued. His breathing felt labored, and he reached for the bottle of aspirin.

"Call ... Kate," Jake rasped.

Max looked up at him.

"Call her. On the radio."

Max finally understood the request and began patting himself down, searching for the radio. Retrieving it from a pocket, he switched the unit on.

"Kate! Kate! This is Max. Are you there?" Max shouted.

Silence. Seconds passed.

"I'm here. This is Kate. I heard the shots. Is everyone... ok?" Kate's voice sounded small and far away. Jake turned to Max and motioned for him to hand over the radio.

"Kate, its Jake. We're all good. Everyone is fine." Jake stared at the radio as if the device could magically make Kate appear. "Come now. I need you."

"On my way," Kate said, clearly on the move.

Jake leaned back, closing his eyes. The adrenaline dump was receding, leaving him wrung out and utterly exhausted. The room began to slowly spin. He tried to lift an arm to reach out to Max, but it wouldn't move. He squinted as an inky darkness filled the corners of his eyes. He opened his mouth, but no words came out. He could hear voices: Max, Jen, the children crying. But no Kate.

The dark tide spread across his field of vision until all was black.

WHEN JAKE AWOKE, Kate was seated on a pallet of supplies directly in front him. She smiled and said something he couldn't quite make out. He felt like he was being slowly lifted from the bottom of a well. The room spun slightly.

"Jake?" Kate said gently, cupping his face in her hands. *God, she was beautiful*, he thought. Was he dead? Where was he?

He turned slowly and scanned the small storage unit. Max held his arms around Jen and their two children. The blood had been washed off his face, replaced by a large bandage on the side of his head just below his hairline. He lifted one arm and gave Jake a thumbs up. Jake stiffly returned the gesture. There was no sign of the two dead men. Max must have moved the bodies. *Good,* he thought.

Jake turned back to Kate and she pulled him into an embrace. They stayed there for a while. Kate finally released her grip on Jake and wiped her eyes. "Sorry," she said. "I thought I was done with the crying." They both started to laugh.

"You can't get rid of me that easy," Jake joked lamely. "Shit, I'm hungry. What does a guy have to do to get some grub around here?"

Kate looked to an open box of MREs. "Tonight... it looks like spaghetti."

"Is there sirloin steak in that box?"

"Sorry, bub." Kate smiled. "This ain't the Ritz Carlton."

She handed the boxed MRE to Jake, who quickly ripped it open, setting the various contents on top of a box of dehydrated milk: spaghetti, mashed potatoes, fruit cup, and M&Ms. Jake chuckled as his mouth started to water.

"We all should eat. It's going to be a long night ahead of us," Kate said, handing out MREs to Max and Jen. Reluctant to let go of each other, but recognizing the need for sustenance, Max and Jen began opening the boxes. The children eyed the peculiar-looking food suspiciously, but were finally convinced the fruit cups could be trusted.

No one had eaten much in the last twenty-four hours, and the little storage unit went silent except for the sounds of ripping foil and eating. After several minutes, Jake turned to Max and said, "What happened?"

Max looked at Jen and then turned back to Jake, "I don't know really. A couple minutes after we got here they showed up. They must've been following us." Jake nodded. Max continued, "At first I thought they would just take some of the stuff and leave. But they stayed. I don't think they really knew what to do with us."

Max looked at Jen. Jen had studied Spanish and was practically bi-lingual. "Could you make out what they were saying?"

Jen just shook her head. Something about her didn't look right. The vibrancy was gone. Certainly, the last few days had been hard on everyone, but Jen seemed distant and disconnected. Max put an arm around her and gave Jake a knowing look. For Jake, this was the hardest part. He just didn't know what to do or say.

"I bet everyone is tired," Kate interjected. "Especially the kiddos." The children were already dressed in their pajamas.

Max looked at his watch. It was nearly 11 p.m. The zodiac, hooked to the compressor, would inflate in less than ten minutes. They would need roughly fifteen minutes to carry the boat to the water and load it with all the supplies they felt they could safely carry. He figured from start to finish the whole operation could be finished in under thirty minutes, and they could be on their way.

"Good idea, Kate. Let's sleep a bit. We'll set the alarms for 3 a.m. Max, you and I will inflate and load the boat. Once everything is set, we'll get everyone loaded up and head out of here. Should still be dark when we hit the other side."

Max nodded. No one objected to the idea of sleep. All the sleeping bags were stored at the cabin, but the storage unit did have a box of army surplus wool blankets. Kate and Jake moved to one corner and balled up extra clothes for pillows. They snuggled close under the itchy blankets.

Jen huddled with her children in the opposite corner. Max flipped off the light and the storage unit filled with darkness. Max felt his way in the dark back to his wife and children and settled in for some needed rest.

Kate lay awake for a long time, listening to Jake's breathing, his chest raising and lowering. Occasionally he stirred, but sheer exhaustion pushed him back under. Her husband could kill but he was no killer. The violence seemed to rip away a piece of him, each time leaving him less whole than before. She wondered how much more of this he could take. Worse, she knew there was nothing she could do to stop Jake from giving his last breath to protect her. What was that word, she thought? A paradox?

She closed her eyes and focused on his breathing. Laying her head on his chest, she could feel the deep, rhythmic beating of his heart. It sounded so steady and strong. Certainly, they would make it through this. Things would be better again. She drifted off to sleep whispering prayers to any god who would listen.

———

THE DOOR to the storage unit flung open and light burst into the room. A dozen men flooded in, each identically equipped with

SWAT type tactical gear and chest rigs, AR-15s with Surefire flash-lights, and communication radios. They moved efficiently, sweeping the storage unit with bright beams of lights, barking orders. Jake and Max were easily overwhelmed. Jake struggled, but two men pulled his arms behind his back and zip tied his wrists. Max fought as well and took a rifle butt to the head. He staggered but didn't fall. His arms were bound.

Jake was confused and seething. How had they been found? Who were they? He hadn't seen any sign of an organized force in days. What did they want? Certainly, they couldn't be coming after their measly supply of MREs.

He struggled to see what was happening. The flashlights were painfully blinding, and he couldn't shield his eyes. He thought he caught a glimpse of Kate trying to shake off two men who were practically lifting her off the ground. "Get her out of here," a voice ordered. Jake blinked into the bright lights, burning his retinas.

"KATE!!" he yelled, "KATE!!!"

"I'm here!" Kate grabbed Max by his shoulders. Max sat up, gasping for breath. He turned his head wildly but the room was pitch black.

"I'm here," Kate repeated, reassuringly. "You're ok."

Max steadied himself. His arms were unbound. He could feel the warmth of the wool blanket against him. He could feel Kate's breath on his face. He exhaled deeply, still rattled by the intensity of the dream. Across the tiny room, the children stirred, and a soft voice hushed them back to sleep. Max pressed the Glo Light button on his watch. It read 2:51 a.m. He leaned back and put his arms around Kate. In nine minutes, they would begin their escape.

At precisely 3:00 a.m. Jake rose and felt his way in the darkness to the front of the storage unit where the light switch was located. He paused, considering whether to leave the lights off and just operate by flashlight. In reality, they needed to leave within thirty minutes, so any extra sleep would be minimal. He flipped the light on and the storage unit was immersed in harsh fluorescent light. Kate was already up and moving. Max slowly pulled the blanket off and carefully stepped away from his sleeping family.

Running his hand over his head, Max winced.

"That's going to leave a mark," joked Jake.

"It's just a flesh wound," Max rejoined.

"Good, because we have a lot to do," Jake said with a smile, "Help me carry the raft out where we can inflate it."

As quietly as possible, Jake pulled up the large door to their storage unit. Stepping outside, he surveyed the immediate area. Seeing no sign of movement, he and Max began carrying out the identical pontoons that formed the base of the large raft. Jake sorted through boxes until he came to the electric air compressor. As Max plugged it in, Jake thought back to the day he bought it. He never stopped to consider how loud it was. He waited for Max to give him the "OK" hand signal and switched the unit on.

The air compressor exploded in a high-pitched staccato "*whirr.*" Anyone within a quarter mile would hear it. Who knows who might show up to investigate the noise? Jake glanced back at Kate. She was busying herself with getting the supplies organized. They couldn't fit everything in the raft. They'd have to leave some of it behind.

The compressor shrilled on, filling the pontoon with air. Another minute and the first pontoon would be finished. Despite the threat of being heard, it was exciting to finally be inflating the raft. It meant they were one step closer to getting out of Jersey.

As Kate busied herself with the supplies, she kept a watchful eye on Jen and the kids, still huddled under the green wool blanket. She knew Jen was traumatized. There was no point in asking her to help. Everyone handled stress in their own way. Kate had never been taken prisoner and tied up. She'd never seen her husband beaten until bleeding. She couldn't imagine what Jen was feeling right now.

Kate surveyed the pile of supplies and started to organize by type: food, water, first aid, etc. As she worked, she whispered prayers of gratitude for Jake's foresight. Every box felt like an incremental greater chance of somehow surviving this madness. Would it be enough? She had no idea. Certainty was a feeling that belonged to her old life. This new world provided no certainties beyond the threat of violence.

Max capped the second pontoon, and they began locking down the inner hull of the craft. It was rated to hold 7 passengers. Jake hoped it would accommodate the four adults, two small children, and a good amount of the most critical supplies. The cabin was outfitted with its own cache of emergency food, water and necessities, but there was no guarantee that it had not been compromised.

"Ready?" Jake asked.

"Ready," responded Max.

"One... two... three," Jake said. Together, the two men deadlifted the raft. At nearly 250 pounds when empty, it was theoretically possible for two fairly strong men to carry it. Jake temporarily lost his balance and had to regrip.

"You got it?" Max asked.

"Got it. At least for now. Let's go." The two men made an unsteady beeline toward the water, roughly 100 yards from the storage unit. It took them ten minutes and two rest breaks, but they were able to lower the boat into the murky water and secure it to the moorings.

Jake looked around. No movement. No sound but water lapping at the decaying pier. The moon hung low over the bay. It would be daylight in a couple hours. Jake considered the raft. If only it had the capacity to take them farther away. Perhaps Australia? Maybe things were better there. Maybe you could still get a Starbuck's Frappuccino on the other side of the world. Have a nice dinner. Maybe share a bottle of wine with your wife. If only...

"Oh shit. Jake!" said Max, pointing toward the frontage road that led to the marina. Jake turned to look. A bulky vehicle with only its parking lights on was slowly making its way toward the entrance of the storage yard.

"Dammit," Jake said. Had they been heard? "Let's go!"

Crouching, they ran back to the storage unit, careful to stay in the shadows. Jake barked out instructions to Max as they ran. "Stay with girls. Help them load the boat. I'll take care of this."

As they returned to the shelter, Kate knew immediately something was wrong.

"What is it?" she asked. Even Jen seemed to perk up and pay attention.

"There's a vehicle coming," Jake said. "Help Max take what you can and start loading the raft."

"Where are you going?" demanded Kate.

Jake grabbed the Mini-14 and quickly checked the action. He glanced around the storage unit but decided there was really nothing else he needed.

"Jake! What are you doing?" Kate repeated.

Jake glanced at Kate and then turned to Max. "Load up what you think the raft can take. Get Jen, Kate and the kids on the boat. I will be back as soon as I can. Don't wait for me here. Get to the raft."

"JAKE!" Kate's voice cracked and shredded.

Jake turned to Kate and regarded his wife.

"Babe, if they get in... we're done. Help Max. I'll be OK. Give me five minutes. I'll meet you at the pier."

Jake turned and sped from the storage unit, not wanting to give Kate the opportunity to protest further. As he ran, he tried to formulate something resembling a plan. The vehicle had already been out of his sight for more than a couple minutes, and that concerned him. A high position on the roof of the storage units would be ideal, but Jake didn't think he had time to climb the ladder and low crawl into position. He had to make sure no one got inside the storage yard. Otherwise, their entire escape plan could fail.

He noted the rusty steel ladder to the rooftop as he passed by. It was tempting, but he needed a visual on the vehicle as soon as possible. Hopefully, it wasn't too late. He rounded the corner and turned into the driveway between the last section of storage units. A small gap about two feet wide ran the length of the unit. Jake slipped into the opening and made his way toward the other end, being careful not to trip or knock over anything that might make noise. Fortunately, the alley was clear and Jake was able to approach his vantage point quickly and quietly.

He leaned out to survey the entrance to the marina, careful to stay within the shadows of the dark alleyway. The vehicle had stopped in front of the entrance, approximately twenty-five yards from Jake's position. From its outline, Jake guessed it was some sort of small van. The engine was still running, but the parking lights had been turned off. A sodium flood light ten yards away helped provide Jake some visibility. A figure stepped out of the driver's side and walked up to the locked storage yard gate. The vehicle had passed one of the cut-out sections of the perimeter fence, but apparently they had not noticed it.

A figure, dressed in dark clothing, carried a large black rifle hung in a three-point sling on his chest. From his size, Jake guessed it was a man. There was something about the efficiency of his movement that seemed familiar to Jake? Former military perhaps? The man seemed to be inspecting the locked chain on the gate. A second smaller figure, possibly a woman, emerged from the passenger side of the vehicle. The man said something to the second person, who then disappeared toward the rear of the vehicle.

Jake pushed the talk button on the radio and whispered "Be ready to move, we've got trouble. I may be coming in with company on my tail."

"Roger that, we're loading up the last of the gear. Kate is helping Jen and the kids to the raft," Max replied.

Jake hesitated.

"Listen, Max. If I am not back in three minutes, get everyone the fuck out of here. Clear?"

Jake waited. No response. "Max, am I clear??" Jake hissed.

The radio finally crackled, "Roger. Three minutes."

The smaller figure returned from the back of the vehicle with bolt cutters and handed them to the man.

Jake considered his options. He could fire a warning shot, but that would reveal his position and probably draw fire. Plus, it would attract more unwanted attention. Jake watched through the scope on the Mini-14 as the man struggled to cut the thick steel lock. It was an easy shot. But who was he killing? A bad guy? Or just a guy trying to get to safety like himself?

Jake knew he had only seconds to decide. He ruled out a warning shot. Too risky. Too many unknowns. There was only one other option. He steadied his breathing and positioned the crosshairs of the scope over the man's chest. The man's arms scissored together and the chain dropped to the ground, along with the ruined lock. It was now or never. From this distance, Jake was confident he could drop the man with one shot. Breathing out slowly, Jake applied the slightest pressure to the trigger, keeping the cross hairs centered in on the man's chest.

A door opened and an orange blur exploded from the vehicle. The man with the bolt cutters turned and began motioning towards the blur. A very small figure, probably a child, emerged from the van as well. Jake swept the area with his scope and the orange blur transformed into an enormous golden retriever. The retriever careened around the van, tail wagging, nose down to the ground. The smaller figure ran after the dog, hopelessly trying to corral it. The dog was enjoying its freedom and not cooperating. Jake could hear voices as the two larger figures chased the dog around the vehicle.

Jake breathed in and lowered the Mini-14. *Bad guys don't have big fluffy golden retrievers,* he thought to himself. *But families do. Families have big, dumb, wonderful, fluffy dogs.*

Jake turned and ran out of the alley, retracing his path back to the raft. How many minutes had passed? As he reached the last corner he heard the Zodiac's four-stroke outboard motor fire up. He had cut it very close.

When Jake reached the mooring, everyone was loaded into the raft. All available space was filled with boxes of supplies. The motor churned the murky water. Jen was tucked under a blanket, two small forms by her side. Her face still lacked expression. Kate sat opposite her. Jake gave Kate a quick wink and then turned to survey the marina. No sign of anyone yet. He figured they would need to get at least three hundred yards across the water from the marina before he would feel safe.

Jake lowered himself carefully into the overloaded raft. Hopefully they wouldn't capsize before they reached land.

"What happened back there?" asked Max, looking both surprised and relieved.

"I'll tell you later," Jake said. "Get us out of here."

"Aye captain," Max replied, releasing the mooring rope and gunning the motor. The raft strained and listed alarmingly to the portside. Jake figured they had exceeded the craft's max payload of 2,200 pounds by at least three hundred pounds. Water sloshed into the low riding raft. Slowly, it gained momentum.

Jake looked back at the receding dock. Still empty. He thought about the family at the gate. Perhaps they had a similar plan and were making their escape from the city. He shivered, thinking again how close he had come to shooting an innocent man. Thank God for the dog. Jake smiled to himself as he realized the man he'd almost killed would never know that big dumb furball had probably saved his life.

The raft bobbed through the cold waters of Delaware Bay. The night was clear and windless. The bay, thankfully, was calm. As the marina disappeared slowly from view, Jake thought he saw movement on the dock. He rubbed his eyes. The familiar heavy weariness was returning, replacing focus and clarity as the adrenaline receded. It would be daylight in a couple hours. The trip across the bay was roughly twelve miles. The raft had a top speed of 25 knots but weighed down they were barely doing six. At this speed, they would reach shore in two hours.

The cabin was a mile from shore and bordered the Bombay Hook National Wildlife Refuge. Jake's family had owned the cabin before the refuge had been designated. It was remote but accessible. Anything was better than Jersey. Max looked back toward the city. A sickly yellow haze stretched across it like a worn blanket. The fires would get worse as the violence spread. He doubted whether fire trucks were even responding. The city would burn until there was nothing left.

He was thankful he had a plan, but the reality of escape had been much harder than he expected. The violence and scavenging had started sooner than he had anticipated. It had seemed like the rule of law had crumbled almost instantly. Perhaps the veneer of stability was thinner than Jake had ever believed.

A thought crept around the edges of Jake's mind. He had ignored it but it remained pawing at the door like a hungry stray. At best, they had food and water for a month. Even that was an optimistic guess based on strict conservation of their resources. One month. A paw scraped at the opening. What then? There was no plan.

Jake pushed away the thought and pulled the collar of his coat tight to his neck. His cheeks were wet with mist. He could feel the occasional spray off the hull. He estimated they would be at the midway point soon. The point of no return.

He turned to look at Kate, but she had pulled her hood over her face. Strands of hair blew out from under the hood. Jake wished she was sitting closer. He desperately wanted to touch her. To feel her face. To be reminded of what made all of this worthwhile. Why was her life worth taking others? He needed to remember.

He dug into his coat pockets and withdrew the small bottle of aspirin. Shaking it close, he heard no rattle. Empty. He tucked the bottle back in his pocket and closed his eyes. A little rest would be good. There was still much to be done.

The outboard droned on. The raft bobbed gently alone in the expanse of the bay, leaving a scar of churning water in its wake. Another scratch at the door. The persistent pawing returned.

Jake's last thought before sleep overtook him was, "One month of supplies. It's not enough. Not even close."

11

THE HUNTER

by JASON ROSS

I SPENT my early years laboring in the tourist universe that orbits around Disneyland, California. I grew up close enough to see the Disneyland fireworks every summer night at 9:30pm sharp and I went to high school in the shadow of a Styrofoam mockup of the Matterhorn. Maybe that's why I'm so cynical when it comes to architected societies and urban living. Beneath the painted smiles of Anaheim, California, there lurks a sun-scorched decay that feeds upon an endless parade of strangers.

That statement is only somewhat melodramatic, in case you were wondering.

One wonders, what monsters would awaken in that land of sunshine and Prozac should the apocalypse cast its shadow over the Land of the Magic Kingdom.

-Jason Ross

The Rapier

It had to have gone in deeper than that, Hunter marveled as he examined the blood on the tip of the sword.

He rolled up another twenty feet closer to the stoplight.

Every stoplight took ten damn minutes during a power outage. Buena Park, California was *packed* with stoplights. Beach Boulevard had like twenty stoplights between the 91 freeway and Knott's Berry Farm. It'd take Hunter an hour to get home, even with half of Orange County running like Syrian refugees toward Nevada and Arizona.

The brown-outs had been going on-and-off for a couple days. But the nuclear bomb in the harbor had been the stake through the heart of the sprawling metropolis. The stoplights weren't blinking like before. Now they stared down at the sun-baked boulevards like empty eye sockets.

When the bomb went off, Hunter heard a bass rumble and ran out on his four-foot by four-foot apartment patio, but he hadn't seen anything special—just the gray-on-gray marine layer that pretty much always rimmed L.A.. He'd thought the rumble was another earthquake at the time, so he hadn't examined it too carefully. He remembered maybe seeing a small cloud poking up a bit from the horizon to the west. He'd tell everyone at work that he'd seen the nuke anyway.

Hunter stabbed his brakes to keep from hitting a pickup truck in front of him and the rapier sword almost slid off the passenger seat and onto the floor.

Leaving the blood on the blade meant a lot to him. But only two inches?

He'd been tracking the man he'd stabbed for years—one of Hunter's favorites. Robert had that perfect pedophile look: thin but limp. Greasy hair. He wore polo shirts from Wal-Mart, buttoned all the way up.

The pedo lived six blocks from Hunter's apartment in a tract home his grandmother had left him when she died. With SoCal going crazy, Hunter had seized his window of opportunity and went to kill the man.

Hunter pulled up to the curb in the middle of the afternoon, walked up to Robert's door, opened the screen and knocked.

The instant Robert opened the door, Hunter stabbed the rapier into the rapist, which was almost a play on words, when you thought about it.

The blade pierced the yellow polo shirt exactly over the heart, and Hunter felt a gratifying slip of flesh parting. He'd practiced with oranges but a pedophile's chest felt nothing like an orange. It felt smoother, like an avocado without the skin.

But something stopped the blade, probably a rib. Hunter pulled back to take another stab, but Robert slammed the door and almost trapped the rapier in the doorframe.

Hunter stood on Robert's stoop for a moment, pondering in the bland sunshine of another California afternoon. He remembered looking around, seeing no one and nothing but the crabgrass lawn and a clump of water-starved gardenias.

Hunter heard whimpering inside but the moment had passed. He no longer had the momentum to force his way in and make sure of the kill. Plus, his blade had already been bloodied. A pregnant droplet worked its way around the edge of the fencing sword as Hunter twisted the blade.

Hunter had found the rapier at a garage sale when he was a teenager. He'd sharpened the tip for days with a file while watching old Bruce Lee movies. Finally, it had been bloodied.

Hunter walked back to his Mazda, fifty percent victorious. He climbed in and perched the rapier on the passenger seat. Then he drove back to his apartment.

Given the stoplights and everything else, he doubted the police would come knocking.

The Switchblade

Later that night, at long last, Hunter retreated to the employee lounge to clock out. The King's Lair had been empty all night and he'd only made sixty bucks in tips. It seemed like most of the tourists had vacated California. At the very least, they weren't at the King's Lair for "Joust and Jubilee." Hunter wondered how they'd all fled the endless tract home bowl of SoCal. There hadn't been an airplane in or out for three days. The skies overhead were strangely empty, unless you counted the intensifying, dingy haze—the love child of hundreds of unchecked apartment fires and whatever radioactive muck the bomb had thrown into the sky.

As Hunter walked down the beige-painted, beige-tiled hallways of King's Lair, he wondered for the thousandth time why they hadn't themed the employee areas like the rest of the dinner and show. Out on "the floor," the Arthurian roundtable motif was inescapable. With all the "mi lady" and "mi lords" from the hostesses and servers, it lent the general impression of being taken back in time—to a medieval Europe where five hundred Chinese retirees per night snapped thousands of selfies. The "KingSlayer," as employees called the dinner/theater venue, even held an audition to become a server. Apparently, not every waiter in SoCal could tap into their *inner squire.* Hunter brought his dad and stepmom to the KingSlayer just once; when they were checking in on him from their new condo in Leisure World—commonly referred to as "Seizure World" by Orange County residents. Thousands of aging retirees lived in the gated, condo community. His mom and his Army Airborne Ranger dad loved Seizure World. It was just minutes from the impeccable beaches of Laguna and without a single lawn to mow.

King's Lair, on the other hand, his father did not like. His old man entertained himself grousing throughout the night.

"Do they have a pilates gym here for the knights? Good thing they're

not real warriors. The food here would make a real warrior fall on his sword."

That evening, Hunter grew to hate his dad a little bit more than he already did. Trudging down the hallway toward the employee lounge, probably for the last time, he had to admit: the place reeked of food that'd come out of the ass-end of a semi-truck. Most of the "Orange Coast" of California smelled the same—the culinary slave to an endless conveyor belt of foreign strangers and their kids.

He washed off his makeup in the employee sink, grabbed his coat and headed into the cool and humid midnight air. Another perfect California night, with just a hint of ash and irradiation.

Hunter thought about his father as he crossed the empty parking lot. His dad hadn't even called to check on him. Everyone was now calling this the "Black Autumn Collapse," but by some miracle, Hunter still had three bars on his phone. Most likely, his old man and stepmom were headed somewhere rural and safe, but they certainly hadn't come by the apartment for him. His dad had taken his hot, young Filipino wife and had "bugged out" just like his old man had been planning for thirty years.

No "come with us, my boy." No goodbye. Not even "we'll catch you on the flip-side."

Hunter bounced the weight to the switchblade in his denim coat pocket. The three buses loaded with "Lords and Ladies" had already headed back to their hotels to take big, steaming shits of processed food. Most nights, there were ten or twenty buses. After one, minor nuke in the L.A. harbor, medieval spectacles of wonder had been scratched off the travel itinerary of thousands. Hunter had been amazed that the three buses had shown up at all. Maybe it had something to do with the KingSlayer's backup generator. Not all SoCal attractions had been so prepared. It'd bought the KingSlayer another couple nights of revenue, but that'd pretty much be it.

After three years of working with Chinese tour guides, he'd learned two things: they were decadently-good tippers and they were easily thrown for a loop if anything changed. The three buses had probably shown up because that's what the paperwork said to do.

He hadn't yet figured out a uniform—a "hero suit" for his *real* work. He hadn't imagined he'd ever follow through with it, so a lot of his plan had been marooned on an island of fantasy.

Six years of conducting surveillance on pedophiles, of collecting weapons and making plans, but it had only ever been a game, something to do in the phony, people-warren of Los Angeles. It'd been like Pokemon Go, only he wasn't hunting Charmanders and Squirtles. He was hunting kid-diddlers. But, when the electricity started going up-and-down and the bomb went off, he'd grabbed his rapier and had gone for it.

His mom died of cancer years before he could ask, but he assumed his dad had named him Hunter. He'd seen it many times with other sons of hard cases like his old man. They named their sons with high hopes of rugged manliness. *Rex. Rocky. Ace. Gunner.* His father had gone with "Hunter." But never once had his father suggested they go hunting. They'd gone fishing off the pier in Huntington Beach a couple times with his dad's buddies, but that'd been about it for the pursuit of prey.

Of course, Hunter had been asked ten thousand times, "Do you like to hunt?"

"No. My parents just picked that name."

HUNTER WAITED outside the apartment building off of Cerritos Boulevard where he'd watched Margarito come and go for two years. Once, he'd even slipped into Margarito's apartment and rifled through his drawers. The freakiest thing he'd found had been some Astro-glide. The pederast must've been a legit homosexual in addition to getting off on boys. Or maybe he just spanked it with Astro-

Glide. Hunter didn't really understand the pedophile life. It wasn't like anyone had written a book. *Zen and the Art of Kid Diddling.*

Margarito's dad had definitely *not* named him for rugged manliness.

A young couple burst out of the apartment building, carting laundry baskets loaded with canned goods and dragging a jumble of clothing; a little late to bail off the sinking ship of SoCal, but they looked like they were going for it anyway. Hunter figured he should be doing the same, but "bugging out" wasn't really for him. That was for his old man and his hot, new wife. Hunter would stick around and pursue justice.

He slipped behind the fleeing couple and caught the security door before it closed, not that the panicked couple gave a damn who got into their apartment complex once they'd left.

Hunter jogged up a flight of stairs and stalked down a long hallway that reeked of Korean food.

That shit must get in the carpet, he thought. Half the apartment buildings in Buena Park smelled like old Korean food. It was a wonder they hadn't outlawed it like they had cigarette smoke.

He reached Margarito's door and dug the hefty pouch out of his back pocket. One of the few skills he'd truly mastered had been picking locks. It was something he could practice at home while watching re-runs of *Dexter.* He pulled out the keys and the tensioner and went to work.

In less than thirty seconds, the deadbolt on the pedophile's door clicked open. Hunter slipped inside and stood against the wall, waiting for his eyes to adjust to the dark. He could hear the kid-fucker snoring lightly in the next room.

No rib would stop his blade this time. He crouched beside the sleeping form of the young pedophile and watched his chest rise and fall, rhythmically, sonorously. Hunter passed the switchblade over his head and chest, seeking the best opening.

Wary of bones, he centered the knife on the side of the

pedophile's throat, rotated it so the sharpest part of the blade was facing up and slid the point into the soft tissue, all the way to the silver hilt.

Margarito sat bolt upright, eyes flying open. His hands groped for the searing pain in his throat. Hunter, still crouched beside the bed, grabbed the handle of the knife and pulled it out and forward, slicing through the larynx and jugular with a massive *whoosh* as Margarito's lungs dumped air pressure into Hunter's face. Margarito flopped back on the bed and began convulsing. Blood spattered across the sheets, and a steady stream dribbled onto the hardwood floor.

Eventually, he stilled.

Careful not to rub the knife on anything, Hunter retreated back into the odorous hallway.

The Tanto

After slaughtering Margarito, Hunter got in his Mazda and headed to a tiny duplex on the Anaheim/Buena Park border to check on another sex offender, Arsenio.

Hunter barged into the duplex just past two a.m. causing Arsenio's roommates to scramble like rats. They had no idea where Arsenio had gone and most of his stuff had disappeared. Likely, he was stuck in one of the massive traffic jams creeping toward the deserts of Nevada and Arizona. Arsenio would probably be sitting in his Volkswagen Beetle—the new version that came with a flower holder—and he wouldn't even know that he'd already beaten the odds. He'd won the pedophile lottery, escaping a grisly death by tanto knife.

The next morning as hazy sunshine filtered through the overcast, Hunter chomped on a cold PopTart and considered his next move. Two days before, he'd organized the six blades on his gleaming, white dinette table. The dining lamp reminded Hunter of three, drooping flowers, nodding their wilting heads over his dinner. Now, they nodded approval of his choice of blades. Seven knives lay perfectly lined out on the tabletop, the switchblade drenched in blood and speckled with chunks of skin "in every nook and cranny," as his mom used to say. The rapier bummed him out a little. He'd been forced to admit that he'd probably only given Robert a nasty poke. Maybe the pedophile would die from infection.

Already, Hunter had been forced to compromise his vision of the perfect outcome. The Robert thing had gone weird. The kid-fucker had defeated him by simply closing the door. Worse yet, Hunter had no choice but to abandon his plans to kill the other guy, Arsenio, which could be rationalized as an honorable reprieve. Arsenio was black, and killing a black pedophile had always struck Hunter as a little racist.

Hunter picked the butterfly knife off the end of the parade of blades and tossed it on the couch. It was a piece of shit anyway. Hunter would rather drop the butterfly than the tanto knife. Plus, the butterfly was on the end of the row and Hunter wouldn't have to rearrange the blades on the table. He'd bought the butterfly knife in Tijuana on a little jaunt across the border to try out a Mexican prostitute. (Which was not as risqué as it had sounded. She'd been a makeup-caked, thick-waisted hooker of indeterminate age; undoubtedly, somebody's mother.)

Five blades on the table seemed more symmetrical to Hunter. He soothed himself with the evenness of the number. Half of ten. But with the butterfly knife off the table, the arrangement looked lopsided. Hunter reorganized them so that the five were evenly spaced. Then he finished his PopTart.

Hunter picked up the tanto knife, the third in line. Hunter had found it at an Army/Navy surplus store in L.A. after a particularly good night of tips at the KingSlayer. Since then, almost a year ago, he'd set the tanto aside especially for Arsenio. But unlike a Chinese tour guide, Hunter could roll with the punches. He could adjust his itinerary, albeit with a slight uptick of anxiety.

In his mind, Hunter moved the albino pedophile, Ben, up on his list to the tanto knife. Ben wasn't actually an albino, but he did have blond-blond hair. Maybe Ben bleached. Maybe he'd been born platinum like the hot chick on Game of Thrones. Hunter didn't know. He liked to think of him as "the Albino," like a James Bond villain.

Admiring the two bloodied blades on his dinette, Hunter wondered if his father had even killed anyone in Iraq. It wasn't something his dad talked about, at least not to Hunter. As of this morning, Hunter had *two* kills to his name. Or, one-and-a-half kills depending on Robert's resistance to infection.

Hunter grabbed the tanto's sheath from the living room coffee table, picked up the knife, sheathed it and slid it into his front pocket. The handle stuck out a hand-span, which made him look like a little kid carrying his dad's knife.

It would've been cooler to belt the tanto to his hip, but Hunter couldn't walk around SoCal with a knife belted to his hip. People would think he voted for Trump.

On second thought, people wouldn't probably spare a second thought for a knife on the hip, given the looting and rioting. The big knife in his pocket made it look like he had a weird boner, and that was the opposite of a superhero.

Hunter searched his room, found his one-and-only leather belt, and threaded it through the loops on his skinny jeans. He definitely liked the feel of the tanto on his hip rather than in his front pocket. The dangling blade at-the-ready made him feel legit.

He'd saved Ben the Albino for this morning because Ben lived just three streets over from Hunter. During surveillance, Hunter would climb over several apartment complexes and homes to get to his observation perch on the roof of the two-story apartment building over from Ben. It felt like being an urban ninja.

That gave him an idea: maybe he should've worked up a ninja-style outfit, maybe updated with military belts and stuff. He didn't think any of the Marvel or DC heroes or villains had done that. But, there might be a G.I. Joe like that—a modern ninja. He couldn't remember.

Today, he'd run the ninja route in broad daylight, so the black outfit would stand out, big time. A ninja outfit only worked at night and Hunter wasn't ready to limit his options.

Back to the drawing board.

Hunter passed his surveillance hide and went in for the kill. He shimmied up a drain pipe to Ben's second story balcony and hopped over to the outside lip of the patio, dangling over a nasty one-story drop. The Albino's mountain bike was chained to the railing, so Hunter climbed over both the railing and the rusty bike. As far as Hunter knew, the Albino never rode it.

Now on the patio balcony, Hunter drew the tanto. He threw open the sliding glass door and swiped the vertical blinds aside in one motion. He landed between Ben's living room and the kitchen, right beside a white-on-white couch. Ben the Albino sat on the couch, literally, with his dick in his hands. Apparently, everyone had their own way of dealing with the apocalypse.

Ben the Albino's lip curled back and his front teeth showed like a threatened chihuahua. He lurched away from Hunter and let out a keening, high-pitched squawk.

"Wha, wha, hurrr-eech."

The Albino's left hand kept a death grip on his erect penis, as though holding it would protect it from the man with the huge knife standing over his couch. His dick-bush glowed red in the sunlight now shining through the balcony glass door.

"Who the fuck are you?" Ben finally whined when his throat relaxed enough to form words.

"Why are you sitting on a towel?" Hunter answered a question with a question.

The glass table in front of Ben was littered with an assortment of pictures of naked, pre-pubescent girls.

The pervert finally regained control over his body, released his engorged dick and tried to scramble off the couch, but Hunter lunged on top of him before he could get his legs underneath him. The pedophile kicked like a donkey and launched himself over the back of the couch, sprawling on the tile of the kitchen.

Hunter jumped over the couch and came down hard on Ben's naked thighs, causing Ben to squeal like a wounded hog. Hunter almost fell, caught himself on the back of the couch and plunged the tanto blade into the mostly-naked man.

Ben had curled into a ball, and the blade sunk deep into his shoulder. Hunter withdrew the knife with a nasty, sucking sound that sent Ben into a shriek.

Down came the blade again, but Ben was too slow and too hurt to avoid the strike. It shot through his neck and passed all the way to the underside. Ben gargled like a vacuum sucking up a puddle. Blood exploded across the white kitchen tile.

Hunter stood up and admired his achievement. The dark blood on the floor stood out like a Rorschadt test against the white tile, white carpet and writhing, albino man. Hunter reached down and pulled the tanto free from the pedophile's throat, went around the couch and past the pictures of naked girls, stepped through the pedophile's front door, down the hallway and walked home down La Palma Avenue.

The overcast was clearing and the relentless sunshine of midday California had re-established its dominion, despite the smoky haze. On such a bright day, returning to his apartment, ninja-style over roofs and fences, would've felt strange.

The Straight Razor/Breadknife

The sight of the three blooded blades on his white kitchen table pumped Hunter up. He was really, finally doing this and there wasn't anyone to stop him.

The one thing he knew for sure, being the son of a "prepper," was that the police and the government wouldn't be around to arrest anyone after the shit hit the fan. Hunter hadn't seen more than a couple of cops in the last two days and they hadn't been doing anything to enforce the law. He felt ninety percent certain that it was open season on pedophiles, which was a good thing since he'd already offed two-and-a-half of them. Hunter again thought about a costume. Maybe it should be something gritty and military. He could find soldier stuff and attach blades all over the camouflage belts and vests. He could call himself *The Avenger*. Except, that had already been taken. Thinking about himself in camo, a dozen swords and knives, bristling from his belt and back, made Hunter smile.

The thought of his next target sobered him up. This pedophile easily outweighed Hunter by fifty pounds. So far, Hunter had front-loaded the wussies. In Hunter's extensive experience stalking pedophiles, they divided into two categories: sissies and creeps. The sissies were like Michael Jackson. They liked little boys and girls because they were probably still little boys themselves and they were still trying to figure out where to put their dicks. You could almost forgive them for being sickos, given they were strangely innocent. Like milk left on the counter for thirty years, though, their innocence had become disgusting.

The creeps, on the other hand, were straight-up evil. They liked to dominate the weak. They weren't hard enough to dominate anyone in the real world, so they went after kids. The pedo creeps were like that fat-fuck Hollywood producer who banged all those hot actresses. That dude was a creep who'd gone Big League.

Hunter had already taken down three sissies—and the fourth sissy had run off into the desert. This next guy definitely needed to die, regardless of his size. Hunter had moved him down the list so he would get some practice before going after one of the formidable pedos. But the time had come for Hunter to super-hero up. The apocalypse wasn't getting any riper.

The California State sex offender's database, available for easy access through the app store (prior to the internet going tits-up,) stated that Bernie—the next guy on his list—had pulled the skanky van routine with four different schoolgirls. He'd also violated parole twice, both times showing little girls his junk.

It made Hunter wonder if he was the first guy to ever use the sex offender registry like a Chinese menu for vengeance. Maybe the creator of the app had even hoped something like this might happen when he coded the app.

Where else did America so utterly and completely shit-can a person's privacy? Pet dogs had more civil rights than these kid-fuckers. They were truly the garbage pile of society. The courts were basically begging good citizens to jack with these guys.

Hunter scooped up his next blade off the kitchen table, an old fashioned straight razor, pocketed it and went out the door. He didn't know how long he'd get to keep doing this—killing pedophiles—but it was really starting to bother him that he didn't have an outfit.

Hunter drove to Bernie's trailer park in Garden Grove, which took forever. It meant going through like forty stoplights. The stoplights weren't even blinking anymore, but fewer people were driving now. Still, it took over an hour to drive the five miles.

It was hard to tell how the apocalypse had impacted this trailer park. There had always been a ton of random shit strewn across peoples' yards even back during the good times.

HUNTER GOT out of his Mazda and, immediately, he heard people screaming at each other. It sounded like a domestic issue, not an apocalypse issue.

It struck Hunter as curious that he could tell the difference between husband/wife kind of violence and the getting-robbed-at-gunpoint kind of violence just by the tone of voice.

The door to Bernie's trailer stood open—probably for ventilation now that all the A/Cs had died. Hunter showed himself in. He came face to face with fat Bernie, on his couch in a track suit, staring at the blank television and eating Top Ramen.

"Who the fuck are you?"

Bernie's spoon, steaming with ramen hovered over his paper bowl.

"I'm *the Avenger*."

The words slipped out before Hunter could think of anything else to say.

"Get the fuck out of my house," Bernie replied, the spoon still hovering.

Hunter pulled the straight razor out of his pocket and whipped it open. Bernie's eyes went wide.

The fat pedophile reacted like a cat; he threw the spoon and the bowl of hot ramen at Hunter and jumped up on the plaid couch. He looked about the room in a panic, searching his trailer for any possible weapon. As Hunter sprang around the table, Bernie grabbed a tattered throw pillow and employed it as a shield.

Hunter lunged at him with the razor, but Bernie had the high ground on the couch. He whipped the pillow and succeeded in entangling the straight razor in the fabric. When Bernie ripped the pillow back, the straight razor flew across the living room and vanished behind a giant stack of old magazines.

For a second, the two men just stared at one another. One, a fat pedophile standing on his couch. The other, a skinny-armed twenty-four year old superhero without a costume.

Hunter ran the three steps to the trailer's kitchen and yanked two knives out of a knife block. One of them turned out to be a bread knife and the other, a huge butcher knife. The fat pedophile responded by grabbing a second throw pillow, still holding the high ground on his couch, crouched for battle in a wrestler's stance.

Hunter went in for the kill, but the pedophile whipped the pillows at Hunter's face like bullwhips. A corner of a pillow caught Hunter high on the cheek and the zipper opened up a shallow gash.

"Bring it, asshole," Bernie screamed, celebrating first blood.

Hunter had come to the moment primed for violence, whereas Bernie had come to the moment primed for Top Ramen, but Bernie the Creep was catching up fast.

Hunter feinted with the butcher knife to the left and Bernie twisted toward the threat, using both pillows to protect his flank. The butcher knife plunged into a pillow. Hunter stabbed at the now-exposed right flank, raking the bread knife through a roll of fat around Bernie's midsection. Like curdled milk, fat cells burst out of the cut.

"Greeeech!" Bernie shrieked like a wounded seal, dropped both pillows and seized the four-inch deep gash. The butcher knife—still stuck in the stuffing of the pillow—went down.

"You FUCK!" Bernie screamed into Hunter's face.

The smell of spittle, ramen and blood caused Hunter to recoil, but he rallied with the bread knife, drawing it from the back of Bernie's neck around to the front. If it weren't for the hard spine, he probably would've decapitated the man.

Both of Bernie's hands released his fat roll and flew to his neck.

He burbled again, "You FUUUU!" then keeled over sideways onto the plaid couch gargling unintelligible insults.

Without bothering to search for his straight razor, Hunter left the trailer straightaway.

As he climbed into his Mazda, a mid-forties couple watched him in silence from their tiny lawn. They weren't arguing anymore.

"Hey dude," the man shouted across the tiny street. "Are you guys okay?"

Hunter didn't answer. He jumped into his Mazda, still holding the bread knife, and cut a hard U-turn across the couple's lawn. They both retreated to the little stoop bolted to their trailer home.

"What-the-fuck-dude?" the man shouted as Hunter's Mazda chewed a runnel in their lawn.

The Kodachi

The whole, endless, stop-and-go drive back to his apartment, it ate at Hunter that the Bernie Thing had gone down with a bread knife. He was glad he'd proven his skills against a full-size pedophile, but this was NOT the trophy he'd hoped for.

Hunter parked his car and headed straight into his apartment, consumed with misgivings. He plowed through the door and made a bee line for the kitchen table. Hunter set the bloody bread knife down next to the tanto knife. He straightened the bread knife—moved it into place perfectly between the tanto and the kodachi sword—but it didn't help.

Rapier, switchblade, tanto, BREAD KNIFE, kodachi. Fuck!

"Whose blood is that on those knives?" Hunter startled, but he knew the voice right away. He turned to find his father sitting on a chair in the living room.

"Um. Hi, Dad. I thought you had bugged out," Hunter stalled.

"We weren't going to leave without you. Whose blood is on those knives, Hunter? Answer my question."

"Bad guys' blood," Hunter said. He hoped he didn't have Bernie's blood on his face. He hadn't really paid attention to that before now.

Strangely, his dad seemed to accept the answer and to move on to his own concerns.

"I had to help Leisure World get their perimeter set up and then

I came to get you. The phones weren't working," his dad explained. "We have food storage for you at the condo. Come home."

"Home?"

"Yeah. Come and stay with Lucinda and I until things are less... violent." His dad stared at the table. The blades were neatly lined up and all of them bloodied, except for the last blade, the Japanese kodachi short sword.

"Did people try to break in here?" his father asked.

"Yeah. And there was trouble at work," Hunter didn't know why he'd said that. But his dad nodded vacantly, as though he'd had trouble at work too; the kind of trouble that led to a row of bloodied knives.

"Come home, son. Can you leave right now? With me?" The way his dad said it, Hunter didn't think he meant it. There had been hesitation in his voice. It was like father and son were meeting one another for the first time.

"Yeah. I'll come right away... but I have a couple things I have to do first." Hunter didn't have anything he needed to do first, but the way his dad had asked him to come, it didn't sound like he really wanted it. So, Hunter gave him the out, just to be courteous.

"Okay. Come soon, though. Today. Things are getting really bad." Again, his dad's eyes drifted to the weapons. "I guess I don't have to tell you that."

It might've been Hunter's imagination, but he thought he saw the slightest hint of pride cross his father's face.

"Can we expect you today?" His dad got up to leave. "I'll need to let the pickets at Leisure World know that you'll be coming so they don't shoot you."

"Yeah. Sure. I'll be there today or tomorrow morning." Hunter followed his dad to door. "I'll see you then."

His dad waved over his shoulder and tromped down the steps toward his pickup truck.

HUNTER HAD one blade and one pedophile left. The incomplete task would've driven him nuts if he'd left with his dad and prematurely ended the project.

The last blade had always been his favorite. He'd found it in a cutlery shop in the Anaheim Plaza Mall right before they tore the place down. The Anaheim Plaza had a swanky Robinson's department store on one end and a May Company on the other. In-between, there were shops with high-end toys, chocolates and expensive luggage. He couldn't remember what else. But it had been nice.

Over the two-and-a-half decades Hunter lived on the flat end of Orange County, the demographic had slid from white doctors and professionals to third generation immigrants. The quality of local shopping had collapsed at the same time as the quality of local food had gone high-order-fantastic.

The cutlery shop where Hunter had purchase the kodachi short sword had long ago been leveled in favor of a TJ Maxx on that spot. The Anaheim Plaza had existed just long enough to provide Hunter's favorite sword: a legitimate, high-quality samurai sword. A short sword, of course, but a samurai sword nonetheless.

The last pedophile on his list actually intimidated Hunter on several levels. Hunter considered him the "prince" of pedos.

Jorge Zorilla owned his own business, owned his own home and had crafted a financial work-around to his sex-offender status. He lived in a house with a pool in an east Anaheim neighborhood commonly populated by attorneys, dentists and self-employed business owners. Likely, his neighbors knew he was a kid-fucker, though it was quite possible that the neighbors didn't talk enough over their slat-board backyard fences to get around to that bit of gossip. The Prince might just be living like any other second and third generation entrepreneur—building a good, California life for himself complete with steak dinners, an annual pass to Disneyland and unlimited streaming video at home.

Hunter had checked on Jorge Zorilla right after the bomb and the Prince of Pedophiles showed no signs of running.

Hunter parked down the street from Zorilla's home and watched as a young gang of ghetto-dwelling teenagers, bounced from house-to-house checking for unlocked doors. It was one in the afternoon and it appeared that the chaos of the ghettos was finally spilling over into the "quality neighborhoods" of Anaheim. Soon, teenagers would be kicking in doors in the middle of the day. Not long after that, they'd start with the apartments.

Hunter considered the threat to himself and knew he should probably pack up and head to his dad and Lucinda's condo in Seizure World, but the criminal threat seemed unimportant with the kodachi laying across his lap. Weapons had a way of making a man *more,* Hunter mused.

After almost two hours, The Prince wrestled his garage door open, the effort obviously costing the aging pedophile. With the power out, he'd either need to open his garage door manually or park in the driveway. The roving bands of opportunists made the garage the better option.

The Prince backed his beefy Lincoln MKS out of the garage, then closed the garage door behind him with a slam that echoed up and down the neighborhood.

For the next two hours, Hunter followed the pedophile as he prowled the streets of Anaheim and Santa Ana in his Lincoln. Never going more than thirty-five, Zorilla skirted the ghetto neighborhoods and favored the neighborhoods inhabited by the middle class. When he'd find a cluster of people outdoors—usually family groups gathered around propane barbecues—The Prince would pause and observe them for ten or fifteen minutes. Then, he'd move on.

Hunter imagined the pedophile was seeking prey. With the

internet down and video streaming dead, Hunter figured he once again had set his sights on the real thing.

As late afternoon approached, Zorilla appeared to find a target he liked. A large, extended family buzzed around a corner lot surrounded by a low, chain-link fence. A fire pit burned merrily in the middle of the yard, generating a huge amount of black smoke that, in former times, would've triggered a response by the local fire department. A huge pot cooked over the fire and a multitude of children ran around the yard playing like it was just another family reunion. The adults appeared to be clustered in the back yard and one or two portly women drifted around to the front to stir the pot every ten minutes or so.

The Prince got out of his Lincoln and meandered toward the fence just as the women finished stirring the pot and returned to the back of the house. He reached the fence and waved a girl and a boy over to him, maybe eight or ten years-old. He pulled something out of his coat pocket, showed them and motioned for them to come toward his car. The boy didn't seem interested, but the girl scampered around to the gate and chased after Zorilla as he went to his car, opened the passenger door and walked around to the driver's side. He gave the corner house a hard look while the girl climbed in and began pawing through something inside the car.

The coast clear, Zorilla dropped into the driver's seat, cranked the engine and punched the gas. The hard start hammered the passenger door closed. The little girl flashed a look up from whatever had captivated her and scowled, maybe sensing danger for the first time. The car rocketed down Westminster Street as the big engine growled.

Hunter barely kept pace in his Mazda, losing ground on the straight-aways, and regaining it on the corners. Luckily, The Prince appeared to be engrossed in the girl, probably talking her into whatever scenario he'd confabulated to keep her from freaking out.

A few miles later, Zorilla swung into an old gas station and pulled around to the back. Unlike most of urban Orange County, this gas station hadn't been rebuilt and remodeled in the last thirty years. The front store contained only a map rack, engine oil and a rusting refrigerator that had once held soda cans. Forgotten by the onslaught of investment capital, the old school gas station would've been unremarkable except for how little love and attention had been afforded it.

Zorilla parked next to the bathrooms around back. Hunter pulled his Mazda against a brick wall festooned with graffiti, slumped down in his seat and waited. Zorilla turned off the big car and remained in the driver's seat talking to the girl. He gesticulated elaborately, undoubtedly weaving a tale he'd woven before.

Just three years back, Zorilla had plea bargained his way out of hard time by lawyering up and working down a bunch of charges relating to lewd acts with minors. There hadn't been any details listed in the Offender Locator app, but Hunter guessed that this gas station bathroom had figured into The Prince's crimes.

Confirming his suspicion, Zorilla got out of the Lincoln and unlocked the men's restroom with his own key. Then, he walked around to the passenger side, opened the girl's door and herded her into the restroom.

As the door closed behind them, Hunter hesitated.

It was almost too good to be true. He'd caught The Prince pulling the exact pedophile crime he had always imagined—right down to the scuzzy bathroom. Hunter had never seen a pedophile do anything that could be considered a crime, except maybe for the Albino looking at kiddie porn the day before.

The apocalypse had let everyone off their leash, Hunter concluded. Those who still remained in SoCal found themselves bored, unchecked and tuning in to their filthiest instincts. The moment felt undeniably *right* for a warrior of justice.

...it would've been so much cooler wearing the right outfit...

Hunter pulled the kodachi from its sheath and stepped out of his car. He'd given Zorilla enough time to commit to his crime, and now, Hunter would catch him in the act.

He tucked the short sword along his side as he crossed the gas station parking lot. He found the key still stuck in the outside lock of the men's room.

Hunter carefully turned the handle and then threw the door wide.

He wasn't ready for how dim it was inside. Without electricity, there wasn't much light coming through the tiny window or the now-open door. When his eyes finally adjusted, he saw The Prince glaring at him. The little girl stood next to him, her pants around her ankles, her panties still up.

Zorilla held his right hand around his back, hiding something. Hunter didn't wait to find out what it was. He lunged forward and plunged the kodachi into the pedophile's gut, double-handed the pommel, and shoved it all the way in, right up to the hilt.

The Prince sucked air through his teeth and stumbled backwards, pin-wheeling his arms. A small revolver clattered to the floor and slid under the toilet stalls. Hunter followed Zorilla into the shadowy bathroom and deeper into the dank smell of old urine and chemical deodorizer. Hunter grabbed the hilt of the kodachi and yanked backwards, sliding it free of the Prince's abdomen.

He cocked the short sword like he thought a samurai might— high and straight from his left shoulder— and then rammed the blade home again, skewering the old pedophile below the collarbone and pinning him to the back wall of the men's room.

Zorilla screamed in agony, and Hunter pulled the sword out preparing for the coup de grâce.

BOOM!

The shot from the revolver deafened Hunter. An immense pain bloomed in his belly. He spun around, the sword held high, and faced the girl. She held the pedophile's revolver, pointed at Hunter's chest. The kodachi clattered to the floor.

The girl whimpered, dropped the gun and fled out of the men's room, pulling up her pants as she ran.

Hunter leaned against the wall and lowered himself to the floor. He looked over at The Prince, who had proceeded him to the ground. Both men wheezed, otherwise silent as their blood pooled on the filthy tile. The dark circles expanded in the dim room, overwhelming the scent of piss with the smell of copper. Eventually, the circles met, joined and became an endless lake of death and life wasted.

Hunter's sight grew fuzzy around the edges. He couldn't tell if The Prince's vacant, unblinking eyes meant his surrender or his death. Either way, Hunter could somehow see his own reflection in the gaze.

What if the cops brought his father down to identify him? What if his dad saw him on the floor across from this pedophile? Would they understand that he was actually the hero?

Would they misunderstand and think that HE might be the kidfucker?

Hunter tried to rise—to get off the floor and move somewhere else—but the most he could do was flail one arm. All his energy had drained away.

At last, he only had enough strength to worry. He worried about the blood. He worried about the kodachi making it back to his kitchen table. He worried about what his father would think.

Would he know that Hunter had been the hero?

If only he had worn an outfit...

MEANWHILE...

The Homestead,
Oakwood, Utah

[Spoiler Alert: if you haven't read White Wasteland, read before continuing...]

Jason Ross sat on his dead daughter's bed, in her room, and cradled her plate carrier vest in his lap.

It held full magazines for her carbine, medical tape, a tourniquet and surgical shears. He ran his hand over them, one at a time, like talismans of her short life. The trauma kit, attached with MOLLE loops would hang at her hip, close-to-hand. The tourniquet was velcroed to Emily's shoulder strap where she could strip it off and save a life.

She'd saved many lives. She'd defended this place. She'd become the woman she'd dreamed of becoming, and now she was gone. She would rest forever in the soil of the bluff overlooking the Homestead.

Emily had died of the flu, allowed through the Homestead quarantine by his wife, Jenna, and by Emily herself. They'd been complicit in feeding and sheltering orphans—sick children who spread the disease of the wasting world into the safe haven that Jason had built.

Did this homestead even matter, when he couldn't even protect his children?

Emily had always been a passionate girl. To risk her life for orphans was fully within her; the beating heart at the center of her. She'd been drawn to study medicine by the orphan children of Africa. Jason should've known that his daughter wouldn't let orphans die in the refugee camp clumped around the gateway to their neighborhood.

Could he have protected her from herself?

Emily had been a passionate idealist, and they had all died in the winter of the collapse.

But *Jenna* should've done better. She should've known better. His wife was a middle-aged woman, well-versed in the serrated backside of life. *She* should've weighed the risks. *She* should've stopped Emily.

Jason lifted Emily's gun belt and hefted the weight of her Glock. It felt loaded, as were all guns these days. Firearm safety had taken a distant backseat to the burgeoning peril of the desperate winter.

"When did you become so cruel?" Jenna's voice startled him. She leaned on the door frame of Emily's room. She'd been watching Jason weep, his legs folded under each other on his daughter's bed. He spun toward the curtained windows and uncurled his legs. She'd seen him grieving and he couldn't brook it.

"My feelings are no longer your concern," he said. "Our marriage was over the moment you sided with Kirkham."

She stood up straight in the doorway. "Our marriage was over the moment you sentenced me to death."

"Right after you sentenced her to death." Jason held up their daughter's plate carrier vest. "Is that when you mean?"

It was a profoundly unfair thing to say, but he meant it. He meant to hurt her.

Jenna turned and fled down the freezing, stone-lined hallway. Jason thought he heard her sob, but it might've been the cold mansion, creaking on its foundation.

Jeff had to go, had to get back to his troops. Tens of thousands of men were counting on him to lead.

"You're *not* leaving. Our son could *die*," Tara drew out that last word like a growl. She had never fought him about a deployment before, but this time, something was different. After almost thirty years as a Special Forces operator, his wife stood against him.

It wasn't only that their son had suffered an amputation. The war, and the air around their family, smelled like stomach cancer, like death lingering in the next room. What awaited Jeff in St. George wasn't a battle like any he had fought before, and despite Doc Eric's assurances, their son's injuries yo-yoed between healing and foul ruin.

"Leif has already lost his hand. Next, they'll take his arm to the shoulder." She choked, sobbed and faced away from Jeff, not toward him. Before, she had always gone toward him, no matter how angry. She had always cried into his chest, screamed into it, and even pummeled it. Turning away pained him more than ten thousand fists.

Last fall, their youngest son had been bitten by a rattlesnake in the woodpile, just another pointless price to a pointless apocalypse. If one collected enough wood, one ran afoul of snakes and spiders. No big deal. Except that everything was a big deal now that modern medicine had been obliterated: every scratch, a potential staff infection. Every broken bone was a lifelong deformity; every sniffle was a slow death from the flu.

Without antivenom, the boy barely recovered from the neuro-
logical effects of the snake bite, but he survived it. But the bite had
been on the meat of his palm, and the flesh up-and-down the hand
and forearm curdled like bad cream. The weal erupted in blisters,
bloody cankers and, finally, loose strips of flesh that peeled away
like string cheese.

The Homestead doctors burned through their shaky supply of
antibiotics with abandon. The wounds festered, healed over, and
then festered again from within. They boiled and broke through
where they should've cured and healed. The original snakebite
became the least of their worries. Myriad infections colonized his
son's flayed arm in a dozen grisly nooks and gouges. His immune
system was laid low by the venom, and even with medicines, the
open meat of Jeff's son was naked against every breeze-borne spore.

Leif's body reacted with a savage allergy to penicillin, struggled
two days, recovered, and his sores exploded again. The doctors took
off his little finger, which had rotted to the bone. Leif then caught
the flu, weakened again, and a long, dark-red weal burst apart at his
wrist. The doctors took a quarter-pound of flesh and packed the
gash with honey and gauze.

But the arm still wouldn't heal, and when it did close up, infection wormed back in from below. In the deepest doldrums of iron-
clad winter, the doctors finally took off half of his arm. They left
enough of a stump so that Jeff might someday fashion a prosthetic.
It was all the solace he would get from this nightmare.

"You can't go. I forbid it," Tara said again. "The Homestead isn't
safe. You can't know for sure nothing will happen here. You can't
leave us like this."

Jeff would leave anyway. He was a warrior and fifty thousand
men had pledged their lives to stopping the iron juggernauts of the
narco army—eighty M1-Abrams tanks staged in St. George, Utah,
poised to cauterize them all with psychotic tyranny. Jeff could fight

them in the middle lands of Utah, or he could fight them within machine gun range of his family. But there was no doubt he would fight them. Tara knew better than to pretend he had a choice. But her shattered heart denied the stark peril.

The day before, their family stood around a tiny hole and laid the desiccated, six-year-old hand to rest where hungry dogs wouldn't dig it up, in the flower bed below the window of their family suite. Perhaps the echinacea flowers would root around the arm and derive small nourishment. Maybe the flowers would provide next year's medicine to heal another boy.

Jeff didn't know if he and Tara would survive this as a couple. Sinking despair settled around his thick shoulders. It seemed as though his family would fall to the apocalypse, one way or the other.

"If you go, I'll take the boys and I'll leave you, Jeff." Her eyes burned like obsidian near the fire.

He knew she wouldn't. There was nowhere to go. There was no one else to take her. This was the end of the road, at the last stand of humanity, at the fall of the world. There was nowhere from here but into the ground.

"I have to go," he said. "I gave my word."

"Damn you," she spat. "Go die, then."

It wasn't a curse. It was her greatest fear.

Jason crossed over into Wyoming in a driving snowstorm. He ran from the howling wind, into the hull of a dead Ford Prius, half-buried in a snow bank. He had only the clothes on his back and the gear inside his bug-out bag, having abandoned his BMW X5 where Interstate 80 cut through Chalk Creek on the Utah side of the border. The trackless snow, eighty miles from the surviving husk of

Salt Lake City, had piled up against the bumper of the BMW and forced it to a stop.

He'd been prepared to walk. He knew his car wouldn't take him far in the shiftless world where snow plows no longer ran and fuel was like liquid gold. When he'd fled his home, Jason had grabbed snow shoes and an ultralight bug-out bag that he'd set up years before the collapse: a one pound tent, winter sleeping bag, water filtration, extra socks, med kit, and eight days of freeze dried food. It weighed twenty-five pounds and he should easily reach his cabin on Bear River, despite the holocaust of snow that entombed everything in nine feet of crystalline stupor.

He pried open the ice-gripped door of the Prius, popped the bindings on his snow shoes, shucked his backpack around to the front and tossed it into the passenger seat. He wormed through the door, scraping his chin, and settled behind the steering wheel. Jason glanced about. The car was perfectly clean, and free of dead bodies. He approved. Not only had the fastidious owner kept the car immaculate, but he'd refrained from fouling it with his corpse.

Jason slapped his gloved hands on the wheel and exhaled a plume of frost. The Prius was an instant snow cave. Bivouacking in the dead car made more sense than setting up a tent. He figured that he was still about five miles outside of Evanston, where he'd take a hard right turn and angle up the north slope of the Uinta Mountains toward the cabin. In just fifteen more miles, a single day of snowshoeing, he'd dig out the front door, slip inside, start a fire in the stove, and begin a few well-earned months of abject grief. As the agony of the loss of his children, and now his wife, abated, he would think and plan, plan and think. His mind would pivot to where his heart held fast, around dreams of black revenge.

When the spring broke the back of this hellish winter, he would return to his home and murder the man who had taken it from him. Jeff Kirkham.

Jason dug the tiny, titanium stove from his back and filled it gingerly with denatured alcohol from a small, plastic bottle. He'd once been a rich man, but the contents of the backpack, and the buried cabin along the frozen river, were everything he now owned. Still, the dainty perfection of the ultralight stove gave rise to that old feeling of superiority. Where other men burned oily-smoke car tires to warm their meal, he burned an invisible, clean flame. He flicked his Bic and the blue tell-tale of the alcohol flickered to life. Jason perched the puck-sized stove on the center console and carefully fished out a zip-locked meal, his titanium pot, and a spoon. He cracked the door open and scooped a heaping pot of snow, cradled it in his lap, stripped off the gloves and assembled the tiny pot stand. With a satisfying clink, he put the pot on the flame and began the multi-phase process of boiling water, then reconstituting the backpacker food.

The sun was going down hard now. The deep snow on the windshield turned from translucent white to gray. Soon, it would be black. The only sound in the cockpit of the dead vehicle was the shushing as the alcohol burned.

How could he have lost so much? It made no sense to him. He'd been the most-prepared person he had ever known. Like his perfect backpack, perfect stove, and perfectly-measured alcohol fuel, he had assiduously readied his property for just such an apocalypse. He'd spent a fortune, earned through a string of business start-ups, to surround his loved ones with layer upon layer of stored food and supplies. And those supplies had held, despite every vagary the dying world had thrown at his Homestead. He had been vindicated in his planning, proven prescient in his foresight and held aloft over Salt Lake City like a monument to his own good judgment. No one could argue that he was not, in every conceivable dimension, *right*.

Yet, those he loved, even those he had saved, hated him for it. They could not bind their envy. They took it all from him and, essentially, cast him out.

But he wasn't a man to wheedle and whine. He was, and would

always be, a man of action. He who had stolen from him had signed his own death warrant. Jason didn't know how, but he was certain that he would once again walk his land, and harvest the fruit of his orchard.

The snow hissed as it boiled. He shook the Ziploc baggie and settled the dry meal to the bottom, some kind of noodle casserole.

The door of the Prius flew open. The night rushed in. Rough hands seized Jason's arm and yanked him into the yammering wind. The contents of the baggie flew into the night air.

"*Kito tih?*" a man shouted in Jason's face through the bristles of a brown scruffy beard. He wore a snow camouflage jumpsuit of a pattern Jason didn't recognize.

"Who the hell are you?" Jason sputtered.

"*Pri-hodit!*" A second man entered the halo of the flashlight of the first, grabbed a handful of Jason's coat and dragged him along the new tracks they had made in the snow.

Jason looked back as the strange, foreign men steered him, snowshoe-less and stumbling, toward a rumbling, tracked vehicle in the middle of the snowbound interstate. The cockpit of the Prius glowed with a slight blue flicker. His last, fine belongings, there remained.

By the time the slow-moving armored transport arrived in the town of Evanston, Jason gathered he'd been taken by Russian military. What they were doing in the United States, in the middle of winter, at the rim of the end of the world, he had no idea whatsoever.

They herded him out of the vehicle in front of a barely-lit building that must've been some kind of county courthouse or city hall. Jason had never tarried much in Evanston, so he didn't know. The men didn't treat him any more roughly than it required to keep him heading in the direction they wanted, up the steps and into the old government building.

Jason had contemplated an escape attempt while locked in the back of the transport, but the Russians' chuckling, easygoing manner belied concerns of rape, torture or cannibalism. They'd rolled him up without prejudice or fury. They'd searched him, but not cuffed him. His gut told him to just go with it.

They passed into the chill of the brick building, through the glass doors, and into a standard, drop-ceilinged conference room, previously home to ten thousand pointless county meetings. Lanterns exhaled on the tabletop, giving light to the otherwise dark room. Around the fringes of the yellow glow, six men murmured in Russian. They looked up at Jason and one barked a question at the soldiers. They discussed some matter concerning him, no doubt, and the Russian officer spoke to him in Cyrillic-dipped English.

"You come from Utah?"

"Correct," Jason said.

"From Salt Lake?"

"Yes." Jason didn't know how to read the man's rank on his shoulder, but he was obviously in command. And he was vulnerable. It was in his eyes, how he glanced to the side when he spoke, like a bird checking its broken wing. It was something Jason could work with.

"We have questions," the Russian officer circled the table to face him. "You answer, no?"

Jason considered those he'd loved and left behind. He weighed his loyalties, and his marriage—what fragment of it remained. He mulled over the injustices committed against him. He pictured Jeff Kirkham.

"I'll answer," he said. *And I'll wager we're going to be very good friends.*

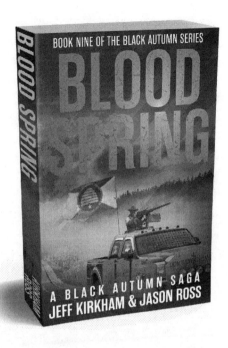

*[Excerpt from **Blood Spring,** the final novel in the Black Autumn Series. Continue reading Blood Spring on Kindle, paperback or free on Kindle Unlimited.]*

ALSO BY JEFF KIRKHAM AND JASON ROSS

The first five books of the *Black Autumn series* rampage through the seventeen days of the Black Autumn collapse, chronicled coast-to-coast through the eyes of thirty-one desperate survivors.

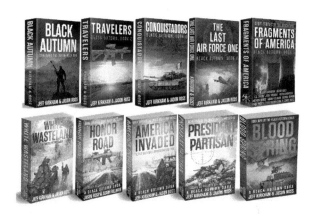

Series in order:

1. Black Autumn

2. Black Autumn Travelers

3. Black Autumn Conquistadors

4. The Last Air Force One

5. White Wasteland (same characters as Black Autumn)

6. Honor Road (same characters as Travelers)

7. America Invaded (same characters as Conquistadors)

8. President Partisan (same characters as The Last Air Force One.)

9. Blood Spring (all characters from all books.)

10. Fragments of America (short stories)

While the unique book order can be a bit confusing, it helps to think of the five "black cover" books as a single, epic novel covering the same seventeen days of collapse, then the four "white cover" novels telling the story of the following, impossible winter. Then, Blood Spring culminates all storylines and characters. Like *Game of Thrones*, or *The Stand*, the Black Autumn series breaks down an epic tale with dozens of characters, fighting for their survival.

Our apologies for any head-scratching that may ensue. We couldn't think of a better way to tell the massive, 2,000 page tale bouncing around in our brain buckets. As usual, I blame it all on Jeff.

— Jason

ABOUT THE AUTHORS

Jeff Kirkham (right) served almost 29 years as a Green Beret doing multiple classified operations for the US government. He is the proverbial brains behind ReadyMan's survival tools and products and is also the inventor of the Rapid Application Tourniquet (RATS). Jeff has graduated from numerous training schools and accumulated over 8 years "boots on the ground" in combat zones, making him an expert in surviving in war torn environments. He spent the majority of the last decade as a member of a counter terrorist unit, working in combat zones doing a wide variety of operations in support of the global war on terror. Jeff spends his time, tinkering, inventing, writing and helping his immigrant

Afghan friends, who fought side by side with Jeff. His true passion is his family and spending quality time with his wife and three children.

Jason Ross (left) has been a hunter, fisherman, shooter and preparedness aficionado since childhood and has spent tens of thousands of hours roughing it in the great American outdoors. He's an accomplished big game hunter, fly fisherman, an Ironman triathlete, SCUBA instructor, and frequent business mentor to U.S. military veterans. He retired from a career in entrepreneurialism at forty-one years of age after founding and selling several successful business ventures.

After being raised by his dad as a metal fabricator, machinist and mechanic, Jason dedicated twenty years to mastering preparedness tech such as gardening, composting, shooting, small squad tactics, solar power and animal husbandry. Today, Jason splits his time between writing, international humanitarian work and his wife and seven children.

Check out the Readyman lifestyle...search Facebook for ReadyMan group and join Jeff, Jason and thousands of other readers in their pursuit of preparedness and survival.

Fragments of America, © 2020, Black Autumn, Book 5, Short Stories of the Apocalypse: *An Anthology of Short Stories in the First Seventeen Days of the Black Autumn Collapse*

Edited by Jason Ross

Published by ReadyMan Publishing, LLC

Written by (in order of publication):

- Adam Fullman
- Josh Brooks
- Paul Knoch
- George Grimm
- Jeff Kirkham
- Chris Serfustini
- R. Chris Yates
- L.L. Akers
- Boyd Craven
- Arthur Dorst
- Jason Ross

.

Made in the USA
Columbia, SC
06 December 2023

27907492R00278